SO-AEL-201

SWEET
AND
LOWDOWN

SWEET AND LOWDOWN

A DORIE LENNOX MYSTERY

Lise McClendon

THOMAS DUNNE BOOKS
St. Martin's Minotaur ❧ New York

THOMAS DUNNE BOOKS.
An imprint of St. Martin's Press.

www.minotaurbooks.com

Library of Congress Cataloging-in-Publication Data

McClendon, Lise.
    Sweet and lowdown : a Dorie Lennox mystery / Lise McClendon.—1st ed.
        p. cm.
    ISBN 0-312-28689-9
        1. Women private investigators—Missouri—Kansas City—Fiction.
    2. World War, 1939–1945—Missouri—Kansas City—Fiction. 3. Kansas
    City (Mo.)—Fiction. I. Title.

PS3573.E19595 S94 2002
813'.54—dc21

                                                            2001058856

First Edition: May 2002

10 9 8 7 6 5 4 3 2 1

To Betty and John, and Barbara and Dean, sources of much comfort, love, and inspiration

AUTHOR'S NOTE

By 1940, EUROPE WAS EMBROILED in a war that Americans wanted badly to stay out of. In June of that year, General Phillipe Pétain, France's hero of World War I, had fallen quickly to Nazi military advances and surrendered the nation. By autumn, the Blitzkreig by German bombers on the island of Great Britain had left that nation stunned but resolute.

But America wasn't at a standstill. She had to elect a new president, or break a longstanding rule and reelect Franklin D. Roosevelt. A peacetime draft was in the works. Fascist sympathizers in the United States still had the First Amendment on their side, but not for long. One Hitler supporter was William Dudley Pelley, who had designs on the presidency himself as the founder of the Silver Legion, or Silver Shirts. Groups like Peace Now and America First were infiltrated by Nazi spies and used to promote isolationism.

People went on with their lives, worried and distracted by world events. Authors wrote books; in 1940 a pulp writer named Raymond Chandler published a book called *The Big Sleep*. Big bands played new songs, as well as those from years before like George Gershwin's "Sweet and Lowdown."

My thanks to Dr. Oliver H. Duggins, who hunted for Nazi spies as an FBI agent during World War II, for sharing his memories. And to the Parmly Billings Library, my local source of every *Life* magazine from the period. I sure wish I had some of those Willkie buttons.

ONE

1940

"WHO ARE YOU?"

"Your new parole officer, Wilma Vunnell. Please take a seat."

"What happened to Lloyd?"

"Reassigned. Take a seat, Miss Lennox. Y'all are staying, aren't you?"

"Do I have a choice?"

"Mr. Francis didn't make very many notes. Did you talk to him?"

"What else is there to do in here? Where did he go?"

"That's not the business of this meeting, Miss Lennox. We're here to discuss your staying out of trouble and having employment."

"Done both. Can I go?"

"Sit down. We have a half hour. I don't know how Mr. Francis worked, but I fill my sessions. We talk about how things are going, the job, the family, problems you might be having."

"I'm not having any problems. Who told you that?"

"I see you're a private detective. And you've been ordered not to have any weapon or instrument that could be used as a weapon on your person. Is that a problem for you?"

"Look, Miss—"

"*Mrs.* Vunnell. I'm a widow."

"Okay. Mrs. Vunnell. It is a problem. I could get hurt on the job. Jumped, dry-gulched—it's happened. There are mean and careless gees out there."

" 'Gees'?"

"Fellas, toughs too slippery for your boys in blue. And they're using things more hurtful than my switchblade, you can bet on that."

"Are you saying you have gotten yourself a gun?"

"I'm on parole, remember?"

"Have you used a gun in the last five months?"

"No."

"Are you sure about that?"

"I'd know, wouldn't I? I could tell you anything, Mrs. Vunnell the Widow, and you got no choice but to believe it. So why don't you just let me go on my merry way and you can go get another piece of pecan pie?"

"Does this questioning make you angry?"

"Hell yes! It's a waste of time."

"Wasting time is a bad thing."

"Oh, sure, you work for the government. Lightbulb, Mrs. Vunnell, the clock is ticking. You won't be around forever."

"Neither will you, Miss Lennox." The widow took a long moment to brush imaginary dust from her desk pad. "What do you plan to do with your life?"

"I plan to live it, outside of these four walls. I plan to—"

"What is it?"

"Nothing—my eye. You know, Mrs. Vunnell, I'm not afraid to die. I've seen people die, and it's not so bad. All their troubles are gone, they don't have to worry about their families anymore, where next month's rent is coming from, or dying in some stinkhole in France. It's peaceful. Don't look at me like that. I'm not going to do the Dutch act. I've seen that, too, and it's not for me."

"You've seen a lot."

"It's my job. That's why I need my blade, to protect myself."

"All this dying, was it all on the job?"

"Some family, like everybody. Were you there when Mr. Vunnell died?"

"No. He was far away, in the war."

"Same with me. They died and I wasn't there."

"You didn't get to say good-bye."

Lennox stared at the woman's face, still as pasty and blocklike as at the beginning of the session. Eyes sunken deep in her flesh, cold and unwavering, probing and examining like icy needles. Dorie looked away, over Vunnell's shoulder. *Didn't get to say good-bye.* She jumped to her feet, face hot, and turned her back to the parole officer.

"Is the time up? I have to be somewhere."

"Sit down, please. We've got fifteen minutes, and I want to hear about the assault and battery charge that brought you here. Mr. Francis doesn't mention it."

"He knew better."

"Was he afraid of you?"

"He had the shakes. Was it me who gave 'em to him? I don't know. I liked him better than you, though."

"I'll like you better if you'll tell me what happened that day."

"And I should care about your opinion."

"You might, if you want to stay out of jail."

Dorie Lennox stood still in the smoky haze of the nightclub. The air was warm, curling around the ankles. There it was, just for a second. A calm pause in the relentless clicking of the clock: a feeling of tenuous perfection, that everything was just where it was supposed to be.

She shivered and it was gone. Untrustworthy feeling, cockeyed, in the way only your imagination can trick you.

Back in Atchison, in the speaks, she'd felt that way. But that was another life. This one was dented and bruised and it wasn't so tender anymore. And that was good, she told herself. She was so tough. Another necessary lie. Life was full of them.

She lighted a Lucky and leaned against the wall by the ladies' lounge. She'd seen the inside of too many nightclubs. In the dark, where anything can happen, and usually did. Closed away, secret, the daytime world forgotten, with its rules and laws and shaking fingers. Easy to pretend to get lost. To forget who you were and what you wanted. Easy to get sidetracked.

The band crashed to a finale. The discordant notes of an unrecognizable tune collapsed into the smoky stillness.

You belong here. The thought crept up like a poisonous snake. That was the feeling. That these dark places belonged to her, and she to them. Was that just a lie to make this life seem normal, or was it such an outrageous lie that it had become true?

The girl stood up suddenly with a peal of laughter, twirled for the gents at her table, and bent to peck the cheek of one. Then she sashayed toward Dorie in her scarlet shift, tossing her hair back. She looked up, her eyes a curious brown, but cold and accusing. Lennox moved aside to let her through the doorway, then sat down at the table across from Amos Haddam. She shouldn't have ordered the whiskey. She pushed it away. Amos fingered his glass unconsciously, turning the untouched gin round and round.

"She's behaving herself tonight. As much as she can."

Amos looked up as the girl maneuvered between the empty tables, back to her gents. He regarded her coldly, from a distance, like the job she was, not as the wayward woman-child she appeared to other men.

"They want me to register for this draft," he said.

"You?"

He straightened his bony shoulders and faked a smile full of teeth but no mirth. His face was as gray as the air in here.

"You a U.S. citizen?" she asked.

"Jolly right. Had to swear on the big black Bible back in my revenuer days. Pinching moonshiners was patriotic work."

As if to demonstrate, he picked up his glass and put it to his lips. He paused, something shifting in his eyes. He lowered the glass, still full, to the tabletop.

"Well, don't worry. You won't pass the physical." Her words were harsher than she meant. "Besides, one war is enough."

He raised his eyebrows. "Aye."

He took a sip, then anger at the war or the liquor hardened his eyes. He shot the rest back in one gulp. She waited for him to keel over. Instead, he stood up.

"Gotta clear the lungs of this bloody smoke."

She watched him go, then splashed the whiskey against her lips. The taste was sweet on her tongue. The girl—Thalia—was dancing now with the skinny gee. He was grinning at her, all his bad teeth showing. Thalia Hines had the worst taste in men. Dorie had watched this week as she was pawed by the greasy-gummed, flop-eared, gap-toothed, and pigeon-toed, the chubby, bony, bald, and smelly. Thalia'd been seen, dancing and drinking and singing, with dozens of men. And, worse yet, she appeared to enjoy their attentions.

A man approached Lennox's table, dressed decent, but with a dirty neck and one misbehaving eye. He asked her to dance. She smiled politely. "Waiting for a friend," she said. She had to keep an eye on the girl. Thalia had proved mostly easy, since she was aware they were tailing her for the Commander. But that could turn in the blink of an eyelash.

The man gave her a harsh look. Dorie gave him one back. The music changed, Thalia was being persuaded to sing by the skinny gee. She shook her head as if she was shy; her chin dipped. Then she leaned against the piano, whispered to the band, and began to sing.

A cheery party song. What was it? From a play, a nondescript musical she barely remembered. She'd gone with Talbot; she remembered that. Harvey Talbot, randy reporter, last seen months ago. Not that she missed him. It had just been . . . well, a dry summer.

Thalia's voice was throaty and tuneless, like Marlene Dietrich's in the movies; her creamy skin and yellow hair glowed in the spotlight. Amos appeared at the top of the stairs, looking flushed. His hair stood up with wax, freshly combed. He flagged down a waitress and asked for water and a gin. When it came, he drank all the water. The telephone rang behind the bar and the bartender answered it. Dorie looked at her watch. Only eleven o'clock.

"Why don't you go home? I can follow her," she said. His eyes were clear enough, only slightly bloodshot.

"Not just following, is it?"

"What's she gonna do?"

"It's not her I'm worried about."

Whether Amos could bully any of these boozers wasn't in doubt. But she worried about a real fight. Amos was hardly a prizefighter. Bad breath would knock him flat. He hadn't mentioned his gun. And Dorie under orders to be easy pickin's. The parole officer's words this afternoon irked her. Mrs. Vunnell, what did she know about street life? She sat there so calm and all-knowing, like a fat Chinese Buddha. The weeks at the gym had made Dorie quicker, lighter on her feet. Her knee felt stronger than it had in years. But still she was naked without her blade.

She patted the empty pocket of the blue suit and sighed.

The suit had been worn only once that summer, at the funeral of a bachelor at the boardinghouse. Sad, really, how little they missed him, a nondescript shadow of a man. He'd gone suddenly. Something about his guts. Everyone picked at their food for a week, until Mrs. Ferazzi burst into tears. They had all felt bad about the bachelor, but it was relief to go back to Poppy's scalloped potatoes and corned beef hash.

Thalia was doing a shimmy as the song ended, running her hands down her hips. Her thin red dress barely concealed her figure. The skinny fella reached for her hand and pulled her down for a peck on the lips.

The way men reached for Thalia, the way she responded so eagerly, so gratefully—it grated on Dorie. Made her feel hollow and edgy. She picked up her glass and took a gulp of whiskey. She knew what it was. That dry summer again.

As the music ended, the girl tossed back her hair, a corn-tassel blond, and smiled her pussycat smile as the men clapped and whistled. This went on for a long minute, until Thalia looked toward the door. She straightened, her smile fading.

The man standing at the back of the room was dressed in a somber gray suit and a darker shirt, which made him look solid, like granite. His hair was also dark and slick. The expression on his moderately handsome face was pure fury. His eyes blazed at the girl, nostrils flaring. His chest rose and fell as if he was barely containing himself. Then, suddenly but deliberately, he took a deep breath and unclenched his fists. He smiled and said her name.

"Who's that?" Dorie whispered. Amos hitched his shoulders. The man looked as hard as the neighborhood Italians, but different. Fairer complexion, slighter build, slender hands. Irish hood, or politician. Or both.

Thalia was heading toward him, pausing for her clutch and jacket at the table. The man who had been buying her drinks grabbed her wrist, but she shook him off, complaining in her mewing way. The man at the door took her jacket, turned her around, and helped her into it. He smoothed back her hair from her face and took her arm.

"Let's go," Amos said, on his feet.

By the time they were down the stairs and out on the sidewalk in the cool October air, the girl was in the backseat of a light green sedan. The man climbed in next to her. A driver in a cap sat at the wheel.

Amos took off toward their car. The skirt of the blue suit was too tight to run in, a liability Dorie had not tested until now. Amos turned to hurry her. She hiked up the skirt, but it was awkward with only the bottom half of her legs working. The Packard was half a block down, near the skinny man's Pontiac.

"Shake a leg," Amos said as she slipped behind the wheel, fishing her keys from her handbag at the same time. "They're around the bleeding corner already. I thought you were a track star. Never saw anybody waddle so slow. Me first, with lungs so damp, they could fill a fish tank."

Damn blue suit. She concentrated on making the turn, avoiding two large coupes on Holmes. The green sedan was up ahead, turning left onto Grand. The night was clear and starry, with little traffic. She felt her mind snap and the corners of her mouth turn up. This was why she liked this job, the jolts of adventure. You paid in hours of tedium, but it was worth it.

At least they'd been at it together. The girl would look at them, smile, stick out her pink tongue. She'd thumb her nose and laugh; she'd wiggle her fanny to Amos. She was hardly inhibited by their presence. The Commander's wishes had little effect on the girl. Girl? Thalia Hines was twenty-one and, as she enjoyed pointing out, had reached her legal majority.

Between them, they'd had a few dull nights watching the girl drink and carouse and go home with—was this number four or five? She'd stayed in one night in the last eight.

"There. Right," Amos said, pointing at a dark intersection where the sedan had disappeared. "Step on it or we'll lose them."

Dorie downshifted and made the turn in time to see the sedan turn left at the bottom of a hill. "Are they trying to shake us?"

The side street was lined with trees and hedges shielding the view of the houses beyond. At gaps in the shrubbery, mansions peeked through, brick, tudor, stately and rich. The kind of people who have chauffeurs and big green sedans. Like Thalia. But this wasn't her neighborhood. The car disappeared into a driveway.

"Park there." He pointed out a spot under a large tree drooping gracefully over the narrow street. "Douse the lights."

She cut the engine and lights and rolled to a stop under the tree. Leaves crunched under the tires. The tree held on to its weathered foliage, making the spot shadowed and cold. A house was obscured by more trees and shrubs, but a sliver of lawn stretched out in golden streaks of lamplight.

"This it?"

"Next one down. Go check the gate, see if there's a name. Stay in the shadows. These neighborhoods have a thousand eyes."

She pried open the car door as quietly as she could. Amos frowned at her. "Give me that jacket." He held out a hand impatiently until she stripped it off and handed it to him.

The door creaked noisily and she left it ajar. Tiptoeing across the pavement and into the grass, she stuck to the shadows, working her way to the first driveway, a long, snaky strip of blacktop. She shivered in the thin navy shell, her summer tan faded from her arms. She skipped into the next batch of shadow.

The air smelled of leaf mold and wood smoke. The bark on the trees rippled roughly under her hand. The house squatted on the front lawn, visible through the trees, a low-slung modern building, windows lit up from inside. Framed against the glass, Thalia stood next to a sofa, across from the man. He gestured, jaw flapping, pointing at her. He walked in a circle, agitated, then pulled the drapes shut with a jerk.

Dorie took off her shoes. The ground, laced with roots, was bumpy through her thin socks. The night was dark and moonless. Heartless, she thought, like Thalia honey. She looked back at the car. Amos was smoking a forbidden cigarette. Why did he tempt fate like that?

She reached the driveway, weathered and potholed brick. There must have been another, older house here once. This one couldn't have been five years old. She peered down the drive but saw nothing but blackness beyond the modern house. On either side of the driveway sat crumbling brick columns topped with limestone. The left one listed to the south. She squinted at a metal plaque: 101.

The house was only twenty yards away. Amos was still smoking.

She stuck her shoes under one arm, dashed along the shadows of trees, bouncing from one to another, until she was on the narrow porch. Inside, voices. The man's loud and strident, then Thalia's, low and soft. In the shadows of the porch, she felt for the mailbox. There was the doorknob. She felt the box and put her face right up to an ordinary mailbox hanging by the door. No name on it.

The voices stopped. Maybe they'd moved into the kitchen, or the bedroom, or maybe they were making up. Easing the lid up, she felt inside the mailbox. There were two letters. Holding the lid open, she tried to read them in the dim light. But it was too dark, even with the dull glow through the curtains.

Eenie, meenie, minie, moe. She chose the smaller of the two, dropped the other back inside, and set the lid down silently.

In seconds, she was back in the car. Amos had the window open.

"See anything?"

She pulled the letter from her pocket. Breathless from her run, another waddle in the tight skirt, this time in damp socks, she wiggled back into her shoes.

"From the mailbox? I never—" He stared at it. "This is going out."

"To who?"

Amos slipped a fingernail under the flap and tore it open. He pulled out a small piece of stationery and unfolded it. "Turn on the lamp."

Lennox flicked on the dome light. "What's it say?"

"Bloody thank-you note. On church stationery."

"Can I see?"

She took the card. "Dear Mrs. Morgan. The blessings of the Creator and all his sheep on you for your generous contribution to the chorus fund. Please allow me to show my gratitude in person at your earliest convenience. Call me on my private line at Hancock 7-1122. I look forward to speaking to you very soon. Your servant, B. Wake."

"Turn off the lamp. Somebody'll call the cops."

The front of the card had a gold crest with—Amos snapped off the light.

"What church is it?"

"One of those big ones down on the Plaza."

"You know this Wake?"

"Not yet." Amos coughed and rolled up the window. "You want a snooze first?"

She put the card back in the envelope and set it on the seat between them. "How long we staying?"

"As long as it takes."

A car passed on the street, very fast. They didn't have time to duck. She ran her hands over the steering wheel. "Can I put my jacket back on?" Amos looked out the back at the passing car. She slipped her cold arms into the jacket, buttoning it up. Sometimes Amos would play word games or tell her stories about England before the war, the first one, but it didn't seem likely tonight. He'd been subdued all week, quiet, as if waiting for something to happen, a letter to come, a draft notice, a telegram. A bundle of waiting, twitching and sneaking cigarettes and rubbing his bloodshot eyes.

"Did you check the mail before you left?" Amos asked suddenly.

"Expecting something?"

He shrugged.

"From England? Nothing yet?"

Amos tightened his jaw and squinted into the dark street. The Blitzkrieg—the Blitz for short—they were calling it, nightly German raids, shelling London. It'd been going on most of the summer and now, in October, good news was hard to come by. His mother refused to leave—at least that was what she'd said in her last letter, a month or more before.

"But that's good news. No news and all that."

"Some truth to that. Almost fainted today when I saw a Western Union boy in the neighborhood."

"She's too busy to write. Helping people."

They sat silently for half an hour, neither close to sleep nor particularly alert, either. Dorie had nothing and everything on her mind: blue suits and naughty girls, Roosevelt and Willkie, airplanes and bum knees, Hitler and Mussolini. The news these days kept them all thinking, wondering, worrying.

She had worried about these long stakeouts, waiting for Thalia to finish her dallying around, worried that the time would be hard on her, that she would think too much about the past and things she could never change. She'd spent the summer checking out reckless spouses and would-be soldiers and corrupt accountants. No time to think about herself.

The stakeouts hadn't turned out to be so bad. Amos seemed more worried about the future than fixed on the past. None of the things that haunted her last year had come to bear, no dreams, no voices, not even longing for male companionship. The work kept her sane; she was sure of that. Even with parole and all those indignities, she had her work. She let her head rest on the back of the seat and sighed. Would it last?

"The third termers make you sigh like that?"

"What?"

"The ones what think giving Franklin a third term is making him our own Hitler. You've heard about them."

"Be hard not to. That parade last week went right by the office, with the elephants from the zoo draped with huge signs: 'No Third Term.' "

Amos chuckled. "If Willkie only knew the huge Republican road apples them elephants leave behind."

"I hear Willkie leaves them, too. Giant turds, everywhere he goes."

Amos erupted again, laughing and coughing, then wiped his eyes. "Sweet Jesus. I'm going to wake the dead."

"You shouldn't be smoking."

"You think anything can hurt lungs like mine?"

"Want another?"

He looked tempted but shook his head. "Too much racket."

They were quiet again, another half hour. She lighted a cigarette and checked her watch. It was nearly one o'clock. Amos slumped in his seat, pulled his hat down, and closed his eyes. "Short one. Wake me in ten," he said.

The patrol car stopped next to them twenty minutes later. Amos was still dozing. Dorie rolled down her window.

"Move along," the cop said, shining his flashlight in her eyes, then on Amos. "Is he drunk?"

"No, sir. Just tired."

The cop's light moved down her neck and arm, then back to her face. "What's your name?"

"Am I doing something illegal, Officer?"

Amos woke up with a snort, his hat falling forward over his face.

"Oh, I'd be willing to bet on it. We got laws against your kind."

"My kind?" She batted her eyelashes at the cop. He was a blockhead, with cropped hair and brains to match. Her voice sweetened like she'd just swum in peach cobbler. She gasped, then giggled. "You don't think I'm *that* kind of a girl, do you? Really, I am quite flattered, Officer."

Amos leaned down to peer at the cop. "Thank you, sir. We'll be getting along now."

The policeman stared at them for a moment, grumbled a few words, then rolled up his window and drove off. He stopped at the corner and waited for them to leave.

"Wordplay gets you nowhere with that type," Amos chided. "Look smart."

"Leave Thalia here?"

"We've been rousted."

"What'll we tell the Commander?"

"Turn the key, girl. We're busted."

TWO

The mansion looked like it belonged in France more than in the wooded hills of Kansas City. The kind of place you see in picture books, a fairy-tale castle, big and safe and magical. As if it had survived attacks by angry serfs, its stone walls unassailable, its secrets safe forever in gilded velvet boxes. Tall stone walls, manicured sloping lawns, spotless circle drive—for people with romantic lives, people unlike Dorie Lennox. When you lived in a cramped apartment over a drugstore, fairy tales seemed important. All grown up, she hardly remembered them.

She'd never been to France—Nazi-crushed Vichy France now—but a visit to the Hines mansion was almost as foreign. She'd been here every morning this week, and still it felt odd, a world apart. The stone building sat in watery shadow under tall trees, as if the builders had known nothing could warm the facade. In the circle drive, a green sedan was being washed by the chauffeur. He'd found a spot of dappled sunshine and rolled up his white shirtsleeves over muscular arms. Water from the garden hose sluiced down the cement into the expanse of grass yellowing in the autumn sun.

Amos wore his brown suit again. Maybe he'd slept in it. Dorie wore tan trousers, pressed quickly in the kitchen that morning. No more blue suit; it would have to wait for another funeral. Lennox shivered at the thought as they were ushered into the drafty front hall by the maid. The smell of funerals hung in the air at the Hines mansion.

The maid disappeared. The high ceiling, complete with wood beams, soared above a winding staircase with a mahogany railing and gray-carpeted steps. They wouldn't be going upstairs. The Commander had taken over the library as her bedroom several years back. What about the bedrooms up there? What were they like—gilded paper, ruffles, thick rugs?

She hadn't slept well. It was after two o'clock when she got back to the boardinghouse. She'd lain awake, waiting for something to happen. What was it? Not the six cigarettes that had passed the time. Something was in the air, like a dark cloud or an unanswered prayer.

"Any mail yet?" she asked Amos. "At the office?"

"No." He paced around a marble-top table, running his fingers along the cool edges. Her question seemed to set him off, and she regretted it. It was driving him crazy, with his mother under attack.

Amos cleared his throat noisily, and she squinted at him. Here it comes.

An explosion of coughing. It sent him looking for a bathroom. He'd been doing so well since last fall's bout in the hospital. Hang in, she thought. Don't leave me here alone.

She drew her arms close to her chest. The stone, the walls, the spotless floor, the tabletop—all conspired to freeze her to the core. How did people live in this icebox? Why *wouldn't* Thalia escape whenever she could? She could still see Thalia in ruby red satin, singing to those googly-eyed men.

Thalia honey, whose hips saw more action than General Pétain. Poor Philippe. His reputation as a French military genius had died a quick death.

Dorie pressed her shivering lips together. She felt suddenly anxious and ready to bolt. She squeezed her arms until they hurt and listened for Amos's coughing. She stood stone-still until the man, a stranger, appeared in the doorway to a dim hall.

"Good morning," she forced herself to say. His sudden appearance made her stomach leap, but she tried to hide that. She rubbed the backs of her arms to warm them, then let them fall at her sides again.

The man stepped out into the bluish light coming from a high window on the stairs. He was slight, with thinning dark hair, but youthful, early thirties, she guessed. Taller if he stood straight. His eyebrows pointed like halves of a roof come apart. He took off rimless glasses and wiped them with a handkerchief as he examined her for a long minute.

"You're the detective," he said finally. His voice was deep, almost a rumble.

"Yes." A tingle of relief: He was human. Silly idea. She strode closer, stuck out her hand. "Doria Lennox. Pleased to meet you."

He wrapped his glasses around his ears. He wore a crisp blue oxford shirt with no tie, soft sweater in green tones, wool slacks. Not the help, obviously. His skin was pale, as if he didn't find any sun. His thin lips matched his eyebrows. He stared, and she squared her shoulders defensively.

"The Commander didn't tell me, you know. I had to find out on my own." His small blue eyes bored into her. She stepped back a pace. Perhaps she'd gotten him wrong.

"You don't say." Who was this jasper? He might be a relative. She decided to be polite. "How is the Commander today?"

The man tipped his head quizzically. "My sources tell me no change. What do your sources say?"

"I . . . um—my sources haven't reported yet this morning."

A smirk transformed the man's face. He leaned closer and whispered, "Sources can be at cross-purposes. I found that out the hard way."

A tangle of emotions danced across his visage, moving from menace to delight, suspicion to disgust. She stepped back again. Too early in the day for a nervous breakdown.

"I'll keep that in mind," she said. She turned then toward the hall, where Amos had disappeared. And there he was, coming toward them, wiping his mouth on a handkerchief, but upright, his color good, walking steadily. Relief flooded through her.

She smiled at her boss as his heels tapped the marble floor and stopped in front of her. He looked up, wiggling his eyebrows. "No admittance to the sanctum yet?"

She shook her head, then remembered the man. "Amos, this

is—" She turned, to find he'd vanished. "Well, I don't know who he was."

"Or where, either."

"Are there more family members? Besides Thalia?"

"Bowl him over with your charm, did you?"

She shook herself, memorizing the man's face, as if he might have been only an apparition. The maid returned; they followed her down a shadowy hallway to the library, through an arched wooden door that creaked as they were ushered in. Where there had once been a billiard table, a large four-poster bed took center stage. Propped on a dozen pillows was the Commander.

"Mrs. Hines," Amos said, bowing slightly. The old woman loved Amos and his old-world ways. She'd served as an army nurse in the same war that had claimed Amos's lungs.

"Mr. Haddam. Miss Lennox." She peered over half glasses, then took them off and set them on a stack of papers in her lap. A dove gray wool shawl was wrapped around her thin shoulders. Her face was stoic, but in her eyes you could see the pain. Eveline Hines was dying, the slow way, from cancer.

"Come closer," she commanded. "Tell me what's happened."

They nodded to Mother Ruth, the heavyset, iron-haired nurse, and settled onto two hard chairs to the side of the bed. Mrs. Hines put a finger on her lower lip and stared straight ahead, as if knowing the report wasn't going to please her. "All right," she said brusquely.

Mother Ruth pursed her lips unhappily and went out the door, shutting it without a creak. If you lived here, Dorie thought, you could slide through without making a ripple. Unless you were Thalia Hines, determined to make all the ripples you could.

"I'm ready," Mrs. Hines said, her voice softer now.

Amos cleared his throat. He began with his scratchy voice, but the Commander raised a thin hand. "Miss Lennox, you take over." She gave Amos a look of disapproval, one of her more common expressions. Dorie glanced at her boss. He sat slumped in his chair, holding back another fit. Make it fast, she told herself.

"She spent most of the night at the Three Owls. It's over on Twelfth, upstairs. She danced and drank a little, not too much. She sang a song and—"

"What song?"

"Pardon?"

The Commander gave her a hard stare. "What song did Thalia sing?"

She looked at Amos. He didn't meet her eye. "Um. I think it was 'Between the Devil and the Deep Blue Sea.' "

She had no recollection of what Thalia had sung the night before. She'd sung at least ten songs that week, none of them memorable.

Amos was staring at her now. The Commander squinted, a venomous look in her eye. She turned it on Amos. "Mr. Haddam?"

"Might have been. I didn't record the song, Mrs. Hines."

"I specifically remember asking for all details." The color rose in the old woman's cheeks. She was angry. Probably what kept her alive. That and the prospect of leaving her only daughter footloose and fancy-free with a big fat inheritance. That worried Mrs. Hines. After a week of acquaintance with the girl, it terrified Dorie.

"You see," Mrs. Hines said, "if I knew the song she was singing, I'd have an indication of her attitude, her demeanor. Almost like I was there. But I can't be there, can I?"

"I'm sorry."

"Don't be sorry, just observe. That is why I have both of you along. I understand it's hard to keep an eye on the girl. Believe me, I understand." Mrs. Hines sunk back again into the white pillows and shut her eyes for a moment. "There is so little time. I must have all the details."

Amos shot Dorie a look. She frowned back. Did they want her to follow Thalia to the toilet, sip her drinks, lift wallets off the men? She could do that, if that was what Mrs. Hines wanted.

She bit down on her molars. How would the old woman react about what happened next?

"Whom was she with?" Mrs. Hines said, eyes open again.

"Mostly the man she saw two nights ago, Oscar Gordon."

"The attorney."

"Right. He lives over in Mission Hills, by—"

"Yes, yes." Mrs. Hines waved a hand. "She told me about Oscar Gordon. There's no mystery there. No danger to her heart."

"Her heart, ma'am?" Stop the presses: THALIA HINES HAS A HEART.

"It's the ones she doesn't tell me about that worry me, Miss Lennox. The men she keeps hidden away, the ones who will break her heart."

Eveline Hines pushed back a wispy strand of copper hair from her forehead. Her face was pale and thin, with old freckles stretched across her sunken cheeks. She had been beautiful once, or at least striking, with her fine skin, fiery hair, and that composure. A portrait of her in her nurse's uniform, her cap in her lap, hung over the fireplace. The steely blueness to her eyes made you look away, as if her strength, her will, took measure of your own. A woman to be reckoned with. Cantankerous now, but one couldn't blame the dying for that. Or for worrying about the future of her daughter. There would be many hearts broken before Thalia was done.

"There was another man last night, Mrs. Hines," Amos said flatly. "He came into the Three Owls before midnight and she left with him."

"And who was he?"

"We followed them to a house on Thirty-eighth Street. Number one oh one. They went inside. The address is that of a Barnaby Wake."

"The chorus director?" Eveline Hines stiffened.

Amos shuffled his notes. He cleared his throat, his neck a violent shade of purple.

"He's employed at Plaza Methodist Church," Dorie said.

"She sings for him," Mrs. Hines said. "In that chorus. You would have seen him when she went to practice on Tuesday." She squinted. "She did go to chorus practice on Tuesday, didn't she?"

Amos flipped pages in his notebook. He wasn't coughing—yet. His Adam's apple bobbed as he swallowed and croaked, "Chorus practice, seven in the evening."

Dorie rose, circled the bed, poured a glass of water from Mrs. Hines's bedside table, and carried it back to Amos. The old woman glared at her. Amos looked up, startled by the appearance of the water. He drank it and nodded to her to sit down. There was an awkward silence while he balanced the glass on his knee and the water at the bottom sloshed back and forth.

"At seven," Mrs. Hines repeated.

Amos didn't answer. Dorie looked at his notebook. "Yes, ma'am. She was there about two hours."

The Commander's eyes hardened. Her fingers, fretting with the edge of the crisp sheet, stilled. "You didn't meet this Wake that night?"

"We waited outside, ma'am."

Eveline Hines squinted at Amos. "Practice begins at eight. For one hour."

Heels tapped by the doorway in the hall, hard against the stone floor. A tree limb creaked and scraped against the roof. Outside the leaded window across from the bed, the yellow leaves of an elm tree floated by, twirling in the autumn sun. What did that mean? Thalia had gone early to get some personal attention, possibly—or not—of the musical variety. Amos handed her the water glass, turned a page in his notebook, and found a pencil in his shirt pocket. The *Kansas City Star* on the foot of Mrs. Hines's bed blared a headline: BOMBS RAIN ON LONDON. Dorie tore her eyes away. War news gave her the feeling of being on a runaway train.

"You know Mr. Wake?" Amos asked.

"I know *of* him," Mrs. Hines said. "This choir, he calls it the Hallelujah Chorus. Through the church. Quite popular, so I hear. A big choir, forty or fifty men and women. They perform around town, for society events and charity."

"Didn't they march in that parade last week?" Dorie asked, remembering the scarlet robes and patriotic streamers as they sang a gospel hymn in the wind.

"The Willkie parade?" Amos said.

Mrs. Hines said, "Thalia didn't mention it." She looked at the heavy oak ceiling. "It doesn't mean she didn't march."

"Do they wear red robes?"

Mrs. Hines frowned, then rearranged her bedding for a moment. "He picked her up at this club?"

"They drove to his house. We followed them there and waited for about an hour." Amos's voice was going. He cleared his throat, took back the water glass, and finished it.

"For an hour?"

"Yes, ma'am. A policeman came by and made us move on. We would have stayed otherwise."

"So you don't know what time she left there."

"No, ma'am." Dorie glanced at Amos. He was taking even breaths and looked better. "I believe, Mrs. Hines, that your chauffeur was driving them. In the green sedan."

The old woman frowned witheringly. "*My* chauffeur?"

"We just saw him out in the driveway, washing the same car."

Amos was staring at her. The thought had just crystallized in her mind. The quick look she'd had of the chauffeur with his hat on, his tanned neck and handsome jaw: It had to be him.

"We think it was the same car, ma'am. I think so at least." She widened her eyes at Amos to make him look away.

"You're saying Barnaby Wake picked up Thalia at this club, this Three Owls, in my automobile, driven by my chauffeur?" Mrs. Hines laid her thin fingers at her throat.

"It does sound—" Ridiculous, but still, she was sure it was the same car. She wanted to jump right up and go ask the chauffeur about it. Prove she was right. Instead, she dug her nails into the chair seat.

"We'll check that out, with your permission, Mrs. Hines," Amos said, recovering his voice. "Is she going out tonight?"

"I haven't heard otherwise, although her plans are always news to me." The Commander sighed. "I'll have you called as soon as I hear."

"Do you know when she came in last night, ma'am?" Dorie asked.

The woman arched her penciled eyebrows. "That is your job, Miss Lennox." After the obligatory guilty pause, she went on. "She did come home, if that's your question. She knows better than that, I should hope."

You *should* hope, thought Dorie. She escaped the sickroom by saying she had to use the bathroom, leaving Amos and the Commander with a few moments together. They seemed to like that. The old woman was dying, and if Amos Haddam could give her a few pointers on pain and suffering, or conjure up happier days, well, more the better. She thought of Mrs. Hines as old, but she was scarcely fifty, less than ten years older than Amos. They had both gone through fire in the first war, emerging battered but alive.

Dorie had her own scars. But a war—that was something alien, a faraway violence to the soul and body. She'd heard the stories, knew the pain. But she knew better than to say she understood.

Haddam gathered his thoughts in his notebook for a few moments, scribbling down a few words about Barnaby Wake. This job, if you could call it that—he didn't—was a favor for Eveline Hines. She'd demanded the first week's billing statement already or he wouldn't even have charged her. She was dying and wanted some peace of mind with a wayward child. It was common enough. But there was nothing common about Eveline Hines.

He watched her pale closed lids, veins threading through the transparent skin, dark circles under her eyes, sagging flesh where once her cheeks had been plump and flushed with life. He'd known her for twelve years, since they'd been introduced at an Armistice Day picnic. Back then, he'd seemed the older one. She'd been a fiery redhead with a wicked tongue, choice opinions on all the candidates, on reform, on women's issues, on everything. Her husband had seemed to understand her need to shine, to be in charge, to be, as everyone called her, "the Commander." Amos never really understood that about Leslie Hines, but he certainly admired the man for it. It took a brave man to endure Eveline's wit, her demands, her harsh nature. Apparently, it had killed Leslie, this bravery, for he'd gone four years before, quickly, of a heart ailment.

It seemed ironic, even cruel, that a nurse should die like this. She had helped so many in the war, bandaged them, held them, comforted them. And now, in her time of suffering, there was no one to hold her. Her daughter was more interested in men and a good time. Amos had his doubts about the girl, although he wouldn't tell Eveline as much. He'd seen her type often enough in this shadowy business of his—the girl who uses her physical charm and connections to the full extent of the law, and then some. She didn't care about any of the men, or she was an actress of star quality. Eveline would like that, in her strange way. Could Thalia care at all? That was an issue that would probably be decided by her own mother's death.

And Eveline's stepson, Leslie's boy—Amos looked up, surprised at himself. That must have been the person Dorie had seen in the hallway. The elusive stepson. What was his name? Julian. Amos had never met him, in all these years. He was married, Amos recalled. And still living at home, watching over the wicked stepmother? Amos scribbled the stepson's name in his notebook, with the notation "Meet?" He was curious, if nothing else.

Amos flipped his notebook back to the appointments section

and checked his watch. He had a meeting with a new client at noon, and it was after eleven o'clock now. He would have to wrap things up soon. He cleared his throat.

"So, my dear friend," Mrs. Hines said, her eyes still closed, head deep against the down pillow, "what will we do with little Thalia?" Her lips curled up. Was she secretly enjoying her daughter's exploits? Her sigh was unconvincing.

"We'll keep an eye on her for you, Eveline," Amos said, patting her arm. "Don't you worry."

"Oh, I do. I worry day and night." She opened her eyes and gave him one of her now-rare smiles. "But having you come and visit me every day almost compensates for the worry."

"I would come anyway; you know that."

"Yes, yes." She squeezed his hand. "Of course." She peered at him. "You look tired, Amos Haddam."

He gave her a brave smile. "No more than yesterday, Eveline."

"Don't give me that stiff upper lip nonsense. Your cough is worse. Your eyes look awful. You aren't sleeping."

He looked at her, lying there dying and worried about him. Still the nurse. His chest ached, not because of gas damage, but at losing her.

"It's nothing," he said. She waited, eyes boring into him. "My mother. I haven't heard anything for some time."

"I'll have Ned look into it. With his embassy connections, he can find her."

"I'm sure Ned has better things to do than track down old fussbudgets in bomb shelters. It's got to be chaos over there."

"All the more reason. What's her first name?"

"Cassandra." He tried to smile, but his emotions were thick this morning, what with the war news and the prospect of more pain for this woman. "Thank you, Eveline."

She squeezed his hand again. "If I can do something out there . . ." She turned to the window. "So." She sat herself up, composed her face. "Europe at war again. It seems so unreal here. So very far away."

Not so very far for someone with a draft notice in his pocket. What had Lennox said last night? *You won't pass the physical.* Then her face had dropped, as if his gas-ravaged lungs were a touchy subject. She was a funny girl, with a warm heart, which it took most of her energy to disguise.

A draft. Here in the States. The war seemed closer every day to him, like a thunderstorm on the horizon, moving into position directly overhead. And his mother under attack—again. He could almost smell the ozone from the lightning. It was not unreal; it was all too horrifying.

She was staring at him again. "But not for you, I see. Tell me what's happening."

Amos fingered his notebook, then shook his head. "Nothing. Really, dear."

She frowned at him. He could see she was eager for details. But he knew no more about it than the *Star*. Maybe telling her Uncle Sam wanted him would give her a much-needed laugh. It was amusing, in an ironic way.

A grimace of pain crossed her face. When it passed, she sank again into the pillows. "You were in France, weren't you, Amos?"

He felt a chill. "Yes, Eveline."

"I remember the quiet, between the battles." Her voice was barely a whisper. "When the shelling was going on, we didn't have time to think, to let anything sink in. We didn't want to. And now all I remember is the quiet. Eerie, breathy quiet. A moan perhaps, a clink of spoon on tin cup. No birds, I remember that. Not a bird in sight. They knew better. So very, very quiet. It was like purgatory. You knew you were dead. You wondered, Heaven or hell? But you knew perfectly well that this was hell's waiting room."

She lay motionless on the white pillow, her face only a few shades darker than the case. Her eyes closed again. She was in France, listening to the nothingness. Amos couldn't take his eyes off her. He wanted to leave, to get away—from her memories and her dying and her pain. But his body wouldn't move. He could hear the quiet, too, as if he lay in the mud again, under the fragile blue sky, waiting for death as his lungs burned with every breath. His ankle had been broken in the crash, the big mapping camera shattered. He'd lain in the soft warm mud, and had been quiet.

He knew how the night would go; he could feel it already. He would lie awake, the windows open, counting the seconds between autos passing on the street, savoring the sound—the hiss of tires, the rattle of engines. He would get up and turn on the wireless, so loud, the neighbors would shout and he would have to turn it down low and lie on the sofa to hear it. Anything to have noises filling his ears, filling the dark, filling the spaces. Anything to feel alive.

Now the silence stretched long and awful, until Mother Ruth opened the door abruptly. The sound echoed like a boom.

"Oh," the old nurse said, "pardon me. Madam, Father Williams is here." She backed out of the room.

Amos blinked, wiggling his fingers to reassure himself. He felt very cold.

The Commander opened her eyes.

"Now. Let's turn our attention to Barnaby Wake, shall we?"

Out in the driveway, the chauffeur was nowhere in sight.

Dorie walked to the green sedan, sitting long and shiny in the patchy sunlight. The wax was fresh, swirling in iridescent patterns on the bulbous hood. Oldsmobile, it said in chrome. Thalia had taken it to choir practice, driving herself that night. How had she managed to bribe the chauffeur into letting her take it? she wondered, remembering the girl's erratic driving.

High overhead, birds twittered in the trees. Squirrels scolded her, then went about their business hoarding acorns for winter. She leaned against the car and crossed her arms, feeling the sun like a stingy gift on one cheek. Autumn was her favorite season, when the air sharpened, losing the turgid humidity of summer, yet without the biting prairie wind of winter. The trees turned magically into their dream coats. It reminded her of school days, which had meant escape, return to order, to duties, to a strangely comforting regimen. She had been told what was expected of her. All she'd had to do to win praise was meet those expectations. If only life were so simple now.

Footsteps tapped the cement driveway behind her. She turned, expecting the chauffeur at last.

"Tom will murder you if you smudge his wax job." The man stood with his hands on his hips, feet apart, chin out. The same man, confronting, questioning, again.

She moved her backside off the fender. "Sorry, I—" She straightened, squinting as the man's aggressive pose. His attitude was tiresome. She walked briskly around the front of the car and stood in front of him.

"I don't believe we've been introduced. At least I didn't get your name."

Another strange look crossed the man's face. He lowered his fists from his hips. "I suppose the Commander didn't describe me accurately." He smiled. "I can believe that. Julian Hines, at your service, *mam'selle.*"

His hand was cool and slick with sweat. Lennox released it gladly. "You're Thalia's brother?"

"Half brother. My mother died when I was a baby. My father married Miss Eveline right after the war. But you've probably heard all the stories. The whirlwind courtship, all the folderol. The stuff of legend."

She hadn't, but she nodded. He continued unabated.

"The famous war heroine, saved hundreds—nay, thousands of lives behind the lines, in the medic tents, in the caissons—with her bare hands! Given a Legion of Honor medal by the French. Famous all over Paris, the toast of the town. One of her many admirers, my father, who had gone to France to look after his import interests. Fortunately, only half the farms were destroyed. Lean for a while, but he got them going. Then he met her. And that, as they say, was that."

"Ran off and got married, did they?"

"How could he resist, a famous flame-haired patriot like the Commander?" The sarcasm sat unattractively on his face.

"She must have been a beauty in her time."

"Good genes, as we see in darling Thalia."

"Yes, Thalia is a stunner."

Julian Hines shifted and stared at her, one finger on his chin, as if she'd said something thought-provoking.

"Nice to meet you, then, Mr. Hines."

"It would be polite to give me a report of your meeting," he said, frowning now, "since I was not invited to attend."

"You'll have to talk to the Commander about that."

"I'm not important enough to know what's going on?"

"Pardon?"

"Wendy was the Commander's favorite; that was no secret. But then, nothing is really fair in the Commander's castle."

She stepped back, bumping into the car. She busied herself shining up the chrome around the headlight with the corner of her sweater. Whatever the man thought he knew, she knew even less. But perhaps the Commander liked it that way. Maybe she was in there right now telling Amos the real mission.

"You'll have to speak to your—to the Commander about that." She smiled to sweeten it, but he wasn't taking it. How did the abrasive old army nurse and Mr. Sunshine Stepson get along? And who the hell was Wendy?

"Swell meeting you, Mr. Hines."

Dorie turned and walked to her car. She hadn't gotten anything from the chauffeur, hadn't even found him. Julian Hines stood staring at her with his hard eyes. She sat behind the wheel, looking at her hands, wishing Amos along. Hurry up, old chap.

When she looked up, Julian had disappeared.

THREE

DORIE TAPPED HER WRISTWATCH, WAITING for Amos. When the door to the Hines mansion opened, she peered over the steering wheel.

Thalia honey. In tennis whites, a sweater and short pleated skirt, and racket. She swung a set of keys over a finger, her hair tied back in a ponytail. She paused, bent one knee over the other as if posing for a photograph, looked at the green sedan, then at the Packard.

Dorie straightened in her seat and rolled her window down a little farther, letting in a mix of scents, grass and burning leaves and auto exhaust. Thalia tipped her head, making up her mind, then strode directly toward the Packard, hips swaying to make the little skirt flip from side to side over her milky long legs. As she walked close to the front bumper of the auto, she paused, gave a little "Oh!" and slipped out of sight below the hood.

Jumping out of the Packard, Dorie slammed the car door. She stepped toward the fender as the girl leapt up from her crouch, yelling, "Boo!" Dorie gasped and took a step backward, her heart thumping.

Thalia's mock-menacing roar switched to a belly laugh as she doubled over, pointing at Dorie with hilarious glee and letting her racket fall to the pavement with a clatter.

"Oh my God, you should have seen your face! You looked like you'd had your last meal. Lord save me from starvation!" Laughter overwhelmed the girl. As she lost steam, she wiped her eyes. "That would have been a hoot. Mommy rapping your knuckles for driving over darling daughter. Or worse." She put her hands on her own throat and stuck out her tongue, making strangling noises. "Poor little detective!"

Her laughter trilled away. Thalia swept gracefully to pick up her tennis racket. She set it on her shoulder, walked to the sedan. With one leg perched in the sunshine, she turned in the car seat. "Don't look so glum. I'm going dancing again tonight."

The sedan's door shut as the motor roared to life. Thalia hit the gas and peeled away down the driveway and into the street, causing a blast of horn from a delivery truck.

Dorie watched until the sedan turned a corner. She felt the black tide inside her drain from her ears and neck, and the thumping in her head softened. She forced herself to take a deep breath and looked down at her hands, clenched at her sides. She opened her hands, shook them out. Out of habit, she felt her trouser pocket for the switchblade. A small lurch tightened her stomach at the empty spot where the blade had always been.

She rubbed her hands together, lacing her knuckles in a clench. An empty grasp. It was so unfair that she couldn't have her switchblade even for its rabbit's foot qualities. Its stabbing qualities, which she'd demonstrated in the spring, weren't its only attractions.

She shook out her hands angrily. God, why was she thinking about the switchblade now? Worthless child. Thalia had no business with a body like that. It was trouble on wheels. Already, Dorie was preparing a scenario in her head. It would end the tailing of Thalia Hines, and it involved nasty things—humiliation, at least momentary pain—why should Thalia be spared?—maybe handcuffs and the inside of a cold jail cell, definitely a good dressing-down from the Commander, which Lennox and Haddam just couldn't save her from, try as they mighty-might-might.

Dorie smiled to herself, feeling her pulse slow. She was perverse, thinking like that. But she would enjoy Thalia's comeuppance. No use denying it. Thalia enjoyed taunting them. It was hilarious that they were following her for her mother, simply hilarious. They weren't to interfere with her activities unless she was physically threatened, and that seemed unlikely, since she would do anything any man suggested. And probably came up with a few naughty suggestions of her own. That man last night, Barnaby Wake, he had an air that was different from her other boyfriends, though. Possessive, that one. And as well dressed as any sharper on Twelfth Avenue.

Dorie stepped into the Packard as Amos emerged from the mansion. She watched him take a breath of autumn air, tipping his nose to the wind like a foxhound. He often had a skip in his step after visiting with Eveline Hines—but not today. Still, he looked glad to be released into the fresh air.

"I caught the chauffeur on the way out," Amos said, settling into the wide seat. "Name is Tommy. Says he gives Thalia the keys whenever she wants them. Like today, she's got a tennis date. And always for chorus practice. He stays around here if she's got a date—usually."

"And last night?"

"He was a bit vague. Says the Commander gave him the night off. Does every Saturday, in fact."

"And the sedan?"

"Part of the job. He doesn't have his own wheels."

"So he's working on the side for this Wake?"

"He denied it. Said he was at a meeting last night, then went out with some friends for a drink."

"That wasn't him?" She could have sworn it was.

Amos shrugged. "We've got bigger fish to fry."

She started the car and drove down the driveway to the street. "Which way?"

He flicked his hand left. "To the Plaza."

They were almost to the end of Ward Parkway, with the Spanish-style red tile roofs of the Country Club Plaza in view, when Amos slapped his thigh. "I have an appointment back in the office in ten minutes. Step on it."

Some minutes later, she pulled up in front of the Boston Building. "Am I supposed to do something at the Plaza?"

Amos turned on the sidewalk, shook his head as if clearing cobwebs, and walked back to the window. "Go check out this Barnaby Wake. He's at Plaza Methodist."

"Where's that?"

"It's the big new one. By the fancy architect. The one in the papers."

That explained a lot. She turned south again on Wyandotte. She read the *Kansas City Star,* but usually just to see what Harvey Talbot was up to. His reporting had been fairly lackluster this summer, just writing about school boards and petty criminals. She hadn't read about any big fancy church. But it couldn't be that hard to find.

Traffic was thick through downtown, even on a Sunday. The war in Europe had lighted a fire under business, and manufacturers were scrambling to predict what soldiers would need. There was a greedy glee to it that left a bad taste in the mouth, but Kansas City had come back to life in a way that Franklin D. Roosevelt had tried to achieve but never quite accomplished. FDR was making noises about airplanes and tanks and bullets and boots, and Kansas City was listening.

A streetcar-auto incident at the corner of Eleventh and Wyandotte had the traffic tangled for blocks. A streetcar hack waved his hat around while jumping on the bumper of an automobile, shouting at the driver cowering inside.

Lennox settled into a slow, stop-and-go rhythm down Broadway through Penn Valley Park—a mistake on a Sunday afternoon, but pleasant and grassy—then on to where Broadway turned into Mill Creek. She turned right on Forty-seventh Street and was in the midst of the Country Club Plaza District, with its Moorish towers, Spanish buildings, fountains, fancy people, and money.

The stores were closed today, making it easy to find the churches. Autos were parked in clusters around them, one at the far western side of the district, which turned out to be a Catholic church, and another near the northeast side. Here was Plaza

Methodist, new, bright, modern. Dorie parked a block away and walked back to the building. She assumed the many vehicles parked nearby meant a church service was under way. It seemed late for services, but she didn't have much contact with churches, hadn't even when she was a kid. Her mother hadn't been welcome in any in Atchison.

She pulled open the heavy wood doors embellished with leaded glass. The foyer was hushed and dark, the stone floor dotted with utilitarian rugs. Lennox stood on one and listened for the preacher. The doors to the nave were closed tight, blocking sound and light.

She stood swaying for a moment on the mat. New construction smells wafted up: paint, varnish, good wood, wet cement. The long green wall that faced her was a clean sweep of color, broken only by a long, low wooden table set with a single brass bowl. If she held her breath, she could hear singing somewhere deep inside the church.

She closed her eyes, reaching out for the edge of the door frame for balance. Was it singing here—or in her head? She gulped a breath and listened hard. Men's voices, young men, a boy's choir, singing a hymn, something in Latin, words she didn't know. It was pure and beautiful, and when it stopped, she was disappointed.

"Can I help you?"

A woman stood peering over rimless glasses, holding a large black notebook tightly against her chest. She wore a plain blue dress and the kind of shoes schoolteachers wore, simple and sturdy. Gray streaked through her light brown hair, which was pulled back off her face with combs.

"Are you all right?" The woman held out a hand as if to show how steady it was.

"I'm looking for Barnaby Wake," Dorie said.

"Oh." The woman gave her a strange look. "I don't believe he's here right now."

"But he does have an office here. For the Hallelujah Chorus? Maybe I can leave him a message."

"He rehearses here on Thursdays. You should come back then." The woman turned to go.

"Wait, I—" She touched the woman's arm, causing her to flinch and frown, then pull her arm away. "I'm sorry. I thought Mr. Wake was the choir director here. I was listening to that choir, the boys. It was swell."

The woman straightened, her posture becoming even more upright. " 'Swell'?" she repeated, then coughed as if spitting the foul word out. "Reverend Nolan does a fine job with the boys."

"Reverend Nolan?"

"The choir director." The woman raised one eyebrow. That's that, the eyebrow said. "Good day."

"Wait, Miss . . ."

Stopped again, the woman said irritably, "Janes. Hazel Janes."

"Doria Lennox. Nice to meet you, Miss Janes." Lennox had no luck getting the woman to shake her hand. Must give it a good wash and manicure. Heck, she'd do both hands—why scrimp?

"One last thing. I was wondering if I could . . ." She pointed toward the doors. "Just a peek?"

In the Packard, Dorie sat for a moment, looking at her perfectly presentable hand. There was a smudge of grease or something on the back. She rubbed it.

Standing inside the nave had been strange. She wasn't sure what she'd expected, since her church visits could be counted on the fingers of one filthy hand. It was huge, she had expected that. With a high wood-beamed ceiling and modernist stained glass, no saints or Resurrection scenes, just geometric shapes in a variety of colors.

Dorie'd stood there, just inside the big heavy door, letting it close behind her. The quiet was dense. Light came through the stained glass, watery but clear, like raindrops, creating a dance of prisms on the long wooden pews. The front of the church was open, with a raised stage. Above a single unimposing podium, a long red-and-gold banner hung on the wall.

She was enjoying the quiet when the smell of lilies came to her. Large vases sat on either corner of the stage, filled with white lilies. The sweet scent of the flowers took her back to Atchison, to a time she had gone to Easter service with her friend Arlette at her father's church. The only white face in the crowd, twelve and awkward and embarrassed by the attention. But the singing. The voices of that choir had been rich and bold, reaching out and grabbing your heart and wringing it out.

She shook herself in the Packard. It had been a long time since she'd heard from Arlette. She hadn't seen her friend in years, not since Atchison, but Arlette usually dropped her a postcard from her travels. Now that connection seemed broken, too.

Just as well, since she never wrote back. Arlette never gave an address, as if to keep the correspondence under her control. As if it was a duty. Dorie never felt her getting pinched for stealing the car, and winding up at reform school, was Arlette's problem. She had made her own choice, the only choice, to take the car, to drive to the doctor in Kansas City, because Arlette was desperate and had to have an abortion. Arlette would have done it for her. There was no obligation, no duty. Still, Arlette had written, little scribbled notes of affection and gratitude, all those years.

Back on Charlotte Street, the boardinghouse had a lazy feel. Two girls sat on the front steps gossiping. The afternoon had warmed and was so inviting that neighborhood children had set up a game of stickball in the street. Dorie threw the ball back to them as she stepped out of the Packard. It was Sunday and she had to tail the rich girl again tonight. She'd be damned if she was going to work all day, too.

Betty Kimble and the new girl, Carol, were laughing as Lennox stepped around them on the stoop. Betty probably telling a joke. They nodded and said hello.

"Oh, Dorie," Betty said as Lennox opened the screen door. "Joe was around earlier, looking for you." She smiled. "He's sweet on you, honey."

Carol laughed, then hung her head to hide it. Joe Czmanski's looks were an object of derision by the girls in the boardinghouse, but it wasn't polite to acknowledge, let alone laugh at, his misfortunes.

"What'd he want?" Dorie asked, frowning at the new girl. The garage across the street, Joe's place, was shut up tight.

"Said he had something he needed to discuss with you. Seemed kinda excited. You two got something to announce?" Betty was enjoying herself, as usual.

"Thanks, Betty," Dorie said, ignoring the implication as she went inside. It was true Joe Czmanski had been sweet on her, off and on, for reasons she couldn't figure. She'd done everything to discourage him. She felt sorry for Joe; he'd had a tough time. Having a car engine blow up in your face changed a man, would change anyone who survived it. Pity was one thing. She believed in kindness; she'd seen the results of too little of it. But that didn't mean she wanted to be his girl.

Lennox used the pay phone on the landing to call the office. "Everything okay?"

"What's shaking." Amos seemed distracted.

"I went over to Plaza Methodist." She told him what she'd found out at the church about Barnaby Wake. It took long seconds.

"Hmm."

"Thalia's choir practice was at the Knights of Columbus. So I guess he's all over town, doing this and that."

"Seems so."

"I'd go check out the Knights Hall, but I don't think he has an office there or anything. And he won't be there today, do you think?"

"Doubtful."

A pause. "How'd your appointment go? New client?"

"What? Oh, yes. Good."

"You didn't hear anything from London, did you?"

"No, not on Sunday."

Telegrams come any day, but she didn't tell him that. "Where do we meet tonight?"

"Pick me up at nine. I'll know by then." He hung up.

Lennox stared at the receiver and replaced it gently. Was the man he was meeting still in the office, or was he losing his concentration? She wished he'd let her go alone tonight. He could get some sleep. He needed it.

Amos Haddam smoothed out the sheet of notebook paper.

The three men across the desk looked back from their polite gaze out the window, worry etching their foreheads. Quincy Gilmore was a dapper man in his forties, a man who liked being the public face for the white owner of the baseball team. He enjoyed dressing the part, from his patent leather shoes and satin lapels to his white felt fedora. It might be Sunday, and these might be his church duds, but Amos had seen him just as spiffed at Chamber meetings. Why he had brought along the young ballplayer, who was dressed, and obviously paid, so poorly, bothered Haddam. The contrast between them was striking. The boy was maybe nineteen and as green as a southern farm boy could be.

"You found this where, Leroy?" Amos asked.

"In the locker room," the boy said. "I been coming in to practice by myself."

"Where in the locker room?"

"On the floor. When I opened the door."

"Just like this? No envelope?"

"No, suh."

Leroy looked at Quincy Gilmore. "Did I do wrong?"

Gilmore reached out a manicured hand to pat the boy's knee. "Course not. You came to me. That was right."

Amos read over the note again: "Niggers. Cancel the Blues game or you'll be more than sorry."

It could mean anything, or nothing. There was no nuance to interpret. He sat back in the chair and folded his hands. He was too tired for this nonsense. Maybe he was too tired for this business. He should just take a train to the coast and go to England. Find out what the bloody hell was going on. Ned Brainard wasn't going to comb the shelters for his old mum, not when he was trying to keep the BBC afloat. Amos rubbed his eyes and rocked back, letting the creaking chair do his complaining.

"You reckon it's just Blues fans, Amos?" Gilmore asked, breaking into his reverie.

"Could be. Who else would be afraid of the Monarchs beating the tar out of the favorite sons?"

Gilmore frowned, his clipped mustache dipping. "There's folks. There's always folks, Amos. Thems who don't like to see the Negro best the white man."

"But you've played the Blues before. Have there been problems?"

"A couple of phone calls from crackers, you know. Some Kluxers. Razzin' in the crowd. Nothing serious."

Amos pushed the note to the edge of the desk. To get rid of it. "But you think this is serious?"

Gilmore raised his eyebrows and shrugged. Leroy Williams sat forward, his muscular arms balanced on his legs. He was a strapping boy, a good hitter when he connected. He played second base like his life depended on it. Maybe it did.

The third man, quiet until now, stood up. He was another player, one Amos had seen play a couple times. He hadn't been on the team long, maybe two years. Older than Leroy by at least ten years, he had an air of confidence the boy could only dream of. His clothes were plain, but he wore them well. He cleared his throat.

"What we have here, Mr. Haddam," the player said, "is a case of intimidation. They want us to roll over, like we been rolling over for many a long year. They think this scrap of paper going to do it. There is nothing you can do to change their minds, Mr. Haddam. Nothing any of us can do really but get out there and play the best damn baseball we can."

"Well said," Amos replied. "I didn't get your name, sir."

The ballplayer leaned across the desk with his hand outstretched. "Gibson Saunders, sir. Third base."

His hand was warm and strong. Amos smiled at him. Muscular, with a wise look in his eye, this player could go far. "I remember you. That game last season."

"Three-run homer," Quincy said proudly. "Over the right-field wall."

Leroy whistled. "Wish I'd seen that."

"You'll hit one yourself," Saunders told him. "Give it time."

"If they let us play," Leroy said, looking again at the note on the desktop.

"They can't make us quit," Saunders said. "Can't nobody make you quit, boy. You remember that." He poked a finger into Leroy, "Remember."

Amos got the hint: Gilmore and Saunders were making this effort for the boy. Leroy had been scared by the note, afraid something would happen to ruin his chances at major-league glory when the Monarchs trounced the Blues. Or maybe just scared.

"How long till the game?"

"A week. It's a Sunday-afternoon game."

"Had a good season this year, didn't you?"

Leroy looked up, pleased. "Oh, yes, Mr. Haddam. It was a good time."

"I don't see how I can do much with this, Quincy," Amos said. "Like Gibson says, nobody can change their minds. But if something else comes up, a phone call or another note, you come see me again. We'll get to the bottom of it."

Gilmore rose and the boy followed. Dressed in faded cotton pants and a too-small white shirt, Leroy towered over the manager, making him look like a dandified midget. Saunders held the door for them as Amos shook their hands, promising to keep an ear out for miscreants.

Saunders turned back. "You'll be coming to the season end party?"

"Mr. Wilkinson mentioned it." Amos hadn't paid much attention to the invitation.

"Tuesday night at Mr. Wilkinson's." Saunders waited politely for a reply.

"Sure. Tell him I'll come."

"Appreciate it, sir."

Giving them a head start, Amos followed down the stairs, catching the Broadway streetcar and walking three blocks to his apartment. By reflex, he checked the mailbox. Empty—Sunday. It hardly affected him anymore. He was becoming numb—with fatigue or depression or anxiety, he wasn't sure. He unlocked the door, then, after a cup of tea and a sandwich, fell into bed, so tired that his bones hurt.

It was dark when he woke. The sound of weeping seemed to ooze out of the walls. From a dream? He touched his eyes, but they were dry. He sat upright and looked at his watch. Half-past seven. He listened. Nothing. Must have been dreaming.

Amos lay back in bed, the crusty sheets reminding him that washing day was long past. He had once been fastidious, but he could hardly remember those days. Now he was just a bachelor, hanging by a thread to sanitary conditions. Thinking about doing laundry, even stripping the bed, exhausted him. The nap had been a drop in a bottomless well of fatigue. His sleep at night was rattled with bad memories of bombs, helplessness, and terror.

A soft moan came from outside. A bumping sound. He got up, tiptoeing to the window. Was the plumber upstairs beating his wife again? No, they'd moved out during the summer. The summer? When the bloody hell had they moved? He couldn't remember things like that anymore.

There it was again. He padded softly to the living room window. A woman, yes, close by. He spread the venetian blinds with two fingers. The street was quiet. His dusty auto sat across the street, neglected. A streetlight on the corner shone a circle of yellow light. A man on a bicycle rode by on the cross street.

Then the sound, a hoarse whisper: "Aaamooos."

He opened the front door. A woman leaned against the door frame, slumped on her shoulder, eyes shut. She wasn't young, but it was difficult to tell much about her face with her light brown hair in disarray. A red felt hat had slipped over her forehead. She was thin and wore a gray coat and dusty black shoes. Her socks were streaked with grime. Amos leaned toward her.

"Are you looking for me?" he asked softly, hoping not to startle her. A vain wish, as her eyes flew open and she gasped.

"Amos Haddam here." He gave a little bow, noticed he was in his shirt, undershorts, and stockings. Two toes were visible through a large hole in his left stocking. He glanced nervously over the woman's shoulder. With his luck, the neighbors, unruly as they were, were out for an evening stroll. He tugged on his shirttail. "Can I help you, miss?"

The woman pushed herself upright. It was a struggle. She swayed on her feet, blinking her brown eyes. Her voice wouldn't come. Her chest rose in quick breaths.

"Amos?" she whispered finally. "Is that you?"

" 'Tis I. And you would be?"

She closed her eyes and whispered, "Dear God." Opening her eyes again, she gulped air. "Amaa. Yaamaa—" Her words blurred. She tilted to one side, then the other. He reached out to steady her, but she swayed the other way.

"How's that?"

"Your mum, she—"

Her dark eyes locked onto his for an instant, then rolled back in her head. And she crumpled into a heap there on the doorstep.

FOUR

THE EVENING WAS STILL AND cool. Dorie wore trousers and a wool jacket. She pulled the jacket close as she knocked on Amos Haddam's door. The windows blazed with light. Usually, a tap on the horn was all it took to bring him out, but not tonight.

The door flew open. Haddam stood in his stocking feet, his suspenders off his shoulders, his shirttail sticking out.

"Are you ready?" Obviously not.

He didn't answer. He wiped the loose hair back off his forehead, dancing in place. She felt her stomach sink. He had heard. He had gotten a telegram.

Amos grabbed her hand suddenly, dragging her over the doorsill. He appeared to have lost his voice.

"What is it? What news?" He was very anxious—that was for sure. He couldn't stand still.

Finally, he said, "Come on," and beckoned her to his bedroom door. He turned, pointing inside.

Streetlight streaked through the blinds. In the dim light, the form of a woman made a lump on his bed. Her shoes were placed neatly on the floor, but otherwise she was dressed as if she'd been out for a drive, a coat, hat, gloves. Her head lay tipped to one side on the pillow.

"Is she . . ."

Amos frowned, looked at the woman. "What? Dead? God no. She just fainted on my doorstep. What should I do with her? Will she wake up?"

"How long has she been out?" Dorie crept closer. The woman was very pale, her skin almost blue in the dark room.

"Hour, a little more. Will she be all right? Should I take her to hospital?"

The woman's lips were purple. "Put some water on. Do you have a bed warmer—a hot-water bottle?"

"Right, yes. Righty-o," he said, relief in his voice as he backed out of the bedroom.

Dorie sat on the edge of the bed and picked up the woman's hand. Slipping off the kid glove, she rubbed the frigid hand between hers. Who was this woman? She had an odd look. Dorie picked up the edge of her coat. Her dress was bunched up. She straightened the dress hem and took a peek at the label on the lining of the coat. Sandington Bros., Bristol, it said.

She found a blanket in the closet and spread it over the woman. Sitting on the bed again, she eased the hat off, finding the pin and slipping it out. She stuck the pin in the hat and set it on the bed, then pushed the thin strops of hair off the woman's face.

She had fine skin, or it had once been fine, but the years and the elements had taken their toll. Rough patches dotted her cheeks and nose, as if she'd been out in the weather. Fine lines around her eyes and mouth, and gray hairs mixed into her light brown ones, indicated she wasn't young. Around her neck was a locket on a gold chain. Lennox picked it up and debated opening it for a moment. She could hear the teakettle beginning to blow in the kitchen. Slipping her fingernail under the catch, she popped the locket open. A tiny photograph of a woman in a silly feathered hat and high collar, a grim smile on her lips, had been pressed into the small oval.

Amos arrived with the hot-water bottle. She snapped the locket closed, then slipped the water bottle under the blanket, half on the woman's stomach, inside her coat, then tucked the blanket up around her again. While they watched the woman's face for signs of life, Amos snatched up the red hat.

"Bad luck," he explained.

"Who is she?"

"Haven't the foggiest. She just arrived on my doorstep."

"She didn't say anything?"

"Nothing. Just my name."

Lennox looked up at him. "She knew you?"

"She's waking up," Amos whispered.

The woman moved her head back and forth and opened her eyes. She stared at the ceiling for a moment, then saw Lennox and Amos. Her eyes flitted around, then locked on Amos. Her hand raised from under the blanket, reaching for him. She said his name.

Amos looked helplessly at Lennox. "Take her hand," she said. He did as he was told, terrified.

"Thought I'd never get here, I did." The woman's voice was barely more than a whisper, but the accent was there. "Your mum sent me. I'm out to California to stay with my aunt. America is so bloody big."

Amos had lost his voice again. He squeezed the woman's hand.

"Did I spark out? Lawk, I ran out of money in Chicago, but I had my ticket here. I thought it would be an hour on the train, and I had nothing for eats."

Dorie said, "When did you see his mother? How long have you been traveling?"

"About a month. Didn't see Cassie for two weeks or more before I left for Portsmouth. But she was fine, Amos. She said to tell you she was just fine."

Six weeks. Anything could have happened to Amos's mother in that time. If anything, the raids had gotten worse. Dorie looked at him. He was trembling so badly, he dropped her hand.

"You don't remember me, do you, Amos?" The woman smiled at him. "When we were fourteen. My parents took that little cottage near yours. The one with the pink roses. We used to go fishing every day."

Amos swallowed and ran a hand over his forehead.

"My mum died the next year and we never went back. Do you remember, Amos?"

With some struggle, he nodded.

"Things were so different then. So different . . ." Her voice trailed off.

"Gwendolyn," Amos whispered. The woman smiled, her face alight. "I remembered," he whispered, eyes wide at the wonders of his memory.

"I'm Dorie Lennox. Amos's associate."

"Gwendolyn Harris. You didn't remember that part, did you? I stumbled across your mother in the shelter—she's part of the home defense. Very important, she is. When I bumped into her, I couldn't remember at first where I knew her. Of course, I've changed a wee bit since fourteen." She looked at Amos. For a fainter, she had a healthy glow in her eyes. "But I'd know you anywhere. Quite the summer heartthrob, you were."

"You look not a day over sixteen," Amos said.

"Lawk! He's gone doolally in America." She smiled up at him, her face revealing the girl she once was.

The woman still looked pale, but she would recover. Dorie stood up, easing away from the bed. At the door, with Amos still staring and smiling at his guest, she cleared her throat.

"Can I speak to you out here, Amos?"

It took some minutes to convince him to stay with Gwendolyn and let her take the night's tailing of Thalia on her own. He wasn't going for it. He reminded her of the sort of men Thalia attracted, and the fact they often brought along muscle. But she convinced him finally. It was getting late and she could argue till hell froze over. In the end, he wanted to stay. She could hear them talking in low voices as she let herself out the door.

A cloud cover lent a blanket to the evening air, keeping the city warmer than the middle of October deserved. Driving with the window down, Dorie felt a jolt of freedom. Behind her, in Haddam's apartment, the old days lived in regret and memory. But for her, the future was now. A prickly feeling of living in the moment. Half fear, half exhilaration. Half pluck, half folly.

Even the possibility of her own folly thrilled her. Reckless, impulsive, daredevil—she hadn't been called those for some time, but they lived inside her, under control most of the time. Too bad she didn't have her switchblade. But the blade was more a talisman than any real help against the trouble boys that roamed the city. The glare of the Widow Vunnell came back to her, chilling the feeling a speck.

The streetlights shone pools of friendly light, the streets in quiet ripples of cobblestone and asphalt. The wheels of the Packard bumped; the springs bounced. She was off; she had a mission. She was a woman alone, off to save and protect, to know and seek, to work and be strong. She was the future, not some failed promise, some bombast of the past. The world was an oyster and she would find that pearl or die trying. Lennox laughed at herself. She hadn't felt this free since the day Amos had sprung her from jail.

But she wasn't free. By two o'clock in the morning, the balloon of exhilaration was bust, the moment ground down to a fine sand and blown away with a hot breath. What was it that seemed so exciting again? She was tethered to a rich girl and the mission—just a job—was as fascinating as navel gazing.

Inside the dance hall, a few couples shuffled in a last embrace. The band played wearily. Their trumpeter had fallen off his chair a half hour before and bruised his lip. He sat at the opposite end of the bar with an ice pack on his mouth.

Thalia and her date swayed to the music. Tonight, her escort was a young puppy who watched her every move with warm, eager eyes. Dorie had been told by a note from the Commander—via the chauffeur—that the man was a college friend of the girl's. Not a threat, the subtext read. Still, she was to be the old woman's eyes and ears, to watch sweet Thalia honey for indiscretions and faulty judgment.

Things had been hopping for a while. Thalia and her date, Lonnie, had taken off their shoes and waded in a fountain. Not just any fountain—the big one with the stone horses down on

Main Street by the Country Club Plaza. The one with the lights that showed off the spewing arcs of water all night.

And what could she do? They hadn't stripped off their clothes. Thalia had rolled down her stockings right there on the grass, laughing at the top of her lungs. Dorie could do nothing but cringe from the car.

She drained her coffee mug at the bar and wondered if they'd get a late supper. She could use some food, not that she'd be invited to eat with them. She was stiff from sitting on the stool. Her muscles ached from the workout at the gym two days before. She had the jitters from too much caffeine and was about to signal the bartender for a soda, when the music stopped.

The bandleader, a scrawny fellow in a baggy green suit, announced they were done for the night. "See you back right here tomorrow night for more swing and more jive!" Dorie slid from her stool, amazed that her legs held her up. Just what she needed, more jive in her life.

She threw two bucks on the bar and waved at the bartender. Thalia and Lonnie walked arm in arm to the coat check and retrieved their wraps. Thalia laid her head on Lonnie's shoulder as he directed her out the door. The girl had dressed more square tonight: a high-necked blue-print dress with a Peter Pan collar, a real coat of rich burgundy wool, low-heeled shoes for dancing. Her date wore pleated trousers with suspenders and a loud shirt.

What was Lonnie studying in college? Dorie missed college sometimes, the idleness, the abstract solitude. What would it be like to be in college now, now that she was older and, hell, maybe even wiser? It was an idle thought she had, watching him dance, overhearing him ask Thalia questions about what books she read, what music she listened to, who would get her vote for president. The girl had let Lonnie down with her answers. She had no time to read books, Thalia told him, laughing. She liked all music, as long as it was jazzy and jivey. And vote?! Dear boy, she had no intention of voting. How common.

Lonnie got over it. He was kissing her now in the backseat of the green sedan. Thalia discouraged that with a yawn. Dorie slid into the Packard and started the engine. She hoped the yawn meant Thalia was packing it in. But she wasn't surprised when the sedan veered right at Southwest Trafficway, then headed north toward downtown and away from the Hines mansion. Some of the barbecue places stayed open all night. Still, it was Sunday night.

Yours is not to wonder why, Dorie told herself, tightening her grip on the steering wheel, keeping close to the sedan. No point in being coy at this hour.

They wove through the market, not far from where her friends were all asleep in their beds in the boardinghouse. The thought did not help her mood. Glare from headlights behind the Packard flashed off the rearview mirror, hurting her eyes. She tipped the mirror and turned onto Broadway. They were going to the bridge.

Now what sort of pie could you get in North Kansas City that you couldn't get here? The Hannibal Bridge took them high over the Missouri River. She chose to keep her eyes on the car's taillights. The bridge was not a place of fond memories.

The vehicle behind her switched its lights to high beam. Was he trying to blind her? She slowed, just for spite. Was he trying to make a late plane at the airport? She could see Thalia and Lonnie up ahead, cuddling in the backseat of the green sedan. Dorie flipped on the radio. At the Palladium in Los Angeles, a dance band was playing, but the transmission was scratchy and weak. Still, it was music, and it kept her awake.

With a roar, the car behind passed on the left. A black coupe was all she saw, one driver, one passenger, both males. The surprise of it delayed her looking until it was too late to see faces. She hit the gas, but the Packard backfired in response.

The coupe was taking advantage of clear sailing to pass the green sedan, as well. It pulled up even with the sedan. Dorie felt her heart skip a beat. She slammed the gas pedal to the floor. An arm with gun attached came out of the coupe's window. The chauffeur must have seen it; he swerved, scraped the curb with the tires, then bounced back toward the coupe.

The shot sounded like a popgun, its flash a puff of orange in the dark. The sedan slowed. Screaming. Another shot. She watched helplessly as a front tire blew out and the sedan went out of control, flopping this way and that. The coupe backed off, let it flop. Dorie gunned the Packard forward, trying to ram the coupe, but it sped up, coming even with the lame sedan. Another shot, for good measure, and the coupe was off, streaking north across the river.

The sedan jerked to a stop half up on the walkway. She pulled up next to it. Lonnie opened the back door and jumped out, pointing at the fleeing car. Thalia sat screaming in the backseat. Lonnie pulled open the passenger door of the Packard.

"Go! Go get them!" he yelled, then slammed the door shut. Dorie obeyed, throwing the car into first, her bald tires squealing. By the time she came to the north end of the bridge, the coupe was gone. She gunned it by the airport. Dozens of autos sat in a large parking lot. The coupe could be any one, anywhere. She drove on, slowing at cross streets, then turned around and went through Harlem following along the riverbank. Her heart thumped. Where were they? She drove for ten minutes, then turned around and sped back to the bridge.

Beside the sedan, on the narrow catwalk along the edge of the bridge, Lonnie held Thalia in his arms. He was stroking her hair. Dorie pulled in front of the sedan and got out, leaving her headlights on. One light was shattered on the sedan.

She ran up to the couple. Lonnie had struck her as nothing more than a gadabout frat boy, but he now was grim, holding the girl against his chest protectively as she sobbed and shook.

"Did you find them?" he demanded.

"Is she hurt?"

Lonnie cupped Thalia's head in his hand. "Just scared."

Dorie frowned. "Get in my car." His anger softened, and he

led the girl toward the Packard. Thalia could barely walk, and she never stopped crying long enough to look up or speak.

Lonnie's words cut like a knife. She hadn't found them. Had lost the coupe. But she couldn't worry about that now. There would be another time for blame. Dorie walked around the rear of the green sedan. The morning's waxing still gleamed in the headlight's glow. The car tilted toward the blown-out front tire. She pulled open the driver's door.

She had imagined—hoped—that he had run off. That the handsome tanned chauffeur had simply disappeared in the gun-play, like a coward or any sane person, even cowered on the floor. That the ruined tire had taken the brunt of it, that the heavy steel body of the car had saved them all. A new car, a new tire: Money solves all. Brush hands, move on.

She sucked in a breath. The gun blast had thrown him side-ways on the seat. His face was bloody and torn. Shards of the window lay scattered like diamonds over his navy uniform. His neat cap lay on the seat next to him, holes eaten into its edge.

He would not be buying a new tire. He would not be brushing hands. He would not be moving on, not in this life.

Dorie sat on the curb, head in her hands. Around her, lights flashed like heartbeats and policemen scurried about, talking to Lonnie and Thalia, making measurements of skid marks, examining the chauffeur's lifeless body.

She had given them everything, but they wouldn't let her go. Lonnie must have said something to them that made them suspicious. Thalia was hopeless; she could only remember the chauffeur's first name, Tom. She collapsed, and Lonnie insisted the cops take both of them home. Dorie was hesitant to mention her uncle, police captain Herb Warren. Herb wouldn't like this. Hell, *she* didn't like it one bit. And think how Tom felt.

They were taking him away now, loading a stretcher into a hearse. Poor sod. If only he hadn't worked for the Hines family.

They were poison. The thought made her sink lower. She worked for the Hines, too.

The lead detective was heading her way. She stood up, wiped off her seat.

"Can I go now?" she asked, aware she sounded testy. But it was after four o'clock and the sun would be up soon. Over the river, the sky was already graying in the east. Barges lined the docks, dark hulks against the silvery water. Her hands were numb with cold.

"Thomas Briggs," the policeman read from his notebook. "You meet him?"

"For a sec, tonight. He handed me a note about the girl."

The detective was short but not bad-looking, with wavy brown hair and melt-away eyes. He didn't seem to hate private dicks like most cops. In fact, he gave her more than one quick once-over. A ladies' man, she figured, pulling her jacket closer. Or maybe he was just checking her pockets for switchblades.

"Dancing at the Pla-Mor."

"That's right. We just left there."

"You were following in your car?"

"Yes, sir." He squinted at her, as if he knew why she always called cops "sir." An old habit, unshakable. She squared her shoulders and looked him in the eye. Another old habit, eyeballing authority. "You talk to Mrs. Hines yet?"

"We got that covered. Now, you say you followed this black coupe."

"After I stopped and saw that Miss Hines and her date were okay. I went past the airport. Circled back down First Street. Under the ASB ramp. But I never saw them."

"Just disappeared?"

"That's right. Poof."

"Do you own a gun, Miss Lennox?"

"No, sir."

He eyed her for a moment, as if thinking again about checking her pockets.

"Ever use one?"

"No."

"I see you're on probation. Stabbed a fella with a blade, did you?"

"It was self-defense."

"That so. I heard about you. They say he called you a name."

"And tried to grab me. Can't a girl defend herself?" She took a breath and felt her temper rise. "What's this got to do with anything? I didn't shoot the chauffeur. Didn't Lonnie tell you what happened?"

"Done some juvie time, too, huh."

"That's not supposed to show up."

"Yeah, okay. We'll talk again later."

"Can I go now?" she called as he turned away. He waved in answer as he walked his cocky walk back to the uniformed men.

As she put the Packard in reverse and eased around the cop cars, she knew why he was questioning her. She was a known factor, a convicted criminal. And on top of that, the black coupe would never be found. Because she had not seen a license number, or even a face, there was not a snowball's chance in hell that a single black coupe could be parsed out from the thousands of look-alikes in the city. The cops would rather believe she was lying about the coupe than try to find it.

She drove down the ramp, back into the wee-hour quiet of the Market. Thalia Hines would be useless as a witness. She probably was kissing Lonnie, or asleep. Or hysterical, under sedation by now, not to mention the protection of one of Kansas City's top hundred families. But Lonnie had told her to follow the car. He had seen it. Could she count on Lonnie?

Parking at the end of Charlotte Street, she shoved her cold hands in her pockets and made her way home. Relying on a frat boy. How had it come to that? She unlocked the front door with her key, pushed it open, careful to pull up at the point where the hinges always creaked, and flipped the latch inside. She tiptoed up the worn flowered stair runner to the third floor, wondering if she might get more than an hour or two of sleep. Wondering if sleep would come at all.

In her small room, furnished with a single cot, a small dresser, night table, and lamp, she eased onto the creaky bed in the dark. The rusty faucet on the sink in the corner was dripping, hitting the porcelain in a dull rhythm.

Dorie felt numb. She knew she should be reviewing what had happened. She wanted a drink but was too stiff to get the bottle from its hole behind the dresser. She sat still on the bed for a moment, listening for Luther's piano music, hoping for its reassuring lilt. But it was quiet outside.

Wiggling under the wool blanket, she closed her eyes. A loud buzz in her head told her to open them again. She obeyed.

Getting up again, she found the gin bottle and took a mouthful from the neck. Her eyes burned as she put in the cork and stashed the bottle.

Lies, she thought angrily, Thalia is full of lies. Dorie frowned. Where did that come from? Had Thalia lied to her? Dorie was more likely to lie to herself. What did the rich girl have to lie about?

She lay down again, holding her sides. The sight of Tommy Briggs lying sideways on the seat made her feel ill. Was Thalia not what she seemed? Was she really sweet and pure inside? Dorie knew about facades, about lies and how they changed you, made you someone you weren't, even if that wasn't what you intended. If you told lies about yourself, and they came true, what did that make you? An actor? A confidence man? An evolved human?

She stared at the ceiling. Was it possible to change who you were? Wasn't that set in your blood, in who your parents were, in the way you were raised? She pulled up the blanket and tightened her grip on it. She didn't want to believe that. She wanted to believe in free will, in self-determination, in the lightness of airplanes and the possibility of changing fate.

But she slept in her clothes again.

Not long after, dawn crept through the gable window. Before

she opened her eyes, a dog signaled daybreak with a series of high-pitched yelps. She lay very still. *There.* There it was.

Tillie's voice, light and sweet. Had she summoned it? It had been months since Tillie had sung to her. Her baby sister, an angel now, had an angel's voice. She sang a gospel hymn "Swing Low, Sweet Chariot," and the words stuck to Dorie like kisses. Her voice was tiny, with breaths at awkward places, full of an innocence Dorie would never feel again. Or could she? Could Tillie restore some purity, a clean, unspoiled charm? Was it possible to go back, to erase the mistakes, the pain, the messy pages of living?

No purity at Verna Lennox's home. Their mother had scoffed at such antiquated notions, seduced by flapper beads and John Barleycorn, and possessed of moxie enough to do as she pleased. To be the rule-breaker, the sinner, that was Verna's banner. Purity was old-fashioned. Plain dull and for those without imaginations.

Coming for to carry me home. The tiny voice trailed off. Dorie wanted it back, wanted Tillie to prove to their mother something Verna had never understood. But it was too late for that. Now only Dorie could understand. She tried not to hold too tightly to Tillie. The little girl's spirit was too much inside her, yet so far away. If she grasped at it, it would break into a thousand pieces.

She stared at the ceiling again. The water stains didn't speak. They didn't answer her question.

Was it crazy to find that your only real friend, the only person you could count on, was a little girl buried high on a grassy hill overlooking a wide river?

FIVE

THE COFFEE WAS RICH AND hot and black. Dorie cradled her china cup under her chin, letting the exotic smell warm her. A big improvement from Mrs. Ferazzi's watered-down Eight O'clock brand, that was for sure.

The scene around the Commander's bed was somber. Many of those present, like Dorie, had gotten only a few hours' sleep. A few had been rousted out of their beds by coppers in blue, like she had. Amos maybe. Why had he brought the English girl? Gwendolyn sat half behind him, like a shadow. She wore last night's clothes, too.

The Commander's secretary was talking about the Willkie visit. As if the chauffeur hadn't been gunned down, as if Darling Daughter hadn't almost bought the farm. Thalia held her coffee cup with both hands, like Dorie. Her matted hair fell over her face. She sat like a child, knees together, heels splayed, wearing green satin pajamas and robe. Sedated maybe. On her feet sat puffs of pink feathers.

The Commander looked pale and drawn. She sat stiffly in bed, following her secretary's words, concentrating hard, as if the Willkie visit was her primary reason for hanging on. At the foot of her bed sat the red-faced oaf, Assistant Police Chief Melvin Michaels, and the friendlier mug of Capt. Herb Warren. Dorie kept her eyes away from her uncle's. She knew that guilt sat plainly on her face.

The secretary, a woman the Commander's age, who had been with her for twenty years, had a screechy voice. She was a tall, solid woman with plain, freckled features and gray hair pulled tightly off her face. Dorie tried to anticipate their questions. No

Lonnie to back her up. He had gone back to Lawrence, she was told.

Her coffee was gone. She wanted another cup. The secretary finished rambling on about receptions and hoorah and who cares which about Wendell Willkie, a man who had never held public office and thought he could fill FDR's mighty shoes.

"Thank you, Mildred," the Commander said. "You may go now."

The secretary looked up, surprised, glancing at the policemen, then at her employer. Mrs. Hines gave her an arched eyebrow and Mildred rose, clutching her notes to her bosom. When the door shut behind her, there was a long pause before the Commander let out a soft sigh.

"Before we deal with this any further," Eveline Hines declared, "I want to thank Miss Lennox publicly for her courage, her persistence, and her presence of mind, all qualities that make for the best sort of soldier. I am proud of you, Miss Lennox, and thank you here in front of all these people for saving my daughter's life."

Dorie sat back in the hard chair. She glanced at Herb. He had a grim smile on his big hard face. She blinked, saw them all smiling at her.

"I've spoken to Lonnie Masterson, who was with Thalia last night, as you know," Mrs. Hines continued. "He told me Miss Lennox tried to scare off the blackguards with her car, putting herself in danger, then chased them into North Kansas City before they could return and finish what they had came for."

Mrs. Hines straightened the red wool shawl on her shoulders. "I am sure these men, whoever they are, intended to kill or kidnap Thalia."

Assistant Chief Michaels was nodding. "I think you're right, Mrs. Hines. There can be no question Thalia was in grave danger. Our thanks, Miss Lennox." He nodded to her nervously.

Dorie returned the nod. She'd met Michaels a few times at her uncle's, and never liked him. Michaels was the rich man's pawn in the department, bowing and scraping whenever society came his way. Only Lear Reed, brought in from the FBI to whip the department into shape after Pendergast went upriver, had kept Michaels from the chief's seat. Reed wouldn't come sit by Eveline Hines's bed and tell her what she wanted to hear. Not hardly.

Herb Warren cleared his throat. "Is there reason to believe someone wants Miss Hines dead?"

The Commander made a huffing noise. "After last night, you can ask that? Really."

"Before last night, I meant."

Michaels turned to him. "The point is, Captain, that she's been attacked. She was almost killed. We need to find out who was in that black coupe."

Thalia made a loud slurping of coffee, seemingly unaware she was being discussed. Everyone looked at her for a second.

"That'll be tough," Warren said, glancing at Dorie. Blame was back, and its name was Lennox.

"But you must try, Captain," the Commander said. "You must."

"We'll put a squad on it immediately, Mrs. Hines," reassured Michaels. "We'll find it."

"There were a few suspicious characters around this week," Amos Haddam said. All eyes turned to him. His face was still lined and pale, but different somehow. "Mrs. Hines and I, and Dorie of course, were just talking about Barnaby Wake."

"What's Barnaby got to do with it?" Thalia said suddenly.

"That's what we're trying to find out, Thalia honey," her mother said. "Did you see him last night?"

"I was with Lonnie. Dancing," Thalia pouted. "She saw me."

Dorie felt her face redden as everyone followed Thalia's dagger glance. "I didn't see Wake last night. Saturday night, she was with him."

"That chorus fella?" Michaels said. "The mayor's wife sings in it, doesn't she? What's it called?"

"The Hallelujah Chorus," Amos said.

"*Everyone* is in it," Thalia said. "I am first soprano."

Michaels had a funny look on his face. "I don't see the connection."

"Find that black coupe, Mr. Michaels," Mrs. Hines said. "I doubt Barnaby Wake drives one. But you could check. Who else, Mr. Haddam?"

Amos ran off a list of names, men Thalia had seen recently: the lawyer, Oscar Gordon; a banker from Columbia; a young playboy who lived a block over; a cattle buyer who smelled like manure.

"Any black coupes among them?" Warren asked Amos. Haddam shrugged his shoulders. Captain Warren turned to the girl. "Any men been bothering you, Miss Hines? Sending notes or making phone calls?"

"I get lots of calls from men," Thalia said, throwing back her hair.

"Annoying calls, Thalia," her mother said.

"I need more coffee."

"Anybody threaten you? Ask you for money?" Warren pressed.

"Money?" Thalia set her empty cup on the night table and stood up. "I haven't got any money. But I will soon, won't I, Mother? Now, I have to take a bath."

They watched her flounce to the door and sweep out. Dorie thought she saw Julian Hines behind the door before it shut again with a slam.

"I am sure you understand, gentlemen," Mrs. Hines said in the silence afterward, "it is easier for the girl to believe she is not in any danger."

Captain Warren frowned. "If she could help, though, Mrs. Hines—"

"If she could, she would."

Dorie waited beside Gwendolyn Harris in the driveway. A few yards away, the men discussed their next moves, guarding Thalia from herself or strange men with pistols. She tried to think of something to say to the English woman. She still looked pale and fragile, but tea and a soft bed had helped. Her cheeks had a little color.

For her part, Dorie had a headache. Lack of sleep compounded with bile. Thalia's biting hatred of her mother, when the woman was dying no less, had turned Dorie's stomach. The girl was waiting for her mother to die, so she could get her money without strings. No wonder her mother was worried. The girl's heart was a cold stone.

And what of her own ill thoughts about Verna last night? Dorie held her hand over her eyes for a moment, blocking out the bright sunshine glaring off the cement driveway. Around her, autumn burst forth in its final blaze of glory: red maples, yellow sycamores, orange oaks, acorns, squirrels, and the smell of decay. She couldn't enjoy it; she shouldn't.

"Are you all right?"

Dorie blinked at the sunlight, dropping her hand. Gwendolyn peered at her, concerned.

"Just a headache. How are you today, Gwendolyn?"

"Much better, thank you. I'm so ashamed about last night. But finding Amos was important, I'm quite happy about that."

Gwendolyn gazed over at Amos. He was talking to Captain Warren and Assistant Chief Michaels. As if feeling her eyes on him, he turned to smile at her.

"He looks pretty happy himself," Dorie said.

"Hearing about his mum."

"What's it like there, in London?"

Gwendolyn tore her eyes away from Amos. "Oh, strange. During the day, we go on, or try to go on, as if we had normal lives, looking for supplies, complaining about prices. And cleaning up the debris, buildings and holes and such. Then at night, we barely sleep. Every night, in the shelters, we die a little."

Dorie examined the thin face, the lines worn from worry, the rough patches on her cheeks. The terror of bombs chilled them both. Up through the trees, the sky seemed so clear and calm. Here, across the world, there was no evidence of suffering, of the thunder and horror of war. So far, it was safe here. And yet, was she missing something vital? Could an ordinary Kansas girl help, somewhere, somehow? Could she fly airplanes, or was that a selfish wish in the face of war? The whine of an airplane echoed in her head. Was it her piloting, or a German dropping bombs?

"You must be glad to have gotten out."

Gwendolyn shrugged. "I had to—I was losing my mind. Claustrophobic, you see. Underground all that time, I began to see things in the dark." She frowned. "Hallucinations." She peered at Dorie. "My screams were bothering the others."

Dorie smiled, then saw the confession in the woman's eyes. And something else—the fear that had unhinged her.

"I didn't want to go. I wanted to stay and help. I'm trained as a nurse's aide, and there was plenty to do. But they made me go. My aunt is in California. I hear the most wonderful things about California, the orange trees and the sunshine. Have you been there?"

"I've never been anywhere." Unless you counted the Beloit Girl's Reform School. No one in their right mind would call that anywhere. "Are you hungry? Because I'm starving. Come on." She pulled Gwendolyn along by the wrist toward Amos. The assistant chief was expounding about propriety and safety and newspaper reporters, but he stopped when the women approached.

"Uncle Herb. We haven't got wheels, because your boys picked us up. And now we're starving." Dorie smiled at her uncle, at six three an imposing old bull with a red neck and little hair. Three rolls over his eyebrows framed hard blue eyes that always reminded her of his dead sister. He squeezed her elbow kindly.

"Always put away more than the men," Herb said, smiling. He turned to Michaels. "We'll get the extra men out this afternoon."

Amos took Gwendolyn's arm. "Ready for tea?"

Captain Warren dropped the three of them off at the Canteen downtown. They slid into a red leatherette booth with a commanding view of dirty sidewalks and boarded-up speaks, then ordered hot turkey sandwiches, biscuits, extra gravy, green beans. The waitress was a sullen lass who needed extra gravy on her bones.

Gwendolyn tucked into her food as if she hadn't eaten in a week. Perhaps she hadn't. Dorie felt the same way, as if days went by without a proper meal because of her odd schedule. She missed all the boardinghouse meals these days. They listened to radio shows she hated, dramas about boys who played football. Boola boola, rah rah rah. The last time she'd eaten breakfast with the boarders, Ronald had regaled the table with gems from the wisdom of America's most beloved racist, Father Coughlin. It was enough to make you lose your appetite.

Amos and Gwendolyn sat side by side in the booth. Two peas in an English pod: Colorless complexions and thin shoulders made them look like sister and brother. Amos was obviously pleased at finding someone so like himself. Dorie wondered if Gwendolyn would ever get to California.

As Dorie finished the last of the biscuits and gravy and wiped her mouth, the night's adventures came slamming back.

"You think they were after Thalia last night?"

Amos shrugged, wiping his mouth with his napkin. "What else? Follow the money—that's all those boys know."

"What boys?"

"That type."

"So they kidnap her?"

"Wouldn't be the first in Kansas City. Mike Katz was hijacked right on Ward Parkway. They got a hundred thousand for him."

"And thirty-thousand for Mary McElroy. Girls are cheaper."

"A hundred thousand dollars?" Gwendolyn said, eyes wide. She stared at her plate, wiped clean of gravy. "Who was the man who was killed?"

"Her chauffeur. Name of Tommy Briggs," Amos said.

"Nobody even brought that up," Dorie said. "Too busy worrying about little Thalia to remember a man had his head blown away."

Gwendolyn cringed, closing her eyes. Dorie was sorry she'd been so crude. The girl had probably seen terrible things in the bombing raids.

"You can go to the funeral. It's Friday in St. Louis." Amos smiled.

"Oh, swell. Just pop over." Dorie frowned. "You don't think he was up to something, do you?"

"Like what?"

She shrugged. Why was he driving Barnaby Wake around the other night? "I need to find Wake. Will we be tailing Thalia anymore?"

"Doesn't sound like Eveline will let her out of the house for a while."

"That should be interesting."

Amos sat back as the waitress cleared their plates, inquired about pie, and poured them all coffee. Gwendolyn stared at the black liquid. "It won't kill you, ducks." He patted her hand.

"So I'm to look at the cars of all Thalia's dates?" Dorie asked.

"Righty-o. All the gents' autos. Some have more than one, remember."

She pulled some bills from her trouser pocket.

"Tsk, now. My treat." He smiled at her. She wondered if she'd ever seen him so content. She blinked and put her money away.

"Call you later at the office?"

Amos nodded. Gwendolyn was braving the sludge in her cup. Dorie slid out of the booth. At the door, she heard them laughing. She turned and saw Amos put his arm around the English-woman's shoulders.

Amos squeezed Gwendolyn's slender shoulder through her coat. She beamed at him and they laughed again. The providence that brought them here, together. Fourteen to forty-one—must be some kind of symmetry. Wait—how old was he? He realized he'd be forty-three in just a week.

Why had she been sent to him? What had his mother seen in her that she sent Gwendolyn and not just a bloody letter?

Not that he was complaining. Cassandra had sent a letter. The note Gwendolyn had extracted from her pocket the night before was comforting, explaining the work the old bat was doing in the shelters, organizing brigades of volunteers to police certain areas, keep them clean and orderly. She quoted Churchill's speech in the letter: "Men will still say: This was their finest hour . . . there will always be an England."

The prime minister's words made Amos curiously sad. He would always be English, but he would always harbor a resentment, a cold corner of his heart, for what had happened in the Great War. He couldn't explain it to his mum, or to Gwendolyn. Anger—and the deep, searing burn in his lungs. He'd done what he was told; he'd been the proper soldier. So had thousands of boys, thousands who never came home. There was nothing left in England for him.

He realized he was smoothing the letter on the tabletop. Gwendolyn was looking at him with a worried eye. He stilled his hand.

"She says nothing about Beryl here. My sister in France. Did she say anything to you?"

"I don't recall. Sorry."

"Tell me again about the shelter where you met."

"It's the tube station two blocks from my flat. Near your mother's, too."

"But you said her house was hit."

"Yes, just before I met her. She was living in the shelter full-time."

Amos winced. He imagined dirty mattresses and rats. "But she was all right? Down there in the tube station?"

"Oh, yes. Better than most." Gwendolyn smiled at him. "I think she rather enjoyed the activity. Organizing the lads into brush-up brigades, finding clean water, cooking up stews from whatever the people contributed. She was very keen on it all."

"Sounds like Mum."

No one had heard from Beryl since the Nazis took Paris. She lived in the north, the worst part of France right now. And she was English. Would that make a difference to the Jerries? And what about the children?

"We'll write today to Mum, tell her you arrived," Amos said. "And to Beryl." For what that futile exercise was worth. Still, on the chance that with the fighting over—what little fighting the bloody Frogs had undertaken—perhaps mail would get through now. If it got across the Atlantic at all.

"Yes, we shall write." Gwendolyn turned to the windows. The sunshine was hitting the sad brick buildings across the street. "Amos, are there some heaths about? Some greens?"

"Of course."

"Can we go to one and sit in the grass? Just look at the clear blue sky?"

The sky. He had once thought of it as clear and blue, and did again. But in between, he was like Gwendolyn. The sky could bear menace. The sky could turn black and fill with enemies. The sky could betray you, hurt you, kill you.

But this was America. This was Missouri. The sky was clear and blue and safe.

He stood and took her hand. "Right this way, mademoiselle."

SIX

DEEP SHADOWS UNDER ARCHING BRANCHES made Barnaby Wake's neighborhood more menacing by daylight. At night, it was possible to imagine that all the shadows were unintentional. In the sunshine, the tall hedges, dense shrubbery, and drooping tree limbs created an atmosphere of mazes and secrecy. Few houses were visible from the narrow, winding streets; even fewer looked welcoming.

Dorie had knocked on Wake's door and retreated to the Packard. Parking was limited on these cow paths, and she'd found the widest spot was under the elm tree where they'd parked before. She went over the list of addresses in her notebook. She'd located two men's cars. The playboy's mother and Oscar Gordon's neighbor had both described their vehicles to her. One new black Buick sedan and one ragtop Oldsmobile. Trips through the bushes, peeking into their garages, confirmed the reports. The cattle buyer, Thalia had gone to dinner with only once; he was from Chicago and came on the train. The banker from Columbia was still a question. She hoped she didn't have to go to there.

The food made her drowsy. Her eyelids were half-closed when the yellow-and-black taxi pulled into Barnaby Wake's driveway. She pulled open her door and was walking toward the house, along the trees that had tried to trip her Saturday night, when the cab backed out again. She paused, waiting for it to disappear, when she noticed the man in the backseat. It was Wake.

Had he been in the house all the time? She clenched her teeth and ran back to the Packard. Following a taxi through Kansas City was usually not difficult, but she almost lost him before he got on the boulevards. She caught up on Gillham. The cab stopped in front of the Plaza Methodist Church. Barnaby Wake hurried up the steps and inside.

She waited until the taxi pulled away before she parked. She climbed the church steps, shook herself to set loose the gloom that threatened to settle between her shoulder blades.

Smile, Miss Lennox. It's a glorious day and you're alive.

Inside the church, she turned left, in the direction of the efficient Miss Janes, although she hoped to avoid her today. The corridor was dark and smelled of disinfectant. She paused, wondering which way Wake had gone.

Muffled voices came from the end of the hall. Treading carefully, she stepped down three steps to a longer stretch of corridor. The sounds seemed to come from one of two closed doors. The first read REVEREND RALPH NOLAN, CHORAL DIRECTOR. The second door's plaque read simply ASSOCIATE PASTOR.

As much as she wanted to eavesdrop, the barren hallway was a piss-poor hiding place. She crept a little closer to the choir director's door. From underneath, a wedge of light spilled onto the hall floor. A man's voice was low and indistinct. A tapping of heels sounded across a floor, then softened. Another voice, hissing with tension.

"You need me. You know you do."

The other man's voice was soft in reply.

"The hell you say. You know who's singing for me?" There was more, but the volume left his voice.

Dorie backtracked to the lobby. Churches, in the middle of a weekday afternoon, were dull places. She didn't want to attract the attention of Miss Janes. Another moment of serenity in the nave didn't appeal. She picked up a pledge card and tried to work up enthusiasm for tithing. Less than a minute passed before the footsteps came up the hallway toward the lobby.

She turned in time to see Wake exit the hallway and head for the door to the street. She caught up with him outside.

"Mr. Wake. Barnaby Wake?"

He turned smoothly on his heel at the top of the steps. Distress cluttered his handsome face, but he smoothed it quickly into a pleasant smile. He tipped his finely coiffed head in greeting.

"Mr. Wake, my name is Doria Lennox. I'm working for Eveline Hines. This concerns her daughter, Thalia."

He smoothed his double-breasted gray suit jacket, tucking in his maroon tie. A tightening around his eyes told her he wouldn't make this easy.

"There has been an attempt on Thalia's life." Excellent ice-breaker.

"Dear Lord." Concern now crossed his brow. It had an automatic quality. "Is she all right?"

"Yes, she's fine."

"What happened?" He put a hand on his forehead. "No, don't tell me. Not here." He looked down the street. "I have to sit down to hear this. Come. Have a cup of coffee and tell me about it."

Inside the coffee shop on the corner, the waitress slicked back mousy hair and moistened pouty lips at the sight of Barnaby Wake. She ignored Dorie as she poured coffee into china mugs.

"I have your favorite pie today, Barnaby," the waitress said. "Pecan."

"Not today, Josie, but thanks, honey." He gave her a wink. He was the kind of man who gave winks and received promises in glances. Dorie felt her nostrils flare, and she huddled protectively over her coffee.

As Josie walked away, he watched her backside for a moment too long. Dorie kept sipping the overcooked coffee. Wake fingered his cup.

"What happened to Thalia? Is she in the hospital?"

"She wasn't hurt. Just scared. Her chauffeur was killed. There was a shooting."

"Lord have mercy. The chauffeur was shot?"

"The car almost went off the bridge. But the cops think it might have been a kidnapping attempt."

His reaction was subdued on hearing this information. He put both hands around the warm mug and stared, frowning, into the coffee as if it would offer him a lie to tell.

Then his mood calmed and he smiled in a businesslike way. "Thalia is rich. She's lucky that way. She should be careful. I'm glad you're watching out for her, Miss—Lennox, is it?"

She cocked her head at him. "What's your relationship with Thalia?"

"She sings for me in the Hallelujah Chorus. I assume you know as much, since you found me at Plaza Methodist." He raised his mug to his lips.

"She has a nice voice?"

"Lovely. She needs a little extra coaching to reach the high notes, but she's improving."

Ah, voice lessons. That's what she was doing at his house. "Just voice coach and singer?"

Wake smiled again, wrinkling the skin around his eyes. "I'm a married man, Miss Lennox. Some of the women in the chorus have other ideas, but I have a reputation to uphold in the community."

"Oh, you're married." She let her eyes drift to his left hand. Bare of jewelry.

"My wife isn't well. She is in Arizona for her health."

"Asthma?" Dorie suggested, being a helpful creature.

"Why, yes." Wake's face opened in surprise. "How did you know?"

"Lucky guess. You must miss her. And the children?"

"No children," he said. "Not yet."

"Well, living apart and all." She smiled, and he nodded, as if grateful for her understanding. And understand she did. "You came here from Arizona, then?"

"The East. Didn't like it much. Too many immigrants. Kansas City is more to my liking. You can live here with your own kind."

She'd heard this litany enough to know not to argue. "Do you own a car, Mr. Wake?"

"A car?"

"An automobile? You know, a boiler?"

"No, I don't." He frowned into his coffee again. "What's this about?"

"I was sent to check on all Thalia's acquaintances. To see what kind of cars they drove. After last night."

"She saw the car—with the shooter?"

"I saw it."

"What kind of car was it?"

"A black coupe. Unfortunately, we didn't get the plate number. So we're looking all over the city for a black coupe."

"Sounds like a big job."

She pushed away the coffee. "But you've got no coupe, black or otherwise?"

"To tell the truth, I haven't had time to get a new driver's license since I moved here. Too busy." Wake stood up with her and rebuttoned his jacket. He wasn't tall, almost eye-to-eye with her, compact though, like he was fit. "So I'm in the clear?"

She tried to smile. "Thanks for the coffee."

He held out his hand suddenly, and she shook it. He held her hand with both of his, so sincerely. "Please come hear the chorus. You'll love it. We're singing Saturday afternoon for the arrival of the Willkie train. At Union Station."

"I'll try." She extracted her paw with some difficulty. "Swell meeting you, Mr. Wake."

"Very nice meeting you, Miss Lennox." He beamed at her, then had a thought. "Will Thalia be at practice tomorrow?"

"I can't say." Halfway to the door, she turned back. Wake was still at the table, looking through a pile of coins on his palm.

"Mr. Wake," she said, startling him. He dropped the pennies and dimes, then laughed at himself.

"The news must have rattled me more than I thought," he said, using what he probably considered his vulnerable look. The man had a future in vaudeville.

She folded her arms. "You knew the deceased, didn't you?" He looked blank. "The chauffeur, Tommy Briggs. You knew him."

"Well, I . . ." Wake laughed uneasily. "Yes. I mean, he drove me and Thalia once, maybe twice." He stepped closer to her, so close she smelled the aftershave on his closely shorn cheeks, a musky blend. "I was hesitant to say anything, you see, Miss Lennox, because of my wife. It's rather delicate, as I'm sure you appreciate."

"I appreciate," she whispered. "But you did know him."

Wake frowned, disappointed with her lack of conspiracy. "We spoke, if that's what you mean. He and Thalia did most of the talking, but I gave him directions."

"On Saturday night? You gave him directions to your house?"

His head jerked up and he looked her straight in the eye. It wasn't a friendly look. She bit down on her molars and held it until he looked away. "You aren't the only one concerned about Thalia, Mr. Wake," she said. "Her mother has us watching her. And that goes for all her dates, formal or informal." She patted his arm. "Word to the wise."

As she looked back through the window from the street, she saw him talking to the waitress. Difficult so far from one's wife.

In the car, she looked at the time. Five o'clock already. Dorie felt beat. The conversation with Barnaby Wake had been a temporary thrill. She loved goading slick boys like Wake a little too much. She shouldn't let her mouth run off. Still, he had admitted being with Thalia; at least he wasn't a fool. But what did that prove?

She drove north to the Market and pulled the Packard into the alley behind the boardinghouse. Frankie was out in the garden at her mother's boardinghouse, across the alley from Mrs. Ferazzi's. They had a beautiful garden full of vegetables—tomatoes, greens, corn, beets, potatoes, they grew it all. And in October, too. Frankie had a basket of ripe tomatoes at her feet.

"Hey, Frankie. Got a tomato for a poor white girl?"

Frankie's dark head popped up over the heavy yellowing vines. She grinned and reached into her basket, depositing a fat red tomato into Dorie's grateful hand.

"It's too bad Mrs. F. lets her land go to weeds like that," Frankie said. They both frowned at the dead stalks in the other backyard. The thistle had been particularly healthy in August.

She felt the warm roundness of the tomato, then sunk her teeth in it, the sweet juice running down her chin. Her mouth full, humming, she patted Frankie's arm in thanks and walked through the gate into the weeds. The stalks scraped against her trousers as she rounded the side yard to the front of the house. She sat on the front steps to finish the tomato, feeling the long day and night in her tired bones.

The sun had disappeared behind the buildings. The air was cool, but still as if rewarding you for surviving summer. She popped the last of the tomato into her mouth, tossed the stem joint into Mrs. Ferazzi's Art Nouveau garden, a fascinating patch of dirt dotted with trash. She closed her eyes. There was nothing like a ripe tomato—it was its own thing, full of life, warmth, sunshine, and summer evenings. To savor one in October was stealing time.

"Dorie?"

She opened her eyes, wiping a drip from her chin. Joe Czmanski stood by the stoop's low wall. "Hiya, Joe."

"I gotta talk to you. You got a minute?"

She remembered Betty's theory. Would he propose to her right here on the street? She stood up. "It's almost suppertime. Maybe later?"

"It's important. Please?" His voice was hushed and anxious. Joe had been badly burned in the engine explosion several years before. His hair was mostly gone, and the odd tufts that remained, he kept neatly cut. His face was scarred and stretched. It was hard to look at him without feeling the suffering of those burns.

She took a breath. "Okay. Shoot."

"Some things've happened. Odd things, ya know?" He eyed her. "You wouldn't know because I didn't tell you, but take my word, odd things. And I think they're related to the fire, ya know? The one that done all this." His hand, also scarred, fluttered around his face.

She moved to lean against the other wall, the weariness settling into her legs. She let out the breath. At least it wasn't a proposal. "What kinda things?"

"Fellas comin' round. Askin' questions. I don't like it."

"Did you tell the cops?"

His lips sputtered derisively. "Oh, sure. Like they care."

"So what can I do, Joe?"

He stepped closer. "Here's the thing. I think I know who's to blame for the fire. I had a lotta time to think about it. But I can't prove it."

"Who do you think did it?"

Joe looked up and down the street nervously. "It wasn't meant for me," he whispered. "It was for Roscoe Sensa."

"The bookie? Well, it was his car that blew up."

Joe was getting excited, too excited. It was obvious the bomb was meant for Sensa. Everyone knew that. Joe was just a mechanic who got in the way. She raised her eyebrows for him to continue. She was hungry again.

"So we find Sensa's enemies. Some other bookies. Somebody he owed money to. Who wanted him dead? The cops never looked at it; they was all crooked then. And then, ya know, Roscoe himself got popped."

"He did?"

"Last month. Right before these fellas start comin' around."

"What did these fellas want?"

"Stuff about Roscoe. Like I even knowed him. I just worked on his heap." He leaned in. "So you'll check it out?"

"I don't know, Joe. That's a big number."

"But you'll do it, won't you?" With his burns and scars, it was hard for Joe to show emotion through his expressions, but his voice still worked fine.

"I'll talk to my boss, okay?" She turned to go up the stairs. "No promises."

He grabbed her hand. "Thank you, Dorie. I knew you'd do it. I knew you would." He squeezed her hand, let it go, and skipped across the street to his garage. She watched him sadly. Snowball's chance she was taking on Roscoe Sensa's droppers.

At supper, Poppy served sliced tomatoes, cold chicken, and white bread. Betty and her new friend Carol whispered behind their hands. The bachelors smeared butter on their bread like it'd been years. On the crystal set, Jack Armstrong's coach took him aside for a word about manly sportsmanship.

In her room in the rafters, Dorie tried to remember if Tillie had liked tomatoes. The tiny things, so ordinary, were so hard to remember. She put a record on the old Victrola, one of her father's old ones with a bad scratch in the second song. She placed the needle on the third song and got back in bed. The slow blue voice of Jelly Roll was tinny but rich: "Tell me baby what you got on your mind." This part always made her smile. "I'll be your wiggler till your wobbler comes." Tillie used to laugh and laugh at that.

She would never be lonely. Not as long as she could still hear Tillie's laugh. Her little sister was six when Dorie had been labeled a delinquent and sent to Beloit. Tillie was only six and a half when she played with the matches that caught the rug on fire. The burns might have left her like Joe, except they didn't; they killed her. Dorie should have been there, but she wasn't; she was busy inside the friendly fences of Beloit, learning the finer points of switchblades. Tillie's death, and the guilt, drove their mother to drink. And drink led her to her own accidental end in a car. One mistake after another, that was the Lennox curse.

Her body felt like lead. She was so tired. She closed her eyes and saw the car on the bridge again, remembered opening the door, the chauffeur's body. A ripple of pain passed through her, the fear of death and the finality of that bullet.

The pain settled in her chest, so that she could hardly breathe. She tried to listen for Tillie's laugh, for Jelly Roll's saucy lilt. They were gone, blown away by the real sounds. The screech of tires, the thud of gunfire—these were the sounds of her life.

She was in a deep, restful place when the pounding came. She rolled over and hollered at whoever it was to go away.

"Phone call, Miss Dorie Lennox!"

Pushing herself upright, she went over and opened the door. The new girl, Carol, stood there with her lipstick smeared and a run in her stocking.

"What time is it?"

"How the hell should I know." Carol turned to the stairs. "Get your phone call, missy. Sounded important."

Dorie went back for her wristwatch and a sweater to cover her nightclothes. Twelve-thirty. She worried the time down to the second-floor landing, where the receiver dangled for her.

"Yes?"

"Lennox!"

It was Haddam. "What?"

"Lennox, there's been a break-in; they've really bashed things around. I'm down here with Quincy, seeing if we can figure anything out before the cops descend."

"Where?"

"At Mr. Wilkinson's. It's a fine mess, it is."

"The Monarchs' owner? I don't understand."

"They're the new client. Some threats—now this."

A scuffling noise and muffled conversation stifled her next question. What had happened? It must have been more than a simple burglary. Finally, Amos came back on the line. "Still there, lass? Guess who showed up with the coppers? Your old swain."

Louis Weston? She hoped not. She hoped never to see her old Atchison pal again. He'd caused her enough trouble. "Who?"

"The newsman. He's snooping around. Chessie cat grin on his mug."

"Talbot?"

"That's the one. Look, Lennox. I need you to go over and see to Gwendolyn. I ran out of there in a hurry, and she was mumbling and carrying on. Wanted me to take her. My blooming shadow, poor girl."

"You want me to check on her?"

"Would you, ducks? Buy you another spot of tea. You weren't taking a kip now, were ya?"

"I was wide-awake. Shall I stay until you get back?"

He explained it might be necessary to stay. Gwendolyn had spells. Dorie remembered Gwen's explanation as she dressed and drove the fifteen blocks to Amos's brick apartment building. Lights were on in the living room. There was an eerie silence as she pushed open the door.

The woman was nowhere to be seen. Dorie called her name. Under the bed: the last place a claustrophobic would hide. She opened the closet, then checked the backyard, alley, bushes. Gwendolyn had disappeared.

Dorie stood in the middle of the living room floor, hands on her hips, trying to work out her next move. Screaming erupted, a banshee wail, high-pitched but muffled. She went to the bedroom door. The screams stopped. She walked to the kitchen, opened the little pantry closet. Another screech cut through the air.

The upstairs neighbor began beating on his floor. "Stop that racket," he hollered. "Stop it now or I'm calling the cops."

"Hold on to your shorts," she called through the ceiling. Another scream. From the bedroom?

She looked around the room, its bed and dresser and lamp stand. A picture of a country house in a lush meadow with grazing sheep hung over the bed.

"Gwendolyn? Can you hear me?"

Screeches came in reply. She opened the closet door again.

Bending down, she pushed aside a pile of clothes on the floor. There, squeezed into a corner, huddled Gwendolyn Harris, her eyes shut tight, hands over both ears. She opened her mouth and sucked in a breath. Dorie put a hand over her mouth. Gwendolyn screamed anyway, harder.

"Gwendolyn, stop. It's me, Dorie." She had to shout. The neighbor pounded on his floor. "Gwendolyn! Please!"

The woman's eyes flew open and she pulled Dorie's hand away from her mouth. "Oh, Miss Lennox, the bombs are coming! Can you hear them? They come so often now, *rat-a-tat-tat*. I can hear the percussion, the echoes. My ears ring and I have to hide in here to get away and the walls come so close. They were moving in on me, suffocating me. I can't breathe unless I suck in the air. And every time I sucked in air, the bombs come again!"

Gwendolyn put her hands around the back of Dorie's neck, pulling her into the coat pile. "Gwen, wait. There're no bombs. Please, Gwen, let go."

Suddenly, the hands left Dorie's neck and she fell back onto the floor outside the closet. Gwendolyn was on her hands and knees, peering wild-eyed at the bedroom ceiling, at the door, at the window. "Can't—breathe—have to—can't breathe!"

She sprang to her feet, then leapt like a gazelle out the door and into the night.

SEVEN

ENGLISH PANCAKE, ENGLISH IN THE loony bin, English strip-tease—these were the scenarios that tripped though Dorie's head as she picked herself up off the floor. Amos's face, his happy laugh, his arm around the girl at the diner—how would she face him if the woman hurt herself?

She ran out into the dark. In the middle of the dry front lawn, Gwendolyn knelt as if to pray. She raised her thin face to the sky, then stretched her arms upward. Her rabbity chest jumped in quick breaths. On her face, a goofy smile stretched the pale skin and she whispered, "Thank you. Thank you, clear and free Yank sky."

A window opened in the upstairs apartment. A burly fellow in an undershirt stuck his head out. A stogie stuck out the corner of his mouth.

"Is she finished? Can we get some ever-lovin' rest?"

Dorie just folded her arms. Gwendolyn's eyes were shut now, her nostrils drinking in the cool night air. Her color was better, pinked by the exercise, but she kept her arms raised so long that they must have ached. The man shut the window after a few more curses. A car sailed by, the driver giving the supplicant a double take.

"Gwendolyn?"

The woman swayed on her knees but didn't reply. Her dress, what was left of it, was rent with jagged tears. A white slip peeked through. Her shoes were gone. Toes poked through holes in her stockings. Her bare arms pointed to the sky, reaching for something out there—a star, a cloud, a certain peace.

Dorie pushed one of Gwendolyn's arms down to her side. Gwendolyn didn't resist, and she let her other arm be lowered.

But her eyes stayed shut, a look on her face that bordered on batty.

Dorie frowned at her. Get up and go to bed, she thought.

"Gwen? Gwennie?"

A smile spread across the woman's face. Her eyes stayed shut. "Mama?"

"Come on, Gwennie." She pulled the woman to her feet, hoping the spell would last a few minutes. "It's all over. Let's go inside."

Gwendolyn's eyes flew open. "Inside? You're not Mama!"

"It's Dorie, Gwen."

She relaxed a little. "Yes. Dorie." A ragged breath shook her and she shivered violently. "I can't go inside." She hung her head. "I just can't."

Dorie looked down the street. Everyone was sleeping. The light had gone out in the upstairs apartment. Amos's door stood open, spilling yellow light onto the sidewalk.

"Try to relax." She patted the woman's shoulder. Gwendolyn noticed her torn dress, running her hands over it and moaning. Her head rolled on her neck like it might snap off.

"My dress, my dress. Dear Lord, what am I to wear? My dress!"

Dorie took her hands. "Gwen, look at me. I have a dress you can wear. You can have it. It'll be just your size." She bent to peer into the woman's downcast eyes. "All right?"

Gwendolyn looked up and nodded.

"What if we go over to my room and you try it on right now."

Gwendolyn allowed herself to be put into the Packard. Dorie ran back to close the apartment door before driving carefully, windows down, back to Charlotte Street. She parked the Packard under a streetlight on the corner and pushed the woman along the sidewalk. As they turned to go up the steps, Gwendolyn balked.

"It's jake, Gwennie. Really." Dorie put her hand on the woman's back. A movement in the still darkness of the street made her turn. In a parked sedan, a man with a fedora shadowing his face sat watching them. Gwendolyn grabbed her arm.

"Who is Jake? Is that Jake in that car?"

"*Jake* means 'okay.' It means you'll be safe here."

"You'll stay? Please, Dorie," she whispered, her fingers a vise like grip. "Don't leave me."

"Shush now."

Dorie led her up the steps. She sounded like the mother here, though the woman was fifteen years older. Strange, like with Tillie, comforting a frightened child. As she unlocked the front door and held it open for the Englishwoman, she looked back at the sedan. The man had disappeared. Hiding? Or gone to see Joe about a bookie?

"Wait here." She patted Gwendolyn's arm. "I won't be long. Stay under the light."

"Where are you going?"

"Just wait here."

Dorie tiptoed back down the steps, nodding back to the woman. Gwendolyn stood gripping the edge of the screen door. Dorie held up one finger, then turned back to the street.

At the corner, a single streetlight burned by the awning of Steiner's grocery. The people who lived on the street, the ones without real homes, had found somewhere warm tonight. Joe's Garage was dark, but upstairs, where he lived, a light burned in a window. The automobile where the man had been sitting was parked in a dark area between Joe's place and the corner, in front of a run-down duplex. She crossed the street, avoiding the porch light on the place. She felt her pocket automatically. Empty.

A movement in the street, near the car, made her jump back into the shadows of bushes by the duplex. Someone getting into the car. A figure outlined against the far streetlight, a hat pulled low, narrow shoulders. The car door was open but he—she?—wasn't getting in. No, the head of the man in the car appeared. Words exchanged. The door closed and the figure backed away as the car engine roared and sent the automobile screeching out into the street. When she looked back, the person—the rouster—was almost gone, disappearing behind the other cars. A glint of gunmetal? In a dark-skinned hand? Was it someone from the neighborhood? Whoever it was, he was gone.

Upstairs, in her third-floor room, Dorie opened both windows wide so Gwendolyn could breathe the night air. The guest put her head out the back window, inhaling the fragrant Kansas City stink of smoke and factories and beef offal. Heights were no problem, it seemed. One phobia at a time.

Dorie found an old dress, a blue shirtwaist, well-worn from dancing and other business. It didn't fit Gwendolyn; the poor woman was mostly bones. But it made her happy to see the torn one thrown out the back window into the weedy yard, where nobody would disturb it for a coon's age.

Gwendolyn lay down on the bed. She frowned then said seriously, "I never liked that dress. My auntie picked it out for me. Said it was a good traveling dress. Wouldn't show the dirt."

"It's gone now."

"Good riddance." Gwendolyn closed her eyes, curled like a spoon. "Thank you, Dorie. For the dress." Her voice floated, sweet and poignant, Dorie was not as good and kind as the tender voice suggested.

"Who was that on the street?" Gwendolyn asked, sleep in her voice.

"Nobody." Dorie pulled the blanket up over her thin frame and tucked it under her chin. "Get some rest now."

Tall and white-haired, in his rumpled evening clothes, Mr. Wilkinson stood with hands on his hips and glared at the mess in his study. He'd been examining the piles of papers and books, records and baseball souvenirs, for more than an hour.

"I don't understand it," he said, rubbing his chin.

The Monarchs' manager, Quincy Gilmore, stood next to him. "Nothing's missing?"

"Not a damn thing. Not even my World Series baseballs."

Amos Haddam walked in from the kitchen, followed by a uniformed policeman. They waited for a moment to get Wilkinson's attention. "We found this in the garbage can outside."

The cop held up a baseball shirt, white wool with black stripes. Across the back it read PAIGE. The men stared at it, where the mud had been rubbed into it and the buttons torn off.

Amos frowned. "I don't like this."

"None of us do," Gilmore said.

"It's just an extra uniform I keep for when Satchel comes back. He always comes back." Wilkinson had a confused, stricken look on his face.

"It's a message, Mr. Wilkinson," Gilmore said. He'd rousted Amos out of bed hours before, but he still had the look of a man who often met four o'clock in the morning looking fine.

"To keep my doors locked?" Wilkinson's dry laugh was painful.

"Your window was broken, sir," the policeman reminded him.

"Put that away now, kid," Amos said. "We get the picture."

The young patrolman cut Haddam a glance but did as he was told. Amos walked into the study and began straightening piles of papers on the desk. Gilmore led Wilkinson into the kitchen by the elbow. Time to clean up and get out. Amos worked awhile in the study, putting some order back to the room, drawers back in their tracks, footstools and chairs and lamps upright. He turned off the light and shut the door, stepping back into the hallway. Gilmore had the Monarchs owner seated, drinking a whiskey at the kitchen table. Amos nodded to the manager and let himself out the front door.

The night air was bracing. The dry leaves from the oak tree crunched under his shoes as he walked toward the car, hands deep in his pockets. He felt dry himself, like he might blow away. He'd seen plenty of hate as a revenuer. In the hills, in the Smokies, around the South, watching his own back. He'd seen this feeling, heard it around Kansas City. It wasn't new. But it sat in his mouth, sour and bitter, like a bad meal that revisited your guts, reminding you over and over of cruelty and ignorance.

A car door slammed on the street and someone called his name.

He stopped short, pulled his head up. The newsman was there, standing in the street. He was grinning. It was much too late for grinning.

"Still here, I see."

Harvey Talbot stuck out his hand and made Amos shake. "Missed the deadline. But I called in a little item. Burglary and malicious mischief at Monarchs owner's. Like that."

"That covers it." Amos turned and kept walking.

"Does it?" Talbot jumped in front of him. "I mean, isn't there something else going on here? Is this some kind of anti-Negro message, do you think?"

"Couldn't tell you."

"But you saw it, the mess in there. I heard nothing was missing, just scattered and all. Is that right?"

"You need to talk to the coppers, boy."

"But why are you here? That's what I don't understand." Talbot kept going, walking backward, talking fast. "I figure you knew something about it, that Gilmore or Wilkinson brought you for something. Not just a burglary. The cops can handle that. So why are you here? That's what I was thinking."

"You think too much." Amos was tired and the reporter's voice was like a chattering squirrel.

They were standing in the middle of the street. Amos realized he didn't have a car. Quincy had brought him. He turned suddenly, and Talbot stepped on his foot.

"Oh, sorry—"

"You can take me home, lad. How about that?"

The leafy streets where Wilkinson lived were close to the chorus director's house, near the blunderbuss palaces that shouted money. The city had such extremes, the very rich and the very poor—mansions, servants, and goose-down, and then those who barely got through a cold winter on a curb with a threadbare blanket. It wasn't strange, this hatred. If you were comfortable, did you hate? If you were satisfied, were you more charitable? He wondered. Maybe not. Were the Nazis comfortable? They certainly weren't charitable. It was a hard world, full of desperation and grasping.

"Here?" Talbot asked, nodding at the apartment building. It was dark, not even a porch light.

"That's it. Home sweet cave."

As he turned off the car, Talbot asked his question. "It was a race thing, wasn't it? Somebody who doesn't want the Monarchs playing ball? They're too good, are they?"

"They're good." Amos put his hand on the door handle, ready to pull it. "Don't write it, boy. It'll stir up feeling. Don't give them that courtesy. They don't deserve it."

Talbot peered through the gloom. "So I'm right."

"There are more important things than being right."

Harvey's jaw clenched and he looked down, fingering the large steering wheel of the Chrysler. "You're probably right. But I'm a newsman, Mr. Haddam. What I think doesn't matter."

"Then what does that make you?" Amos got out of the car. "Thank you for the ride, Mr. Talbot." He shut the door and walked around through the flare of the headlights. For a moment, he thought the newsman would call out, tell him to go sit on a stick, or at least ask about Lennox. It was a rare man who didn't want the last word. Amos stepped up over the curb, negotiated the sidewalk toward his front door.

Behind him, the Chrysler revved to life again and roared away.

Inside the apartment, Amos looked for Gwendolyn and let out a sigh of relief at her absence. The woman barely slept, and when she did, she had nightmares. He listened to the quiet, feeling aches in his back and neck. Then his eyes fixed on the pile of mail he'd brought in but abandoned.

Sifting through the bills and newspapers, he found the envelope. It was thin, stiff paper, scorched brown on two corners.

Someone had traced over his faded name and address, but he recognized his mother's schoolteacher handwriting. His heart skipped. He walked stiffly to the sofa and sat down. Outside, the birds had begun chirping. Light was creeping into the gray sky.

He smelled the envelope. It had an odd odor, like ash. The postmark read August 20, weeks before Gwendolyn had gotten on the boat. He relaxed a little and tore open the flap with his thumbnail. There was only one page.

Son,
A short note to let you know things are fine here. The house is quite safe, and although I've taken the precaution of packing up all my china and silver and sending it to your cousin Luella's, I'm determined to stay right here. Nothing can hurt this solid old thing. So not to worry about your old mum.

I've heard from your sister at last. She hasn't seen any fighting, but the Germans have occupied the area. She says she may be going to the south. I don't know how she'll manage that unless she's joined the Resistance. Frankly, a bit of a stretch for our Beryl. She talks about going with her friend Jean-Luc, a painter. I do hope she knows what she's doing. The children are safe, she says, with their father. I am glad of that.

All for now. Ta-ta, love.
Mum.

EIGHT

Dorie pulled the heavy door closed behind her, the iron hinges creaking. She felt a wave of relief, then guilt, at passing off Gwendolyn to Amos. He looked so tired, so drawn, yet he'd called this meeting with Eveline Hines. Or rather, Eveline had called it through Amos, unhappy as she was with the police escort for Thalia.

"I told her over and over again, 'Thalia honey, you have to let the men stay with you,'" Eveline said. "But she won't do it. They have uniforms, she says. It takes all the fun out of it, she says."

Dorie exchanged a glance with Amos that said taking away Thalia's fun wasn't a bad thing. In the silence, Gwendolyn piped up. "I've always been a bit afraid of bobbies at home. They carry the largest sticks. So serious. And their chin straps!"

Eveline arched an eyebrow. Dorie found an excuse to slip away. Mrs. Hines didn't look well. She looked thinner, paler, more tired. Her mind was still alert. That was something. In the dank, shadowy hallway, Dorie said a quick prayer for Eveline Hines as she walked the uneven floor. "And Lord, don't forget Thalia honey," she muttered as she reached the front foyer.

"Is she a decoy?"

Dorie almost bumped into the huge vase of gladiolai on the round table. There, in the same hallway as before, stood Julian Hines. He wore tennis shorts and a white polo shirt.

He stared at her from behind his glasses. "Because she looks like Wendy from a distance, but she's much too old. She wouldn't fool anyone up close." He stepped over to the table and looked cagily through the sprays of gaudy orange and yellow flowers. "I'd get someone younger."

"Mr. Hines," she said, recovering herself. "How are you this morning?"

"Fine."

She stared at him. "What is it you're talking about?"

"The woman you brought in."

"Gwendolyn?"

"When is the meet? Tonight?"

She moved around the edge of the table and grabbed his wrist. He smiled lewdly, enjoying the contact. "Stop, sir. Gwendolyn is not a decoy. And who is Wendy?"

"My wife." He pulled his arm away and stepped back. "You are the private detective. My stepmother told me."

"That's right. What does that have to do with your wife?"

"She's gone. Missing for almost a month. I thought—" He frowned, looking down the dark hallway to the sickroom. "She's not looking for Wendy?"

"She may be. I'm not." She suddenly felt sorry for the man, confused and obviously cut off from his own family. "What happened to your wife?"

He blinked behind his glasses. "Disappeared. Went out and never came back." He scratched his neck. "It was several days before I realized it. That sounds callous, doesn't it? But it's true. We . . . well, we hadn't been together much lately."

"I see."

"Three weeks ago Saturday. I wasn't here."

"You don't know where she went?"

He shrugged. His face was childlike, bewildered. "The Commander loves her. She always thought the world of Wendy. I thought—" His shoulders twitched. "I guess she only cares about Thalia."

"She's worried about Thalia. I would be, too, if I were dying." She watched him for a reaction, but he examined cracks in the stone floor. "Have you looked for her? For Wendy?"

"I called her aunt in Pittsburgh. She hadn't heard from her since Christmas."

"Well, good luck." Dorie moved toward the door, hoping the man had uncorked enough vapors. He reminded her of a loose balloon careening around a room, spewing hot air as it bumped into walls.

"I guess I could hire you, couldn't I?"

She turned at the door, her hand on the knob, hesitating before answering. Hoping he'd answer it himself.

"I have money; that's not the problem. My father left me some, not a lot, since the Commander is still alive, but some. I could hire you."

He had flushed, nervous now. He put two fingers to his lips, a girlish gesture, then flung his arm wide.

"But if she wants to leave me, then let her go!" His voice bounced off the hard walls of the tower stairwell. "Who am I to stop her! A mere flyspeck of a husband? What's that to a woman? That's what you want to know, isn't it? I can see it in your eyes. Why wouldn't she leave him? She squeezed him for every cent he had and then ran off with some gambler. That's what you're thinking."

Julian stomped up to her, sweat dotting his brow. He jabbed a finger in her face. "You want to know what I think?" He stuck his reddened face so close that spittle sprayed her cheek.

"To hell with her! Straight to hell!"

In the noonday sunshine, Dorie shook herself like a dog. What other secrets lurked in that house? She didn't need to know why Wendy had run off. That was plain as the nose on your face. She thought about the dull boardinghouse where she and Gwendolyn had had breakfast this morning. The whining, bad jokes, lame-brain theories about the economy, the war, Roosevelt, Willkie, Eleanor, Hitler. How reassuringly dull those opinions seemed now.

She shook herself again as she walked down the long circle drive to the sidewalk. "La-di-da, la-di-da," she muttered. Whenever Betty at the boardinghouse said it—Betty, who'd seen *Gone with the Wind* four times—she cringed. Now it was just the ticket for cleaning out the head. "La-di-da, la-di-da. Let's think about that tomorrow." She ran her hand down the high wrought-iron fence.

A tall hedge grew behind the fence, shadowing the sidewalk. She stopped, looked back at the Hines mansion. She should go back. Amos wouldn't be long with the Commander today.

She grasped two iron rods of the fence and put her face up to the hedge.

"La-di-da, fiddle-dee-dee."

But Julian's words pounded in her head; then they became her mother's words. Her father was taking a trip. *So go to Tennessee. Go to Oklahoma. Have a great time and then go straight to hell.* He had gone on that trip. Dorie had gotten a postcard from him in Tulsa or somewhere.

He didn't go to hell. He just didn't come back.

"Fiddle-dee-dee, straight to hell." She leaned against the fence, the vertical bars poking her shoulder blades. The sky was clouding up, promising an afternoon shower. She heard a rustling behind the hedge, then singing.

The voice was small and light, like a child's. The breathy words were hard to understand. Then the tune clicked. It was one of Tillie's, one she had sung to her father because he sang it to her. She'd been so little, four maybe.

Dorie closed her eyes and listened. In her mind, she saw her little sister with the white-blond hair, sitting on the braided rug on the floor. The rag doll that Verna had made for Dorie sat beside her. Tillie held the doll's hands.

"And if that looking glass gets broke, papa's gonna buy you a billy goat. And if that billy goat won't pull, you'll still be the sweetest little baby in town."

The voice behind the hedge had forgotten the words and began to hum. Dorie opened her eyes, smelling the spicy cedar of the hedge. She tried to peer through it. Movement, something blue, a hat perhaps.

Then, as if it was all in her imagination, gone.

———

Back at the office, Amos gave Gwendolyn some money to go fetch them all pastries and coffee from the coffee shop down the street. It was lunchtime, but no one complained.

Dorie sat in the client's chair across the desk from Amos, gazing out the window. The song through the hedge, Julian Hines's spleen, the ache in her back and neck from sleeping on the floor. She longed for coffee and a buttery kolache.

"Your newsman gave me a lift last night," Amos said. "This morning, actually."

"What time did you get in?" She ignored the personal comment.

"Five or so." He rubbed his bloodshot eyes and seemed to evaporate a little into his brown suit. "Got the paper?"

Dorie retrieved it from Shirley Mullins's desk. "Will there be something about the break-in?"

"And the murder." Amos scanned the columns, turning pages for several minutes. "Just a wee item. Nothing but the address."

"What about the murder?"

"They're keeping a tight lid on it."

Yesterday's paper had a double column with a splashy header: GANGLAND SLAYING. No mention of Thalia or her college boy. "Nothing today."

The lack of facts wasn't surprising. Eveline Hines was a friend of the *Star*'s publisher.

"Do we watch her again?"

"At least until the end of the week. Eveline's in a twist about the chorus director, Barnaby Wake. They've got some extra practices this week to rehearse for the Willkie rally at Union Station."

"What do we know about him? Besides the fact that his wife lives in Arizona and that he comes from the East Coast."

Amos folded his hands across his belly. "Rumors of women. Don't put a lot of stock in that, but worth asking around. I hear he's from New Jersey, so I'll send a telegram to a friend of mine back there."

He sat forward. "I need you to work on Wake today. I've got to see about some things regarding this Monarchs mess."

"The break-in?"

He rocked in his chair. "Somebody doesn't want Negroes playing white boys. That's what it looks like."

"Reds?"

"I doubt it. They're pro-Negro. But the Negroes don't like them." He smiled and shook his head. The hate was hard to keep up with; it changed and hardened, was swept away, then returned on an ill wind. "No, it's somebody who doesn't want the Negroes besting the hometown boys."

"But they've played before."

"Some cracker's got a bee in his bonnet." He held up both hands, perplexed. "Not the first and not the last." They sat quietly for a moment, digesting that, listening to the creak of the office chair as Amos rocked. "Eveline told me Thalia and that chauffeur had a thing going about a year ago. Lasted just long enough for Eveline to find out about it."

"It was over?"

"Seems so."

"She didn't fire him?"

"Apparently not."

Footsteps echoed through the door. Gwendolyn opened the door for a scrawny young man dressed in white, carrying teapot, cups, and a plate of pastries. He looked breathy and sheepish as he set the tray on the desktop, arranged the items, and stepped away, tray in hand.

"Leave the tray, Ernest," Gwendolyn said, holding out her hand. "We'll get everything back to your shop. Very soon, I promise."

"No hurry, miss." Ernest handed her the tray and backed to the door.

"I told you to call me Gwen, Ernest. You promised."

Ernest beat a hasty retreat. Gwendolyn propped the tray against the wall and poured the tea. "Isn't this nice? Now, this is a proper English tea. A bit early, but still proper. Don't you think, Amos?"

She handed Dorie a cup and saucer. "Milk?"

Amos took a cup and picked out a Danish from the pile of sweets. "Very nice, Gwendolyn. Just lovely."

"No milk. Thank you." What happened to the coffee? "Amos, do you think this fling between Tommy and Thalia could have had something to do with the shooting?"

Gwendolyn sat on the edge of the desk, as there were no more chairs. She looked uncomfortable perched there. "Sit here, Gwendolyn. Please." He jumped up, almost spilling his tea. "See, I'm better standing anyway."

Gwendolyn moved around the desk, cradling her teacup in both hands. She smiled at Amos and sat in his big wooden chair. She looked like a different person from the one cowering in the closet the night before, ripping her clothes, tearing her hair. She'd taken a bath and found another of Dorie's old dresses. This one was red and white, and fit much better. Her complexion looked better. She'd gotten some sun on her face and the rough patches were healing over. Kansas City agreed with her.

"The Tommy lark," Dorie prompted.

"Connected with the shooting?" Amos sipped his tea and frowned. "Only if Eveline had him done in herself because Tommy boy couldn't keep his hands off Thalia. Not bloody likely."

"Did you tell her about Thalia?" Gwendolyn asked Amos.

"What?"

Amos shook his head. "Thalia singing, that's all. We've heard her before."

"She was going up that wonderful staircase, very slowly, singing a lullaby in a peculiar voice." Gwendolyn sipped her tea. "It made me wonder at her mind a bit. Truly."

"What lullaby?" Amos and Gwendolyn frowned. None of them was good at song titles. "We are supposed to write these down." More frowns. "With a mockingbird?"

"That's the one." Gwen began to mumble through the words. "Little baby don't say a word/mama's going to buy you a mockingbird. . . ."

"Papa." Dorie stood up and set her cup on the desk. Gwendolyn looked puzzled. "Mama just tells you to hush. Papa buys you things."

Gwendolyn frowned into her tea. "So that's the way it works."

Out on the street again, Dorie's chest lifted. It was good to be away from Gwendolyn and Amos. The way they matched, the easy way they had—it made her skin itch. Better to work, to focus. The lilt of Thalia's voice would be in her head all day. That was bad enough.

In her rush, she hadn't asked Amos about Wendy. Had Eveline mentioned her? Too concerned with Thalia, and her past and present paramours. The information about Tommy intrigued her. Easy to carry on with the chauffeur, with him living at the mansion, without your bedridden mother finding out. Thalia wasn't stupid, just young and careless. The kind of girl who makes priests tear off their collars.

But Wendy. Was her presence important to Eveline, to Thalia's well-being? Something—no, everything—about Julian bothered her. His vanished wife was only another riffle on a very stormy sea.

Amos Haddam escorted the Englishwoman to the streetcar and paid their fares. As he took her hand to help her up the steps, he felt an unaccustomed flush of happiness. It had been so long since he had a lady in his life. This one was a bit batty, but having her close made him feel like the war was winable, that Beryl would somehow find her way to the south of France and safety, that his mother would live through another German barrage. She was sunlight in a cloudy sky.

Gwendolyn smelled fresh, her thin brown hair wispy in the afternoon breeze, a shapeless, innocent nest. The dress brightened her face and she smiled up at Amos. They stood next to each other, swaying in the aisle, their shoulders bumping as the street-car lurched up and over the hill toward his apartment.

The morning chat with Eveline Hines had made him seek out the old nurse. Mother Ruth had not been forthcoming. She couldn't—or wouldn't—predict how long Eveline had to live. Days, weeks, months? She wouldn't say, but her eyes were dark and shadowed.

The Commander was very weak. Her voice still had that edge, that sharpness, but it came in spurts, with long pauses in between. Upset with the police, she wanted them back on the job, following Thalia every evening, staking out the mansion in case she went out unexpectedly. Lennox seemed to do well with the girl, but Amos felt guilty giving the job to her alone. She wouldn't be able to save Thalia if another attack came. But then, what could he do that she hadn't done on the bridge? Would he have shot at the black coupe? He made a mental note to clean his gun and find some ammunition. The thought soured him.

"Who was Mrs. Hines talking about, the person named Wendy?" Gwendolyn asked over the clanking of the rails.

"Didn't hear that, love."

"You were out with the nurse. Is it a friend?"

"I'll ask the nurse next time. Maybe somebody who needs to come round."

"The poor dear doesn't have long."

Amos put his arm around her waist. "Want to go to a little party tonight?"

When she smiled up at him, a sparkle lighted her eyes.

Dorie walked toward the exit of the gym at Fourteenth Street and Harrison, feeling the low-grade ache in her knee. In the boxing ring two fighters sparred lazily. If only the change were imme-diate, one would keep up the exercising. She picked up a copy of last week's *Kansas City Call*, the Negro newspaper, on the way out. The wind gusted out of the north, crisp with a promise of winter, cooling her damp skin. The sidewalk was empty as she walked to her car.

"Hey, Dorie!"

Grinning behind the wheel of a police cruiser was Chet McMillan, a cop she'd dated a few times. She hadn't seen him since her arrest. The romantic appeal of cops had paled.

"How are you, Chet?"

"Going to this war. Did you hear?" He drummed his hands against the steering wheel.

"What?"

"I'm in the reserves—remember? Navy. Word is that we'll be called up real soon."

She didn't know what to say. Congratulations?

"We have to get draft numbers and all, but it won't matter. We're going. We could be at sea in just a couple weeks."

She found her voice. "Gee. Have you ever been at sea?"

"Hell no, never even seen a beach. I'm from Garden City!" His sturdy farm-boy looks would be oddly right in a sailor's uniform. She envied him his adventures, his enthusiasm, being part of history and democracy and all that.

But it was war. What would happen to him? Would he come back? Would he die at sea, his cutter torn in half by a U-boat torpedo?

She shivered.

"Don't worry, Dorie. You'll get your knee back in shape. You'll be flying a plane in this war. I know you will."

"We'll see." His words made her dreams real. Then they dissolved, as childish and temporary as sugar on the tongue. "Amos got a draft notice."

"That old jasper? He's more than thirty-five, isn't he?"

"He was in the first war. He has to be."

"Tell him to forget about it. You'll see me there, draft or no draft. I'm hitting the high seas and getting me some Nazis!"

They said good-bye, wished each other good luck. She wondered if she'd ever see him again. She felt a sort of doom, like a storm cloud passing across the sun. This was the first of many times she would wonder about seeing someone again. Already, she felt a loss, as if just the speculating diminished living. What had her father once said? *Hold death close and it never comes as a stranger.* Was that the only way to go through life, clutching death to your bosom?

Dorie opened her car door as a strong wind blew up the street, tugging at her jacket. She reached up to pull it in and saw the man staring at her from in front of the gym. She looked back at him so long, it was too late just to get in the car and drive away.

Harvey Talbot had an odd look on his face. For a second, she thought he would nod and move on. She hadn't seen him since the third of May, the date popping embarrassingly into her mind. Two days before the stabbing. Where's he been? What's he been doing? she wondered.

He looked at his shoes, then in her eye. "What are you doing around here?" His voice was a little accusing.

"Nice to see you, too, Talbot. I could ask the same."

He glanced at the windowless facade of the brick gymnasium. "A story. Somebody tells us there have been some threats."

"Threats?" She closed her car door. "Racial threats?"

"Why do say that?" he snapped, then frowned at her. "Have you been inside?"

She stretched out her knee. "Trying to get my knee back in shape. Just in case."

Harvey squinted at her trouser leg and shoe as if confused. The look on his face shifted, softening. Just before he reached the door, he looked back at her. "Did you have a good summer?"

She could barely remember summer.

"Peachy. Swell." She smiled so sweetly, bees might have swarmed around her mouth—if she'd been in a song. "You?"

Talbot nodded, frowning, and opened the door to the gym as a muscular man with cropped black hair exited, a large bag slung over his shoulder. She'd seen him by the barbells and thought he looked familiar. Talbot nodded to him and said hello.

"Isn't that one of the Monarchs?" she whispered.

He nodded. "Gibson Saunders. I've got to go."

"Talk to Moses, the old trainer. He knows everybody."

Sounds of men arguing and laughing and pounding each other spilled onto the sidewalk for a moment; then they, and Harvey, disappeared.

NINE

DORIE IDLED THE PACKARD IN the driveway. Sleek and baby blue, the shiny new Plymouth roadster caused a spasm of jealousy in her heart. What a car, and for such a girl. In a moment, Thalia Hines burst out the front door, a scowl on her beautiful face. She paused, her hand on the door handle, not even taking time to appreciate the fine curves of steel, the nifty trunk, the chrome. Instead, she frowned at the Packard, squinting as if her glare had fire.

Fortunately, the girl didn't know where the gears were. Dorie had no trouble following her through the winding streets, over to the Country Club Plaza, and north to the Knights of Columbus Hall on Sixteenth Street. Light hung in the sky, the last fringe of the day. An unexpected warmth lingered, too, radiating off cobblestones and the tall columns that fronted the hall. Thalia parked the new roadster badly across the street and stalked up the steps. Dorie found a spot in a gravel lot down the street, then followed the girl inside.

Despite the classical facade of their building, the Knights of Columbus weren't known for lavish interiors. The Episcopalians had built a modern church on Ward Parkway two years before, abandoning this one. Unfortunately, they'd taken all the pews with them. Folding chairs covered the large wooden floor. A choir loft with fancy carvings and a bit of gilt was the only trace of Episcopalians. Most of the windows had been boarded up to save on the heating bill.

She settled onto a hard chair halfway up. The rest of the choir hadn't arrived. Barnaby Wake looked through sheets of music as Thalia dug through her purse on the edge of the stage. They whispered to each other. Then turned their backs. Thalia climbed the stairs to the stage, took a sheet of music from Wake. He put his arm around her shoulders as they pointed at the music. Wake went to the piano and picked out a set of notes. Thalia sang them, sounding rather off-key. He played again; she sang again.

After ten or fifteen minutes of this, Thalia threw down her music and cried, "I can't do this. She's watching me!" Dorie was jostled from her reverie. She lighted a Lucky and smiled at the girl.

"I hate her! How am I supposed to learn this with her sitting there staring? She is like my mother, her eyes, always judging me. I feel this—this tide of spite, of jealousy. She watches me and wants everything I have! Well, she can't have it. It's my life and she should stay the hell out of it!"

Wake put his arm around Thalia again, whispering in her ear. Thalia's face was red; she shook her head angrily. "No. No!" Then she burst into tears.

Dorie took a deep drag on the cigarette and blew smoke toward the high ceiling. A drama in her honor. How special. It would have been more enjoyable if Thalia wasn't half right.

Wake stomped down the aisle. Dorie stood up, took a last smoke, and smashed the butt under her shoe.

"Miss Lennox, this is intolerable. I don't know what you've done to that poor girl, but—"

"Done?"

"To make her so upset. You must have said something to her. She's never like this."

"I haven't spoken a word to her all day."

Wake scowled. "I'll have to ask you to leave."

The choir director seemed a little haggard now, less confident of his charms than at the coffee shop. He was dressed to the nines in a well-cut gray pinstriped suit, flaming red tie, and cream-colored shirt starched within an inch of its life. But his tan had faded, leaving his close-shaven cheeks gray and his dark eyebrows hooding low over his blue eyes. He seemed to ooze a sort of musk some men had. Left over from the cavemen days. Dorie suppressed an urge to grunt cavewoman-style.

"That's the nicest request to scram I've had all week, Mr. Wake."

"Barnaby. Please." He gave her the eye-contact treatment.

"Barnaby." She sat down again and shook out another Lucky. The hall was littered with butts. She reached over a few chairs and grabbed a sandbag ashtray. "Somebody's going to burn down this place."

"Miss Lennox. I asked you politely, but I can ask you again if you want."

"Ask away. I'm always curious to hear the way men from the East Coast phrase things."

She lighted another cigarette and dropped the match in the ashtray. Wake looked back at Thalia, who was sitting on the stage, blinking wet eyelashes. He reached down and pulled Dorie up by the arm, his hand tight. The heat off him was palpable as he spat his words.

"I'm warning you. This is not a public place. This is my rehearsal, my choir, and you are trespassing. Get your sorry pinko derriere out of here before I call the police."

"The police know I'm to follow Thalia, to protect her, to be her mother's eyes and ears. Go ahead and call them." She smiled. *Derriere?*

He pushed her away, disgust on his face. His jaw clenched, then his fists. It was a race between words and action. She raised her eyebrows and took another drag. Wake's face turned crimson, nearly matching his tie. Suddenly, Thalia appeared at his side.

"Come on, Barnaby. She's not worth it." Thalia pulled his arm, breaking the fever. He blinked at her, coming back. "Come on, baby," she whispered.

The door opened at the front of the hall, bringing in a gust of wind and dry leaves. Two women wearing fur stoles and delicate hats squealed as they held on to their hair. They walked toward the front, a jump in their step as they spied Wake.

"Barnaby darling! Everyone is so excited about the Willkie rally, I can't tell you! It's got quite a stir going all over town." The younger woman, slender and bright in a green dress and matching gloves, threw herself at the choir director, smothering him in a hug.

"Thank you, Agnes. Good news." He patted the fur across her shoulders, stroking it as Thalia stood by stiffly. Extricating himself, he smoothed his suit and cleared his throat. "Oh, look, Mrs. Wintraub."

Dorie sat back and watched the parade. Mostly women, dressed as if this rehearsal were a meeting with the King George, in their elegant furs and long gloves, scarves and silks, they impressed her as a very social lot. Chattering, stroking one another's clothing, squealing, hugging, smiling with all their teeth—it was quite a drama, almost as good as Thalia's. Some men arrived, serious types, some with wives, some solo, their girths suggesting rich food and deep voices.

One by one, they eventually lined up on the stage and began to sing a rousing American anthem Dorie had learned in fourth grade. She had never understood about the grapes of wrath back then. Now, thanks to Steinbeck, the grapes were everywhere, angry and forlorn. The voices echoed around the hall, thin and high, as if the air weren't rich enough to carry them. Wake waved his arms energetically. They reached the end of the first verse. The accompanist started in on the music for the second, when Wake beat his skinny stick on the podium.

"People, people! Let me hear you say *hallelujah*!"

In unison, the choir said in a weak voice, "Hallelujah."

"With spirit! With the love of God and country in your soul!" They tried again, louder.

"Deep in your heart—what lies there? Is it not the love of all things American, for the red, white, and blue, for the rights and freedoms we hold so dear? Do you love America?" He paused, but only a giggle came from the choir. The women looked around nervously. "Do you love America?"

"Yes! I love America!" The squeaky voice of Agnes piped up. Others chimed in. "Yes! Yes! Hallelujah!"

Finally, things reached a feverish pitch, hearts opened, love of country aroused. The song continued. And, Dorie had to admit, it sounded better. A big old amen to better music. What would democracy do without it? Oh, the terrible swift sword.

She lighted another cigarette. It was almost over.

They all went home alone. That was perplexing. Dorie figured Thalia and the choir man would take off for some clubbing, or a rendezvous at his place. But she marched to her roadster alone. A gray sedan came for Wake, driven by a chauffeur, with a man in the back. Thalia's expression was icy but reserved as she watched him pull away. They hadn't had a chance for more whispers after the rest of the choir arrived. Dorie would have bet her pinkie finger that they had more to say.

Dorie followed the girl home as she wrestled with the transmission again. Watched as she went into the house and turned out the porch light. A deliberate kiss-off, too deliberate. But her charge was safe at home, wasn't she? It was not quite ten o'clock. She drove to the corner and parked in the shadow of an oak, waiting for Thalia to leave. An hour later, she hadn't. Dorie threw out the last cigarette butt and drove home to the boardinghouse.

Autumn chill had arrived. Time for gloves and wool jackets and scarves. She didn't have a fox stole. Didn't have to wear it to church. That was something. This was the first night in weeks that she'd beat eleven o'clock and didn't need her key at the boardinghouse. An entire blissful night of sleep awaited her.

At the steps, her name was hissed in the darkness.

"Who is it?" She looked up and down the sidewalk, barren in both directions. An automobile passed by quickly. She looked up at the peeling gray mass of a house, windows yellow through filthy glass. She spun around. The shadows across the street were still.

"Miss Dorie." The voice again, an old, creaky one.

She walked to the corner of the house and peered into the dark alley of dirt between the boardinghouse and the Ballard house next door. Someone was playing a piano in the Ballard's parlor. The notes spilled thinly into the shadows.

"Who's there?"

"Down here, miss."

At the far front corner of the Ballard house, beyond the patched siding and withered chrysanthemums, the bent figure of Old Jenny tilted against a fence post. Her hair was wild and tangled, as usual; a tattered green shawl dangled from one shoulder. Her quilts and signboard lay in a heap. Dorie walked toward her until she could see the old woman's face. Her wrinkled expression had a crazed, frantic quality that Dorie had seen before.

"It's cold tonight, Jenny."

Jenny jerked a nod, her eyes darting over her left shoulder into the shadows.

"What is it?"

Jenny took a ragged breath. "Come closer. Somethin' you gotta see."

She stopped within an arm's length. "What is it, Jenny?"

The old woman's face began to dissolve, as if she had been frozen. Dorie could see now the blue cast to her complexion, the bloodless sockets, the dry lips, the tremors in her hands. Jenny's head lurched on her neck. Dorie put out a hand to hold her up. She weighed less than a bird.

"Are you sick?" The old woman had a powerful odor to her always, but now, in the sharp air, there was a smell of death.

Jenny collapsed in Dorie's arms, her legs giving out, her mouth falling open as her head fell. She lowered the old woman to her quilts, arranging her head. She pulled the shawl and the quilt around her. Jenny had lost her mind in the heartaches of the Depression. And now, as she had so long predicted, the end was near. Should she haul the old lady to the hospital? Or did she want to die where she had lived, here on the dirty sidewalk?

The powerful arm that hauled Dorie to her feet spun her backward against the lamppost. Her head bounced off the metal pole, the clang surprising her as, stunned, she fell forward before catching herself.

The man stood in the shadows, but close enough. He wore the same hat as the man in the car the night before—a brown fedora with a silk ribbon. Otherwise, she didn't recognize him—squat and muscular, wearing a dark suit, with a face out of a boxing magazine. She did recognize the piece in his right hand.

"Let's go, girlie," he growled.

"Jenny needs medical help. We can't just—"

"Sure we can. And we is. Move."

She held on to the lamppost at her back. She looked up at the quiet boardinghouse, a picture of evening solace, down at green awnings of Steiner's grocery, across at Joe's Garage. Why did things like this happen in her neighborhood? She really was going to have to move.

"Nobody's coming for ya, girlie. Let's go."

"You sure? You all alone?" She gauged his itch. He waved the gun back and forth, an extension of his arm. What would he do if she hollered? What did she have to lose?

"*Hey.* Help! Somebody help me!"

He swung at her then, catching the back of her head with the side of the pistol, throwing her against the lamppost again. She slid to her knees, stars blinking on the pavement in front of her eyes. "I told you to shut it. Get up." He pulled her upright then and pushed her toward the corner. "Move your feets."

A light came on in Joe's Garage. His door opened, then shut. Dorie took a step in the monkey's direction to keep him from lobbing another on her. So much for help from her friends.

Old Jenny lay with her eyes shut, mouth still hanging open. A huff of vapor came from her. She was still alive.

"Faster now." The man poked the gun in her back. "See that

boiler on the corner? That's where we're going. And shut up, or you get it between the shoulder blades."

Not that there was much choice. She felt her empty pocket again. Her head was booming with pain. And then there was the piece in his hand. She'd never been a fan of bullet holes.

The midnight blue sedan loomed shiny and ominous. She stopped. A prickling sweat rose on her back. Once inside, it would be over. She'd learned that much in this business. Her head was clearing, and she glanced back at the goon. He wasn't so big. And careless with the pistol, swinging it. Could I kick it out of his hand? she wondered. And then what?

He was opening the door. She stepped back, cold fear running down her spine and into her feet. She couldn't get in. No. She took another step back.

He pointed the gun at her, wagging it toward the open door. "This way, girlie. We're going for a ride."

A whoosh of air behind her was the only clue. The figure sprang in front of her, from nowhere, shoving her back toward Steiner's, into an empty fruit box.

"She's not going anywhere with you, bud."

A woman. Her voice was raspy but rich. She wore a man's suit, or trousers and a smart blazer, and a low-brimmed hat over her twisted black hair. In her hand, her dark-skinned hand, was a small pistol. She pointed it at the goon. He stumbled in surprise, falling off the curb and catching himself with the car door. Before he could get his breath, the woman hit his elbow with her knee. The gun spun out of his hand. It clattered to the gutter, where she scooped it up.

"That's right. Get into your beater and get on your way. Your business is done here." The woman stepped close to him, her tall, trim figure overpowering him where he crouched in the open car door. "And tell your boss to stay off Charlotte Street. This here's sacred ground. You got that?" She poked her gun in his face for good measure. "You got it?"

The woman stood on the curb, pistol pointed, as he scrambled into the car and drove away. He took the corner at full speed, tires squealing. The woman laughed, watching him. Then she spun on her heel and cocked her head at Dorie.

"You can't let men march you around like that. They'll be marching you down the aisle before you can blink, then making you wear an apron all day, fetch their slippers like a dog."

Dorie stepped out from under the awning, pulling her jacket square again. She rubbed a lump forming on the back of her head. The Negro woman put her pistol into her handbag. She swung the man's gun around her fingers, examining it before sticking it in her jacket pocket. She had striking features, a straight nose, full red lips, beautiful dark eyes, and cocoa skin. The whites of her eyes seemed to glow.

The woman pursed her lips. "I read in the *Star* you got pinched for using that blade of yours. Your knife and your temper never did mix well."

"Well, he deserved it. He'll be all right."

"As soon as his liver heals." The woman grinned, her teeth setting off sparks.

Dorie leaned in. "Do I know you?"

"You need some help watching your back. You can count on me." She tapped Dorie lightly on the shoulder. "Try to stay away from trouble, honey."

The woman walked around the corner. She moved like a dancer, almost at a run, but too graceful, too smooth. Dorie watched, numb. She shook her head, feeling the sore spots and cursing. Then it hit her.

"Hey, hold up!" Dorie ran to the corner. The street was empty. The woman had vanished into the shadows and the night. She stood gasping, heart pounding faster than it had when the man put a pistol to her back. She pulled air into her lungs and felt a strange burn in her chest. She blinked into the dark.

"Arlette?"

Joe hunched over the prostrate figure on the sidewalk. He had covered Jenny with a blanket from the garage, an oil-stained scrap of quilted cloth. Dorie crouched down beside them, touching the old woman on the cheek.

"She's still breathing," Joe said.

"Barely." Her chest rose slightly on short, choppy breaths. "Let's carry her inside." Dorie ran up the boardinghouse steps and opened the front door. She propped open the screen with a broken flowerpot and went back to Joe and Jenny.

"She don't look hurt. Do you think she's dying?"

"I don't know, Joe. Help me. Take her feet."

She jostled Jenny's head and shoulders into her arms, the woman still cradled in quilts. She weighed almost nothing, skin and bones and a bit of cloth. They carried her up the stairs and into the boardinghouse, coming through the door as Mrs. Ferazzi came out of her rooms under the stairs.

"Here, here. What's this?" Mrs. F. clucked, tying her robe tightly around her middle.

"She collapsed outside," Joe said.

"She can't come in here; she's probably got fleas and lice and who knows what. Dorie, please, turn right around and take her back outside."

Dorie continued toward the parlor. Mrs. F. followed, chattering on, her voice increasingly high-pitched as they ignored her. Her hands flapped around.

"Not on the sofa, for God's sake. Not that pillow. Mother of God, what are you doing? She's filthy! She smells like the sewer."

Dorie spread the quilts over Jenny, tucking in her arms. "Do you have an extra blanket, Mrs. F.?"

"I certainly do not. Not for street urchins and crazy old biddies."

She turned to stare at the landlady. "Could you please call an ambulance, then?"

Mrs. Ferazzi was dumbstruck. She held her sides tightly and didn't move.

"Now, Mrs. F. Before she dies in your parlor."

Joe was digging in his pockets. "I'll do it."

The ambulance took a long time. Dorie rubbed Jenny's hands and feet to warm her, then had to wash herself. Mrs. F. finally relented and brought a hot-water bottle. It was all Dorie could think of to help Jenny, since reviving Gwendolyn. The old woman was still blue and stiff, barely breathing, when the crew loaded her into the ambulance.

Dorie and Joe stood on the steps and watched the ambulance pull away.

"Think she'll make it? They musta beat her up bad. I saw some bruises."

"I don't know, Joe. She's old."

"Who was that fella, the one with the gun?"

"Wish I knew."

"You talk to your partner about me, about finding Roscoe Sensa's enemies?"

She blinked and fixed on Joe, his face a mask of scars. She'd almost forgotten about his accident, but he never would. "Sorry, I haven't had a chance."

"But you will?"

"Sure, Joe. As soon as I can." She looked at him. "But remember. No promises."

He stepped down a stair, hands in his pockets. "I remember."

The door opened. Mrs. Ferazzi, still in pink chenille, held the oily blanket between a finger and thumb.

"Does this belong to someone, or can I burn it?"

In her room, the smell of an overripe banana had to be dealt with. Dorie threw it into the bathroom wastebasket and opened a window. The heavy sweetness lingered, finally mixing with smoky city smells and the sirens wailing. The long wait for Jenny's saviors had been maddening. If the old woman died of shock, or bleeding, or whatever was wrong with her, it would be the fault of those boys in the white pants as sure as it was the attacker's. Tomorrow she would go to City Hospital and see if Jenny was alive. She rubbed her forehead. She had no great hopes.

On the edge of her bed, she eased the bottle of gin from behind the nightstand and looked at it. The colorless liquid sloshed— half gone, half left. She stared at it for a long time, then finally got up and poured a short one, recapped the bottle, and stuck it back in its hidey-hole. Mrs. Ferazzi didn't like drinkers. She was partial to Swedish bachelors, especially if they spoke no English. Also partial, in a negative way, to her own people as boarders, prone as they were in Kansas City to foul deeds and whoop-'em-up. But to hear her talk, she was proud as all get-out to be Italian, wouldn't hear a bad word against Il Duce, the goose-stepping nincompoop who made Leonardo da Vinci roll over in his grave.

The juniper and its after-bite rolled around her tongue and down her throat. One drink, Mrs. F. Just one. Because tonight a ghost from the past came back to save me.

Could it really have been Arlette? Dorie heard her voice again in her head, that sassy talk. It had to have been Arlette. But why had she run away? What was she doing in Kansas City? Why had she appointed herself protector? And how could Dorie ever pay her back?

She shivered, thinking about the yawning door of the sedan, waiting for her. Who did the goon work for? The same one who'd tried to snatch Thalia and tore Tommy apart instead? She stared into the gin for answers but received only a call to pour it down the hatch. Which she answered.

The last time she'd heard from Arlette, her friend was in Chicago. They'd grown up together. They'd discovered speakeasies and moonshine and men together, too early. The favor Dorie'd done for her when they were both fourteen, a favor that had almost killed Arlette, had bound them together. Even through the years and the miles between them, it was there. Yet Arlette had stood in front of her tonight and she hadn't recognized her. How could that be?

Did Arlette think she had to repay her? There had never been a question of that. She'd never blamed Arlette. It had been only six months in Beloit. Six months on the inside, and several lifetimes on the outside. When she'd gotten out, Tillie was gone. Her mother was on her road to destruction. But there had never been a question of owing.

But what had Arlette written in postcards over the years? Dorie opened the cabinet over the sink and found the stack held together by a rubber band. The crumbling band snapped in half as she pulled it.

On an Easter card from two years ago: "I think about those days you spent in Beloit for me and sometimes I go to church. A Catholic one near my place, with a Spanish priest. I sit in the back and think about the good things you did for me."

A year earlier, more cryptically: "Don't think I forget."

There were other short comments. She stacked them all up, some twenty-five postcards over nearly ten years. Dorie had never replied. Never knew how. Arlette somehow found her, at Beloit, in Atchison, in Kansas City with her aunt and uncle, at the university in Lawrence. And here. She should be a private detective.

Dorie washed out the glass, dried it, and set it back on the shelf. She replaced the postcards without the band and shut the cupboard. It took so little effort to keep order in her tiny world. And so much to find it out there.

She lay on her bed. There were so many things she wanted to ask Arlette. Where she'd been, who she'd seen, where she worked, if she was happy, whether she had children. That had always worried her since the botched abortion. Would Arlette be able to have children? Was she married? Dorie smiled, remembering her fierceness on the street. Not likely with that comment about marching down the aisle. She was so strong, so fearless! The way she kicked that gun out of the fella's hand as if it were candy. The familiar way she handled her own piece.

Was Arlette a criminal? A thief, a burglar? Or worse, did she do hits for the trouble boys? No. Not Arlette.

So many questions. Where is Wendy? Who is Barnaby Wake boffing? Who whacked Roscoe Sensa and burned poor Joe? Why is Harvey Talbot so cold? Who beat up a crazy doomsdayer? Who is harassing the Monarchs?

As she drifted into sleep, the questions jumbled in her head, Wake and Wendy, Sensa and Jenny, Arlette and . . . She saw Arlette on the sidewalk again, examining the man's gun, a knowing look on her face.

A look that said, This will come in handy.

TEN

THE SEASON END PARTY AT the Monarchs owner's house hadn't been a festive affair, and Amos Haddam was ready to go by ten o'clock. The owner's mansion had been cleaned and straightened. One would never know there had been a break-in. Gwendolyn had one cocktail and sat, slightly drunk, in an armchair while he talked to Wilkinson and Gilmore about the threats.

"I will not be cowed by these bastards. Cowards, that's all they are. Stinking cowards," Wilkinson declared. "I have seen this dozens of times over the years, and it's absolutely ridiculous to think we would take this seriously."

The boy, Leroy, dressed tonight in another secondhand outfit of black pants and shoes, white shirt, and an oddly attractive red sweater, turned his head to stare at the owner. His face showed the fear that Amos had seen in his office, but it had deepened now.

"Absolutely, sir," Haddam said. "It's just that it upsets the boys. Some of them."

"It upsets me, goddamn it!" Wilkinson pounded his fist into his palm. "This has got to end, this hatred. It has to. God knows, I'm doing everything in my power to bring the races together, to find common ground."

Gibson Saunders stepped into their circle. "Beg your pardon, sir, but that is just what makes 'em crazy. Maybe we should think about canceling the Blues game."

"Never! How can you suggest that, Gibson? To give in to idle threats, to this—this hillbilly nonsense! I won't do it. Let them come and get me. Let them just try to stop the game."

Saunders stepped closer to Quincy and Wilkinson. "Some of the boys, you know," he said in a low voice, glancing back at

Leroy and his bunch, "some of them seen some lynchings up way too close. That's all."

Haddam shivered. He'd seen some—too many—during his revenuer days in the South.

"Dear Lord," Wilkinson muttered.

"We don't have things like that in Kansas City, Saunders," Quincy said. "You tell 'em not to worry. This ain't the South."

Saunders nodded, straightening and taking a breath. "I'll tell them."

"There's a lot of money riding on the game, Gib," Quincy Gilmore said. "Not just betting money, either."

"We make a good gate at that game, Mr. Saunders," Wilkinson explained. "Last year's was the best turnout of the year. We need it to get us through to next season."

Saunders demurred. Haddam watched him drift back to a group of players standing in a corner. They looked awkward in their best clothes, their wives and girlfriends nervous in a white man's fancy house, their big hands wrapped around delicate crystal. Amos felt for them. He didn't feel much more comfortable.

Gibson Saunders was wearing a plain but well-cut suit and a fancy bow tie. He was a good-looking man, but he'd brought no woman with him. Well-spoken, too, Amos thought. Not afraid to speak his mind even if it meant getting slapped down by management.

Amos caught Gwendolyn's eye and nodded. She frowned as if she didn't understand. Amos looked at his watch meaningfully. Then Quincy bumped his elbow.

"Got any money on the game, Haddam?" he whispered.

"I'm not much of a betting man."

Quincy nodded, brushing the sleeves of his jacket compulsively. "Good idea. If you were a betting man, it would be hard to not hedge a little. Monarchs got good odds. Almost too good."

Haddam squinted at him, trying to decipher a message, if there was one.

Quincy smiled. "If you was a betting man."

"There." Amos Haddam smoothed the freshly laundered case, plumped up the pillow, and placed it on the clean sheet. "Now you'll be comfortable."

"I was comfortable before," Gwendolyn said. "But this is quite lovely, Amos."

She stood in a tattered dressing gown scattered with yellow roses, her thin ankles blue in the pale light. Amos had spent the afternoon washing the linens in the bathtub, drying them on the line in the yard, pressing them with his sputtery old steam iron. He knew he should be tired, but he was only relieved that he still had it in him to do all that work—and that he hadn't scorched the fabric. He pulled back the sheet. "All right now, hop in."

The nights in the shelters in London had made Gwendolyn easy about her body. All shyness was gone. She pulled off the dressing gown and draped it on the end of the bed. She wore a thin pink slip underneath but made no motions of distress over his seeing her in it. Her body was thin, even bony. Still, he felt a reverence at seeing a woman's body again. She stepped in and pulled the covers up to her chin.

"You'll leave the window open?" she asked, glancing at the street.

"It may get chilly."

"You put the extra blanket on the bed, Amos. I'll be cozy as a clam."

He rubbed his chin. "No screaming?"

She smiled. "It seems to have left me. The sky is so blue here. So safe."

"Yes. Sleep easy." He thought about his own poor sleep, about the deaths he'd seen here, about the way the past had haunted him. He cleared his throat. "Good night, Gwendolyn."

At the door, she called his name.

"Can you sit here? For a minute or two while I fall asleep?"

He eased down on the edge of the bed. It was a double bed, though he had rarely had a need for it. So strange to have a woman in his bed. He patted her hand and she grasped his tightly.

"The dark still bothers me. Just a little."

"I'll stay, love."

Her eyes sparkled in the dim light of the bedside lamp. "Do you remember the time you took me fishing? You were so certain you knew the best places to fish, the best type of bait. You had that old bamboo rod, remember that?"

"It was my father's when he was a boy."

"I don't remember your father."

"Neither do I. Not much."

"What happened to him?"

"Nothing. He didn't come out to the cottage that summer but a weekend or two. He was a bond trader, always working."

"I didn't know bond traders worked weekends."

"He didn't think much of relaxation. He'd been through a few crashes. Lost a few shirts."

"Is he—"

"The last crash killed him. He'd saved enough to safeguard my mother, but the losses for his clients did him in."

"I'm sorry."

"Don't be."

"I caught a very fat fish, do you remember? A smelly old pike. And you caught nothing."

He couldn't remember, and he wanted to so badly. It seemed he could remember the things that hurt, and none of the other.

"Lie down here, Amos. Put your head on the pillow. For a moment."

He lay on his side, looking into her small, tender face. She drew her hand across his cheek. "Has America been good for you?"

"Good enough." He took her hand in his. "Yes, good."

"Do you love it? This country?"

He frowned. "I'll always be English." The letter crinkled in the pocket of his jacket. "I heard from my mother. But the letter was written in August. Before her house was bombed."

"Poor Amos. You'll hear again soon."

Their talk petered out, their voices tiring. Memory and regret. It wore Amos out, all this trying to remember. He watched Gwendolyn's eyes close and her breathing slow. He kept her hand in his a long time, its soft palm against his rough one, the tips of her fingers like tiny pillows against his neck. Behind him, the open window let in cold air, chilling his back through his suit. He shivered, watching her sleep, the tiny veins in her eyelids so delicate. He dreaded the day she'd go on to California. Having her here, even with the exhausting nature of memory, brought back a piece of him he had lost, a piece of his Englishness that was good and honorable.

A piece left behind in a sea of mud.

Gwendolyn fiddled with the knobs of the wireless, which had recently been installed in the reception area. Shirley had come in early to type up some letters and found the office of Sugar Moon Investigations full of music. She and Gwen laughed. Their happy voices came through the doorway into Amos's office, where he sat rubbing his tired eyes. Lennox sat across from him, her hair freshly done, the blond streaks arranged in clips, a turquoise sweater tight on her not-so-ample chest. She looked a little wide-eyed at the commotion and had even given Gwendolyn a grilling about sleeping arrangements—which Amos found amusing.

On the wireless, Ella Fitzgerald was trying to convince listeners that "A Chicken Ain't Nothin' But a Bird." Gwendolyn's laughter cut into the song, and abruptly it was gone. Dorie started to say something but closed her mouth, overpowered by the annoying static.

"Pick something, Gwendolyn, would you, ducks?" Amos called. "And lower it a touch?"

The static crackled madly between snatches of news programs, studio applause, game-show numbers. The dial fixed on a sonorous voice. A preacher. He was going on about the "yellow peril" and "the enemy within: Jews, Catholics, Negroes." Drivel that sat sourly in the morning stomach.

"Not Father Coughlin, Gwen. Please," Dorie called over her shoulder. She turned to Amos. "He's trying to start a war inside this country."

Amos cocked his head, frowning as the dial moved again. Finally, Ella came back. "What of last night?"

She told him about Old Jenny, the man with the gun, the mysterious protector. "I think I was set up by Wake. He sent Thalia home early so he could send goons around."

"Only one."

"I'm not very dangerous. Everyone knows I don't have my switchblade." The *Star* had reported all the details, if anyone cared to read the back pages. Dorie squinted her eyes, then looked at the ceiling with an odd, dreamy look, as if something nice had come out of being shaken down and almost taken for a ride. "I did get Wake's goat last night. He tried to throw me out."

"Got angry, did he?"

"Threatened to call the law." She had a malicious twinkle in her eye. "That choir isn't half-bad."

"Glad you enjoyed it, since you'll be hearing a lot of them."

Haddam had other things to do tonight. Like take Gwendolyn out for apple pie. He felt guilty about it, but not as much as he should have. "First, we go visit the Commander."

"Again?"

"Every day now." He opened the door for her. "She's fading fast. It won't be long."

A half hour later, they were arranged around the large four-poster bed, the shrinking world of Eveline Hines. Her bedding looks even cleaner than mine, Amos thought, wondering what sort of massive laundering machinery was necessary for this household. Odd little thoughts, domestic details, came at him.

SWEET AND LOWDOWN 117

What sort of bleach does she use? This morning, he had made a note to buy butter for toast and cream for tea.

Eveline looked no worse than on the last visit, nor better. She rested her head against the tower of pillows at her back. The top pillowcase was embroidered and laced on the edges, a beautiful old piece. My mum would have loved that case. Amos shook his head, annoyed by his wanderings.

They said good morning. Dorie looked rested and fresh in the bright sweater. The silver beads on one shoulder caught the sunlight. Eveline rallied as she blinked at the reflection.

"Goodness, Miss Lennox. Don't you look chipper this morning."

"As do you, Mrs. Hines. I hope you had a good night."

Eveline closed her eyes. "Could someone get me some water?"

Dorie did the honors, pouring a small glass of water and holding it to the sick woman's lips. Haddam felt useless. He had left Gwendolyn with Shirley at the office, and he missed her. Absurd, missing the fawning attention of a half-wit. Ah, but one English half-wit was as good as most full-witted Americans. He smiled to himself. How ridiculous he was.

"Appears one of us had a good night," Dorie said, catching Amos's eye. "Thalia came home about ten. I waited an hour here, but she didn't leave again, so I went home."

Eveline Hines blinked. "I wasn't awake." She looked embarrassed.

"That's what we're for, Eveline," Amos said. "Dorie had an unfortunate incident later on that we think might be related to Barnaby Wake. Someone tried to force her into his automobile at gunpoint."

"Whatever for?" The Commander squinted at her. The girl put her hand to her throat as if rankled by the attention.

"We can only guess," Amos said. "The abduction was foiled by another woman with another gun."

"Good Lord, how lucky. You think Barnaby Wake was behind this?"

Amos looked at Dorie. She said, "He tried to throw me out of the hall last night. Thalia was in tears. Said my presence upset her."

Eveline Hines sighed and sunk deeper into the pillows. "Pleasing that girl . . . Well, that is not my concern. Her safety, her future, that is what we must think about."

"We've been trying to find out more about Barnaby Wake," Amos said. "He's proving a bit difficult."

"Oh?"

"He has no driver's license, car license, or land title here. We think he's from New Jersey or thereabouts, but we haven't heard anything from our contacts there. The workings of the chorus are very hush-hush. He says he's married and his wife lives in Arizona for her health."

"Wife?" Eveline said, eyes widening. "He's married?"

"So he says."

"Miss Lennox, run and fetch Julian. Beulah will know where to find him."

Dorie straightened, surprised, then did as she was told. When Amos looked back at Eveline, her body was tense with pain.

"Amos. My pills," she whispered through her teeth. He found a prescription bottle by the water glass and shook out two.

"How many, love?"

"Three."

Putting a hand behind her neck, he pulled her forward. She threw the pills into her mouth and swallowed them with water. Amos sat again and waited for the medicine to take effect. Finally, Eveline opened her eyes and smiled wanly.

"Thank you, Amos."

"I wish there was more I could do for you, Eveline."

"There's nothing anyone can do," she whispered. "Watching Wendy for me is all the help in the world."

Amos frowned. "Wendy?"

"Did I say Wendy?" She blinked and bit her lip. "I meant Thalia." Eveline looked at him seriously. "Wendy is—was—my daughter-in-law. Julian's wife. Appears to have run off and left him. I miss her terribly. She was the only person in this house I could really talk to. She lost her own mother to cancer. We would talk late into the night."

"I'm sorry."

"I do miss her." Eveline's eyes began to mist. "Oh, dear me."

Amos handed her a handkerchief. "Where's she gone?"

"Ran off without a word to any of us. I must say that it struck me as odd. She didn't even say good-bye."

He took her hand and squeezed it. She pulled away, embarrassed. "Of course, once you meet Julian, you'll probably understand why she did it. Please don't mention Wendy to him. He's terribly fragile."

Dorie came through the door and held it for the man. So this is Julian Hines, thought Amos. A thin-haired scared rabbit in plaid casual pants and a bright green shirt and saddle shoes. He looked flushed, his hands thrust nervously in pockets.

"Good morning, Comm—Eveline. How are we today?"

"You sound like Mother Ruth. Sit down. All of you." She made introductions between Julian and Amos Haddam. "You met Miss Lennox?"

"Several times." Julian smiled boldly at Dorie, all of his teeth a gripping white. Amos felt a sudden animosity spring to his breast. "How goes the battle, Miss Lennox?"

"The battle, sir?"

"Good versus evil? Men versus women? The Hines versus the rest of the world?"

"Stop it, Julian." Eveline said. "I want you to tell them what you said about Barnaby Wake yesterday."

"Oh, that." He stuck his plaid legs out and smoothed the phosphorescent madras fabric with delicate hands freckled by the sun. They shook a little, no doubt a temporary ailment, lasting until cocktail hour. "Just some flap I heard."

"Tell them," the Commander ordered.

"All right. I'll tell them." He glared at her briefly, then smiled at them. "The word at the club is that Barnaby Wake is dallying with Agnes Marchand. Her husband is a vice-president at Security Fire and Life. On track to be bigwig there, I hear. A damn good golfer, too."

"I saw her last night. She gave him a hug," Dorie said. "At least he called her Agnes. Reddish blond hair, stylish?"

"Flirty and fluttery? That's Agnes. Wake must work his way through the sopranos to the altos. Haven't heard about him working on the baritones. Yet."

"Thank you, Julian. That'll be all." Mrs. Hines's nostrils were flaring.

"Do the folks at the club know he's married?" Dorie asked.

Julian smirked in merriment. "Better and better."

"I have an idea, Amos. Tell me what you think," Eveline said. Even her weak voice held the command of respect and authority. "We go to this Agnes and have her put the screws to Wake. If he doesn't leave Thalia alone, she'll expose him as a Don Juan."

Amos bit his lip, glancing at Dorie. She was picking at a button on her sweater. Julian linked his fingers across his belly, enjoying the intrigue.

"I'm not sure she'd agree to that, Eveline," Amos said gently.

"And why not?"

"Because it would expose her, too."

"We can hold that over her. Make her do it, or we expose them both. No more society matrons and their money and favors."

Amos tried a smile on the Commander. Eveline was staring at her portrait over the fireplace. No one spoke for so long, even Julian grew restless, wriggling on his chair.

Finally, with a small sigh, Eveline spoke. "You'll go to her, Amos. Unless you feel Miss Lennox would be better, give her the womanly touch. But we must be very firm. Make her see she will be ruined unless Wake gives up his attentions toward Thalia."

"We don't know absolutely that she and Wake are involved," Amos said.

Julian snorted and waggled his eyebrows.

"You have some proof?"

The stepson said, "There's always a grain of truth in this talk. If she's not actually bedding him, she wants to."

"That would lessen any power we might have over her."

"Enough!" Eveline cried, raising a palm like a policeman signaling. "You will go to her and make her see the lay of the land, Amos. Today."

Dorie was staring at Amos, disbelief in her eyes. This was a bad idea. It wouldn't work, and they both knew it. A shiver went up Amos's spine and out of the blue a vision of Gwendolyn lying on the clean white pillow, her hair in a fan, swam into his mind.

"Of course, Eveline. We'll talk to her today." He stood up. "We'd better get busy. Shall we call on you later?"

"Tomorrow morning is soon enough," Eveline said, the indignity of the situation draining color from her face, leaving her pale as a cloud. "Julian. Tell Mother Ruth I need her now."

Dorie watched Julian walk to the door, shooting them a resentful look over his shoulder. She stood her ground, not wanting to accompany him to the foyer again. Amos held his open notebook, frowning into it as if it would tell them how in the world they were to lean on Agnes Marchand. She stared at him, willing him to look up. But he sat down again, crossed his legs, and continued the examination of his chicken scratches in the notebook.

"I'll be out front," she said finally, nodding to the Commander. Unnecessary, as her eyes were closed.

"Won't be long," Amos muttered, folding up the notebook and slipping it into his jacket pocket. "I'll just wait for Mother Ruth."

The hallway was deserted. Maybe Mother Ruth was out having a smoke. Lennox tiptoed on the stone floor, hoping for a quick getaway. She walked down the corridor toward the front hall, until she heard the voice. From upstairs. High and light like through the hedges—it had to be Thalia. At the doorway into the icy foyer, she stopped. The voice came floating from upstairs.

"Full of the old paprika, loaded with dynamite, come on down, come on down, I'm throwing a ball tonight. . . ." Her voice was reedy but full of pep, the way one sang to the mirror.

"Invited Wendell Willkie, invited FDR . . ." The voice trailed off as she hummed through several verses before declaring again that she was throwing a ball tonight.

It was the song Thalia had sung that night in the Three Owls. From a musical play. What was it? At least she could tell the Commander what song Thalia was singing now, or hum a few bars anyway.

Thalia's voice was surprisingly sweet, like Tillie's. Hearing it had an odd effect. A warm spot grew in Dorie's chest, the part of her where she kept her memories of Tillie. The singing—Thalia's singing—cast a new glow over Thalia. She was different suddenly, as if hearing her sweet voice altered Dorie's picture of her, filling in superficial planes with warm color, even depth. Could it be that Thalia wasn't really as shallow and coldhearted as she seemed? Perhaps she cared about her mother, but the old woman, with her military ways, hadn't allowed any feeling. How hard it must have been to grow up with Eveline Hines and her sharp, critical tongue.

Heel taps on the stone floor. Mrs. Hines's secretary, Mildred, rounded the big table adorned with gladiolai and headed toward the hallway. Tall and officious, with her big nose and half glasses, she didn't see Dorie until the detective cleared her throat.

Mildred's step stuttered and she clutched a sheaf of papers to her bosom. "Good morning. I hope you haven't been tiring Mrs. Hines."

"It was a short meeting."

"She has a very busy weekend coming, what with the Willkie rally and some visitors connected to the campaign," Mildred said, nose high in the air. The attention of the Willkie people was obviously a coup. "They are coming to the house, you know. We shan't be having a reception per se. But they are coming to visit and commune with Mrs. Hines. She needs her rest."

"I wouldn't dream of interfering—Mildred, is it?"

"Miss Miller, if you please."

Mildred Miller carried on down the hallway, having communicated her importance. Dorie smiled. What would the uppity Miss Miller do if she saw a switchblade, felt its sharp swish of steel? Crumple into a million flaky pieces, no doubt.

Dashing across the foyer before someone else collared her, Dorie escaped into the open air. The switchblade thoughts reminded her that today she had to visit her parole officer. One more month. That was all she had. She shivered. She had to hang in and clear things up.

Amos Haddam appeared at the door before she got in the Packard.

"You want me to talk to Mrs. Marchand?" Dorie asked when he settled into the seat.

"I'd better. She's not going to take it from another woman."

She nodded. "You know that song that goes *'Invited Wendell Willkie, invited FDR?'* "

"Don't try for a singing career."

She made a face. "It's from a show. Thalia was singing it that night at the Three Owls when she went off with Barnaby Wake." She hummed a few bars and threw in the "come on down, come on down."

"Forget about that. We've got a bucketful of stuff to throw out today." Amos waited until she started the Packard and headed north again, toward the office; then he cleared his throat loudly. "Listen, I've been hearing things about somebody named Wendy."

A sound—no, a feeling like a thud—hit the interior of the car and bounced off Dorie's chest. They stopped at an intersection where a boy in blue was directing traffic, white gloves and all.

"Julian's wife?"

"You know about her?"

"A little."

"Eveline says she ran off without a word."

The cop waved them on. "That's what Julian says. Peeved as hell." That was anger, wasn't it?

"We've got to find her," Amos said. "Eveline is dying. She's going fast. Mother Ruth told me she won't last the month."

"Does she know where Wendy went?"

"No idea. What did Julian say?"

"Not a trace. Oh, he talked to an aunt back east. She hadn't heard from Wendy since Christmas."

"Give it a go, will you? Talk to Julian again, find out her haunts. Maybe she's hiding out with some friend."

"Or shacked up somewhere." Dorie pulled into a parking spot right next to the Boston Building. Her lucky day. "What about Wake?"

"Stay away from him. He's liable to send more of his fun boys around. Make like you got the message, righty-o?"

"Righty-o, old boy. What about tonight?" She slammed the car door and stood in the breeze.

He rubbed his chin as the wind flopped his hair forward. "I'll watch her tonight. You take a night off."

"If you say so, boss. What will you do this afternoon?"

"More trouble with the Monarchs. I've got to go hold a few hands over there."

The door to the stairway at the Boston Building opened. Harvey Talbot stepped out, pulling on a fedora, adjusting the brim as he spied them. He looked anxious, although eager to see Amos Haddam.

"I've been waiting upstairs," he told Amos. "Can we talk?"

"About what?"

"The other night. And some new developments." Talbot moved closer to Amos. Dorie eased around the front of the Packard. "Rumors of Kluxers. That they might try to close down the game."

"That's bluster and fluff and you know it. There's no story there."

"What happened at the gym?" Dorie asked. Talbot squinted at her coldly. Couldn't he even be civil? What had she done to him? Then she remembered. A cold ache rose up her back, into her neck. She folded her arms.

Talbot turned to Haddam. "Maybe if we fill each other in, we can find some rhyme or reason."

Amos coughed into his handkerchief. "Let's get out of this wind." He looked at Dorie over his shoulder.

"Find her," he said.

ELEVEN

YOU SEEM JUMPY TODAY, MISS Lennox."

"Let's get on with it."

"You don't like people observing your behavior? It makes you nervous?"

"It's *my* job, observing people."

"And what do you see?"

"Liars, cheats, thieves. People with more money than smarts, people with smarts still looking for easy street."

"You don't think much of people?"

"It's the nature of the job."

"To dislike people?"

"To deal with the cheating type, the tough guys, the scam artists."

"Is that what you're working on now?"

"Not really." She waited for the Widow Vunnell to react, enjoying the taunt of withheld details. "More like trying to stop a girl from ruin."

"Ah." The chair creaked as Vunnell leaned back. "Any similarities between you?"

"Me and her? She reminds me a little of my sister. She sings a lot. Tillie did that." Dorie paused and looked out the window. In the distance, purple clouds were gathering over the bluffs, blocking the afternoon sun and giving a melancholy autumn glow to the city. "She's mixed up, wild, mouthy. But the mother is a tyrant. She drove the girl to it. Maybe."

"Is it usually the mother's fault? What about your mother?"

"My mother was a drunk and a floozy."

"Is that what the man said, the one you stabbed?"

Wilma Vunnell had the most insidious way about her. Dorie frowned at the solid form behind the desk, her passive face and dark, unreadable eyes. "More or less. It wasn't friendly."

"He was unarmed?"

"I never saw anything. He tried to jump me."

"That's not what he said at trial."

"And you believed him. Because he's rich and has society friends."

"He doesn't appear to be the sort to jump women on the street."

"We weren't on the street. We were in his car."

"On a date, then."

"He took me flying. It wasn't a date. He rents a plane and takes people up sometimes."

"So you accepted his invitation?"

"Just for the flying. Not for anything else." Dorie dug her fingernails into the arms of the chair. "This wasn't the first time he'd tried something. And he'd been drinking."

"At noon?"

"It happens, Mrs. Vunnell. People who drink too much start early."

"If he assaulted you before, jumped you, why did you agree to go on this flying date?"

"I was stupid."

Mrs. Vunnell sat back in her chair, a very small smirk on her bowed lips. Amazing how the woman could smirk without moving a muscle. She smoothed back her volume of gray-streaked hair, a complicated tangle of nutty brown held with combs. Something Dorie had said apparently satisfied her, as if she'd been digging for treasure and found it. Her smirk made Dorie angry all over again.

"You satisfied? Yes, I was stupid. Call the papers. I wanted to fly, to get up off this crummy, hell-strewn prairie for a few minutes of peace. Is that a crime?"

"Only if you stab the pilot afterward."

"I won't be stabbing anybody for some time. You've got my blade."

"That sort of switchblade should be illegal, Miss Lennox."

"Let me know when they do that, would you?"

"You seem rather attached to it."

She shrugged. Her attachment to the switchblade *was* irrational, and she knew it. She hadn't been able to sleep for a week after they took it away. She still woke up sometimes feeling for it under her pillow. She sneaked a look at her watch. Ten minutes to go. Mr. Francis would have let her out, but the Widow Vunnell was a stickler for the half-hour head-shrinking session. Dorie got out her deck of Luckies.

"No smoking." Mrs. Vunnell made her eyes even smaller and pursed her lips. Her gray dress reminded Dorie of prison matron garb. Her other persona? "Do you get jumped often?"

"Often? No." Dorie felt a chill suddenly as the yaw of the midnight blue sedan swam back through her head, the open door to all sorts of possible nastiness. "The blade is good to have when it happens, though."

"For protection."

"It gives them second thoughts."

"Against a gun even?"

The gun from last night, tucked safely inside Arlette's jacket—had that been Arlette? Dorie had begun to doubt now, to look at the possibilities, the coincidence. Who else could it have been? How could she find this woman who had appointed herself protector? She squirmed on the chair, willing the seconds to pass. She had to find Wendy Hines first.

"Miss Lennox? Do you find the switchblade adequate protection against a gun?"

"Of course not."

"Then why bother?"

"You're absolutely right. I should have a gun." She smiled mischievously. "What a brilliant idea."

The widow's eyes darted to the clock. "Our time's up, Miss Lennox. Try to stay out trouble."

"It'll be my pleasure, Mrs. Vunnell. My complete pleasure."

To call the main building of the Shawnee Fields Country Club a "clubhouse" was technically correct. The rambling cream stucco building, with its red tile roof, green shutters, and curving ironwork, could have pinch-hit as a summer palace for Mussolini or a small cottage for Douglas Fairbanks.

Dorie stepped inside and listened to the tapping of spiked shoes on the slate floor, so like that musical goose-step in the newsreels. A golden light shone in squares through windows that overlooked the lush greens dotted with yellow sycamores and red oaks. Then the sound of tinkling glassware and laughter drew her toward the barroom.

As soon as she stepped into the doorway to look for Julian Hines, a man jumped to his feet, waving his arms.

"Stop! Against the rules. No women allowed." His red face made her step back, frowning. The official shagger for the manly domain.

"Is Julian Hines in there?"

The man had ceased paying attention to her, but he blocked the doorway, his chunky arms crossed. He laughed with a group of men at a table nearby. He looked surprised she was still there. Dorie repeated her question, louder this time.

"Hines? He's not a member, is he?" Some of the gents tippling nearby asserted that he was. One turned to her, an older man dressed in baggy knickers.

"Finished his game awhile back. Try the putting greens."

A friendly caddy pointed her toward the putting greens, around the west wing of the building and down a short hill. Four egg-shaped greens were manicured to perfection and sunk with several holes apiece. They were quiet in midafternoon. Three men bent over their sticks and eyed the trajectory over the grass. One of them was Julian Hines.

The mild weather, autumn sunshine warming the fields and fairways, had enticed Julian into a pair of royal blue knickers and matching blue-and-white-checked short-sleeved shirt. His high socks were white, his footwear brown-and-white saddle shoes. His hair fell forward over his glasses as he concentrated on his putter. Dorie stood quietly at the edge of the green, wondering how long it would take for him to notice her. After several more balls knocked toward but not into the hole, Julian straightened and walked toward a wire bucket of balls on the far side of the green. He looked up at the man at the next green. The other man nodded toward her.

Hines brought his bucket of balls to greet her. "Is it the Commander?"

"No. She's fine. As far as I know."

"She'll never be fine again." Julian surprised her with at least a smidgeon of feeling for the old lady. "What brings you out here, then?"

"We need to find Wendy before the Commander . . . before it's too late. Mr. Haddam has given me the beef. That is what you want, right?"

Julian was fiddling with the golf balls. He set the bucket down. He struck a nonchalant pose, perhaps remembering his screeching monkey routine in the front hall. "Search away."

"I need to know some of her haunts. Where she went, who her friends are."

"She didn't have many friends. She wasn't shy; it was just hard for her. She had strong opinions." Julian rubbed his chin. He looked tanned and fit from a day on the links. She guessed work wasn't an option, just which golf course. "Harriet Fox. She lives down the block. Um. Agnes Marchand."

"Agnes Marchand was her friend? The one you heard the rumor about?"

"The same." Julian looked unconcerned. "Agnes is a great gal. And her husband is a real ass."

"Any restaurants she liked, clubs, women's groups?"

"She played bridge with a group from Grace Episcopal. I don't know their names. We ate at the Muehlebach once in awhile. Don't think they'd know us there particularly." His eyes cut sideways. "I told you. We weren't together much the last six months."

She blinked into the breeze that blew up from the creek, full of moldy odors. An omen for *the* question. "Did she have a boyfriend?"

Julian bobbled the golf ball in his hand, dropping it onto his foot. "Ah—no." He took a deep breath. "Not that I know of."

"But it's possible?"

"Anything's possible, Miss Lennox." He squinted at her. "You think she ran away with somebody?"

"You got any ideas? Men she fancied, a friend?"

"She isn't like that. You don't know her. She isn't a flirt. She's very serious-minded. She was in charge of all kinds of civic and charity work. Ask the Commander. She'd do anything Eveline wanted—all the causes, the righteous indignation, the flaming letters to the newspaper. Like she was Eveline's right arm."

"Didn't that make Mildred jealous?"

Julian smirked. "Sure, Mildred did away with Wendy. That's a brilliant theory. Oh, you're kidding, aren't you? Come to think, Mildred might know something. They were close."

He picked up the bucket and held it awkwardly to his chest. Such a puppy dog, Dorie thought. Wendy must have felt sorry for him, if nothing else.

"Is that it?" he barked. "Because I'm due inside for a martini."

What was it about piecing together a life from a few scraps, the inadequate and foggy memories of the nearest and dearest, the petty barbs and long-held grievances, the woeful lack of giving a flying damn. It made her tired. She spent the rest of the balmy afternoon, what precious little was left after the drive back to the city, trying to track down Harriet Fox and the bridge club ladies from Grace Episcopal. The third woman in the club depressed

Dorie the most. How hurt she was—how incensed!—that Wendy hadn't arranged her own substitute for the game. They were left with an odd number for cards. And after all, she had made baked Alaska.

Harriet Fox proved elusive. Her mother, at a rambling, porch-fortified joint down the street from the Hines mansion, reported indignantly that the young woman had moved out of the house. She gave out a telephone number but was suspicious enough that she wouldn't provide an address for Miss Fox, age twenty-seven but still coddled. The telephone at Harriet's rang a lot, but no one answered.

Dorie would check the reverse directory tomorrow in the office. But tonight, she went back to the boardinghouse and ate dinner with the gals and bachelors, with Mrs. Ferazzi, with her elaborate hair and flowered apron, with her son Tony, sporting a scrawny new mustache, with the prim old maids and shop girls who made up her life.

What would they say about her if she disappeared? She knew it wouldn't be much. A shadow, they might call her, a strange and private person. Never knew her, they would say.

Dorie looked at them around the table, trying to summon the strength to speak, to ask them about their day, their jobs, their loves. But the plates were cleared, pudding brought in by Frankie, and they ate and left, in ones and twos, off to live their solitary lives. She sat alone, wishing she had spoken, wishing she could do something for them, touch them, let them know they mattered, that everyone mattered. Why couldn't she? It was so little, just a small moment that could have been so much more. And yet, it had passed unnoticed.

"Somebody to see you, Miss Dorie."

She turned in her dining chair, to see Poppy holding a bowl, drying it, and bobbing her head toward the front hall. Just inside the door stood Joe, hat in hand.

With a sigh, she rose. Her legs felt heavy as she moved toward the hall. Joe had cleaned himself up; his hands were as grease-free as she'd ever seen them. He wore clean blue pants and a starched white shirt.

"How are you, Joe?"

"I'm going to the hospital to see Jenny. Do you wanna come?"

The ward for the poor at City Hospital was a large room with a long line of white-sheeted beds, a little dying sun coming through high windows facing west. The dusty panes defused the light, turning what should have been another depressing moment into a momentary slice of orangy heaven scented with disinfectant. She stood with Joe Czmanski at the nurses' station as he tried to describe Jenny to the nurse. Dorie watched the dust motes in the stream of color, high above the misery.

"Jenny. Old lady." Joe looked at Dorie. "You know her last name?"

She shook her head.

"Well, we've got several older women here. Twice as many men. Young ones, too—sometimes they fool you on their ages," the nurse said, standing. She was close to fifty, pretty still with her chestnut hair. She had a plaster cast on one wrist. "Better come take a look."

"She came in last night, late."

"I've been off for a week," the nurse said, holding up her cast. "I slipped on a wet floor."

They had to look at each ravaged face, bandaged, twisted with pain, sagging with age, decrepit, with rotting teeth and clouded eyes. This is what happens. This is where we're all headed, Dorie thought, shuffling slowly, looking ahead of Joe and the nurse, eyeing the other side's beds, hoping to spot Jenny. There, that hair, three beds down. She trotted to the bed.

"Over here," she called in a loud whisper.

The nurse picked up the clipboard hanging on the end of the bed, balancing it on her cast. She frowned as she read. Joe stood at the side of the bed and picked up Jenny's limp hand.

The old woman had seen better days. One side of Jenny's face was discolored and swollen. One eye was puffy and red. Both were closed now and she appeared to be resting. The hand Joe wasn't holding was streaked with blue bruises that continued up her arm, inside the stiff hospital gown.

The nurse set the clipboard back on the hook and walked around to Jenny's side, touching her head gingerly. Dorie stepped closer, seeing the goose-egg bump and bruise on the old woman's scalp.

"Did she wake up?"

"No. They think she has internal injuries. Did she take a beating?"

"We don't know."

Joe spread her hand out again on the sheet. "Will she wake up?"

The nurse's face softened. "Time will tell."

"How long will you keep her?"

"As long as it takes."

Back in Joe's car, they were quiet on the drive to Charlotte Street. As he pulled the car into his garage and turned it off, Joe made an odd squeak. Dorie turned and saw that his shoulders were shaking, and tears rolled down his cheeks.

She waited. Finally, his sobbing ebbed. He gulped for air and wiped his face with the back of his hand.

"Sorry, I—" He stopped, put his hand on the door. He let out a moan.

"It's okay, Joe. She's old and off her nut. But we'll miss her around here."

"I should have helped. I saw that man talking to her," Joe said. He made a fist and hit the steering wheel, not hard but angry. "Then I heard you shouting. I just hid inside. I saw the gun and I didn't do anything."

"No sense both of us getting shot."

"I'm yellow. Ever since Sensa's car blew up—no, before. I've always been yellow."

"I doubt that very much." She put her hand on his arm. "Besides, I was scared, too. Anybody would be when somebody comes after them with a gun."

Joe glanced at her for reassurance. She nodded and let her hand slip away. "I was just lucky last night. And Old Jenny wasn't."

Joe hung his head. "Do you think she'll die?"

"We all die, Joe."

They got out of the car inside the dim garage. Joe watched her over the roof of the car. Dorie was sure he would ask again about finding Roscoe Sensa's enemies, the scum who'd burned him. But he didn't. She said good-bye and walked out into the street, where the streetlights provided watery spots of light in the dark. Pausing, she checked the autos parked along Charlotte Street. The street and sidewalks were deserted. She wondered if Arlette—if it had been Arlette—was still watching her back.

The night air was cold. Dorie shivered, not just from cold, then walked deliberately across the cobblestones and up the stairs into the boardinghouse, feeling silly in the relief she felt as she locked the door behind her.

TWELVE

Amos Haddam knocked on the heavy oak door. Built like a little Norman castle, the house had a front door built into a round turret stuck onto the front. Amusing how so many of Kansas City's houses had recently been built like this. In England, they would be the butt of jokes, the occupants considered martinets full of pompous gas. He glanced back at Gwendolyn in the car. She had one cheek lying on the seat back, her eyes closed.

The door opened suddenly, creaking on heavy black hinges forged by a smithy, no doubt. A tall, imposing man with a tanned athletic face and a cocktail glass in one hand stood glowering in the doorway. He raised dark eyebrows that matched his thick brilliantined hair.

"Yes?" His voice was a baritone growl.

"Sir." Amos removed his hat. "Mr. Marchand? Amos Haddam, sir."

He offered a hand, but the man needed more information. "Do I know you, Haddam?"

"No." And you'll wish it had stayed that way, Amos thought. "I'm sent here on a mission by Mrs. Eveline Hines. It's a matter of some delicacy. Is Mrs. Marchand at home by chance?"

Amos had called the house an hour earlier, from the Monarchs offices, and knew that Agnes Marchand was due home by four o'clock. It was now an hour later, cocktail time. Mr. Marchand sipped his while making Amos stand in the chill evening breeze. It had been a long, trying day and a small refreshment wouldn't have been refused.

"Eveline? How is the old girl? I've been meaning to pop in and see her."

"She'd welcome the call, I'm sure. Is Agnes about, then?"

Marchand suddenly remembered his manners and ushered Haddam through the tiny turret into an overly decorated living room complete with fringed footstools and green tasseled drapes. The pink sofa with its gold cording looked delicious enough to eat. Amos was shown a chair covered with a fabric printed with gigantic rose-colored flowers. Peonies? He didn't know his flowers anymore. Damn uncomfortable for something so pretty.

"Drink, Haddam? I'll get Agnes." Marchand was now the suave fellow.

"Whatever you're having, thanks." Haddam settled into the hard chair. Anything wet would be welcome. Emotions had been running high at the Monarchs office when he arrived. The fact that he'd brought Talbot along only made them more volatile. Probably a mistake. The reporter was so passionate about the Monarchs, he was beside himself. Amos had been able to calm the nerves a little by telling them he thought the latest threat, a letter sent from somewhere in Kansas City, wasn't worth the paper it was written on. The sender was a coward, not even signing the letter, trying to scare them—again—into stopping the game on Sunday. If they listened, he won, whoever he was. If they carried on, they won. He advised carrying on.

"Stiff upper lip and all that?" Talbot had asked as they left the offices.

"Onward, mate."

"You really think it's all groundless, that there's no basis for alarm? Because I've been hearing this stuff other places, and maybe there's some group getting riled up. Because of the war, the election, who knows."

"What would the Kluxers or some such group gain from threats?"

"They scare the players. Maybe they play badly. If they play at all."

"Do they want publicity, to boost their own candidates? Like that Silver Shirt fellow—what's his name, Pelley?"

"Or the Monarchs don't show up. The game is forfeited. Or only a skeleton crew is there to play the Blues."

Haddam and Talbot had run through a few other possibilities, but this one rattled around in Amos's brain as he waited for his drink and Agnes Marchand. He hoped to have a bit of liquid sucked down before she showed up. He needed the courage. If the husband was present—but of course he would be. He'd be hanging on her arm, and every word.

The other *if* was more intriguing: What if the Monarchs had to play on Sunday with a nominal team? No substitutes, no relief pitchers, no pinch hitters. They could still probably beat the Blues, but it would be more difficult. What if somebody had money on the Blues—a lot of money?

The boy, Leroy Williams, who had found the first note in the locker room, had no doubt infected others with his fears. Quincy Gilmore seemed unflappable, but Mr. Wilkinson was in a cold sweat. Wilkinson probably took plenty of heat at his old-boy clubs as it was, being the white owner of a black baseball team. Not only an owner but an advocate, an enthusiastic drum-beater and all-around booster for colored baseball.

Gilmore had a plan, he'd said. Amos hadn't had time to hear more than a few details—a ballplayer, a statement of solidarity to the press. If they have a plan, he thought, more power to them. It was more than he had.

"Manhattan, how's that?"

Marchand had crept up on him on the thick carpeting. He handed Amos a stout glass of reddish liquor with a cherry. These fancy new drinks were unappealing to Haddam, but he wasn't in the position to refuse. He thanked Marchand as the man brought his wife out from behind him. Introductions were made and the couple settled into the candy pink couch, next to each other but not touching. No holding of hands.

Agnes Marchand was a pretty woman, maybe ten years younger than her husband—by her looks, not yet thirty. She wore her reddish hair waved, a curl plastered to one cheek in a silly fashion. Her tight green skirt below a matching sweater crept up, revealing shapely legs, which she crossed. The heel of one shoe slipped off and she bobbed it from her toe impatiently, her tight face unhappy.

"Mrs. Hines sent you over?" the husband prompted.

"Is this about Wendy?" Agnes asked. Her nasal voice was impatient and sharp. "Because if it is, I don't know anything about where she is. Julian already asked me if I'd heard from her."

Amos sipped the sweet cocktail. "You know Wendy?"

"You're a private detective, right? I read about you in the paper." Marchand grinned like a baboon, so happy was he. "So she's looking for the runaway wife. Got the gumshoe on the case."

"I was surprised as everybody," Agnes said. "Took off just like that. Not a phone call or a by-your-leave. I don't think she'll be checking in here. She doesn't want to be found, not by that husband of hers."

Amos wished an attack of narcolepsy on this husband. Instead, the liquor suddenly caught in his craw. He coughed delicately, then with fervor, sounding, he knew, like a bawling goat. Agnes looked alarmed and went for a glass of water. Marchand walked to the window, as if ignoring the hack would make it go away. A tactic Haddam had tried unsuccessfully for years.

With water in hand, the moments passed and the cough with them. Agnes resettled edgily on the couch. Marchand remained at the window. A sigh from Haddam. He closed his eyes briefly.

"If I could speak to Mrs. Marchand in private, sir, it would be most appreciated." Haddam found his Englishness was suddenly back in force: stiff, formal, and mostly effective.

"Anything you say to my wife, you say to me."

Agnes flinched, then composed herself. She looked at her varnished nails, a vibrant rose that matched the chair, then back at Amos. Her face was placid, a challenge.

"I don't know a thing about where Wendy's gone," she said. A broken record, this one.

"Your concern is welcome. But I didn't come here about Wendy. I'm afraid my mission is more to do with Mr. Barnaby Wake."

Agnes took a silent gulp of air. Her husband spun from the window and barked, "What about him?"

Amos took a breath and felt the hot burn in his lungs. This was no time for an attack. He set the Manhattan down on the precious gilded coffee table. Agnes darted forward and slipped a woven coaster under the glass. In the face of a confrontation about her lover, she is worried about water rings on the furniture.

"There has been some worry, at the Hines residence, that is," Amos said flatly, "that Mr. Wake has been taking—what shall we call it? An unusual interest in Miss Hines. Thalia Hines."

Agnes sat back on the couch, tucking her hands under her thighs like a schoolgirl. Her blue eyes darted up at her husband and back at Amos, blinking furiously. Was she flirting with him, relieved, or about to lie? One of those.

"What if he is? What business is that of ours?" the husband growled.

Agnes cocked her head. "Yes, what business . . ." She lost her train of thought, or nerve.

"May I ask if you have heard any talk about Miss Hines and Mr. Wake?"

Marchand stepped closer, crossing his arms. "We're not in the business of repeating gossip, Mr. Haddam."

Business and more business. What did Julian say this man did for a living? Insurance? Amos rubbed his cheek and looked at each of them. Should he quote them percentages? Just how was he supposed to work on this woman in front of her husband?

"There has been gossip; I think you should know that." He looked pointedly at Agnes. The color drained from her face. "And sometimes just the hint of scandal is enough to ruin a person's reputation. If you know what I mean."

"You are a font of information, Haddam. Christ." Marchand shook his head, walked to a buffet, and poured clear liquid out of a metal shaker, refilling his martini glass.

"I have, um, I have heard a few things. Little things," Agnes said, her voice a squeak.

"So have we," Amos said. "That's why we need your help. We were very much hoping, Mrs. Marchand, that you could use your influence, as a member of the Hallelujah Chorus, to talk to Mr. Wake and make him see what a predicament this could be, for him and the choir. You see, we would hate it if the talk got back to Mrs. Wake."

"*Mrs.* Wake?"

"In Arizona, I hear. For her health."

Agnes curled in on herself for a moment, then smiled wanly at her husband. He glowered at her over his martini. "You can do that, can't you, dear?" he asked coldly.

"Of course, Eddie." She gave Amos a twisted smile. "Sure. I can speak to him."

"You see," Amos continued, "he gets most of his backing from society people such as yourselves, business, banks, insurance. The type of business that relies so much on personal integrity and contacts. I expect your company might have given him some donations, Mr. Marchand. And that backing isn't likely to continue if there's a scandal involving married people."

Eddie Marchand threw back his cocktail in one gulp.

"I'll tell him to stay away from Thalia," Agnes said. "I'll take care of it."

"Mrs. Hines will be most grateful."

Amos made himself scarce. He might have enjoyed that scene, as a fly on the wall, when Eddie confronted Agnes with his suspicions. But he looked like a brute; she was already afraid of him.

The arms of Barnaby Wake, ladies' man, crooner, and fast talker, were probably a safe harbor, even if she had to share him with several other ladies. Amos hoped he wouldn't read about Agnes Marchand in tomorrow's paper.

After a dinner in a café downtown, Amos tried to talk Gwendolyn into going back to his apartment while he followed Thalia. But she was having none of it. He drove back through the dark streets to the apartment, the feel of the car alien after so many months. Surprising the old beater had even started up. Things were so busy these days, what with the Monarchs business, Mrs. Hines going in several directions, and sweet Thalia's shenanigans.

Amos parked the car. "Can you drive, Gwen?"

"Me? Oh, yes." She smiled at him in the shadows from the streetlight.

"All right, then. You're hired."

Gwendolyn laughed. "Hired? As your driver?"

"Mrs. Hines can afford it. Why not?"

She laughed again. He did so love the sound of her laugh. "Why bloody not?"

The call from Mildred, the Hines secretary, came early, just after eight o'clock. Gwendolyn mastered the gearshift after the first intersection, groaning a bit about the size of the car, an old Buick, well made but tanklike. It took a strong pair of arms to take a corner slowly, and Gwendolyn soon learned the art of the quick get-around. Amos got his exercise by hanging on to the door handle and grinning at her exuberant laughter. A year's worth of repressed happiness was now bubbling out of her uncontrolled, a geyser of glee. It made him forget about his mother mashing tea in a tube station, about his sister sneaking around France with an artist, about bombs and Nazis and Hitler.

Gwendolyn took a curb at a hop on Twelfth Street, trying to park the Buick, barely avoiding a red Pierce. Amos took a breath. "Well, here we are. One piece, more or less."

She yanked on the parking brake and turned off the engine. "I said I could drive; I didn't say how well." She laughed. "You aren't hurt, are you?"

"A few gray hairs, no problem."

"Is she in there, then?" Gwendolyn nodded toward the Reno Club on the corner, its marquee bright with the name of an orchestra. The brassy sounds of jazz music amplified as a couple opened the doors and disappeared inside.

"That's the plan." As he got out of the Buick, he had a niggling feeling in the back of his head, a spark of guilt. He should have gone to the Hines mansion, followed Thalia from home to wherever she was going. She had assured her mother that she was going to the Reno Club, then to chorus practice. The combination sounded unusual enough to be true. But now he wondered if she really would be inside.

But there she was. Thalia Hines sat with another woman and a man, both of whom looked like decent citizens, sipping cocktails and listening to a warm-up band with a shapely, out-of-tune singer and a loud drummer. It was only 8:30. The main event wouldn't start until at least ten o'clock at which time Thalia would be singing hymns with her man.

The only interesting thing at the Reno Club at that hour was watching Gwen get tipsy. Thalia Hines left, alone, at 9:15 and drove—badly, so Gwendolyn, her reflexes a bit slow, could keep up easily—to the Knights of Columbus Hall. A group of about twenty people, mostly women, gathered on the platform stage and were already singing when Thalia made her entrance. Barnaby Wake stopped the song midway to usher her into place.

Haddam and his shadow settled into the last row of folding chairs in the old church. He scanned the faces of the chorus members and didn't find his new friend, Agnes Marchand. Of all the dirty things he'd had to do over the years, informing a woman's husband of her infidelity ranked low on his list. Was it a rare thing, a woman seeking affection outside the bounds of marriage? He doubted it. He'd seen plenty of men who deserved a good cheat. Those who beat their wives, bullied them like Marchand, scared them to keep them in line. He thought about his sister Beryl, a decent woman, if not strong-minded, living in common with that Frenchie. Where was she? Was she safe? His mother's letter hadn't reassured him. Just the opposite. And now, even with drowsy, happy Gwendolyn at his side, he had too much time to think about Beryl.

The chorus lacked most of its tenors and baritones. Two men tried their damnedest. The sopranos, including Thalia, weren't bad, but Amos particularly liked the rich alto voices. Hard to sing harmony, to assist rather than shine. Like a marriage, he supposed. One part would always be louder, stronger, but the supporting part—equally important—made it glow.

Amos took Gwendolyn's hand. She smiled up at him, sighed as she laid her head on his shoulder. A thought, a possibility, bloomed in his mind. He'd never thought of marriage with any-one but Eugenia. He'd always thought it would be a betrayal of their love. But Eugenia had been gone these twenty years. Surely she wouldn't object to a good-hearted English girl.

The music was rather lovely, and Amos felt slightly mesmer-ized. Then the chorus broke up suddenly, gathering coats and handbags and heading to the door. Ten-thirty. Quite early for Thalia to go home. On the edge of the stage, Wake helped her on with her wool coat. She had dressed tonight in a chic blue suit, with a string of pearls and little dove gray gloves. Her hair was pulled up and she wore a small gray hat with a feather in the back.

Amos helped Gwendolyn to her feet. The poor girl had dozed a little, relaxed from the cocktails and music. Haddam shook himself. Barnaby Wake and Thalia came down the aisle, her arm through his, defiant, head high. They paused next to Amos and Gwen.

"All ready, then, for Wendell Willkie?" Amos asked, tipping his hat to Wake.

The choirmaster squared his shoulders, a hard glint in his eye. For a moment, Amos thought answering a simple question was beneath the man. Then Wake said coldly, "I hope you enjoyed the entertainment."

"My mother has no right—*no right*," Thalia blurted. She caught herself, biting a lip. "Leave me alone or I'll call the police. I'm warning you."

"You'd rather the boys in blue follow you, then?"

Her nostrils flared in anger. "I'd rather you—you jumped in a lake."

Thalia pulled Wake into action and they made for the door. Amos waited until they disappeared, then burst out laughing.

"Jump in a lake?" Amos choked. "Oh my, I am so tempted."

At one o'clock, or a little past, Thalia Hines backed her new roadster out of Barnaby Wake's drive. Gwen stepped up to the challenge and kept up with her, only hitting three curbs and two muddy flower beds. The telephone pole she brushed really didn't count, as it sat far too close to the street. She braked the Buick in front of the Hines mansion as Thalia pulled around to the garage hidden behind the house. In a moment, the lights in the front hallway went on.

"Drive on?"

"Home, Jeeves," Amos said, patting her arm. "No hurry, dear."

"But I am getting good at these fast corners, aren't I?"

"A little more practice and we'll take you on the racing circuit."

She parked, badly, across the street from the apartment building, in the place the Buick had occupied for the last year. Four tire marks and a rectangle of dirt marked the spot. They walked across the street together, Amos watching the way the glow of the streetlight attached itself to her cheeks, her hair, the line of her neck. So long since he'd thought of the future with wonder or curiosity. He wasn't so old. He wasn't so sick. He still had a future.

Halfway up the walk, Gwendolyn stopped suddenly, jumping

backward as she gasped. Amos followed her gaze. A man stood in the shadow under the canopy. The light was out. It wasn't until he pushed off the brick and stepped forward that his face became visible.

"Haddam. I've been looking for you all night."

"It's bloody late. What are you doing here?"

Irritation was Amos's first emotion at the sight of the reporter. Then he remembered his manners. "This is Gwendolyn Harris, my friend from England."

Harvey Talbot nodded quickly at Gwendolyn, turned back to Haddam. "Haven't you heard?"

"Heard what?"

Gwendolyn shivered violently. "Can we go inside. Please?"

Amos unlocked the door, punched the lights. The overhead fixture was dusty and dim, giving them all sallow complexions. Talbot looked anxious, barely containing himself. He didn't sit when offered a chair.

"It's Saunders, Gibson Saunders. The third baseman." He paced, arms waving. "They did this press conference—you heard about that?"

"Quincy said he was planning something." Amos had found a bottle of ale in the back of the refrigerator and popped it open. Gwen sat on the sofa, a frown on her face as she watched the reporter.

"He wanted Saunders because he's well-spoken." Talbot stopped suddenly. "He's from the North, from Michigan. He gave this little speech about how the game would go on, that it would show unity between the coloreds and the whites, all that. Togetherness. Nothing wrong with it, except you know and I know that one little speech isn't going to change people."

Gwendolyn crossed her arms. "Change what?"

"Race feelings," Amos said. "Then what happened?"

"The meeting broke up about eight-thirty. Not too many people there, the sports reporters scratching their heads. I went back to the *Star* to write my story, and about midnight I get a call from the police reporter downtown."

Harvey pushed his hat back on his head. He stared at the ceiling, his voice flat. "Saunders was shot. In his bed at home. Nobody saw anything. He lives in a shack, behind a house on Troost. Somebody came down the alley, I guess. His landlady heard the shot and called the police."

"Is he dead?" Gwendolyn asked.

"Yes," Harvey said, standing in the middle of the floor, hands limp at his sides. "He is dead."

THIRTEEN

Ballplayer Found Shot.
Blues-Monarchs Game Under Wraps

BY HARVEY TALBOT

Negro League ballplayer Gibson Saunders, a third baseman for the Kansas City Monarchs, and a starter for three seasons, was found shot to death last night in his Troost Avenue home. Police say an intruder crept in at approximately 11:00 P.M. and shot Saunders at close range. He was pronounced dead at the scene.

Earlier that day, Saunders had participated in a press conference in the Monarchs locker room, decrying a series of threats to the team if they played the all-white American Association Blues, who won the pennant this year. The game was scheduled for Sunday afternoon at 2:00 P.M. Monarchs' owner J. L. Wilkinson said he will confer with the Blues management about rescheduling the postseason game.

The Monarchs have received several anonymous letters in the last weeks, threatening harm if the Blues game was played. Management was concerned enough to bring in outside security consultants. The consultants downplayed the serious nature of the threat, claiming it was all "fluff and lather."

Earlier in the week, Monarchs owner Wilkinson's home was burglarized. Little of value was taken, but in one blatant message, Satchel Paige's jersey, kept for when (and if) he returns to the team, was smeared with mud. Someone, it appears, has it in for the Monarchs, who won the Negro Athletic League pennant again this season.

Are the Monarchs better than the Blues? Are the Blues the team they could be? If they don't play, it's all talk. If they do play, can more violence be far away?

DORIE STALKED INTO THE SUGAR Moon office and slapped the copy of the *Kansas City Star* on Amos's desk. He and Gwendolyn were sipping tea from the cups they'd never returned to the café around the corner. Steam curled from the spout of a sturdy white teapot on the tray. The morning sun reflected off the building across the street, creating spots of blinding light on the desktop.

"What the hell is this?" She jabbed at the paper. "He might as well have said you bought the gun that killed him. That shady, scheming, underhanded yellow dog." She threw the newspaper on his desk. "I've half a mind to march down to that scandal sheet and—"

"Have a seat, ducks. Tea?" Amos stared at her over his teacup.

Gwendolyn had spilled her tea, startled by the outburst. She dabbed at the dress Dorie had given her, the blue one that didn't fit.

"How can you sit there and sip your stupid tea?"

Amos set down his cup. "Sit down, will you? You're scaring Gwendolyn. She's had a bad night."

"Not as bad as Gibson Saunders, it seems."

He sighed. "Please. Sit."

Dorie dragged in the spare chair from the waiting area and sat, fuming. "What is wrong with that son of a bitch?"

"He was just quoting me. He's absolutely right: I didn't take it seriously. I thought—" He rubbed his brows. "I don't know what I thought. That it was just a crank letter."

"Of course you did."

She felt her blood pressure go down. She noticed Gwen's hair was a mess, and the woman continued to stab at the wet spot from the tea on the skirt of the dress. She looked as bad as Amos, both of them with dark circles under their eyes.

"Did you find out like me—this morning?"

"Talbot came by last night," Amos said, his voice tired. "We were up most of the night, talking about it, what would happen. Who could be behind it."

"Did you figure it out?"

"You'd think Kluxers. But it's not their style."

"They'd drag him outside and burn him with torches."

"Or string him up and burn a cross in the yard."

Gwendolyn gagged on her tea. It dribbled down her chin. She blinked at them, lips pursed.

"It's a dirty business, love," Amos said gently. "Do you want to step out?"

She shook her head. The look on Amos's face was one of such tenderness that a shiver went up Dorie's spine.

Amos sipped his tea and said, "So the answer is no. We didn't get any ideas."

The anger was gone, for now, and she felt the awful suddenness of the ballplayer's death. "Saunders was good. I saw him hit a homer this spring during tryouts."

With Talbot. Not more than fifty people in the stands. The day had been warm and lovely.

She rubbed her temples now. Her head hurt. She'd had bad dreams about Old Jenny last night. In them, she was running to save the old woman from being sucked into a huge black hole. She threw the doomsday placard across the abyss, to give Jenny a stepping-stone to get out. But Jenny was too far away, or too weak to grab it, or the wooden placard proclaiming THE END IS NEAR smashed into her face, leaving her bloody instead of saving her. Pathetic dreams, all too vivid in the morning. Why couldn't she think about warm spring days instead? Would it be so bad to think about Talbot?

"What did he say—Talbot?" she asked. Her voice sounded funny.

"He doesn't like the race angle, although I'm not sure why," Haddam said. "Everything points that way. Talbot is looking at it more from a sports viewpoint. Baseball."

"Betting, that's what he said," Gwendolyn said.

"He's got a point," Amos said. "If there's heavy betting on one side, somebody stands to lose a bundle."

"Bookies?"

"And the various organizations they work for. Just because

Old Tom is wearing prison stripes doesn't mean gambling has vanished. We're a far cry from clean."

They thought for a second about Boss Pendergast, whose own betting had made him greedy and led the feds to him. One minute, running an empire the size of Kansas City, the next, one the size of a cell at Leavenworth.

"But how would Saunders's death change things? He was good, but he doesn't—didn't—carry the whole team."

"Talbot had some theories. Not that I like any of them."

Dorie raised her eyebrows. "Well?"

Gwendolyn opened her eyes wide. "A fix," she said.

"The Monarchs in on a fix?"

Amos held up his hands. "Only a theory."

"So the Blues can win—the Monarchs throw the game?"

"Happened in the World Series."

"I don't believe it. There isn't a straighter fella than that J. L. Wilkinson. He loves baseball and he loves his team."

"And we love him with all our bleeding hearts," Amos said. "*He* doesn't have to be in on the fix, however."

With the game only days away, she doubted the managers would postpone it, despite what Harvey had written, even for the murder of one of the players. There was too much money at stake, both for the players themselves and for the owners. Not to mention the enormous citywide betting that must be going down, Blues against Monarchs, Negroes against whites. It would be a matter of pride to the Monarchs not to back down, not to run scared, not to walk away first. The game would go on. But Talbot's warning—would there be more violence?

"What are the odds on the game?" Dorie asked.

"Talbot says it's five runs to the Monarchs."

"So if the Blues win, the payout would be big?"

"Even if the Monarchs win by only one."

"Do you think Saunders is in on it?"

"Was. My guess is no, he wasn't. If this was the reason he

was . . . eliminated, it's possible he wouldn't agree to the fix. *If that's why he was snuffed.*"

Gwendolyn stood up suddenly, her teacup clattering to the desk as she set it down. "Pardon," she whispered, and ran out of the office and into the hall. They listened as her footsteps stopped down the corridor.

"Is she all right?"

"This has upset her. Reminds her of the things she saw back home." Amos looked at the door. "I suppose she thought no one died over here."

Dorie stared at him, trying to see what was different.

"What?" he asked.

"The way you said that—'Home.' "

"Having her here has made me realize how English I am." He frowned. "Am I very English?"

"*Veddy,*" she said, making him smile. "Don't you feel English?"

"It's been so long. I've forgotten so much. I've wanted to forget. But now, I don't know. I want to remember good things, and there aren't bloody many."

"Except Gwendolyn."

He gave her a half-baked frown. "Did you find Wendy Hines?"

"She seems to have disappeared without a trace. I can't find her friend Harriet Fox, either, but I'm on that. Agnes Marchand is Wendy's friend, too."

"Aye, but she can't tell you anything. I talked to them yesterday."

"Did you show her the handwriting?"

"On the bloody wall. But it were invisible, more or less, with her husband right there."

She grimaced. "He wouldn't leave?"

"He's got that girl scared to death of him. Might check back around this afternoon, make sure he hasn't laid into her."

"What about Thalia? She behave last night?"

"She was with Wake at his house for two hours or so after rehearsal. You think there's singing going on in there?"

"Of a sort."

Dorie checked the reverse directory for Harriet Fox's address before they picked up Gwendolyn in the washroom and headed down the stairs. The Englishwoman insisted on driving Amos's Buick, although, God knew, she didn't look up to it. Her red patches stood out in relief against her English skin again, but she stood straight and tall and wouldn't discuss anyone else driving.

Before they settled in around the Commander's bedside, Dorie stood at the end of the bed, waiting until she had the old lady's attention. It didn't take long. Sick, weak, worried, Mrs. Hines still had a keen, unforgiving eye.

"What is it, Miss Lennox?" Impatient even in dying.

"I'd like to speak to Mildred—Miss Miller, if I could. About Wendy's disappearance."

The Commander glanced at Amos. "She should be in her office."

On her way out, Dorie caught the eye of Mother Ruth. The iron-haired nurse pointed her heavy black eyebrows toward the back of the house.

The door was open, light streaming in from the east to warm the small room. Since the mansion's library had been turned into a sickroom years before, Dorie wondered what spare corner had been given Miss Miller. But this was no closet. Small, yes, but larger than Dorie's third-floor garret. The window's diamond-patterned stained glass cut the light into colorful patterns. On the windowsill sat two African violets in bloom, one white and one purple. The tidy space was dominated by a large battered desk placed at an angle, behind which sat Mildred Miller. She was writing out a letter on creamy stationery with blue ink from a fountain pen, the nib scratching across the paper.

Dorie rapped with one knuckle. "Good morning."

Mildred startled, ink flying in droplets from her pen. She rose angrily, blotting the letter with a handkerchief. Her face was flushed as she tried to compose herself. "Miss Lennox. What can I do for you?"

"Sorry to interrupt. If you have a minute, I'd like to ask you about Wendy. Her disappearance."

The study was papered in a nubby yellow silk, very tasteful. A small oil painting sat alone on the wall, a hunting scene with horses and dogs. "May I come in?"

Mildred pointed to a small oval-backed chair done in needlepoint, then sat again behind her desk. She discreetly covered the letter she'd been working on with a plain sheet of paper. "I don't know why you'd think of me."

Dorie walked to a small bookcase. Miss Miller had a affection for Henry James and his gang. "You like Edith Wharton?"

Miss Miller stiffened. "Very much. A great lady."

"And not too shabby a writer." She eased down on the tiny chair. "It was Julian—the reason I thought of you. He said you and Wendy have done work together on charity projects and such."

"She is quite public-spirited."

"Can you tell me what she was working on just before her disappearance?"

The lines in Mildred's forehead deepened as she frowned. She wore her hair like Mrs. Ferazzi, piled up in twists and bunches, combs here and there. It probably took an hour to construct each morning, not to mention the mandatory hundred strokes each night. God bless the flappers for doing away with all that.

"Let me think." Mildred tapped a finger on the desk. She opened the desk drawer and pulled out a large notebook. "When did she . . . disappear, as you put it?"

"September twenty-first. You would use a different word?"

Pointing at her place in the calendar, Mildred looked up over her half glasses. "We don't know she disappeared, do we?"

"She didn't come home. That's disappearing to me."

Mildred pursed her lips. "On the twenty-second, she was to meet with the Ladies Auxiliary of the Veterans of Foreign Wars, to work on plans for war support. She believed we would go to war very soon."

Thank God she was wrong. But was she? What about the draft, and the plants turning from autos to tanks? She thought about Chet in his sailor uniform and shivered.

Mildred flipped a page. "Nothing on the twenty-first. I didn't keep all her appointments. On the nineteenth, she and Mrs. Hines had a luncheon in the house for Randall Newcomb. He's running for state legislature."

"I didn't know Mrs. Hines was strong enough for luncheons."

"She does like the company."

"Anyone interesting at the luncheon? Someone she might have run off with?"

Mildred's eyebrows jumped. She expelled half a surprised laugh. "Oh! Humorous. Very humorous." She frowned. "There was someone there she talked to quite a bit. I'm not sure who he was, to tell you the truth. It's unlike me to not know everyone at these functions."

"That's jake, Mildred. What did he look like?"

"Short man, rather . . . swarthy. But charming, maybe a politician."

"Not Barnaby Wake."

"Who?"

"The choir director. Hallelujah Chorus, the one Thalia sings with."

"Oh, no, not him. I know who he is. Wendy sang in that group, too. No, this was someone else."

"Wendy was in the Hallelujah Chorus?"

"Oh, yes. I heard them once at the Nelson Art Museum. Quite good."

For a few more minutes, she probed Mildred Miller's recollections and appointment calendar. Miss Miller had a high regard for Wendy Hines. She thought Wendy had a good heart, even if she had been a little hasty in marrying Julian Hines before she knew his character. She worked hard for charity events and political candidates she believed in. She was a devout Episcopalian, attended church regularly. She wasn't particularly happy in her marriage but was resigned to it, Mildred thought. And she loved Mrs. Hines like her own mother.

Dorie thanked Mildred and stepped back into the corridor. Where was she going with this? How did you find someone who vanished without a trace, someone who likely did not want to be found at all? To her left, the corridor ran to the back of the house, offering a view of the yard. It drew her down the three steps to the window seat. She perched there in the sunshine, trying to think about Wendy and her motives. All she could figure was that the woman had run away from this stone-cold house, its death and dying, its madness and pretense. Any sane woman would cut her losses. But was Wendy that sort? Mildred didn't think so. Sane or insane, at least content enough with her situation.

To the west, the brick garage cut off the verdant lawn. A movement from behind the garage caught Dorie's eye. She leaned close to the glass. A streak of black and white crossed to the bushes: a maid, running. Odd. She'd only seen the one maid here, the one who often opened the door for them. Plain, with a flat chest and a face full of freckles.

Dorie pressed her nose against the cold pane. Julian Hines stepped out from behind the garage into the sunshine. He put his hands on his hips and shouted. The words were lost, but the attitude was clear. His chin thrust out, he walked stiffly toward the shrubs. He stopped, called again, and plunged behind the hedge.

She rubbed the condensation on the pane with her coat sleeve. Time to go; she had to find Wendy. As she stood up, glancing outside, the bushes began to shake and scatter leaves. Suddenly, the maid's starched white hat poked through the leaves, then the top of her head. Then Dorie saw Julian kissing the maid's neck as she arched back through the shrubbery.

Julian's hands were all over the girl. From this angle, it was impossible to say whether the maid was enjoying it or not. Maybe she was. Maybe they played cat and mouse through the garden every morning.

Dorie turned her back on the window, put her chin down, and squeezed her eyes shut to blot out the image.

The drive back to the office was uneventful, which was a blessing. As she was now hardened to Gwendolyn's style of navigation, Dorie just hung on and planned out her day. She usually did this in the morning, driving to the office, but this morning she had been distracted by Talbot's article. She couldn't stop looking for his byline, and yet he aggravated her with his writing more often than not. She wouldn't mind telling him so.

By the time they smashed the Buick's rear tire into the curb and parked with one wheel up on the sidewalk, she felt a comfortable rage simmering inside her. Anger was her friend, her companion. It had kept her alive all these years. But—and there always was a *but,* wasn't there?—it had its edge, its dark side. If only she could feel bad about stabbing Louie Weston.

It was going to be one of those days, she could tell, where anything could set her off. Probably just as well she didn't have her switchblade.

They climbed out of the Buick—a slide out of the backseat, with the trunk up in the air—and were gathered on the sidewalk when the Western Union boy rounded the corner at a dead run.

"Mr. Haddam! Mr. Haddam! Telegram, sir!"

Amos turned slowly and faced the running boy. All the delivery boys knew him. Since the war had begun in Europe, he'd chosen Western Union over a slow boat.

Amos's face was white as a sheet. Gwendolyn clutched his arm, either to hold him up or herself. She put her hand over her mouth.

The boy handed the telegram to Amos. Dorie dug in her handbag for a dime and tipped the boy. "Hope it's good news!" he called out, running down the street to his next delivery.

"Oh lawk," Gwen whispered, glancing at Amos. "Why'd he have to say that?"

"He says that to everybody." Dorie peered at Amos. He stared at the envelope with his name and address scribbled in pencil.

"But it will be good news. Amos?"

His Adam's apple bobbed as he swallowed hard. He squeezed the envelope so hard, his fingers turned white. With a jerk, he thrust the envelope to Dorie. "You open it."

"Let's go upstairs."

"Open it."

A gust of wind came down the street from the west, as if something bad was on the way. A raunchy slaughterhouse smell, a river stench. Earth smells. Just a temporary stay. Your time on the planet was limited, by everything that made it grand—sunsets, bluebirds, rose scent on the wind, a morning song, a winter's evening. It was all time, and time was cruel, arbitrary, capricious. The earth went round and round whether you breathed its pretty breezes or not.

And yet, here they were on the sidewalk, standing in the prairie wind, with no choice but to face it. Dorie ripped open the seal and pulled out the folded sheet. "Western Union Gram," it said. She scanned the message quickly and looked up, smiling.

"It's not— It's okay, Amos." She touched his arm. "It's not from England."

He blinked. "Beryl?"

"No, that private eye on the East Coast, the one you wrote about Wake."

"Let's see it." He yanked the telegram away, embarrassed now about his moment of anguish.

WAKE HAILS YORKVILLE NOT JERSEY STOP MARRIED KUHN COUSIN SIX YRS STOP WIFE KIDDIES YVILLE STOP MUSIC TEACHER RUN OUT AFTER KUHN PRISON STOP STREET TALK NAZI SYMP STOP OWE ME FIFTY BUCKS STOP LEONARD

Dorie was grinning, reading it over Haddam's shoulder. "He's a Nazi!" She laughed.

Gwendolyn stared disbelievingly at Dorie, then asked Amos, "Who?"

"Barnaby Wake, the choir director. Thalia's boyfriend!"

"I don't see that's cause for amusement." Gwendolyn looked insulted.

Dorie tapped Amos's arm. He was still staring at the words on the telegram, watching in case they changed. "Explain it to her, Amos. I'm off to find Wendy."

She hissed in his ear, "We found his heel!"

The apartment in Independence, over a lawyer's storefront office, brought back unpleasant memories. The long, narrow stairs, filthy with trash and dirt, dimly lighted, leading to two doors in dire need of paint. It wasn't the type of place for a Mission Hills girl like Harriet Fox. She rapped lightly and listened. Inside, the sound of a radio being clicked off cut off a low drone of music.

She knocked again, harder. "Miss Fox? My name is Dorie Lennox, I'm a friend of Wendy Hines. I'd like to talk to you."

As she raised her fist to knock again, the door opened suddenly. Harriet Fox wore a faded flowered housedress and slippers, her dirty blond hair uncombed. A thin, skittish woman with a pale, sickly complexion. The apartment smelled of camphor.

"Miss Fox?" Dorie stuck out a hand. The woman shook it, then wiped her hand nervously on her dress. She told Harriet her name again, and the name of the detective agency.

"You said you were a friend of Wendy's." She started to close the door. "You lied. You said you were her friend."

Dorie put her foot out and held the door. Harriet was angry, but her strength was gone. "I am her friend. Because I want to find her and bring her back to Eveline Hines before it's too late. You know Eveline is dying?"

Harriet blinked. "She's been dying for years."

"She's close now. We need to find Wendy. Can I come in?"

Harriet frowned but stepped back to open the door.

The musty apartment had the look of a much-lived-in furnished walk-up: scuffed linoleum, one sprung chair covered with a tattered plaid blanket, a moldy cooking space with a sink and ancient icebox, a sagging bed in a curtained alcove. The walls were covered with torn paper in a gray chicken pattern. The only window faced the street and was covered with grime.

Harriet Fox sat down on the upholstered chair and looked at her hands. Dorie pulled around the solitary dining chair from the table to face the woman.

"I guess you talked to my mother," Harriet said flatly.

"She gave me your telephone number and I tracked you down from that."

Harriet nodded, resigned to whatever fate held. Dorie watched her rub the back of one hand with her fingers, then the other. "What do you want?"

"I want to know if you've seen or heard from Wendy in the last month. Since the twenty-first."

The woman shook her head. "We were supposed to go to lunch a couple days later, but she never showed up. I called the house and the maid said nobody'd seen her for days."

"Would you say you were Wendy's best friend?"

"Oh, I don't know. She was kind of secretive. Never passed on gossip, hated for people to talk about her. Made her pretty quiet. Not the best type of friend."

She watched Harriet. Mousy and afraid—of what? Did either she or Wendy have any friends? The two of them must have been a regular Laurel and Hardy routine.

"Do you know any of her other friends?"

She shook her head.

"None? You didn't meet any of them?" Another shake. "Did you work on projects with her?"

"Projects?"

"Charity work, political campaigns, that sort of thing."

"We both belonged to a Ladies Aid through Grace Episcopal."

"Did she have any particular friends there?"

"Not that I recall."

"You don't belong anymore?"

"No!" she cried, suddenly nervous. "And Wendy, well, she's gone, isn't she?"

"Do you have any idea where she might have gone? Did she have any reason to leave town that you know of—boyfriends, trouble of any kind?"

"She never said. Unless she's visiting her relatives back east."

"How did she meet Julian?"

"In New York City. He was traveling, business with his father. I'm not sure what Wendy was doing exactly, working somewhere. A couple years later, they got married. I had the idea it was a match made by the parents somehow, that she was talked into it."

Harriet's voice was weakening. By the end of the speech, she was winded and doubled over, as if the effort had depleted her. A little groan came out of her.

"Are you okay?"

"It'll pass." But she blinked hard; then her eyes rolled back in her head. Dorie jumped up to catch her as she rolled off the chair, but by some miracle, she caught herself. A light sweat had broken out on her forehead and she pushed strings of damp hair away from her face.

"Are you sure you're all right? Do you have some juice? Can I call your mother?"

"No!" Harriet's eyes widened in either anger or fear. "I mean, she wouldn't care."

Dorie sat again, leaning toward the woman. "Is she the reason you're out here in Independence?"

"Technically, I suppose." Harriet laughed bitterly. "But it is really my own fault." She leaned back in the chair, tilted to one side. "I could drink a little water."

Dorie Lennox, aka Gunga Din. She fetched more water than an Arab. The tap ran brown, then finally cleared. She carried a small cup of water to Harriet Fox and stood over her while she drank it. When she finished, Dorie said gently, "You haven't done something to yourself, have you?"

Harriet shook her messy hair and pinched her lips. "Not that I haven't thought about it."

She took back the cup and set it on the table. "Did you sing for Barnaby Wake, Harriet?"

The woman looked at Dorie and beyond, eyes wide like a deer's, her face expressionless. Then Harriet began to rock in her chair, back and forth. Back and forth. Dorie closed her eyes, the sight so pathetic. When she looked up again, Harriet had streaks of tears on her cheeks.

Dorie walked to the girl and put hands on her shoulders to still the rocking.

"How far along are you?"

Harriet gulped. "Four and a half months," she whispered.

"Harriet, this is important. Did Wendy know?"

"No. No one knew."

"Not even Barnaby Wake?"

"No one. Except my mother."

Barnaby Wake: philanderer, fascist, worm. Her anger belonged to him today. But that feeling wouldn't help Harriet Fox.

Dorie looked around the depressing apartment. More than a personal crusader, Harriet needed a square meal and some fresh air.

"Put some clothes on, Harriet. We're going to get us some lunch."

Gwendolyn held the telegram in one hand while she wrapped an arm around a hot cup of tea Amos had poured for her, cuddling it like a baby. Amos had worked out a deal with the dentist downstairs for hot water. He skipped the milk in his tea but heaped an extra spoonful of sugar and stirred. Since Gwendolyn had come to town, his system had never been so clean.

"Who is this Kuhn?"

"Fritz Kuhn. A brownshirt. German American Bund. Did you hear about their big rally in New York last year—at Madison Square Garden?"

Gwendolyn shook her head. The bird's nest she called a hairdo needed help. A good brushing at the very least.

"American Nazis, lots of 'em. The mayor of New York, La Guardia, said it was their right to say whatever they believed. The Bill of Rights, freedom of speech. So there were thousands of brownshirts and Jew-haters of all stripes."

"Sounds disgusting."

"By all accounts, it was. This man—a Jew—jumped on the stage, he was so angry. The brownshirts beat him and kicked him and the police had to save him."

"Barnaby Wake is his relation?"

"By marriage, it appears. And shares his beliefs, if you trust this." He took the telegram from Gwen and read it again. "Says he was run out of town." He frowned.

"You don't believe it?"

"Hard to know at this distance. Running a person out of town usually means he was about to be arrested. Or worse." He looked up at Gwen; she was frowning hard into her cup. He tried to make his voice light. "And if Leonard thinks I'm paying him fifty bucks for this . . ."

"Does it mean he's doing Nazi business right here? In Kansas?"

"Missouri," he corrected. "It's our job to find out. You might not want to come along on this, Gwendolyn. Nasty business."

She blinked hard, took a gulp of tea. She didn't argue.

"What happened to Fritz Kuhn?" she whispered a minute later.

"Put in prison. Nobody took them seriously for years. Walter Winchell used to call them 'ratzis.' Then what Kuhn had been saying started to come true. He did have thousands of followers. He went to Germany and chatted up Adolf. Called Roosevelt a Red."

"Mr. Roosevelt? But he's a saint. He's saving us."

"The government tried to deport Kuhn. Finally got him on tax charges, like Al Capone. He tried to run to Germany when the war started, but they nabbed him."

"And his followers?"

"Still running around. Just not so bloody vocal."

"But not around here? It's so pleasant. Peaceful."

He looked at her drawn, frightened face. He thought about the pictures he'd seen in *Life* magazine, the ones showing the Nazi groups still finding friendly pastures out there in the prairie somewhere.

And fragile, innocent people like Gwendolyn caught in their ugly thoughts and ways. Who said war didn't make victims of us all? Amos mused.

"How about a trip to the beauty parlor, love? Get your hair done?"

FOURTEEN

HOWIE DUNCAN WAS THIN AND dark, with a squirrel face and a tendency to jitter his foot and crack his knuckles—and the only Bureau man Amos Haddam knew. He was an ex-policeman who'd joined Hoover's boys after the Union Station massacre. His partner on the Kansas City police force had been killed in the shoot-out to rescue Pretty Boy Floyd's cohort Frank Nash from the government's clutches. Amos had caught up with Duncan as he was going to a late lunch and now sat across from him at the greasy little diner in the Scarritt Building.

"Buy you a sandwich?" Amos asked, trying not to be too ingratiating, and failing. "Piece of pie?"

"Never eat here. That's an order," whispered Howie. "Stick to coffee."

Duncan rubbed the spoon the waitress brought him on his shirttail, polishing it until it shined. He dumped four cubes of sugar into his cup and stirred methodically. By then, Amos was half-done with his own burned java. He thought of Gwendolyn at the salon all by herself. He hoped she wasn't afraid, that there was no screaming, and that the ten he'd slipped the hairdresser had been enough to keep Gwen busy for several hours.

"So it's this fella we're watching for a client," Haddam began. "Corrupting a young girl, we think. Well, we know about that."

"How young? Turn him in."

"She's twenty-one."

"Tough luck." Howie grimaced at his coffee. "What's the name?"

"Barnaby Wake. Has that Hallelujah Chorus?"

"Never heard of him. He been in dutch around here?"

"Don't know. He's been in the area only a year or so. We just got word he might be connected back east to Fritz Kuhn and the Bund."

Howie wrinkled his nose. "Peeeuw."

"Any way to find out if he's been at that line of work out here?"

"You can ask the espionage boys."

"Think they'd tell me anything?"

"Nope. Cloak-and-dagger, sunup to sundown and into the night." Howie moved closer. "They just added more spook-fighters. Got nearly seventy-five now. Like the war was going on right here."

"Here—at the Bureau?"

"They travel around some, but, yeah, here. They're hot on America First. Think they can tie it to Hitler. Lucky Lindy won't be so lucky when the Bureau gets done with him."

Amos raised his eyebrows. "He appears to have a screw loose."

"Or is blind in both eyes. Some of these folks, well-meaning people, God-fearing, churchgoing—they are being taken down the river. They come back, most of them, but without their wallets."

"Or their good names. What about brownshirts? Any talk around here?"

"Nothing I heard. But those boys are closedmouthed, even inside the Bureau." He pointed a finger at Amos. "St. Louis, that's what I heard. That's where those people are swinging."

Amos put down his coffee cup. He was disappointed, as he usually was, with the information from Howie Duncan. He took his last shot. "Anybody in that unit who might talk?"

"As much as any cigar store Indian."

Amos twirled his cup on the diner's scratched tabletop.

"Hey, listen," Howie said with sympathy. "I'll pry a little. I love trying to get those stiffs to talk. I can't promise anything, though."

"Thanks, Howie. What would Chief Reed say?"

"He'd say forget the fascists, hunt for Reds. But he don't work for us anymore."

"Couldn't you take him back?"

"Guess not. He's yours to fight the corrupt ways of the Kansas City Police Department, until the end of time."

"Thank you very much."

"My pleasure."

Amos Haddam didn't dawdle. He paid for the coffees and left a tip, then took the streetcar down to the Country Club Plaza, where he and Gwendolyn had discovered a small tearoom that catered to society matrons and bridge club ladies. He bought himself a plain ham sandwich, and a fancy cucumber one for Gwen, and dropped it by the beauty salon in Westport.

Gwendolyn sat under a huge hot blower, her cheeks rosy and eyes bright. She waved as he held up the sandwich. He set it on the counter as a strange feeling washed over him, mingled with the smell of permanent-wave lotion. What was it—hope, fear, love? A bit of each? It held him, this tumult of emotion he hadn't the faintest idea what to do with, until he swallowed hard, making it go away. His eyes were burning from the chemicals.

He raised his hand, a small wave, and ran out.

That evening was the dullest of the week. No one complained.

The pall of Saunders's killing hung like black crepe. Amos volunteered to take Thalia again, and Gwendolyn would tag along and do the driving. The night was cut short when Thalia went to dinner with one of her girlfriends and the friend's parents, then straight home afterward. Amos didn't mind. He was suspicious, of course. They waited half an hour for her to emerge from the mansion again, her plain dress exchanged for a torch singer's.

But she didn't show. Haddam called from his apartment and was given the report that Thalia was in the bath and not to be disturbed.

Dorie, too, found solace in hot water. The third floor of the boardinghouse was unnaturally quiet. The twin sisters, Norma and Nell, had gone out to a polka concert. Carol, still the "new girl," despite three months' occupancy, was also out. Dorie used too much hot water, washed her hair, and went to bed early.

Hard on the nerves, this calm, she thought as her eyes fell shut.

The cops were plainclothes detectives typical of the Kansas City crop of the Pendergast era: distracted, shady, and not too sharp. They'd been parked at the curb when Dorie pulled the Packard into what she was beginning to think of as her very own spot in front of the Boston Building. How they recognized her, she wasn't sure, but they'd hopped out of their unmarked sedan immediately.

The morning's meeting with Mrs. Hines had been canceled. The quiet was becoming habit-forming, a sleeping potion. Not that she'd been twiddling her fingers here in the office, contemplating the sins of Thalia Hines or weighing the pros and cons of Wendell Willkie.

No, she'd had company. These boys in blue, up early to nab her in the office. Richards was the older man, sweaty and red in the face from the hike up the stairs. Stewart looked like he'd recently completed toilet training.

"Following up on the homicide on the bridge," Richards explained, dropping into the chair and letting the boy stand. Dorie sat behind the battered metal desk and fiddled with a pencil. "Could you explain to us what you saw?"

"It's all in the report. I don't know anything else."

Richards nodded, flipping open a notebook. He mopped his forehead with a large white handkerchief. He was close to her uncle's age, with a paunch and more hair, black with a little gray.

"You said you saw the gun. Can you describe it?"

"What happened to O'Brian? He was at the scene."

The younger man shook his head, saddened by her unwillingness. Nice pantomime.

"We're following up, Miss Lennox," Richards continued. "The gun?"

"A pistol of some kind, a revolver. I couldn't see it well. And frankly, I don't know much about guns."

"So it was not a shotgun or a tommy gun? You're sure."

"Looked like a pistol. Did you find a weapon?"

"Not at liberty to say." He crinkled his eyes in an attempt at a smile.

"Then what?"

"Sometimes," Stewart said suddenly, his voice surprisingly deep, "the type of weapon tells us which group to focus on."

"So if it was a tommy gun, then that means gangsters?"

"Correct." Stewart was short and blond and heavily freckled. She imagined him growing old and even more boring, entertaining his cat with love songs.

"So what does a pistol mean?"

Richards shrugged. "Means we look elsewhere."

"Have you found any enemies of the chauffeur?"

"Miss Lennox. I prefer asking the questions."

"And I prefer having answers, but, like you, I don't."

Richards and Stewart exchanged a look. She felt her temper rise. "Is there anything else?"

"You were following the car because you were acting as a bodyguard that night? For Miss Thalia Hines?"

"Not really a bodyguard. I was just watching her, to report to her mother."

"So you were armed?"

"No. I didn't have a gun."

"Or any other weapon."

"No. What is this about? I've told you fellas this a dozen times, to O'Brian, to Assistant Chief Michaels. To Mrs. Hines, who seemed to think I was a hero."

Richards blinked girlishly. "And were you—a hero?"

"They did their damage. They'll probably make another attempt to snatch Thalia, when things have died down a bit. Or maybe make a grab for some other girl."

"So that's your take," said Stewart, folding his arms. "A botched kidnapping."

"What's yours?"

"We're running on that theory," Richards said. "But we plan to keep an open mind."

"Good luck."

Stewart squinted at her. "With the investigation," she added.

The telephone rang. Amos, summoning Dorie to the police station to have a powwow with him and her uncle. He was whispering because he was in the station, he said, but he sounded excited, as if some new information had come to light.

She saw the cops to the door, then waited three minutes for them to get in their car and drive away. More conversation with Richards and Stewart might be injurious to her sleep patterns.

At police headquarters, Dorie drove around for ten minutes, looking for a place to park the Packard. Finally, she paid two bits to an attendant at a lot across the street, even though it was highway robbery, a scam run on people late for court. Getting a parking ticket, when you were already in dutch, was not recommended. You didn't want to be hunted down like a dog.

And Dorie was already in dutch, as any visit to these hallowed halls reminded her. She felt her blood run cold as she mounted the granite steps, same as each time she visited her parole officer. Anyone who has been behind bars must feel the same. Or underground and batty like Gwendolyn, screaming her head off in the closet. Bone-crushing, heart-stopping panic.

Ahead, two uniformed policemen opened the big brass-trimmed doors like hotel doormen.

"Doria Lennox?"

She stopped on the top step, squinting. Had she missed an appointment with Wilma Vunnell? No, she'd just been. Were things so bad inside that her uncle had arranged an escort? She shivered in her wool jacket in the cool wind. "Did Captain Warren send you?"

The two uniforms came toward her, letting the doors swing shut behind them. She stepped back down the stair.

"We have a search warrant for your vehicle," the cop said sternly, producing a folded sheet of paper with court stamps on it. Her mind raced as her body went rigid with anger and fear. The policeman was big, the kind who played football without a helmet. "Take us to your automobile and we can get this taken care of."

The other cop took her upper arm in his paw and didn't let go. The footballer with the warrant made a "This way, madam" motion, as if they were going to a fancy dress ball. She turned, by force, to head back down the steps, across the street to the parking lot, and back to the beat-up black Packard 120. She hadn't gotten any repairs done since the chase last year, the fender still bashed. Joe Czmanski had fixed the light so it functioned, but she'd never put the glass back over it. It hadn't looked too good before, and now it looked dusty and sad.

"What's this?" the escort cop asked. He poked his finger through a hole in the trunk.

"Was there when I bought it. Ask my uncle, Captain Warren. He bought it for me at a sheriff's sale."

"Getaway car," the cop said. "My cousin got one for fifty bucks."

"My uncle paid twenty-five. Hey, you can let go of me."

The cop sized her up. He released the clamp on her arm. She felt the blood pulse down through her fingers.

"What's this about? Did Mrs. Vunnell send you?"

"Received a warrant, all I know."

"I'm on probation. I wouldn't carry anything in my car. I don't know who told you that."

What had she said to the widow? Something about a gun. But she'd been joking. The widow had to know that.

The other policeman had his head inside the front seat, rummaging through the glove compartment. He straightened, clutching something with his handkerchief.

"What have we here, Miss Lennox?"

"Wha—"

She stopped, now seeing the object the cop held high like a piece of rotten meat. The gunmetal gray was unmistakable, the barrel round and long. She stared at the pistol, dumbstruck.

The policeman closed the car door. "I'd say we done our duty, wouldn't you, Griff?"

"Oh yeah."

The big paw circled her arm again with the righteous strength of democracy. It squeezed a squeak out of her throat. "It's not mine. I don't own a gun." She made herself take a breath, her head swimming with cells, blackness, shame. No, be smart, she told herself. Don't be a dunce.

"I—"

Griff looked at her expectantly. Her stomach turned a back flip and she blinked hard to clear her vision.

"I want my lawyer."

He smiled. "There's a good girl."

The cell was like any other cell: square, dim, and confining. That was the purpose of a cell, to confine, to restrict, to hold. Dorie felt her throat shut down as she tried to breathe, sitting on the edge of the cot with her arms wrapped around her sides. Be brave, she told herself. This will pass. But the words bounced off the shell of her consciousness. She couldn't fool herself, even if the people on Charlotte Street thought she was brave and hard.

She lay back on the cot and stared at the ceiling with its water stains and mildew spots. She closed her eyes and was back in booking, the flashbulb in her eyes. Hours ago, although time had taken on a strange quality, elastic and free. It was the only thing that was free around here. At first, there had been company, lots of it—cops, Amos Haddam, more cops, matrons.

No lawyers. Amos called, but none had appeared. It was Friday night. Late now. Getting a lawyer to come down would be hard. Still, she had done so much for the firm.

Her eyes flew open. Amos wouldn't call the firm, would he? Vanvleet & Wintraub was Amos's biggest client. But Louie Weston worked there. Louie Weston, who was the cause of all this. Louie, who flew airplanes, and wanted more than kisses in return. Louie—the cause of all Arlette's troubles.

And her own.

No. She'd brought on her own misery. She had no one to blame. No one had forced her to stab the jerk. She had wanted to. And now the only lawyers she knew were his colleagues. Dutch Vanvleet had gone on semi-retirement after the trouble with his son. So who was running the place, old Wintraub? She shivered on the cot. Not Louie.

She closed her eyes again. For a second, she savored the moment when she'd switched out her blade and stabbed Louie Weston in the gut. The switchblade served to scare off people, to keep them away from her. It had worked most of the time. Louis Weston had been too drunk to stay away. She smiled to herself. No, she'd poked him. She had. She'd poked him good.

Then came the blood, and the remorse set in. She'd known on the spot that he would make things bad for her. And she'd been right. He'd pressed charges. No one had believed her story that he was grabbing and pawing her. In fact, her lawyer—some low-rent Johnny she'd found in the phone book—hadn't even let her mention it during the brief hearing. She'd spent a week in stir and gotten six months on probation.

The door at the end of the hallway clanged open. Dorie sat up on the cot. She bit her lip, then made herself stop. Amos Haddam stepped up to the bars, a sorry look on his face.

"Hey," she said.

He grasped one of the steel bars that separated them, grimacing at it. "Seems like only yesterday," he said. "There's trouble with Vanvleet."

She waited.

"No one will come down until morning."

"Who put that pistol in my car?" she said, standing, angry now. "Does it have any marks?"

"They're not saying."

"What about Herb? Can't he find out?"

"He's gone for the weekend. He took your aunt to the Ozarks to see the leaves."

"What?" She sat down on the hard cot.

"They left at noon today. No way to call him."

"But you called and said he wanted to have a meeting."

He looked at her sideways. "I never called you." Amos walked a few bars back and forth. "Some of these boys want you for the chauffeur. They think it's bloody convenient."

"Those two that came to see me, I bet."

"Who was that?"

"Two dicks named Richards and Stewart." She stood up. "Do you think they planted it?"

"Cops?"

"Why not? You think Reed's got all the bad apples out of the barrel? You think none of them are taking some on the side? And what about Wake's man, the one Arlette scared off?"

Amos looked at her funny. "Arlette?"

She waved off the subject. "We're getting close to Wake. We know things about him, and he's scared."

Amos Haddam put his hands deep in the pockets of his old brown suit and looked at his shoes.

"What?"

"I went to see him at the church this afternoon," Amos said. "He wasn't there. But the choir director, man named Nolan, had nothing but good things to say about him. He's foul, no doubt about that, especially with the ladies. But I'm not sure I can connect him with the brownshirts."

She jumped to her feet, grabbing the cell bars inches from him. "Amos! He's a Nazi—a sympathizer. He's using this front, this Hallelujah Chorus, to drum up business and make money for the cause. He's sly about it; he gets into their underpants first. Like Thalia. Do you think it's her voice he's after? He's a fascist, Amos. You know he is."

Haddam looked up at her. "I don't," he said quietly.

"What if they're responsible for Gibson Saunders's murder, too? What if the German American Bund and the Kluxers got together to create a little havoc? You've seen those posters: THE JEWS MUST GO, THE POPE MUST GO, DEMOCRACY MUST GO. Then the KKK and the swastika right next to each other. It's a brotherhood, Amos. They may not hate the same folks the same way, but they're a white brotherhood. You know that."

"What I don't know, Dorie," Amos said, his voice still calm in comparison to her shriek, "is if Barnaby Wake is involved. I don't want to set off half-cocked. This is a climate for accusation and defamation. I don't want to be a part of that. I could be wrong and ruin a man's life. Wake just doesn't seem the type."

"The *type*?" She stamped her feet in frustration. "Those are the most dangerous ones, don't you see? The ones that look like preachers! Amos, what's wrong with you?" She lunged at the bars. "Are you in love? Has your brain gone soft?"

Haddam looked up slowly, flushing from his neck into his cheeks and ears. She watched him go from cool to simmer in seconds. She ran her hands through her hair. She had to get out of here. What the hell was going on? Who was Amos talking to?

When she looked over at him, he was turning his back to her. He walked toward the door, hands still in his pockets.

"Amos, wait!" She rattled the bars. "I didn't mean that. I like Gwendolyn! Is she all right? Wait, Amos, wait!"

The door closed with a metallic echo. Dorie lowered her forehead to the cold iron. Her chest filled and released air just like she was alive and breathing, just as if she had a future, just as if she wasn't alone and powerless and afraid. Behind her eyes, tension mounted. In her heart, a battle felt ready to burst with torpedoes.

She would have liked to cry. That would have been something.

Painstakingly, she licked her finger and picked up the crumb of bread from her blanket, placing it on her tongue. The faintness she'd felt earlier had passed, helped by the small hard roll the matron had brought when she complained. Hours had passed, observed only by the beating of her heart. Or had they? What had happened to her sense of time?

Dorie lay on the cot, under the thin sheet and blanket, still as death. She held her breath for as long as she could, making the blood pound in her ears. She'd done that as a kid, made herself blue in the face if nobody was paying attention to her. It was childish. No one noticed it back then, either. She let out the air and closed her eyes. At least it made her feel alive.

Sometime past midnight (announced by the matron as she clomped by), Tillie's voice came to her. For a moment, Dorie thought it was Thalia's, their sugar-fine airs so similar. Then Tillie laughed. She always laughed at the end of "Lavender Blue." Sometimes she sang the nonsense words as "Tillie Tillie," holding her petticoat with tiny fingertips and dancing around the room. When she sang them right, "dilly dilly" always made her laugh. So funny, "Like a pickle," she said. "A purple pickle."

She let the singing wash over her. Once she tried to fight Tillie, to tell her to rest, to stay away, but now that her small voice came so infrequently, Dorie lay still. She might be crazy. So be it.

When I am king, dilly dilly, you shall be queen. Yes, Tillie Mae, if lavender can be green, then it can be a pickle. Why not? Anything is possible.

A smile fixed itself to her face as the music faded away. A short song, a silly one. Tillie had wanted to be somebody's queen, to be cherished and adored. What happened to the wishes of lost children? Were they stored somewhere—for someone else to discover and hold on to like a wilted flower, past its prime but still fragrant? What did lavender smell like anyway—someone's lost dream?

Dorie hoped lavender could be green in heaven, for the tow-head's sake.

'Twas my own heart, dilly dilly, that told me so.

FIFTEEN

THE MATRON NUDGED HER FORWARD through the doors of the courtroom. The clock on the wall said it was just after nine o'clock. Light poured in gray and dull through the high windows. So it was morning. Saturday? She'd assumed she would mold in stir all weekend.

Dorie looked around the room for a familiar face. The courtroom, high-ceilinged and wood-lined, with a big yellow chandelier, was nearly empty. It smelled like lemon wax and shoe polish. Up front, a gray-haired judge sat stoop-shouldered at his desk and frowned down at two men. One—the defendant, she guessed—in a rumpled blue suit, was short, round, and mostly bald. His lawyer wasn't anyone Dorie recognized, but his air of bored superiority pegged him.

The matron sat her down in a seat and lowered herself between Dorie and the aisle. She was a big woman with a hard, bloated face and wore a blue scarf over her dark hair. She hadn't bothered with handcuffs.

"Don't I get a lawyer?" Dorie whispered to the matron.

"Shush."

Up in front, the man in the wrinkled suit mumbled something. The judge hollered, "Speak up, man! I'm deaf in one ear!"

The attorney nodded at his client.

"It was an accident, Your Honor. I had too much to drink and she was just there, in the street."

"What is his plea, counselor?" the judge demanded.

"Guilty, Your Honor."

The judge banged his gavel and rattled off plans to sentence the gentleman at a future date, then let him go without bail. Rumpled erupted in delight, shaking the hand of his lawyer as if Oliver Wendell Holmes had just made legal history.

Another case came up, a streetwalker dressed in a hotcha number, dispatched quickly. The judge was in no mood to chat, even to curvaceous chippies.

How, Dorie wondered, was she to explain to him that she had no lawyer and that she was innocent and that the gun had been planted and that her probation was almost up and she really had been good despite His Honor's stupid employees? How?

Her name was called by the bailiff. She slumped lower in the chair. The matron hit her with a plump elbow. "Get up."

Dorie drew herself up. She felt the trembling as she walked toward the judge and wondered if it was because they were trying to starve her in Jackson County Jail. As if she could smell the fried eggs and bacon at the Top Hat on Franklin, where they put something magic in the grease.

"Miss Doria Lennox, you are charged with a parole violation," the judge read. Even in his bored impatience, he sounded like a stern father. She searched his face for kindness. What did that look like in an old man—warm eyes, a gin-blossom nose, a turkey waddle? This one had none, all sharp angles and bloodshot eyes.

"Where is your representation, young lady?"

The words stuck in her throat.

He smacked his lips. "Counsel. Your lawyer. You have a lawyer?"

"I—no, I don't have a lawyer."

The judge stared at her over his glasses. "What they get you for the first time, then?"

"Oh. Ah . . ." Dorie looked down at her hands, clasped in front of her. Could you phrase a rollicking good stabbing in a way that sounded remorseful? She was a gentle person, wasn't she? Except for a few moments when the anger roiled up and took control of—

"Your Honor!"

The doors in the back of the courtroom swung shut as the man stumbled forward down the courtroom aisle as if propelled. He straightened, collected his dignity by tugging on his camel-hair jacket and pushing back his blond hair. "I represent this woman."

Louis Weston didn't look at his client as he walked deliberately toward the judge. He spoke as he walked, a swagger in his step and a shit-eating smile on his mug.

"I represent Miss Lennox in this matter, Your Honor. Louis Weston, sir, of Vanvleet & Wintraub. We had a case last month, I recall, the man with the horse." He smiled his winning smile, strutting down the aisle. The judge actually seemed to chuckle.

"Yes, Mr. Weston," the judge said. Amused, he still gave the lawyer a gimlet eye. "Can we carry on here, or are you due on the golf course?"

"Carry on, Your Honor," Louie said. He had the most charming blue eyes. As he turned them on Dorie, they dropped in temperature a few degrees.

She looked away. Why had he come? He would send her away and she'd never get out. She'd be up the river for weeks, months. Maybe years. The blood drained from her head and she tilted toward the judge's desk. A hand caught her, Louie's hand.

"Are you all right, young lady?" the judge asked.

"Probably ate some jail food this morning," Weston joked. The judge harrumphed. The proceedings entertained someone at least. Dorie took a breath. The stars spinning around her head dimmed.

"Get on with it, counselor."

Weston cleared his throat. "Your Honor, Miss Lennox was initially convicted of assault and battery. She has been on probation for the last five months, with only three weeks to go until the end of her parole. She was directed to steer clear of any sort of weapon for the duration, but yesterday a firearm, a pistol, was found in her automobile. She hasn't had any other trouble during her probation, and she has met successfully with her officer. She claims the gun isn't hers. She would like to plead not guilty, Your Honor."

She stared at him, her mouth agape. Who had given him this information—Amos?

The judge was sizing up Louie anew. "I remember this now. She jabbed you with a knife, didn't she?" His gaze turned to Dorie. She shrank under the discerning stare. "And now you're representing her in court."

He sounded mystified. That made two of them.

"We're requesting—"

"Are you healed, Mr. Weston?"

Louie, to his credit, tried to stay off that topic. "Mostly, Your Honor. Thank you for your concern. We request that Miss Lennox be remanded to my—"

"No!" Dorie blurted, then clamped a hand on her mouth.

The judge cocked an eyebrow. "You wish to remain as a guest of the county, Miss Lennox?"

Louie lowered his head and hissed at her, "You want out or not?"

Dorie ignored him.

"Your Honor, I have made every parole meeting. I'd like to be released on my own. I promise I'll show up for the trial. I have always shown up; you can ask Wilma Vunnell. I live right here. Near here."

Louie turned to the judge. "Your Honor, we request that she be released into my custody and supervision. I will make sure she completes her probation requirements and appears in court at the appropriate time."

Dorie stared at the judge, her temper flaring. She tried to calm herself as her fingernails dug into her elbows. A few more minutes of this insanity. *Just get out.* She told herself to agree with Louie, with the judge, just to get sprung. She dropped her hands, but they were shaking so badly that she clasped them together again.

Just get out. That was all that counted. She bit down on her molars to keep from talking. Louie's smell, aftershave mixed with bourbon, drifted over her. She felt queasy again.

"Do you have any prior convictions, Miss Lennox?"

"No, sir," Louie said quickly. "Not as an adult."

The judge grimaced at the lawyer. "Mr. Weston. Why would you want that sort of responsibility for a woman who sliced you in the—liver, was it? If I were you, I'd want to be as far away from her as possible."

Dorie stared at Louie. Good question.

Louie laughed under his breath as he looked at his fingernails. "It's complicated, Your Honor. I feel a responsibility toward her, to get her rehabilitated and all. She's not a bad person; she just did this one thing. And I do think someone planted that gun in her car, sir."

"That we can discuss at trial. All right, Miss Lennox, you are released without bond into the custody of Mr. Weston and ordered to appear in court on Wednesday, November sixth, for parole violation."

He banged his gavel and waved them off as the bailiff called the next defendant.

She turned away from Louie Weston.

She was out. Free.

At the back of the courtroom, a woman rose to leave. Her blue hat was pulled low over her face, like before; her fitted red jacket pulled tightly across her hips as she turned her back to the court. Dorie froze, staring.

"Arlette!"

The judge banged his gavel again and called for quiet. By the time she looked at the judge, apologizing, then back, the woman had gone through the doors. Dorie ran down the aisle, Weston on her heels.

The hallway was dimly lighted by yellow glass globes hanging over dark marble floors. She skidded to a stop and looked one way, then the other. Where was she? How had she disappeared? And why?

"Did you see a Negro woman go by here—wearing a hat?" she asked, tugging on the sleeve of a woman standing by the door. The woman shook her head. Dorie ran to the stairwell and looked down. No one there. Arlette was gone. Again.

"Here she is."

She spun on her heel, hope coming back. Louie knew Arlette; he would find her.

Louie stood with his hands on his hips and a deep frown on his face. Next to him stood Harvey Talbot. Of all the bastards she'd seen this morning . . .

Louie smirked at her groan. "You didn't really think I was going to take you under my wing, did you? And risk life, limb, and liver?" He turned to Talbot. "She's all yours. Make sure she gets back for the trial." He wiped his hands down the front of his blazer as if wiping off the last of her, then skipped down the stairs. Always the schoolboy.

She turned to Harvey, her mind doing tricks to set the pieces of the morning's events into place. Talbot and Weston—working together? For what? It didn't make sense in her rattled brain. Then she knew what it was: Harvey had somehow gotten Louie to come down and defend her.

But where was Arlette? Her mind strained toward the fleeting image, wanting to give chase. Dorie blinked a few times, frowned at her hands. What could she say to Talbot? The shame of the moment, of him seeing her in court, in trouble again. She couldn't think of anything to say. She turned to walk away, down to the end of the hallway. What was down there? Who cared? It was away from Talbot's stare.

Her heels tapped on the marble. She was out of jail. She didn't care who had sprung her. It could have been the devil himself, or Santa Claus; she'd still be out.

She wasn't going to be grateful to Harvey Talbot; he just wanted a story out of it. She could see the headline now: BLADE

GIRL NABBED FOR GAT. He'd like that. She kept walking, her indignation giving her strength. She reached the end of the hallway and tried to open a door. It was locked. She tried another. Locked. No more doors.

She leaned her head against the wall and closed her eyes. Why did everything have to be so difficult? Where had Arlette gone? Why wouldn't she stay and talk? Was she in trouble? Dorie bit her lip and tried to breathe normally. Maybe it wasn't Arlette. Maybe she was seeing things, dreaming things. She turned. Talbot stood where she'd left him, by the stairwell.

"What do you want?" Dorie stood her ground, not close, but not so far she had to shout.

He looked at her sheepishly. There was no other way to describe it. He twisted his neck, looked at his shoes. "Are you hungry?" he asked quietly.

"What?"

"Want to get something to eat? I'll buy."

"What else are you buying?" She crossed her arms. "I'm not one of your stories."

He looked up at her. He had been so cold that day at the gym, so what was this? It looked like a plea of some kind, an apology in his eyes—but for what? What had he done that he needed to apologize? It was she who had broken off with him in May. All that ugliness, humiliation, degrading—and more of the same today.

"I was thinking about the Top Hat for eggs and bacon," he said. "Just breakfast, Dorie. That's all."

The grease did its magic.

Harvey knew her all too well. She ate four fried eggs and six strips of bacon. Nobody counted toast. He ate something, too, but she didn't pay attention. When the waitress brought more coffee, she pushed back her plate and stared at him.

Talbot didn't look well. He had dark circles under his eyes. His dark hair needed a trim. His clothes had that Haddam look—

slept in. He wore an old blue cardigan that looked like something of his father's, and his shirt collar was dirty. With a full meal in her belly, she felt a little kinder toward him. He hadn't asked her a single question.

"Thank you. For getting Weston down here. That can't have been easy on a Saturday."

He shrugged.

"Amos said last night that none of them would come," she said. "How did you do it?"

"Blackmail," he said flatly.

"Ah."

Dorie watched the street outside the Top Hat get busier with shoppers and campaigners. A group of girls came by in perky patriotic uniforms, handing out buttons for Willkie. Today was the rally at Union Station. And Mrs. Hines would receive her Republicans, as well. She felt like she'd been in Oz and suddenly was back in Kansas and no one had missed her.

Except Talbot.

She frowned at him. "Why *did* you do this, Talbot?" He stared at her, mute. She lowered her voice, leaning in. "After the last time, when I stabbed him—"

She gulped her words. Did I really say that—"when I stabbed him"? But what else could she say? She *had* stabbed a man. Talbot knew what she was.

She took a breath, determined to continue. "I was too embarrassed. Too ashamed to talk to you, to talk to anybody about it. I'm still . . . humiliated by the whole thing. I just couldn't explain it away. I couldn't tell you about it."

He swallowed. "And now?"

"I still can't."

She felt the heat rise into her cheeks. *Oh hell.* She took a deep breath and tried to will away the blush. "Look I—" She closed her eyes for a second, trying to figure out what the hell she was feeling. "Talbot, I'm not the one for you. I have a bad temper and—"

He leaned forward suddenly, his voice hissing. "Don't tell me what I should feel. Don't do that." He stared at her, eyes blazing. "You don't know me that well."

She reached out suddenly, touched his cheek. Stubbly and dark, it was rough and warm to the touch. He grabbed her wrist, color rising to his face. A spoon and fork clattered to the floor. Dorie felt her pulse against his fingers. Her breath was hot and short. Talbot blinked and let her hand go.

She thought about his words. Didn't she know him well? A spot of hurt from the words filled her. Did he want her to know him? And did she dare let him—or anyone—know her?

A shiver went up her spine. She slid out of the booth and brushed crumbs from her trousers. She blinked, smiling to the old couple in the next booth. She took a breath, trying to be normal.

"Come on, Talbot. Drive me home. We've got a rally to cover."

On the drive to Charlotte Street, she watched him. He didn't seem like the same man as last year, cocky, full of brass. He had charmed her with his good heart and warm body. Now he seemed tired and angry. She wanted to talk to him, she realized. To know him. Even if it was hard. Also, she understood this much: She wanted the spotlight off herself.

"What have you been doing with yourself, Talbot? You look like hell."

He rewarded her with a small smile. "You don't look so hot yourself."

"I've been in stir. What's your excuse? Are you sick or something?"

He shook his head. "Unless sick at heart counts." He glanced at her. "Gibson's funeral was last night."

"Oh. That must have been rough."

Talbot turned a corner. The Plymouth had a floating suspension and fat tires, which made the cobblestones seem like tiny waves. She hadn't gotten her keys back for the Packard, hadn't

even tried. Apparently, she was contented enough to let her bene-
factor drive her home.

"Do the cops have any leads about who did it?" she asked.

"Leads? No. Theories? Plenty."

"What are the theories?"

"Kluxers, for starters. Then Blues fans."

"They think Blues fans killed him?"

"They're grasping at straws. They don't have any idea. Then
there are the old standbys—debts, drugs, making it with somebody else's wife, being a player in some racket."

"Any of them valid?"

"Not that I can tell. He wasn't that sort of a guy."

"You knew him?"

He nodded.

They drove in silence around the last corner. Talbot idled the
Plymouth in front of Mrs. Ferazzi's boardinghouse. Carol and
Betty sat on the front steps, painting their fingernails. The day
was sunny now, warm enough to remind you of summer again.

Her hand on the door handle, Dorie turned to Talbot. "Somebody planted that gun in my car. I think I know who, but I'll
never be able to prove it."

"Who?"

"Barnaby Wake, the choir director for the Hallelujah Chorus.
We've been investigating him. There's a story there. A big one."

He didn't bite.

"I guess there're stories everywhere these days," she said. She
moved across the seat. Taking his chin in her hand, she kissed
him quickly.

"Thanks, Talbot." She slid back to the door and opened it.

"Are you going to the Willkie rally, then?" he asked.

She nodded. "See you there?"

Across the street, Joe Czmanski stepped into the sunshine in
the doorway of the garage, wiping his hands on a greasy cloth.
He raised his hand in a wave and she nodded back. What was
she going to do with Joe?

"Somewhere," Talbot said.

She looked at Harvey. "How is your mother?"

"Good. No big complaints."

"That's great." She closed the door again, turned in the seat to face him. "I hear Luther is playing at the Blue Room."

"Once. He was pretty nervous."

"We don't see him much on the street anymore. It was great, that story you did about him." She paused. "What would you think about some more digging on Charlotte Street?"

He looked suspicious.

"See that fella? In the garage?"

"The one with the scars? I met him—name's Joe?"

"Czmanski. He wants to find out why that car blew up in his face. It was Roscoe Sensa's, you know."

"Sensa?" Harvey squinted at Joe, who remained in a patch of sunlight, working over his palms. "When was that?"

"About two years ago. Now somebody's coming around, since Sensa was hit, trying to put the squeeze on Joe." She sighed, laying the drama on thick. "He wants me to find out who planted the car bomb so these fellas will leave him alone, but I just don't have time."

"Who are the squeeze guys?"

"Don't know. Sensa's droppers, I guess. But I don't get it. Why would the trouble boys who hit Sensa care about the fella they burned by mistake?"

He was considering it, watching Joe, then examining his own fingernails.

"What do you think?" she asked.

"Might be worth a follow-up story." Harvey turned to her, a spark of his old self in his smile. "Or do you just want me hanging around Charlotte Street?"

"Better than the county jail." She wanted to kiss him again, but she backed out of the car. "See you at the station, then. I'll be the one in red, white, and blue. Thanks for bailing me out, Talbot. I won't forget it."

Dorie watched the Plymouth roar away, down past Steiner's grocery and around the corner. Why had he done it? Did he still care about her, after all she'd done to him? After all she *was*—a convict, a criminal, capable of violence, full of anger and voices from the dead? If only she hadn't stabbed Louie Weston. But she had, and she knew herself well enough to know she'd do it again if she had to. She just couldn't see how a girl who did that could end up with a man like Talbot. He was too good.

She stepped up the curb. Carol and Betty whistled in unison, loud and sassy.

"Guess who spent the night with tall, dark, and Har-veeeee," Betty said, teasing. "Who was a naughty girl and didn't come home last night? It's all over the street, Dorie—you are a loose woman."

Carol threw back her head and laughed like a hyena. Betty had a smirk plastered on her mug. Carol, with her hotcha lipstick and blue shorty shorts—what a laugh. She straightened her long, curvy legs and wiggled her platform shoes in uncontrollable glee.

Dorie stopped to stare at the pair of them. Their nails were a racy shade of scarlet. Betty had turned hard under Carol's influence. Now she wore tight sweaters over pointy brassieres and looked like a magazine ad for eye shadow.

Dorie stepped around them, going up to the top of the stoop. "What sort of fun did you girls have last night? Milk and cookies? Walking the dog?"

Carol looked over her shoulder. "Oh, I walked the dog all right. I walked him all night long." Betty slapped her thigh and guffawed.

"They pay well for dog walkers these days, Carol? Twenty bucks? Fifty if you can get them to do tricks?"

Carol and Betty stared at each other, suddenly quiet.

"Hey!" Carol spat, rising as Dorie let the door slam behind her.

———

At the Hines mansion, the door stood half-open. Amos Haddam leaned in and could hear voices, a commotion, running footsteps. He pushed the door wide, alarmed.

"What is it?" Gwendolyn whispered, peering over his shoulder.

Pulling her into the foyer, Amos skipped down the hallway to Mrs. Hines's bedroom. He had a bad feeling. Her empty bed made his heart sink. Something had happened to Eveline.

"Oh lawk," Gwendolyn said. "Has she gone to hospital?"

They backed out into the hallway. Noises came from the front of the house. There was a formal parlor and dining room off the foyer, rarely used, and a wing of private rooms Amos had never seen. He dragged Gwendolyn toward the sounds. A clatter came through large double doors. Amos put his ear to the door, then turned the wrought-iron handle plundered from a medieval torture chamber.

"Over there. Yes, yes, by the window. And fluff them, will you? They look like a horse stomped on them."

The sound of Eveline's compelling voice rang out in the parlor. Amos pushed open the door. A fire burned in the massive fireplace, warming the keeplike room with its stone walls and leaded windows. On the sofa lay the Commander under a pile of blankets, barking orders to a squadron of servants. The maid, her cupcake hat askew, struggled with a huge bouquet of lilies and glads in a crystal vase. In the adjoining dining room, the kitchen crew were setting out a lavish display of food and drink. Mother Ruth hovered behind Eveline, plumping pillows and looking at her watch. Miss Miller paced in front of the sofa, talking to herself while consulting a notebook. Panicked, she barked at Amos and Gwendolyn.

"Too early! Go away and come back in an hour!" The secretary flapped her hand in a shooing gesture. "You'll wear her out."

"Mildred, help her, will you?" the Commander said. "She

hasn't a clue about floral arranging, but then, who thought she would? Please, Mildred, now. The flowers."

Miss Miller turned to the maid. Amos stepped into the room, circumventing a poorly placed footstool. Eveline's face creased with a smile.

"Dear Amos. So good of you to come early to help."

Gwendolyn took Amos's arm. "Good morning, Mrs. Hines. Everything looks lovely."

"Does it?" Eveline looked around the room with a critical eye. "This room was full of dust. I specifically told the staff to keep it clean, but they simply don't have the discipline."

"Good to see you out of bed, Eveline." Amos surprised himself by giving her a kiss on the cheek. "To what do we owe this unexpected pleasure?"

The maid, en route to the kitchen, said with great excitement, "The Willkie people, of course!"

The words caused a new glow in Mrs. Hines's complexion.

"Wendell Willkie?" Gwendolyn chirped.

The Commander tsked. "Just some of his advance men. I'm a supporter of the party and they want to thank me. That's all. Just a few old friends in for tea."

The bustle continued around them, Mrs. Hines barking orders, getting reports from Miss Miller about the food, flowers, air temperature, and last-minute cleaning. She demanded someone wash the front windows again, as she could see streaks where the sun was hitting them. She ordered pots of chrysanthemums placed by the driveway. She rearranged the placement of the hors d'oeuvres on the table. Finally, she sank into her pillows for a moment of rest.

Amos snagged Miss Miller. "When are they due?"

The secretary glanced at the tall grandfather clock against the wall. "Ten minutes ago."

Gwendolyn craned her neck to look down the driveway. "No one yet." She threw a worried look at Eveline.

Amos squatted by the sofa. "We need to talk about Thalia. But we can do that later if you like, Eveline."

"Oh, yes," Mrs. Hines said, as if she'd forgotten about her daughter's troubles. "It can wait, can't it? She has been coming home early. I hate to think of you wasting all your evenings."

"I don't consider it a waste. Shall we come by later?"

A roar in the drive cut him off. A large black auto with American flags pinned to the aerials pulled up to the door. The maid squealed; Miss Miller shushed her. Amos and Gwendolyn tried to melt into a corner.

"Should I be this excited?" Gwendolyn whispered, hugging Amos's arm.

He squeezed her hand. The previous night, they had gone to Gibson Saunders's funeral in the small Baptist church on the East Side. His wife and mother from Michigan had huddled in the front pew as the congregation sang gospel hymns that sent chills down the spine. One of the worst nights of his life, Amos had thought, then shots of memory—worse, much worse—had flitted in and out of view. But they were frozen, timeless. The freshness of this pain, this loss, made the old wounds pale. Chasing the wayward daughter around the city afterward had been little comfort.

Amos put his arm around Gwendolyn's waist and pulled her close to him. The night before, they had found comfort in each others' arms. He had been afraid, once he recognized his desire, that he would fail. Not much practice the last few years. But she was so genuine, so lacking in the false coyness of American girls, so up-and-up about the nature of love in the moment. How could he not love her? It wouldn't be forever; he knew that.

The world wasn't made that way. Not anymore.

SIXTEEN

THREE MEN AND A WOMAN, all dressed in navy blue suits, as if they were stumping for the Salvation Army, stepped reverently into the parlor. The maid, in high color, ushered them forward and took their hats. Her voice squeaked as she introduced them as the "Willkie people."

The woman smiled at Mrs. Hines. She was slim, perhaps thirty, and wore a stylish small hat with a red feather in it over her neat brown hair, and solid-heeled shoes made for walking. She slipped off gray kid gloves and stepped toward the reclining hostess.

"Mrs. Hines, this is such a pleasure." She extended a hand. "Roberta Adams. I'm Mr. Willkie's women's campaign chair. After Mrs. Willkie, of course."

Mrs. Hines shook her hand quickly, saving her charm for the men. "Pleased you could come, Miss Adams."

"My pleasure. Call me Robbie, please."

Eveline nodded politely, looking over the woman's shoulder. A short dark-haired fellow—probably trading bonds on Wall Street with Wendell this time last year—stretched his neck to smile.

"Mrs. Hines, Brewster Nielsen. We met, oh, it must have been—"

"Six years ago, in Chicago, at the Board of Trade Ball."

Nielsen blushed deeply. He recovered, stooping to kiss Eveline's hand like a Prussian general.

"I was devastated to hear of your illness. Mr. Willkie sends his warmest regards and wishes for your speedy recovery." His voice was warm and low. Standing so close behind the sofa, Amos and Gwendolyn had no trouble hearing.

"How is the campaign going?" Eveline asked. "Wendell couldn't have picked a better man."

Nielsen smiled modestly. "Uphill, as we knew it would be. Going very well though. People seem ready for a change. They don't want a monarchy in this democracy; they want a real man, one who is close to the people, who—"

The second man tapped him on the elbow, stopping the diatribe. Nielsen rolled his eyes. "What am I doing? Sorry."

"Preaching to the converted, Brewster," Eveline said with a weak smile.

Nielsen backed up to introduce the other two men. The one who cut off the speech was a young man, not more than twenty-five, with red hair and freckles. His name was Muncie and he was the pressman in charge of newspaper and radio coverage of the rally. As soon as he was introduced, he looked at his wristwatch and made for the food. Robbie Adams joined him, exclaiming loudly over the shrimp.

Eveline was wilting. She closed her eyes briefly. Mother Ruth, hovering in the background, leaned down and whispered in Mrs. Hines's ear. Eveline brushed her away. Brewster Nielsen waited for her eyes to open, then said, "A little surprise for you today, Eveline."

She frowned up at him. The light from the large leaded-glass window behind them made it difficult to see faces.

The tall man behind Nielsen took a step forward. He was older than any of them, fifty if a day, with gray hair cut precisely. He towered over Nielsen. Amos imagined he had been an impressive figure in his prime, broad of shoulder, military physique, the proud head with exacting dark eyes.

The Commander stared at him from under a gathered brow. Her lips whitened.

"Eveline, dear. It is wonderful to see you again."

The gentleman—he was a classy fellow—had a kind, formal voice. But it was clear they had known each other in a way she had not known any of the rest.

She didn't speak. Brewster Nielsen bowed slightly as he backed away. He joined the others around the dining room table.

Eveline blinked, still staring at the tall gent. "Teddy?"

"Yes, dear. I've changed a bit, haven't I?"

"Come . . . closer." Teddy went down on one knee like a suitor and took both her hands in his, pressing them to his lips.

Gwendolyn tugged on Amos and whispered, "Let's see about some tea." They backed away for a few steps, bounced off the wall, and turned to round the corner into the dining room, casting a glance back at the scene in the parlor. Mother Ruth took the hint as well, grabbing Mildred as she ducked into the foyer.

The maid was pouring tea and coffee in the dining room. Amos and Gwendolyn each took a cup of tea, taking time with the milk and sugar. The Willkie people were huddled on the far side of the dining table, whispering and looking at watches. The pressman was obviously in a rush. Nielsen kept sneaking looks into the parlor. Gwendolyn sipped her tea, then sidled around the corner of the table, examining the delights: shrimp with cocktail sauce, crab Louis, petits fours in a variety of colors and shapes, iced cookies, cheese cut into little cubes, rolled salami held with decorative picks. She plucked an olive from a large bowl and popped it in her mouth, smiling at Robbie Adams.

"Lovely eats, eh?" said Gwendolyn. Robbie smiled politely. "So who's the gent with Mrs. Hines?"

"An old friend of hers from the war. They knew each other in England, I think."

"Mrs. Hines was a nurse in the war, wasn't she?"

Robbie nodded. "Were you in the war yourself?"

"Oh, aye. Just arrived from it this week. Bloody dreadful."

"Oh," Robbie said. "I meant the first war."

"Right. I was young then, if you must know. Just a girl. But Amos was in the war. He lied about his age. He was so brave."

Amos set down his teacup and reached around with his hand to Miss Adams. "Amos Haddam. Pleased to meet you."

"Do you two work for Mrs. Hines?" Robbie asked.

Amos stiffened.

"Oh, I'm sorry," the Willkie woman said. "I've offended you. It's been such a long, hard Campaign. I'm afraid I'm running out of tact."

"No, Miss Adams," Gwendolyn said, "It's quite all right. I am the help. Amos here is a friend of Mrs. Hines, and I'm his driver." She grinned her silly smile at Robbie Adams, who frowned into her teacup.

"Are the children coming down?" Amos said.

"You'd think so, wouldn't you," said Gwendolyn. "Thalia—that's the daughter—she's a bit of a handful."

Robbie Adams raised her eyebrows. "Really."

Amos tapped on Gwendolyn's foot under the table. She made a chirping noise and jumped. "Just a spirited girl, that's all," he told the Willkie woman. "Spoiled a bit—you know the type."

"Who's that, then?"

Robbie had turned toward the parlor, where Julian Hines now stood in front of the sofa and suffered introductions to the gentleman known as Teddy. The older man shook his hand and spoke warmly of Julian's father for all to hear.

"You were in Paris, then?" Julian asked. He smoothed his tie obsessively. He wore the little glasses, taking them off and wiping them, examining them in the sunlight repeatedly. A distraction technique, unhappy hands. Amos moved around the dining table, desperate with curiosity. Who was this man out of Eveline's past?

"London. While your stepmother was there—when was it, July and August of '18? March? She was gathering supplies for a month or so. A difficult time for all of us but she was so forceful, so brave. Back she went to the lines."

Teddy saluted her with a hand empty of a glass. The maid just then brought him a cup of tea. She wasn't such a bad servant. She even stopped in front of Julian and asked him for his preference. His answer was too low to hear. She smiled demurely and went away.

Eveline pushed back a stray hair from her forehead. "Mr. Lafferty was at the consulate. What was your title, Teddy? That I do forget."

"I was attached to the naval commander, his civilian liaison at the embassy. Mostly, I shuttled information from my British counterparts to ours. Nothing so brave as Eveline."

"You're embarrassing me. There were many braver than I." She looked over her shoulder at the dining room. "For instance, Amos Haddam here. He was a mapper, flew behind the lines. Nearly lost his life there."

Introductions ensued. Amos found it oddly pleasant to talk to the American about the war days as if it had all been glory and honor. He'd done it before. Many men—and some women, as well, particularly those who had never seen action—real action, actual battle—retained a uniquely American romanticism, as if they were still saving civilization from the savages. For Lafferty and Eveline, the honor of helping win the war remained, glowing on their skin, resting their minds at night. How he'd thought it would be that way for himself, once. He looked at Lafferty and wondered if his life was better than it might have been, because he'd been high and dry behind a desk somewhere, doling out life jackets and torpedoes instead of wet and moldy in a trench.

How did one rate a life—by years lived, by women loved, by children sired, by fortunes made? Was there some way short of landing at Saint Peter's gates, whereby a man could judge his life, his worth, his goodness? Amos didn't have a clue. But from the look of Lafferty, the tanned cheeks, the ease of money, the glow of health—his life was definitely not worse now because of that desk job. Longer, healthier for sure.

With a burst of air, the door to the foyer opened. A voice trilled: "I'm off, Mother! I'm late, so—"

Thalia stood tilted into the open doorway, a powder blue suit clinging to her figure, a white ermine collar ringing her lovely pale face. Her blond hair fell across her eye and she pushed it back. She stood, stunned for a moment at the gathering of people. "Oh. I was just going, Mother."

"Come join us, Thalia," Julian said, walking toward her. She shrank at his approach, stepping sideways.

"Yes, honey, come in. There's someone I want you to meet." Eveline's voice had such mark of authority and sweetness in it, Amos wondered how she did it. Even on her deathbed, the Commander never lost her touch.

"There she is," Amos heard Gwendolyn whisper behind him. "That's the handful. And looking quite smart today, she is."

Thalia stepped toward the sofa, glowing with youth and innocence, despite the high heels and the soft wool suit. She sat on the edge of the sofa, crossing her ankles. She gazed down at her mother, solemnly examining the ravaged face. A look of sympathy, of real feeling, flashed across Thalia's face, and she leaned down to give her mother a kiss on the cheek. Then she blinked, patting Eveline's hand.

"I have to get to the rally. The chorus is singing today."

"This is an old friend of mine, Thalia." The girl rose and turned. "Thalia, this is Mr. Lafferty. Teddy, my daughter, Thalia Louise."

Thalia wrinkled her nose as she extended a gloved hand. "Oh, I hate my middle name. Please, Mother." She laughed, backing away. "Pleased to meet you. Bye now."

She disappeared out the door. In the silence that followed, Amos felt a thud of dread in his chest. Thalia was so obliging today. So charming, so kind to her mother.

She was up to something.

The Hines mansion sat silently in the afternoon sunshine, its dark windows like empty eye sockets. The stone made Dorie shiver as she walked up the driveway. She'd taken the Brooklyn streetcar from the boardinghouse, past Union Station, through the hills, and along Ward Parkway. A crowd was gathering outside the station, even though there was an hour until the Willkie train was due. The rally would last for some time, at least a couple hours, she figured.

For reasons more personal than professional, she felt a need to concentrate on the chauffeur, Tommy Briggs. She knocked on the door at the mansion. The maid let her in and showed her to Mrs. Hines's sickroom, chattering on about the Willkie people, who had decamped a half hour before.

Mother Ruth opened the door and frowned. "She's very tired. This isn't a good time."

"Who is it, Ruth?" The Commander's voice was strange, as if a change had taken place and a new person had replaced the dying one. Not that this voice was strong; far from it. Dorie peered past the nurse. Eveline Hines looked the same, sunk into a dozen pillows, a red satin comforter tucked around her.

"Miss Lennox, ma'am."

"I just have a favor to ask. I won't be long."

"Let her in, Ruth."

Mother Ruth sighed and waved her in. At the Commander's bedside, Dorie sat on the edge of a chair. Mrs. Hines looked pale as a ghost, her lips blue. Her eyelids fluttered as she focused on her guest. She had put on extra rouge and eyebrow pencil, which only made her look more deathly.

"You had guests? How nice." Dorie said, trying to be polite. A hard lesson, awkward, but she'd learned how.

Mrs. Hines raised a trembling hand to her face. She'd never shaken so badly in Dorie's presence. Her hand touched her eye as if to shield it from view. But it was obvious that tears had come to her eyes, unwillingly.

Ruth patted her other hand, concerned. "There now. You're overtired."

"An honor to you," Dorie said.

"No. No," Eveline Hines said, wiping away the tears angrily. "You don't know; none of you know."

Dorie looked helplessly at the nurse. Ruth had a look of sympathy on her broad face. "I'll get you some tea," Ruth said. She closed the door behind her as she left.

The Commander composed herself, sighing in little breaths until her breathing was more or less normal again. She raised her left hand, a chain and locket clutched there. Mrs. Hines opened the locket, then passed it silently to Dorie.

"Go ahead. Take it," Eveline said. "I want you to know."

Dorie frowned. She didn't like this, whatever it was. But she took the locket. Inside was a small photograph of a man, a handsome man in a stiff collar and formal tie, smiling benevolently. "Your husband?"

Mrs. Hines shook her head. "Everyone thinks Leslie was her father. That we married because I was pregnant. If they know at all." She looked seriously at Dorie. "Thalia's father. The children don't know about Teddy. Thalia doesn't know. I never thought they'd meet."

Dorie stared, confused, at the tiny photograph.

"Finally, today they met. And it was so unexpected, so . . ." The Commander couldn't finish. She held out her hand for the locket and gazed again on the handsome face. "When I saw them together, I realized how much she looks like him. Their bearing, their chins, their eyes. I was filled with happiness. And dread."

"There's no reason they have to find out."

"No. They can't find out. You can't tell them, Miss Lennox. But someone—someone should know." She frowned. "I know I sound confused. But no one can find out. Thalia must get her inheritance. You must promise me you will safeguard the secret and make sure she gets her inheritance."

"Of course. Does he know?"

Mrs. Hines cast down her eyes. "No."

"Do you want him to know—someday? Is that what you're asking me?"

"I don't know. I just had to tell someone."

And why have you chosen me? Dorie squinted at her hands. She disliked secrets, resented holding them for others. What was the point—spread the burden? She squirmed on the chair. She hadn't come for this. She fumed, trying to regulate her breathing, her heartbeat, her anger. Then she glanced at Mrs. Hines. So alone in dying. So alienated from her family, her children. Of course she couldn't tell them, not even Thalia, who might take it as an excuse to run off to San Francisco and become a fan dancer. Who else did she have? Why not Amos? But he was part of her past, too. He revered her, and might think less of her. It didn't matter what Dorie thought. She was just a girl. She clenched her teeth and tried to be forgiving.

It wasn't Eveline's fault. She was dying. Make some concessions for the dying, she reminded herself.

If this got out, Thalia would be disinherited. Julian would no doubt see to that. So why couldn't Mrs. Hines have died with the secret? Why did she have to tell? What could possibly be the point of telling someone such a secret, one you didn't want anyone to know, on your deathbed?

She bit down again on her molars. She couldn't figure it out. Did someone suspect? Julian maybe? Was the Commander worried that someone besides herself had seen the resemblance today?

When she looked up again at Mrs. Hines, her eyes were closed. Her head had dropped to one side on the pillow. Her mouth hung open a little, revealing strong white teeth and a sad string of saliva.

"Mrs. Hines? I'd like to look through Tommy's things, if that's all right." The Commander didn't answer, or move. "Mrs. Hines?"

Dorie took the woman's hand. It was cool and skeletal, almost weightless.

Mother Ruth came through the door, carrying a tray. Dorie stood, trying to control the sense of alarm that ran through her like an electric shock. "She's—she's—"

"Fallen asleep? Good. Well, you and I can have some tea, then," Ruth said.

"She dropped off so quickly."

"She's very tired. Lemon or sugar?"

"Can you check her, please, Ruth?"

"No one asked you to come in and bother her with your questions." The nurse set down the teacup, annoyed, and picked up Mrs. Hines other hand, checking her pulse. She frowned a little, set her palm on the patient's forehead. "I'll not be waking her up now when she needs her sleep."

Dorie backed away. The Commander was only sleeping. The locket remained in her hand, secure. "I'm going out to the chauffeur's quarters. To look at Tommy Briggs's things."

Ruth had her eye on the patient. "I believe Mildred's got them in her office. You know where that is?"

Mildred Miller's office was empty, the door open. Dorie considered a search for the secretary around the mansion. She was probably back in the kitchen, directing the staff on the leftover hors d'oeuvres, or sitting somewhere with her feet up. Where were her rooms?

Too much time. Besides, Dorie could see the canvas bag, an old brown army duffel, standing in the corner. She slipped into the office and shut the door. A key sat in a lock above the knob, and she turned it. With luck, Miss Miller wouldn't be back for a while.

She worked quickly, pulling out uniforms, clothes, boots. A bundle of letters. A hairbrush and shaving kit. A few books. One was a tattered old novel, the binding broken and pages loose, entitled *The Greater Glory*. The next was a small Bible inscribed to Thomas Edward Briggs at his confirmation in 1927. Inside it was tucked a small pamphlet advertising a college in Asheville, North Carolina. They had correspondence courses. Someone had circled a course: Economics for a New America.

She was about to put down the pamphlet, when she noticed a name on the back. The president of the college, William D. Pelley. She turned back to the front. The name of the place was Galahad College. There was no biography of Pelley on the brochure; none was required. He was infamous as the founder of the Silver Shirts, his own special brand of brownshirts. He was running for president but had been kept off most state ballots. He was a fascist. He was a national socialist.

A Nazi.

Her blood ran cold. She looked back at the piles of clothes, pawing through the neatly folded shirts. One had been folded inside another. She pulled them apart, and there it was: the silver shirt, more a rich gray, with military cording looped over one sleeve, an *L* embroidered on the breast pocket.

If Briggs was a Nazi sympathizer, and Wake was, too—what did it mean? Were they working together? Had Briggs planned to turn in Wake? He must have known Wake. Had he tried to blackmail him? It must have been him driving that night Wake found Thalia at the nightclub.

She didn't have time to think. She bundled everything up into the duffel bag the way it had been, keeping the pamphlet to show Amos. She tucked it into her pocket and stood the duffel bag in the corner. Unlocking the door, she looked up and down the empty hallway, then back at the duffel.

"Oh hell," she muttered to herself. She fished out the silver shirt.

Tommy Briggs wouldn't be needing it anymore.

Rolled up, tucked under her arm on the streetcar, the shirt seemed to stink and become heavier at the same time. What if the police found her with it? Dorie began to sweat. If she'd had her beater, she could have stuffed it under a seat. But here she was, in public, swaying with the rest of the patriots on the way to the Willkie rally. Cold sweat trickled down her backbone.

The crowd at Union Station had doubled in the last hour. Despite Kansas City being a Democratic stronghold under Pendergast, plenty of its voters were interested enough in Wendell Willkie to give him the eyeball test. Was he as short as they said? Did his hair always fly around in the wind? Was his wife pretty? Would anyone hit him with an egg? Or a tomato, a chair? Critical matters of state would be determined here today.

She told herself she was here to keep an eye on Thalia. But she'd wanted to come, to see the man who might be president. She would vote for FDR; there was no question of that. But Willkie was breathing hard on the old man's heels. He just might win. And he wasn't a bad sort. He knew better than to openly attack Roosevelt when the world was at war. What did Willkie think about war, really? She didn't think anyone knew. He probably didn't know himself. After all, he was just a Wall Street man. He only knew how to make money.

She made her way through the crowd to the station, pushing through a group of students blocking the door. Inside, she found the checkroom and paid the attendant an extra fifty cents to keep the shirt for two days in a basket in the back. He gave her a key on a pin, which she stuck in the lining of her handbag.

The north waiting hall was packed with people waiting for Willkie. She hoped people weren't trying to get on trains. Moving was difficult, but she inched her way around the edge of the room. When she got to the pay phones, she stood in line. After ten minutes, she got into the booth and shut the door.

With a sigh, she sat down. It was quiet in the phone booth, comforting, with the smell of oak. She found a nickel in her purse and dialed the operator.

"Lawrence, Kansas. Lonnie Masterson."

She waited. The operator came back and told her there was no such listing. She asked then for the University of Kansas Housing Office. When the operator gave her that number, she dialed it and waited. Finally, an operator came on. The office was closed; it was Saturday. She sighed and hung up.

A man was banging on the glass. "Come on, I got to make a call!"

"Buzz off." Dorie picked up the receiver, slugged in another nickel, and dialed the Hines residence. She asked for Julian Hines. It was some time before he came on the line.

"Lonnie Masterson? That college playboy? What do you want with him?" Julian said. His attitude didn't quite match his words. He seemed distracted and breathless.

"I guess I want to talk to him."

"About what?"

"About the night Tommy Briggs got shot. Do you have it?"

Another long pause. She smiled at the impatient man outside the booth, who informed her the train would be arriving in five minutes.

At length, she got Lonnie's number and dialed it. A sleepy male voice answered.

"This is Masterson. Who's this?"

"Dorie Lennox. I was in the car following you the night of the shooting on the bridge?"

"Yeah." It sounded like he'd sat up and gotten the blood flowing to his head. "I remember you. Lady dick."

"Listen, Lonnie. Can you tell me any more about what happened that night? Like how you happened to be going across to the north? Whose idea was that?"

There was a long silence. She could hear him breathing, moving around. "Lonnie?"

"I'm here." He sighed. "I don't want to get into anything. I better not talk to you."

"Wait. The chauffeur who was killed? He was a Silver Shirt. I need to find out if he was involved in something that got him killed that night."

"I thought it was a kidnap thing."

"Tommy Briggs might have been up to something."

"Oh." Another pause. "I guess it doesn't matter now. I got a call. They said I would get a hundred bucks if I got Thalia out on a date and went to North KC afterward. That was all. Just go dancing and get some dessert."

"Who called you?"

"No name. A man. He said an envelope would be given to me

by the chauffeur at the end of the night if I did what they said. It wasn't exactly unpleasant, going dancing with Thalia Hines. I figured, easy money."

"Did you get your envelope?"

"No, ma'am, I did not."

"Did anyone contact you again?"

"Never heard another word except from the cops."

"Did you tell them this story?"

A breathy sigh. "No."

Back in the throng, Dorie felt bombarded with sensations: chanting from one side, echoed from the other, signs everywhere, touting Willkie and declaiming against FDR and the third term. One man had an entire coat and hat covered with Willkie buttons: WE WANT WILLKIE. NO FOURTH TERM EITHER. ELEANOR—NO SOAP! THANKSGIVING DAY NOV. 5. WILLKIE OR BUST. MY FRIENDS—GOODBYE! NO ROYAL FAMILY. The crowd kept the man from toppling over from the weight of them.

Farther on, one of the Willkie Girls plied buttons on the crowd. WE WOMEN WANT WILLKIE was pushed into her hand. She passed it off to a little girl. A man shoved a handbill at her. It read A VOTE FOR WILLKIE IS A VOTE FOR HITLER. She scowled at it and let it fall to the floor, joining the thousands already littering the station. Elbows jabbed. Someone stepped on her foot.

Then she saw him. Talbot was taller than most in the crowd, his dark hair falling across his eye. He stood close to the platform doors. Hundreds of people between them. When he looked her way, she waved and shouted his name, jumping, but he didn't see her.

The train was coming! A cheer went up in the crowd, nearly drowning out the hoot of the steam whistle. She realized at the exact moment as hundreds of others that it would have been better to stay outside. Soon a voice was heard on the public-address system outside. Another cheer went up. Everyone pressed toward the doors. She was carried along, her feet off the ground.

People cursed and hollered, shoving one another, telling one another to stop.

As the crowd around her pushed closer to the door, she had to gasp for air. The woman in front of her wore a large hat; the feather stuck Dorie in the eye. She put her hands against the woman's wool coat and pushed, trying to get some air. A surge of panic went through her. She thought of Gwendolyn, underground in the dark, the pressing down of bombs, war, starvation, destruction. She felt close to that narrow ledge of panic.

These thoughts flitted through her mind as if she were somewhere else, analyzing crowd hysteria. Then she was thrown to the right, up against the wall. The man behind her fell into her neck, pressing in unpleasantly with his bristly mustache and belching. She pushed him off with a muttered curse, only to have him apologize with garlicky breath inches from her face.

Forty-five minutes later, she was outside. The sky was still blue. She'd missed Willkie's speech. She'd missed the singing of the Hallelujah Chorus on bleachers she'd failed to notice. She'd missed seeing Mrs. Willkie and admiring her hat. She'd missed the hecklers and smearers. She'd been squeezed and bruised and cursed and poked, and missed it all.

She walked north toward the Market. All the streetcars were packed to overflowing, passengers dangling from the steps. The mayhem at Union Station had taken the starch out of her. She wanted to see Barnaby Wake and Thalia again, too, and had botched it. Maybe the best thing to do would be go back to the boardinghouse and take a nap. She was useless for anything today.

"Give a lass a ride?"

Haddam stuck his head out the passenger side of his Buick, grinning like a monkey. She stopped on the sidewalk, trying to stand up straight, but failing. She climbed in the backseat. Gwendolyn was driving again, but slower and more carefully, as if she finally had command of the big car.

"Hey. Thanks." Dorie put her head back on the seat and closed her eyes.

"Some speech, huh?" Amos was saying. "Old WW is finally getting the drift of oration. It's about time. Lennox? You asleep?"

"Almost."

"What did you think of the speech?"

"Didn't hear it. Busy trying to keep from being trampled to death."

"Squat little blighter, isn't he?" Gwendolyn said. "What'd you call him?"

"Wee Willie Willkie. Shorter than his missus." Amos snorted.

"Did you hear the chorus?" Gwendolyn asked, turning a corner, throwing Dorie across the seat. "They sang 'Swing Low, Sweet Chariot,' and that 'terrible swift sword' song. 'Mine eyes have seen the glory.' Ooh, they were lovely. Don't you think, Amos?"

"Bloody lovely." He paused. "So the lawyer showed up this morning?"

Dorie opened her eyes and sat up. "Weston."

Amos frowned. "Weston came down?"

"And ever so friendly."

"He got it kicked out?"

"Not quite. No bail bond—good, since I have no money."

"I would have paid it; you know that." Amos put an elbow over the seat. "Where's the Packard?"

Charlotte Street was deserted. Unusually so for a Saturday afternoon, but not unwelcome. Dorie parked the retrieved Packard and began the climb up to the third floor of the boarding house. Her bed began to take on epic proportions in her mind: soft, warm, safe. Large as a floating dock in a choppy sea. It had taken close to an hour to spring her auto at police headquarters.

She reached the second-floor landing as the pay phone began to ring. She stared at it, willing it to stop. It didn't.

"Charlotte Hookshop," she said. "You itchum, we scratchum."

Breathing for a second, then: "Dorie Lennox, if you please."

She put the receiver to her stomach. Who was this? "She's out." She used her low voice.

"Can you please have her call Miss Miller at the Hines residence." Mildred rattled off a number.

Dorie did a fast mental review of her packing of the duffel. Miss Miller didn't sound angry. "Oh. Wait. There's the broad now." Phony foot scuffling. "Hello?"

"Mildred Miller here. I remembered we had talked about Wendy's schedule on that last day. I went up to her room and looked around. I felt a little . . . well, foolish, but I thought it was important."

"Did you find anything?"

"Another calendar. She kept her own. She had written in several things I didn't have."

"Such as?"

"Such as on Friday, the twentieth, she had lunch with Mrs. Hines. Not unusual, but rather so to put it in the appointments."

"Do you know what they talked about?"

"No. But then on Saturday night, she had written this in. 'Eight-thirty. *Tommy*. Two forty-five East Fifteenth.' "

"Tommy Briggs?"

"I don't know."

"Anything else?"

"Nothing out of the ordinary. Nothing else for Saturday. We didn't see her again."

Done hung up and climbed the stairs. The only person who might know what Wendy had been doing that last night was dead. Coincidence? What had happened that night? What sort of a place was 245 East Fifteenth? Could it have been a Silver Shirt meeting? Or was Wendy having a fling with the hired help, like her sister-in-law? What had Wendy and Mrs. Hines discussed at that lunch that it was so important to pencil it into the book?

In her room, she lay down on the bed. Rubbing her face hard, she thought of the song the Hallelujah Chorus had sung, "Swing Low, Sweet Chariot." She'd lied to Gwendolyn; she had been able to hear the chorus from inside the station. And that song, Tillie's song, had caused a physical pain in its simple beauty.

She closed her eyes. Where was Tillie today? Dorie felt so tired, so low, she wanted that sweet little voice to soothe her into a peaceful sleep. Listening hard, she heard a faraway tinkle of a piano. Luther perhaps. No Tillie.

She rolled over on her stomach and punched up her pillow. Sinking her face deep into it, she smelled a man. Though he'd never been in her room, she could smell him on her pillow, as if the smell of him—cinnamon and hair oil—had rubbed off on her hair.

She rolled onto her back again and hugged the pillow to her chest, drawing in the scent. That look he'd given her in the diner, so lonely, so sad. She'd wanted to hold him, to make it right. To tell him she didn't mean it, to promise him the moon.

In the theater, Amos Haddam put his arm around Gwendolyn's shoulder and pulled her close. "The March of Time" was showing last week's bombings in the Battle of Britain, complete with daytime raids of London. Saint Paul's Cathedral had been hit, and the statue of Richard the Lion-Hearted outside the Parliament buildings. The sound of the planes made him shake, so real it was. How was old Cassandra bearing up? Was she still down with the rats in the Underground? Would she catch some awful crud down there, just when she was needed? When would he hear from her?

Gwendolyn shrank in her seat. She had been eager for the cartoon with the mouse, then a pleasant feature with Joan Fontaine and some handsome bloke.

Trembling, she put her hands over her eyes and made little squeaking noises.

She'd seen enough.

SEVENTEEN

DORIE TUCKED THE BAG UNDER her arm, adjusting the strap over her shoulder, then looked at her wristwatch. She was on time; it was 8:35, but there was no one here. The room, upstairs over a stationery and greeting card shop, was obviously for meetings. It was unlocked. No one had bothered. There was nothing of value anyway, not even a chair. Just a bare room, its wainscoting painted a dull green, with two windows that overlooked Fifteenth Street. The smell of cigar smoke lingered in the air.

She tromped down the stairs and peered through the glass door of the card shop. The door was locked, but a light shone in the back. She knocked on the glass. After a few minutes, a young woman appeared, wiping her hands on an apron.

"Closed."

"Just a question," Dorie yelled. "About the meeting room."

The woman glanced upward. Maybe she wanted to rent the place. Whatever the reason, she pulled keys on a ring from her apron and unlocked the door.

"Hi. I've been out of town," Dorie said, smiling. "I have been to some of the meetings upstairs, but now no one's there. Did they change the time?"

The woman, in her twenties, but rough from hard living, was expressionless. She looked Italian, and not long since she'd seen the old country. Dorie nonchalantly pulled the bag from her arm, setting it on the floor between them, its mouth gaping. The young woman glanced at it, then back again.

"They do not meet there now. They move," she said, her accent soft. She glanced over her shoulder.

"Where to?"

The woman shook her head, frowning. "Call them. They tell you."

"But I want to go tonight. They'll all be at the meeting. I'm late already."

The woman rubbed the bridge of her nose. Dorie knew that sign. She reached into her handbag and pulled out a five-dollar bill. As she bent to get her bag with the silver shirt, she let the bill fall to the scuffed wood floor. The woman stiffened, looked around, and snatched it from the floor.

"There was some trouble and they had to move."

"Trouble? Like cops?"

"No, no," the woman whispered. She made one hand into a pistol. A *whoosh* came through her lips, and a *pop*.

"Ah. No cops, though."

"No. They go to the Hotel, um, Bellerive. That's what I hear."

"Bellerive. You sure? That's pretty swank."

The woman frowned. "I not know swank."

Dorie didn't know swank, either. But she could get used to it. She stepped into the bright lights and brocade sofas and plush carpets of the lobby of the Hotel Bellerive. Women in satin gowns and furs draped themselves over arms of men and furniture. Tuxedos and polished shoes mingled with watch fobs and cigars. A man was playing the piano in one corner. She stepped behind a mirrored column and straightened her jacket. Where would the meeting be in this sort of hotel? In a private room? The basement? Surely not right out where the banquets were served.

The bag was over her shoulder. It was awkward, both physically and mentally. She didn't want to get caught with it, by anybody. It was an abomination, a symbol of the kind of evil wrongheadedness that was making a mess of the world.

Finding the service stairs behind swinging doors, she tiptoed down, listening for sounds of something besides the big steam boiler. The boiler was obvious before it was seen, its sputtering and hissing—and its heat. The basement was a good ten degrees warmer than upstairs.

The central hallway, scuffed and worn, led straight to the back. She poked her head in doors, finding the laundry, the dish-washing room, and a variety of storerooms. At the end of the hallway, nothing.

She backtracked to the stairs, continuing up to the second floor. A large banquet was winding down in the big ballroom, the crystal chandeliers glowing down on the guests. She stared at people in sequins and evening wear. A man with sharp, cool eyes stood at the door. He demanded to know her business. She moved on.

Several small meeting rooms stood empty. Around a corner, down a badly lighted hall sat a man outside a closed door. His arms were folded across his chest. He wore tall leather boots with trousers tucked into them, with puttees over the boots.

She stumbled, slowing her feet. The guard stared at her, his face menacing. What exactly was she planning to do? Even if she'd had her switchblade (and being freshly sprung from the joint, she had no wish to provoke the fates in that direction), what did she think she would do—slice through the room? She would hardly get by one guard without a lot of luck. She kept going forward slowly, trying to think. The guard stood, putting his ham-sized hands on his hips and frowning with his consid-erable brow.

Knowing that a local Silver Shirts group existed should be enough. Enough to ruin Barnaby Wake? Did she need hard evi-dence that he was attached to it? She had evidence of Tommy Briggs's membership—could she go through Wake's closet, too?

She stopped ten feet from the guard. The bag with the shirt sat under her armpit like a tumor. Hot streams of hate spewed from the guard's nostrils. She blinked at him and smiled. Said good evening.

Then turned on her heel.

———

Under the awning outside the front doors to the Hotel Bellerive, she stood and bit her lip. The doorman glanced sideways at her but let her be.

What? *What?* She was a coward, a pip-squeak. She racked her brains. How was she going to shine a light on these bigots? How could she save Thalia Hines from their clutches? She could be brave, and foolish, and confront the whole band of fascists upstairs. But what would she do, *could* she do? What would the Silver Shirts do to her if she burst in, screaming about Nazis?

The woman at the greeting card shop—what had she said? Trouble. A gunshot. Dorie saw Wendy doing what she had almost done: barging into a clot of angry fascists, accusing them of being what they were, recognizing certain people around the room. Had Wendy followed Tommy that night, confronted him? Had she been killed for it? Had she seen Barnaby Wake? Had he killed her?

A commotion behind her. She turned just in time to be run down by two cops hustling a group out of the hotel. Dorie stumbled, dropped her bag, and fell almost to the cement sidewalk. A policeman grabbed her arm and hauled her upright.

"All right, miss?"

A large group of men and a scattering of women in furs and plumed hats paused behind the cop. A man with a mop of black hair, wearing a well-cut pinstripe suit, leaned over and picked up the strap to her bag. The bag stayed shut, but she could barely breathe.

The man passed her the bag. "We shouldn't have been taking more than our share of the sidewalk. My apologies."

Dorie blinked. The cop was grinning at her. She took the bag, holding it tightly to her chest. "Thank you, Mr. Willkie," she managed to say.

Wendell Willkie touched his hat and gave her a wink. Then the party moved on down the sidewalk, chattering and laughing and slapping one another on the back. She watched them with something like awe, the cool breeze that came up from the river not even registering.

"Looks like you've been touched by the Willkie magic."

She pulled her eyes away from the man himself. Talbot stood with his little notebook and pencil, looking like the cocky reporter again.

"What's in the bag?"

"Nothing." She released her stranglehold on it and fit it over her shoulder again. She looked down the street. The party had gotten into autos. "What—what are you doing?"

"Just writing this up." He squinted at her. "You want to come down to the *Star* for a minute?"

She shook herself. "My car's near there."

They started walking slowly south, toward the newspaper office. Her car was parked north, actually. She had no idea what she was doing tonight. All day, if she was honest. Something about being in jail had curdled her brain. The evening had turned cold and she didn't have gloves or a hat. She shivered, pulling the bag close for warmth.

"I didn't see you at the rally," he said.

"The crowd was enormous."

He nodded and kept walking. She lengthened her stride to keep up.

"I should thank you for that lead about Roscoe Sensa," Talbot said after walking a couple blocks in silence.

She stopped. "Did you find out who snuffed him?"

"No. But I think I know why."

He smiled and kept walking. Dorie had to pull on his sleeve. "Well? Spill."

"Can't tell you yet. I think it's related to Gibson Saunders's murder, though."

"What?"

"I'm off to Chicago tonight on the late train. I'll know in the morning, if all goes well."

They stood at the bottom of the steps of the *Kansas City Star*. It was built like a federal building, a rock-solid institution that you could trust, depend on, believe in. At least the building conveyed that. Harvey Talbot tucked his pencil behind his ear.

"I've got to go write up the Willkie piece. Is your car nearby?"

"I can't believe you're holding out on me, Talbot. After all the help I've given you. After all we—" She stopped, biting her upper lip.

"Meant to each other?" His voice was harsh, accusing. Or was it? He looked at her sideways. "I have to go."

"Talbot? Can I use your telephone?"

He looked at her hand on his arm. "On one condition," he said.

"What's that?"

"That you—"

He looked down at her from under his eyebrows. She felt her heart thump. It was so aggravating having feelings. Why couldn't you just go through life with a friendly dog and a pint of gin to keep you company? Why this longing? How did you get rid of the damn longing?

"What?"

"Pick me up at the station tomorrow night," he said.

Dorie followed him up the broad steps, then up the stairs to the newsroom. Reporters sat scattered around the floor, banging on typewriters, answering ringing telephones, tossing balled-up paper. She found the place fascinating in its ordinariness. Astounded that proclamations came from these grimy quarters, that lives were ruined, made final, elevated, celebrated. Such a leap—from inky words to real life. A sort of magic.

But reality was a filthy chair by a messy, scratched desk. She sat on the chair, wondering why she was here, feeling in an odd state, almost suspended. She was tired of worrying about Thalia Hines. She remembered she had come to use the telephone. Talbot was reading over his notes at the typewriter. She dialed Amos's home number.

"Where are you?"

"At the newspaper. I ran into Talbot downtown. And Wendell Willkie." She winked at Harvey.

"Listen. Eveline Hines has been calling—or rather, Mother Ruth. She's worried about Thalia tonight."

"Why tonight?"

Amos sighed. "It's Eveline. She—" His voice broke.

She felt her stomach lurch. "No. Not yet, Amos."

"No . . . no. She's just slipped off. Unconscious."

Perhaps she'd been right this afternoon, then. Just a matter of time. Hours perhaps. That was what he didn't say.

"Her last wish, Ruth says, was that Julian and Thalia be with her at the end."

The Commander must have liked Julian more than she'd let on. Had Mrs. Hines told anyone else about Thalia's parentage? God, Dorie hoped so. Was the request for both heirs of Leslie Hines at her bedside a last attempt at legitimacy? Did Amos know about the man called Teddy?

It didn't matter at this stage. Eveline was dying.

"Both of them, Ruth said," he repeated, as if reading her mind. "She was so happy today. Saw her old friends, chatted and laughed. Held court. She put on her last party, Lennox. I wish you could have seen her. Flushed with a last small joy, she was."

"The Willkie people?"

"And an old friend from London. Thalia popped in, too, looking quite lovely. It must have pleased her mother. I have to hold on to that."

"An old friend? Who was that?"

"Some fellow from London. She knew him during the war." A voice in the background. "Gwendolyn says his name was Lafferty. She called him Teddy."

"No one you knew?"

He cleared his throat. "We have to find Thalia. She didn't come home after the Willkie rally."

"Where do we look—Barnaby Wake's?"

She had good reason to believe Wake was in a meeting. Would Thalia be there, too? Amos muttered something about having no bloody idea.

"Amos, listen. I think Barnaby Wake is a member of the Silver Shirts. Both Wake and Tommy. And I think Wendy found out. That would explain why Tommy was killed. He could link Wake to the murder of Wendy. It didn't matter at first because Wake didn't know who Tommy was. He was just another dumb fascist. But then Wake started to date Thalia and things got a little uncomfortable. Maybe Tommy even asked for a little hush money."

Talbot stared at her under his hank of untidy hair. She didn't care what he heard, what anyone knew about Barnaby Wake. What about Harriet Fox, heartsick, alone? So like Arlette years before, and there was not much Dorie could do this time. Arlette—where was she? The thoughts, the memories, popped by like frames edited into a strip of celluloid.

"Is this a theory?" Amos demanded. "Do you have proof?"

"The meeting is going on right now at the Hotel Bellerive, right down the hall from the Willkie dinner." She looked at her watch. It was after ten o'clock already. "They may still be there."

"You have proof?"

She sighed. *Goddamn Amos!*

"You can't go around calling people fascists, Lennox, as much as you dislike them. Or murderers. We've been through this, lass."

"I know, I know. But I have—"

Dorie reached for the bag between her feet as Talbot shoved the early edition of the *Star* in her face. He pointed to a small item on the second page, down in the right-hand corner.

"What do you have, Lennox?" Amos said.

"Just a sec."

She set down the receiver on the desk and grabbed the newspaper. The small photograph of Barnaby Wake in his smiling best set off the headline: CHOIR DIRECTOR SUED FOR ALIENATION OF AFFECTIONS.

"Holy Mary." Dorie skimmed the article quickly, picking out the name Edward Marchand. He was divorcing Agnes and blaming it all on Barnaby Wake. She picked up the phone.

"I'm reading the early edition. Have you seen it? Here's the headline." She read it, then the first paragraph. "The reporter talked to Marchand. I can't believe they print this stuff. These ink monkeys'll print anything." Talbot smiled and wiggled his eyebrows.

"What else does it say?"

Mrs. Agnes Marchand was not available for comment. Mr. Marchand told the *Star* that he feels Mr. Wake's behavior needs to be known. That is why he is making public his private marital difficulties, despite the blow to his own pride.

"I'm told by good sources," Marchand said, "that at least one member of the choir is 'under distress,' and has been disowned by her family."

He refused to elaborate.

"Did you go back to the Marchand's?"

"Tried. She was in there but wouldn't open the door."

"You think he beats her?"

"He was the type. Although I have to say that I'm fairly impressed with his tactics. Not only is he divorcing his wife but he's telling the world who cuckolded him. That takes guts."

She folded the paper. "Do you think it's over for Wake? Can somebody really be sued for alienation of affections?"

"It's the scandal that'll get him. I'm sure that's what Marchand had planned," Amos said. He sighed. "What are we going to do about Thalia?"

"I'll drive by Wake's and see if I can find her."

"We should have been with her tonight, of all nights."

Neither of them had an excuse. Except they were bored with Thalia's antics, and she was tired of them.

"You've got to find her, Lennox."

Amos hung the receiver back on the telephone. He felt guilty laying all that on the girl. Eveline's sudden decline today had hit him hard. She'd seemed so lively, so animated, at the reception. He recalled her bright eyes while she'd talked to the Lafferty fellow. She must have used up whatever reserve of energy she had. Maybe she would awaken and hang on. But something told him she was tired of fighting.

Gwendolyn was wrapped in a tartan blanket on the sofa. The sight of her warmed him, brought him back. If he let himself, he could be back in France, watching Eveline bandage soldiers. He'd had a dream like that a few nights before, with mud grabbing his feet as he struggled in vain to run to her, warn her, because mortar shells were coming. He hadn't known Eveline Hines during the war. Yet it had been their common ground all these years.

And now, he was going to lose her. And with her, another fragment of the past, the memories that linked them. Without her, would he be able to recall any of the pure motives, any of the good they had all embraced going into the conflict? Without her, would a piece of him die? A chill racked his frame. He made himself look at Gwendolyn.

"Some tea?"

"That'd be lovely." She smiled at him, letting her eyes dash to the letter on the table for a second. It had been waiting for them in the postbox when they returned from the picture.

He put the kettle on, got out the cups and the tea. The ritual was soothing, after all these years in America drinking scalding coffee. He wiped off the tray, set two spoons on it, the sugar bowl, poured milk in the creamer. His kitchen hadn't been this clean and organized in—well, ever. He looked through the doorway to her musty little head bent over the letter, her hair doing its odd dance in the draft.

The draft. At least he could quit worrying about that. He'd run into his city councilman at the rally today. "Too old, old boy!" the politician had shouted to all and sundry, as if it were hilarious. As if he was not just old but ancient, decrepit.

"Top age is thirty-four! Besides, we got so many volunteers, looks like nobody'll get drafted."

Too old.

Tonight, he felt old—dried-up, useless. He set the tray down in front of Gwendolyn and poured them both tea. He added a healthy dose of milk to his own and let Gwen mix her own. She used masses of sugar, rationed at home.

They sipped their tea silently. Amos both wanted and didn't want to know what was in the letter. She would tell him when she was ready.

Gwendolyn finished her tea and sat back on the sofa, letting a small sigh escape her. Her color had improved dramatically in her time in Kansas City. Her cheeks were rosy again, the dry patches had cleared, and her haircut framed her small face with a sophisticated shape. Amos felt the age again inside him, an aching weight, trouble and regret, what he sometimes called "the Dreadful." It wasn't age really, but tonight it felt that way, as if his years were more than they should be, and killing him inch by inch.

"My aunt," Gwendolyn said. Amos raised his eyebrows, noncommittal. "She wants me to come. She sent me money, and a train ticket."

He had expected as much. He felt no worse, curiously, and hoped this didn't mean he hadn't really become attached to Gwendolyn. He took her hand.

"I don't want you to go. You know that."

She patted his hand briskly and gave a brave smile. "You saved my life, but I can't be sponging off you forever, now, can I?"

"Marry me, Gwendolyn."

The words spilled out of him. He surprised himself, and as her eyes widened and lips stretched, they both laughed in a nervous explosion.

"Silly man," she said.

"I meant it." He dropped off the sofa onto one knee. "Marry me and be my wife." He kissed her slender fingers with their broken nails.

She laughed again. "Get up, you ridiculous creature. Do you want more tea?" She pulled her hand away and went for the teapot.

Amos sat back on the sofa and assessed his heart. Resilient, warm, unbroken. And yet, he did mean it. He would marry her. In a flash, in a snap. He gazed at her, pouring more lukewarm tea into their cups. She was so lovely, so English. She reminded him of himself at fourteen, with love and fortune and good things ahead. She made him feel young, or at least remember what it had been like to be young.

She passed him his teacup and he saw the tears on her face. He set the cup down and took hers from her shaking hands. She sat straight-backed on the edge of the sofa, the tears running over her delicate freckles, eyes gleaming.

"I'm the ridiculous one. So sorry," she said.

Then he held her close for a long time, smelling her hair, feeling her breath on his neck.

Life would go on. This war would be over and he would see her again. Perhaps even marry her. Who knew?

His timing—not to mention the world's—was off-kilter again.

EIGHTEEN

Dorie held her wristwatch up to her face and squinted at the dial. Four o'clock. Her eyes blurred. She had to find a bathroom soon or suffer the consequences. Her coffee was cold, but at least there was still a cup left in the thermos bottle. She sighed and looked at the back of the Wake house. The alley wasn't the best vantage point, but so far it hadn't mattered. All was dark, and had been since midnight, when she'd arrived.

Stretching her bad knee across the seat, she yawned. Drummed her fingers on the steering wheel. Drummed her fingers across her cheek, her chin. Pulled her hair horizontal.

The life of the private eye. One sensational adventure after another.

Forty-five minutes later, she eased out of the Packard, leaving the door ajar. Night was still thick in the sky, stars shining around the wisps of lavender cloud. The cool air made her shiver and brought the urgency of her physical needs to a head. The hedge between the alley and Wake's house had lost half its leaves. Since midnight, there had not been a light on or a noise. They weren't home; she was sure of that. But would they leave a door unlocked? Just in case a local snoop needed to use the bloomin' loo? Fat chance.

The front of the house had neither a porch light or streetlight. Cupping her hands, she looked through the small garage door windowpanes. No auto. She tiptoed around to the backyard again and tried the side door. Locked. There was one other door, possibly leading to a den. She stepped over piles of leaves on the brick patio and quietly rattled the knob. Locked. She moved to the windows, all at level in this ranch-style house, pushing on the sashes.

Striking out again, she veered into the shadows, and found a bush sheltered from the street, alley, and neighbors. Zipping her trousers back up, she heard the crunching of leaves by the street. Then the figure, darting from tree to tree. She froze, shrinking back into the shadows.

Had someone seen her in the alley? The Packard, hulking and far from invisible, might have given her away. She cursed under her breath. She hadn't been too careful. Thalia was aware of them. What difference did it make? But now, a chill ran up the back of her neck. She wasn't alone.

She reached the defoliated hedge without snapping any major twigs underfoot. She was still in the shadows when the figure dashed along the other side of the hedge, a flash of dark fabric, dark hair, movement, air. Leaves crunched lightly, then a gasp— *Oh!*—somewhere near the Packard.

Dorie looked behind her for somewhere to hide. The yard was barren of features. Not a single chair or table on the patio. No trees except on the lot line and in front. She veered right, into the shadows by the edge of the yard. She squatted, leaning against a small tree. It was cold and damp. She was no longer sleepy.

Her knee, the bad one, had just begun to throb, when a pop of a gunshot broke the silence. She toppled over backward in surprise, catching herself on something sharp on the ground. She blinked, pulled her hand away. Listened for another shot. Someone kicked the car door, slamming it shut. Voices. Angry.

She pulled herself upright. Who was back there? Had they been shot? *Are they after me?* It made no sense. Yet someone had tried to force her into a car by gunpoint. Wake's men? But who had dashed through the front yard? Someone light on their feet, someone small.

Wendy.

Of course! Wendy had escaped Wake's clutches (had she been a prisoner in the house?). Or she had been watching, waiting for her chance to get back to Eveline, and now they had shot her. Good, virtuous Wendy, married to that crazy bastard. Wendy, the woman she was supposed to be finding.

Dorie stood behind the hedge again. Her palm was bleeding. She had no weapon, not even a big stick. Trembling, she made herself stand still and wait. No sounds from the alley. Then footsteps, fading. Christ, it was dark.

Then a car engine roared to life, down where the footsteps had gone. Lights shone away. Had they taken Wendy? Had she been left for dead?

This thought propelled Dorie through the hedge. Branches scratched her face and hands. She bolted onto the alley as the car turned out onto the street. A big dark car—the black coupe of Thalia's shooting?

The Packard sat dark and silent. The passenger door was open.

She crept around the auto, keeping her head down. She looked down the alley both ways as she moved toward the Packard. A foot, in a small shoe, stuck out the door. A moan.

She threw open the door. "Wendy?" she whispered, peering into the dark interior.

Across the seat lay a woman all right. A bleeding woman. But it wasn't Wendy, unless someone had forgotten to mention a mixed marriage.

The woman wore a dark fitted suit with trousers and was holding her ribs with one hand. Her head lay back on the seat, eyes closed.

I found her. Dorie felt a thrill run through her. Then she saw the blood.

"Arlette! Are you hit?" Stupid question: Red oozed over her fingers. Arlette only moaned again, teeth clenched.

"Don't worry, I'll take you to a hospital. Come on, feet in." She closed the passenger door and ran around the car, throwing herself behind the wheel. She turned the engine over, flipped the lights, then looked down at Arlette. Her eyes were open now, looking up from the seat.

She patted Arlette's shoulder. "I'll take care of you, honey. Never you mind."

The Packard screeched to a stop at the Emergency entrance to City Hospital. The trip had taken less than five minutes.

Dorie jumped out and ran around to open the side door. "Come on, girl." She took Arlette's free hand and tried to pull her upright. The woman groaned and pulled her hand away.

"No. No hospital."

"Arlette, you've been shot. You're losing blood." *Just like last time*. Dorie wiped her hair off her face and realized she was sweating. Her heart beat wildly. "Please, Arlette. You're going to die if I don't get you in there."

The woman lifted her head. "I'm not gonna die. Get me over to Doc Friedkin." She fell back and closed her eyes. "He can help me," she whispered, her strength gone.

"But we're right here, Arlette." Dorie looked back at the comforting lights and glass doors. Nurses in clean white uniforms waited, their caring hands at the ready, their minds bursting with first aid. "This is quicker."

Arlette didn't answer. Could she drag Arlette inside without hurting her? No. She looked at the Emergency doors. "Stay right there."

Pushing through the door, she ran to the desk. No one was there.

"Hello? Help, please! Gunshot wound!"

A nurse in a white cap stuck her head out of white curtains in a large room behind the desk. Dorie slapped the desk with her palm. "Please, come help! She's in the car!"

Finally, two orderlies and the nurse followed her out the doors, carrying a pallet. The door to the Packard was still open. But Arlette wasn't there.

"She was right here." Dorie felt the seat, coming up with warm blood on her fingers. "You see? She was hurt."

The orderlies scoured the street, behind bushes and curbs and mailboxes. Dorie went to the end of the driveway and called for Arlette—cursed her loudly, too—until the nurse took her arm.

"She's run off. You tried to help. Let's go inside and wash that blood off your hand."

"Do you know a Dr. Freidkin?"

The nurse, a sallow-cheeked woman, frowned. "Why?"

"Just tell me. You know him?" She gripped the nurse's arm. "Where does he live?"

"Friedkin lost his license. A long time ago."

"Where is he?"

"If your friend is going to Friedkin, she's in trouble. Maybe that's why she ran away. But I guess you knew that." The nurse's frown softened. "He used to be off Troost, on Twentieth. I don't know if—"

Dawn was breaking. The pearl sky turned rosy, glossy in its enthusiasm. The apartment building sat dull and brown and square, with dirty windows and burglar bars. The name on the mailbox was faded but readable. The apartment was on the third floor, in the back. Dorie ran up the stairs, consumed with fear. Arlette would never make it up these stairs. She would die somewhere, walking—crawling—to find this quack.

Why, Arlette? Why go to another quack when one almost killed you?

She pounded on the door. No answer. She pounded louder. "Dr. Friedkin?"

Across the hall, a door opened. A fat man, wrapped in a plaid robe, glowered under tufts of black hair. "Hey. It's five o'clock in the fucking morning, toots."

"Doc! Friedkin! I know you're in there!"

The fat man stood beside her, his robe revealing unruly body hair. "I told you once. Have a heart for a working stiff. It's five o'clock in the morning." His tone darkened.

"You seen Dr. Friedkin? Did he go out?"

"Do I look like I seen Friedkin? I was sleeping like a fucking baby."

She raised her fist to pound. The fat man grabbed her wrist. "Leave it, toots. I ain't gonna tell you again."

She swiveled and brought her knee up hard, twisting out of his grasp. He fell to one side, sagging against the wall. As he bent over, gasping, she took the stairs, pausing for a moment at the first landing.

"Nobody calls me 'toots.' "

On the second floor, an old woman stuck her head out of the door of the apartment directly under Friedkin's. Her hair was covered with a pink shower cap. She waved at Dorie.

"I heard his phone ring and ring, and he yelled at whoever it was. Then he left." The old woman scrunched up her nose. "He wears big boots. *Clomp clomp clomp.* I hear him every time."

"Do you know where he went?"

She shook her shower cap. "Can't hear words through the ceiling, only yellin'. And bottles breakin'."

The neighborhood was waking up out on the street. The Packard sat at an angle to the curb, abandoned in a rush. A paperboy came by, delivering the *Star,* and Dorie found a dime for it. Distractions, that was what she needed after a long night and a day of anticipation of tomorrow's headlines: WOMAN FOUND SHOT. BLED TO DEATH.

She sat behind the wheel, spreading the front page before her. The headlines blurred. "Goddamn it, Arlette. Who appointed you anyway?"

She smoothed the wrinkles in the paper. There was Barnaby Wake with that headline. What would he do? Would he tough it out? Smooth things over with his society gals? Did the bund—or the Silver Shirts—need him here? Had he and Thalia already flown?

Or did these homegrown fascists plan treason, destruction, sabotage? Were they recruiting American citizens? Were they traitors—or just misguided? Would Hoover let them alone?

That seemed unlikely. But Hoover's G-men had their hands full. They might overlook a bunch of goons in shiny boots for a while. Should she be a true-blue citizen and tell the FBI what she knew about Tommy Briggs? What she suspected about Barnaby Wake? She hoped to hell she didn't have to.

And where was Arlette?

She slept hard. At noon, she woke to smells of Sunday dinner coming up from the kitchen of the boardinghouse. She splashed water on her face, tucked her hair behind her ears and her shirttail in her trousers. The turnout at table was low, just Mrs. Ferazzi, her son Tony, one Swedish bachelor, and Carol. Dorie sat at the far end of the table from all of them, until Mrs. Ferazzi made her move in beside Carol. They gave each other a cold stare.

The hot food made her feel human again, and she was scolded by Carol for having thirds of sweet potatoes. Even Carol's snide remark, "At home, we feed sweet potatoes to the hogs," couldn't ruin supper.

Mrs. Ferazzi dabbed her mouth with a napkin. "Father told me after Mass that the Ford auto plant is going to be making tanks soon." She shuddered. "Are we really going to war?"

"It's to send to the British," Carol said.

"I'm going," Tony said. "Nobody can stop me."

"We'll see about that," his mother said. "You'll be going to trade school next year in Wichita. That's where you belong."

"Not if there's a war. You won't stop me."

Mrs. Ferazzi's eyes blazed as she turned an Italian shade of scarlet. Dorie turned to Carol: "Where's your best pal this afternoon?"

Carol slumped over her plate. Her nails were bare of paint, and her hair needed a good comb. Gone was her eye makeup, and her brashness.

"Don't worry, Carol," Mrs. F. said. "You're paid through the end of next week and you'll find something. With men enlisting there'll be plenty of jobs."

"Get canned, Carol?"

Carol squinted hatefully at Dorie, and she regretted her words. "Sorry. I—What happened?"

Carol stuck out her chin. "I did nothing wrong. They said I was too—" She glanced at Tony, who was ogling her chest. His mother slapped his shoulder. "They said I flirted too much. They didn't like my clothes."

"That's ridiculous," Dorie said, although it wasn't. "Maybe you can get a job in the Ford plant. Build us some tanks."

Carol snorted, then laughed, her false cheer settling over them, making them glad that there was no dessert to endure.

Only the third inning, but Amos Haddam had sat long enough. The Monarchs were down one to nothing in uninspired play, swinging at everything and connecting at little. The Blues didn't look much better, though they were jaunty and waved to the crowd. Could the players have decided on a fix now that Saunders was out of the picture? Or were they just short-handed and dispirited? Amos had a sick feeling in his stomach that had nothing to do with the wieners he and Gwendolyn had bought downstairs.

They sat five rows up over the first baseline. The best seats Amos had had all season. He'd made it to only six games, but the Monarchs played a short season, with plenty of road trips. The weather was brisk and sunny, with fast-moving clouds skidding across the sky. Gwendolyn sat quietly after a short explanation of the rules. She stared intently at the players, as if trying to figure out why no one was hitting the ball.

Haddam patted her knee. "I see somebody I have to talk to. You'll be all right?"

Her eyes darted nervously, but she nodded.

Amos made his way down the bleachers. This side of the ball

field was all white, all Blues fans, or at least white fans. He shouldn't assume they were for the Blues, a team mostly popular for their skin color, even though they'd had a great season this year. True baseball fans went to watch Joe Greene and Hilton Smith and Zip Matchett and Buck O'Neill. And some years Satchel Paige, Turkey Stearnes, Bullet Joe Rogan, Big Train Jackson. So many great ones, personalities, that the other side of the bleachers was packed to the top with dark faces, cheering.

Should be sitting on that side, Amos thought. Would be if it wouldn't cause a race riot. Tensions were high after the death of Gibson Saunders.

Rumors had linked the murder now to the Kluxers, the German American Bund, and other unnamed underground groups. The *Kansas City Star* was uncharacteristically silent on the subject. Amos Haddam had hashed it out with Talbot but was only now ready to find out what the management of the Monarchs thought.

He made his way across to the box seats behind and to the left of home plate, where owner J. L. Wilkinson, Quincy Gilmore, and a few assistants and friends sat. Wilkinson was frowning, arms crossed on his chest. He looked up and waved Amos over. Haddam eased into a folding chair. As he did, he noticed black armbands around the left arms of the men.

"Mr. Wilkinson." Amos turned to see the left fielder Booker McDaniels hit a line drive between second and third plates, then get thrown out at first by an unusually fast arm on the Blues left fielder.

Gilmore slapped his thigh in disgust. Wilkinson's frown didn't change.

"News on Saunders, Haddam?" the owner asked.

"No, sir, I'm sorry."

"You did your best. I only wish these boys would." Wilkinson glanced at Gilmore. "You better go down and light a fire under them, Quincy."

Gilmore, dressed to the nines as usual, eased his way out toward the dugout.

"They'll come back. They always do by the sixth or seventh inning," Amos said. "Saunders's murder must have thrown them for a loop."

"As it did all of us." Wilkinson took a deep breath and spread out his hands on his knees. "It's a game, Amos. That's all it is. It's America. Look at that." He gestured to the field, where the Blues were now heading to the dugout as the Monarchs took the field. "Black and white playing together. Playing a game. What is wrong with that? We're all Americans. We all love baseball. We all love sitting out here in the sunshine on a Sunday afternoon and cheering our boys, eating our peanuts, watching a game. *We're all the same.* Am I wrong, Amos? Tell me."

Haddam looked at his dismal face, a face that had seen and heard every angle of colored baseball for the last thirty years. He hoped the reporter was wrong, that nobody on the team was guilty of fixing.

Wilkinson was staring at him. He looked away, at the new Monarchs pitcher, Lefty Bryant, warming up on the mound.

"No, sir," he said. "You're not wrong."

"Did they win?"

Dorie pulled the Packard up parallel to the Buick. Amos's auto was easy to spot, parked with one wheel up on the curb at a creative angle outside the stadium. He was already inside the car, talking to Gwendolyn.

"Sure did," he called back.

"No trouble?"

"Oh, yes," Gwen said, excited, "they were batting terribly. Awful. They were behind most of the game; then in the tenth section"—she glanced at Amos—"the ninth inning, a very big man hit a home run!"

"Joe Greene," Amos added. "And no, no trouble. Seven to four. Come get a bite with us?"

Dorie followed them to a diner in Westport that served bar-becue all night. They sat in a booth and ordered. She thought the couple looked happy, and sunburned, from the game. But she had other things on her mind.

She pulled the photos from her purse. Amos immediately picked up the one of Julian and his wife, Wendy.

"That's her?"

"She's a bit horse-faced, isn't she?" Gwen said. "I mean, he's nice-looking and all."

Unfortunately, Gwen was right. Wendy had little in the looks department. She must have brought her family's wealth to the marriage. In the photograph, taken in a garden, Wendy stood apart from Julian, her hands gripped tightly in front of her. Julian had a lewd half smile on his face, but he wasn't sending it Wendy's way. His eyes pointed off to the left, presumably where the maid stood. Or some other young lovely.

Dorie turned the photograph around for another look. Wendy was plain all right, with straight bangs and perm-waved fringe above her shoulders. Her hair looked perhaps light brown in the black-and-white photo, and her lips were pinched tightly together under a large nose and slanted, sad eyes.

"I took these down to Fifteenth Street, to that place where the Silver Shirts met." Dorie fingered the other two photos: Tommy Briggs and Barnaby Wake. Wake's was a nice publicity shot with his hair waved and shiny. Tommy's was less good: muddy, tiny, unclear. Mildred had found it among his belongings. Dorie had lurked around the front of the store, where the Italian woman had talked to her before, but it was closed and no one appeared inside. Finally, she'd gone around back.

"I found these boys playing craps in the alley. Some not so old, but others old enough."

"To play craps?" Amos said, wiping his chin.

"To have their palms greased. Two of them, brothers, live right next to the meeting room. They knew what meeting I was talking about."

"They in the group or cell or whatever you call it?"

"I don't think so. Maybe." She pointed to Wake. "They knew him. Barnaby'd been around every Saturday night for months. Since the spring. They also were pretty sure they knew Tommy, especially when I described the green sedan. They're Italian, these brothers, and they know their cars."

"What about her?" Amos asked, his eyes flicking to Wendy.

Dorie couldn't help a tiny smile. She covered by taking a bite of ribs and chewing vigorously while Haddam fumed. Finally, she wiped her mouth, took a long drink of water to kill the flames, and told him.

"They saw her. They remember the last meeting because of the commotion."

"What commotion?"

"Gunplay. They heard the gun go off, then shouting, and people scattered. Later, after midnight, they heard footsteps on the stairs and a last car took off, squealing its tires."

"And Wendy?"

"They saw her go in. Not many women at these meetings, just an occasional girlfriend, and she looked strange to them, dressed up and proper. Obviously rich. She looked at the number over the door and then checked something in her hand, the way you do when you first arrive someplace."

"And she went upstairs? They saw her."

"They saw her go upstairs. And nobody saw Wendy after that night."

Haddam set his napkin down gently. He stared at her. "Last sighting," he said. "Good work."

"Last sighting," Dorie agreed.

"Good enough for me," he said.

"Do you think so?" For the last hour, she had been trying to think of alternative scenarios, that Wendy had run off with somebody, as unlikely as that seemed now.

They would never know, in all likelihood, what had happened at that Silver Shirt meeting. And it rankled her. She liked absolutes, dead positives. But this identification of Wendy at the meeting was probably the most they would get. No one at the meeting would probably tell. She tried to imagine torturing Barnaby Wake, or that storm trooper at the fancy hotel. Wake maybe—he didn't look unbreakable. But he was the sort who skated away from trouble. His pants might be dragging, hanging off, but he somehow slinked away.

"Oh, I think so," Amos said. "One of two things happened. Wendy confronted Wake at the meeting and Tommy saw Wake kill her. Or Tommy, afraid he'd get the can back at the Hines now that Wendy had seen what he was up to, did it himself."

"Maybe Tommy shot her for Wake."

"Too complicated. They can't have expected Mrs. Julian Hines to march right into a Silver Shirt fascist meeting. She's hardly the type. To risk her upper-crust reputation, her society matronliness, on this chauffeur—who would have thought? She surprised them. Tommy could link Wake to both the Silver Shirts and the Hines. He could blackmail Wake into keeping quiet. Or maybe he still had an eye for Thalia honey."

"Jealousy?" That sounded cleaner.

"Unlikely, but stupider reasons, if you need one for murder, have been used. For whatever reason, we can put both Barnaby Wake and Tommy Briggs at that meeting. No doubt they were at the same meeting the night Tommy showed up with Wake to sweep Thalia honey away from the Three Owls. At any rate, Wendy followed Tommy there that night to get some dope on him for Eveline. What a report that would have been. Tommy slips a gasket when she walks in. Starts running or hiding, then figures that won't work, gets out his gun, or grabs somebody else's, and starts shooting. It's a bit too late to pretend you aren't really a fascist when you're standing around doing *sieg heils* in your special uniform."

"Then Wake realizes, after he starts getting heavy with Thalia, that Tommy can rat him out to the Hines. Maybe Tommy asks for hush money."

"Bingo. No more Tommy."

Gwendolyn turned to Amos, frowning. "The chauffeur shot her, then?"

"My best bet," he said. "But all in the past." He patted her knee.

The Englishwoman looked up at Dorie, her pale eyes solemn, a dab of sauce on her chin. "I'm leaving. Going to California to live with my aunt."

The glow of putting the puzzle pieces together drained from Amos's cheeks. He swallowed hard, glanced at Gwendolyn, then at his hands.

"So soon?" Dorie said, trying to smile. "Stay another week or two. Amos and I would love it."

"Oh, I'm sure I would, too, but I'm out of money and my aunt is waiting for me. She sent me a ticket."

"We'll miss you, Gwen." Dorie let the silence yawn for a minute, then changed the subject. "Shall we tell anyone—the cops, Uncle Herb?"

Amos blinked. "What do we know? What evidence do we have?"

"I've got his shirt." He stared at her. "Tommy's silver shirt. I've got it."

He nodded. "Nice insurance plan, Lennox. Money in the bank."

She stood for a moment inside the doors to Union Station. The high ceiling was shadowy and full of echoes, a far cry from the high excitement and crowds of the Willkie rally. The floor was buffed and shiny, all the handbills gone. Moonlight trickled in through the big round window. On a wooden bench in the waiting room sat a box of Willke buttons, abandoned to the whims of nonbelievers. Small groups of travelers clung to carpetbags and relatives.

It was late, almost midnight, and the sunshine that had warmed the city was long gone. Dorie walked back under the clock to wait. Talbot had said his train was due in at 12:05, but the board by the door to platform four said fifteen minutes later.

She felt wide awake. She thought again about Amos's sorry face at the prospect of Gwendolyn catching a train right here, out to California. He was more attached to her than he let on.

Where, oh where, was Arlette? Not in any hospital. She'd spent the evening canvassing them. She only hoped that quack doctor had kept sober long enough to patch her up. Arlette, such an odd duck. Almost had a death wish, didn't she? Flirting with darkness, and guns. Dorie considered if she was any different, and decided, not much.

No meeting with Eveline Hines today. She was still unconscious. Mother Ruth had the doctor coming round twice a day, but she expected no change. When Gwendolyn said quietly, "Looks like her time has come," no one disagreed.

Dorie curled into the corner of a wooden bench. The train was late. Thalia Hines had been on her own all day. After last night—futility, danger, gunshots—they had thrown up their hands. She was a big girl, old enough to mess up her life, if that was what she wanted. Amos speculated she had left town with Wake.

God and the Commander couldn't stop Thalia. Still, it felt like they were taking advantage of Mrs. Hines's illness to stop carrying out her orders. It had been their own idea—and Mother Ruth's—to deliver Thalia home to her mother's bedside. The burden of unkept promises lay on Dorie's shoulders as she sat hunched on the hard bench.

If she were my sister . . . What would I do? Cut her loose? Try to persuade her? I would talk to her, make her see reality. Who he really is, what he believes.

But Thalia didn't have a sister. She isn't my responsibility.

Is she?

The bench was cold. Dorie got up to walk around. A train arrived; passengers came up the stairs from the platform and out the door for platform six. A porter said it was coming up from Memphis. She stuck her head outside the main doors and saw the clumps of passengers readying their baggage, tipping porters, finding cars.

The Chicago train was late. Finally, at 12:50, it rolled in. The brakes screeched through the floor of the waiting room. She made her way through the door and down the stairs. The lights were very dim next to the passenger cars.

Talbot climbed down the train car steps, his hat on the back of his head, looking rumpled. There was a jump in his step, and she knew he'd found out something juicy in Chicago. He put his arm around her shoulders and gave her a peck on the cheek.

"You came," he said.

"I said I would. I don't break my promises." A rush of feeling hit her, as if they were still a couple. "You're in a good mood. You get what you were looking for?"

"Oh yes." He laughed. "You might say that."

"Can you link Roscoe Sensa to Gibson Saunders?"

He squeezed her shoulder. "Just watch me."

They stepped around a pile of baggage at the end of the platform. Moving up the stairs toward the doors to the terminal, she felt a lightness that came from a place she didn't get to often. She smelled Harvey's cinnamon breath near her ear, felt his ribs next to her shoulder, and thought she might do something rash. It was so compelling, it scared her a little, and made her back away.

Just inside the doors, she stopped, turning to block his path. She put a hand against his chest. "Just wait a second, buster—"

"Lennox, look. There's Wake," he whispered, looking over her head.

She turned back to the shadowy terminal. "Where?"

"Getting out of that cab. He's with a woman." Talbot grabbed her hand and pulled her behind a cigarette kiosk closed for the night. "Christ, he's running away with that married woman."

Dorie peered around the kiosk. Barnaby Wake was picking up a large suitcase. He wore a hat and overcoat, but he was easily recognized. Next to him stood a slim woman in a black hooded cape, black gloves, with a pile of luggage near her. Wake set his bag down and looked around for a porter.

"Is that Agnes Marchand?"

"Who else? All they've got left is each other, after her husband ran them up that flagpole."

"Unfortunately it could be many women. Including his so-called wife."

"He's married?"

She moved around to the other side of the kiosk. "Talbot, let's just walk by and we'll find out. We'll never see who it is if we hide back here."

He stuck out his elbow gallantly and she took his arm. "You are in some mood," she whispered as they strode out from the kiosk, making for the front doors of Union Station.

"You would be, too, if you had perfect hunch-making machinery rattling around in your head."

"Maybe you'll start putting some money on the ponies now. Make a small fortune."

"I could. A large fortune." Wake and his companion were close now. Dorie tore her eyes away from them and smiled up at Talbot.

"You don't say, big boy," she said, batting eyelashes.

Wake and the woman were walking in the other direction, around a porter's cart, toward the door to the platform for the Memphis train. Dorie pulled to a stop. "Turn around. Turn," she hissed quietly at the departing couple.

"Damn," Talbot said. "Well, au revoir."

"Little Red Riding Hood and the Big Bad Wolf."

"Look out, Granny."

The couple disappeared through the platform door. She stamped her foot. "Who is that woman?"

"Does it matter? He's gone. Good riddance."

She squinted up at him for a second. "Hell yes, it matters."

She ran across the marble floor to the platform door. Inside the baggage room, porters were loading carts onto the elevator to take below to the platform. The trains ran right underneath the terminal's waiting room, all twelve lines going to the north and south, east and west. She skidded around luggage and hit the stairs. Her knee wrenched on a step and she winced, slowing. She could see the train was still in place.

The platform was nearly empty, just a single porter handing up luggage into the baggage car.

"The woman and man—she was wearing a cape with a hood. Which car, do you know?"

"Cape?" He looked at her quizzically.

"A cloak. A long, billowy thing. The man had an overcoat and a brown hat."

The porter shook his head. She dashed past him along the passenger cars, jumping to see into windows, tapping on the glass. Annoying but effective—story of her life. In the next to last car, she saw Wake's hat, then his hair, then his profile. Climbing the car's steps, she went down the aisle. It was a first-class car, with closed compartments. She peered into the window of each one, finding a large family, a single salesman, then Barnaby Wake.

She tried the door. They had locked it and pulled the shade down, so only a crack let her see the choir director. The woman was still in her cloak, huddled in a corner. Wake had his hand on her knee, talking to her.

Outside on the platform came the call: "All aboard! All aboard for St. Joe and Chicago! All Aboard!"

Dorie looked down the aisle at the exit. She should take Talbot home. He was waiting for her. She didn't know who this dame was, and what's more, she didn't care what woman Wake tangled with. Let him wreck marriages; it was out of her hands. For Harriet Fox's sake, she wanted to throttle him, but that wouldn't do anybody much good now.

She looked back at the pair in the compartment. Wake was

taking her cloak off now, touching her face, smoothing her hair as he pulled off the hood.

Thalia. Sweet Thalia honey. Her heart sunk.

Dorie jumped from the steps to the platform. Talbot stood at the bottom of the platform stairs, a pained but patient look on his face.

She thrust her car keys in his hand. "It's Thalia. I have to go."

He held her wrist. "Wait." He dug in a pocket and pulled out a knife, one like hers, with an ivory handle. He slipped it covertly into her palm, rolling her fingers over its handle. "A souvenir from Chicago."

The blade felt warm and solid in her hand. She could tell by its weight that it was a fine one. She looked up, expecting his mocking look. But he was serious, his cynical expression gone, as if he'd come to some conclusion in Chicago, had some epiphany. Like he'd accepted who she was, what she did, in a way that she couldn't even manage for herself.

He gave a small smile and a wave of his hand. She looked at him for a second to memorize the color of his eyes.

"Go," he said.

NINETEEN

THE TRAIN BEGAN TO PICK up steam as it moved through the city toward the bridge, heading north. Dorie stood in the aisle, watching the buildings, stores, houses, apartments, and mansions go by in a flash of light and shadow. The night wasn't as dark as it should be, not with streetlamps and car headlights and squares of windows where insomniacs drank warm milk and did the crossword.

From here, the city looked like a picture: serene, calm, untroubled. A place to live a well-mannered, prosperous life, free of danger and hunger and poverty. Like when she was up in an airplane, watching the tiny cars crawl like ants along the threads of highway. But here it was closer, more real—but distant and manageable, too. They passed the cemetery, a moonlit sea of choppy waves of the dead. Then feed yards and acres of boxcars, then more small, silent houses.

Then the city was gone. The river ran far below, a flickering ribbon reflecting the half-moon in the clear sky. Dots of man-made shine bounced and dipped, there, then gone.

She held her breath, passing over the Missouri, as if the ghosts could feel her so close. As if her breath became their breath and they lived again. From somewhere, a prayer shimmered wordlessly through her mind. Then both the river and the prayer were gone.

She stepped up to the compartment. The shade had been pulled lower. She tried to hear their conversation, but the rumble of the train drowned it out.

She pulled out Talbot's gift. The knife probably wasn't really a gift for her, just a souvenir from his hasty trip to Chicago. She would give it back to him. Her fingers tightened around the handle, her thumb on the switch. She didn't want to use it. She didn't think she'd have to, not with Barnaby Wake. He didn't look like the scrappy type. Thalia, however. You never knew.

The thought of jail flitted through her mind like a shudder. She wouldn't go back. No one would know she had a knife. No one but Talbot.

The knife slipped back into her trouser pocket all too comfortably. Its presence would be just a good-luck piece, a new rabbit's foot. That was all.

She turned and faced the door. Squaring her shoulders, she raised her fist to knock. But the door slid away, scratching metal on a track. Barnaby Wake was chuckling as he straightened his tie. He looked up, startled.

"What do you want?" he hissed. "Get out of here."

"I need to speak to Thalia." Dorie tried to catch her eye, but Wake moved into her line of sight. "It's important. Please."

"She has nothing to say to you."

Wake moved outside the door, sliding it shut behind him. He had taken his hat and overcoat off. His tailored suit fit him as well as Wendell Willkie's did, snug on a muscular frame. Barnaby Wake was a proud man, and his clothes showed it.

He smoothed his hair. "What are you doing on this train? I'll have the conductor throw you off." He seized her elbow, but she didn't budge.

He stared at her, anger in his eyes but a stoic expression on his face. Dorie braced her other hand against the window frame.

"It's a free country." She smiled. "Wouldn't you say, Herr Wake?"

He dropped her arm and jumped a step back. A trembling hand went up to his mouth, rubbing sweat off his upper lip. He glanced at her, then at the corridor leading off into the shadows, as if he planned to bolt.

"Go ahead. I'll stay here with Thalia. I'm sure you have some business to attend to, rallies and such."

Wake grabbed her shoulders then, pushing her against the window. "You weasel-faced cunt. You stay away from me or I'll ruin you." He was spitting on her. It was fairly disgusting. "I have friends, powerful friends. They'll make you wish you'd never met Barnaby Wake."

"But I wish that now."

He pushed her to the floor. "I'm getting the conductor. Get up."

Brushing off the seat of her trousers, she got to her feet. "Is one of your powerful friends Agnes Marchand? Or Wendy Hines? Or maybe the parents of Harriet Fox?"

The door slid open. Thalia was wearing her powder blue suit. Her hair was pulled up into a French twist. She clasped her hands together, scowling.

"What the hell is this?"

Wake patted her arm. "I'm taking care of it, honey. Go back inside."

"I need to use the powder room," Thalia said. She pushed past him and moved down the corridor, swaying on her high heels with the motion of the train.

Wake took Dorie's arm again, squeezing her bicep hard and dragging her in the direction Thalia was going. One knee gave out and she stumbled. "Come on," he barked.

They passed the ladies' rest room as Thalia was closing the door. Her eyes caught Dorie's for an instant, just long enough for Dorie to see the frightened girl in them. Well disguised under the haughty exterior, but it was there, giving Dorie hope. Thalia was only a girl, after all, running away with a man twice her age, leaving behind a dying mother and a hefty inheritance. The money, at least, mattered to her. Somehow Dorie had to talk sense to her.

But now, Barnaby Wake yanked the detective through the doors between the cars, where the noise of the train rattled her teeth and the deep cold of the coming winter hit them like an ice ball. A flash of prairie under starlight, then into another first-class car. Then cold and noise and prairie again, plus rolling hills. Then a car she knew: rows of cracked padded seats, passengers bobbing in the sway.

He paused to change hands, grabbed her again, then moved on. Finally, in the next car, there was the conductor, chatting with a woman as he looked at her ticket. He wore a blue uniform with brass buttons, a smart cap. Wake pushed her forward, holding both arms down at her sides.

"This woman is bothering me and my wife," he declared loudly, waking a few surrounding passengers. Some moans, a baby started to cry. "I want her thrown off the train."

The conductor, a kindly-looking gent with wings of white hair under his cap and sagging eyes, looked Dorie over. He cocked his head, peering closer. "Is that so?"

"I was minding my own business, sir," she said. "This man is taking liberties with my person. If you could get him to let go of me, I'd be grateful."

"She barged into our compartment. She's been following me for days," Wake cried.

The conductor rubbed his chin, almost laughing down at the lady he'd been talking to. She was gray-haired, watching the scene with bright eyes under her feathered hat. She looked up at the conductor, gloved hands clutched around the handle of a large umbrella, and raised her eyebrows.

"Unhand this woman, sir," the conductor said dramatically, half-winking at his lady friend. "Go back to your wife. I'll take care of this one."

Wake held firm for a moment, then dropped his hands. The conductor dismissed him with a wave. Dorie rubbed her arms where he'd pressed his fingers into them, then turned to watch him retreat. He looked back at her from the doors, a black expression on his face.

"If only," she whispered to the conductor and his lady friend, "he wasn't a fascist—and the lady was really his wife."

The old woman sucked in a breath, eyes bright with intrigue.

"And what's all this about, miss? Let's see your ticket."

The conductor was done playing games. Dorie made a show of checking her pockets, hoping the switchblade didn't show as she did.

"I left it in my pocketbook. Where is my pocketbook?" She'd had it when she gotten on, hadn't she?

"Did you drop it when he grabbed you?" the old woman suggested.

"I should go back and look for it."

"Is that safe?" The old woman peered up at the conductor.

He sighed. "I'll go with you and take tickets on the way back."

The conductor followed her into the next car, then tapped her on the arm. "Have you been following him for days?"

"Never saw him before in my life."

"Right. Sure," the conductor said. "And I got a bridge you can buy. Okeydokey, whatever you say. Get going."

In the corridor of the next car, she turned back to the conductor. "All right, I have been following him. He's running away with a girl, and the mother wants her back."

"You're a cop?"

"Sort of."

She turned to continue down the darkened corridor. She hoped she'd been honest enough that he would give her a break. He seemed nice, but then, he didn't know she hadn't bought a ticket yet. How was she going to get Thalia alone?

They crossed the last gap into Wake's car. Dorie made a pretense of having trouble with the door, biding her time, checking the corridor ahead. Deserted. Where was her handbag? She couldn't see it down the hallway.

As she pushed open the last door, the door to the ladies' rest room opened to her left. Thalia stood framed in the yellow light. She stepped out, looking up sharply at the two of them. Dorie took the call. With a quick jab, she pushed Thalia back into the small rest room. Ignoring the cry of the conductor, she reached back for the door and locked it.

Thalia bounced off the toilet, bumping her head on the light fixture as her knees gave out. She howled. Dorie caught her before she hit the floor, pushing her sideways onto the closed toilet lid. Outside, the conductor was beating on the door.

"Thalia, listen to me." Dorie knelt in front of her. "I'm sorry I had to do this. But listen to me."

"Get away from me! You're a savage." She struggled to get her feet under her. Dorie held her knees. "Let me out of here!"

The conductor rattled the knob. His muffled words came through the door. Thalia opened her mouth to cry out, and Dorie put her hand over the girl's mouth.

"Just be calm for a minute and let me say something."

Thalia's eyes were round with anger and shock. She tried to speak, to pull off the hand, but Dorie grabbed one of her hands and sat square on the girl's lap. "Just listen." Thalia slapped her on the head and shoulder with her free hand. "Stop that, will you? Just listen to me. I'm not going to hurt you."

Thalia quieted for a moment.

"We don't have much time. First, your mother. Since the Willkie people were there she hasn't woken up. Mother Ruth thinks she's going to die any day. Her last request was that you be with her at the end. You have to come back. It won't be for long, but you have to be there. She's your mother."

Thalia stopped struggling. Dorie rushed on, hoping the spell would last a minute more.

"Then there's Barnaby. You must have read the paper; you know he had a romance with Agnes Marchand and broke up her marriage. What you may not know is that he also dallied with Harriet Fox and got her pregnant. Yes, it's true. Her parents kicked her out of the house. I talked to her myself."

Thalia closed her eyes, shaking her head.

"I know you don't believe it, but it's true. Harriet says he's the one. And there's the Nazi thing. No small potatoes. He loves Hitler, Thalia, and he wants this country to be a fascist colony of good old Adolf's. Tommy Briggs was a Nazi, too. Your old boyfriend. That's why they killed him. It was Barnaby's boys.

Tommy saw Barnaby at the Nazi meeting the night they killed Wendy. Tommy could have told everyone. There's been a lot of killing to keep Barnaby's dirty secrets."

Dorie got up off her lap and took away her hand. Thalia spat into the sink and rubbed her cheeks. She looked up, disgusted.

"You make me sick. Let me out of here."

"So you can be a Nazi hausfrau? Is that what you want, Thalia?"

"Why not? Hitler has some really good ideas. I believe in him."

"You're not that stupid, Thalia."

She looked indignant. "Roosevelt is a Red. Everybody says so."

Dorie stared at the girl. "Oh. So you're running away with old Barney because he's such an upstanding fascist gigolo murderer?"

"You don't have any right to tell me what to believe." Thalia stood up and tugged on her jacket. "This is a free country. I can believe in anyone or anything I want."

Dorie stepped right up to her face.

"You're right, Thalia. This is a free country. But there's one thing that isn't free. That's what you owe your mother. She loves you, Thalia. She cares what happens to you. Why do you think Barnaby Wake is running away with you? Because you're a good singer and you love Adolf? You're going to inherit a fortune. How you spend it is up to you. You can give it to Adolf, for all I care. But do your mother the final courtesy of being at her side when she goes to meet her Maker."

"He loves me," Thalia whined.

"Just like he loves Harriet and Agnes and his wife. So much he couldn't let Wendy or Tommy tell you who he really is."

"And who is that?"

"A cousin of Fritz Kuhn by marriage. A Nazi."

Thalia rolled her eyes. "He told me that. I don't care. He loves me. He'll take care of me."

"With your mother's money, sure he will. And his wife and children. And his fascist friends."

Thalia sucked in her lips, her eyes watering.

"Go back and see her, Thalia. One last time."

"We're going to Chicago," the girl said, summoning up her defenses. "We'll cable her."

Dorie reached into her pocket. "Don't make me force you. You know the right thing. I know you loved her, once."

"What do you know?" Thalia looked away, but the mirror reflected them standing toe-to-toe.

"I know there is something there between you and your mother. A bond, despite her harsh words, and yours. Something that you need to honor, one last time. Give her that courtesy. She loves you and she's dying."

"She's been dying for so long."

Thalia drooped, her face in her hands. She sat down on the toilet lid and began to cry.

They stayed in the rest room until St. Joe. Wake pounded on the door; the conductor left and returned, pounding more before leaving again. When the train stopped Dorie unlocked the door, Thalia's hand clasped tightly in hers.

The brakes were still squealing. Somewhere, a car or two down, a conductor was calling out: "St. Joe, St. Jo-seph!" Wake's door slid open.

"Come on, girl." She pulled Thalia out of the rest room.

"Thalia!" Wake's voice boomed. The girl tugged against Dorie's hand.

"Don't look at him. Your mother will be gone soon. You have your whole life ahead of you. Without her looking over your shoulder."

"I should . . ." Thalia's voice trailed off. She *should* go home. She'd promised she would.

"Don't do it, Thalia. Don't make the mistake of not saying good-bye."

Wake kept calling her name. Dorie pulled Thalia out through the doors. Behind them, Wake was charging like a bull. She pushed Thalia down the corridor to the end of the next car, then down the steps to the dark platform. The girl caught the handrail, stumbled, and cursed under her breath.

"What the hell are you doing? Thalia, get back on this train!" Wake barked, grabbing Dorie's arm.

"We're going back to Kansas City," Dorie said. "Wanna come? Maybe not the friendliest place for you right now, but it's where Thalia has to be."

Wake had his eye on the girl. She stood with one hand on her hip, looking away.

"Come on, baby," he called. "Get back on the train. We've got things to do."

"You can do them later," Dorie said, trying to twist out of his grasp. Wake gave her a shove then to get to the stairs. But she anticipated it, tripped him, and ducked under his shoulder to block the way.

"I don't want to do it this way, Herr Wake."

Her new blade twinkled in her hand. New, sparkly, and sharp. It was beautiful, and deadly. Sweet but low-down.

She glanced at the switchblade, made sure he saw it. She was not going to stick him by accident.

"Mrs. Hines is dying and Thalia needs to be there. Where you go is your own business."

She backed down a stair toward the platform. Wake stood frozen, dark eyes jumping from Thalia to the knife. Dorie backed all the way down, checking quickly for cops or other with uniforms. The only one was a porter halfway inside the station, pushing a cart of luggage into the terminal. She waited a beat, then held out her blade, spinning it in the glare of the platform lamps.

A lovely thing. She would have to thank Talbot.

Wake was on the bottom step. She straightened, frowning. "Stay where you are, Wake. Go to Chicago. Have a nice life."

All right, the train can leave now, she thought.

"Thalia, baby. Come back up here. We'll have champagne and

forget all about this. You don't believe that about your mother," Wake said. "This is a scam to get you away from me. Your mother doesn't like me."

Thalia stepped up beside Dorie.

"Oh, baby," Thalia said, her smooth self back, "sure she does. She just doesn't know you like I do."

Dorie tipped a hip toward the girl to keep the blade between them. Wake reached out for Thalia.

"You think so, honey?"

"Wendy liked you, too, didn't she, Barnaby?" Dorie said. "You remember Thalia's sister-in-law, don't you? You met Wendy at a Silver Shirts meeting."

"Wendy?" Thalia pulled away her hand.

A shadow crossed Wake's face. "Don't listen to her."

"Tell her how you and your Nazi friends killed Wendy. Was it an accident, just meant to scare her? Tell her, Barnaby, how Wendy threatened to tell everybody you were a fascist. Especially Eveline Hines."

Wake's expression hardened, skin crinkling around cold eyes.

"Barnaby?" Thalia squeaked.

The head of a conductor popped out of the next car, calling, "*All aboard!*"

Dorie put her free arm across Thalia's waist. Wake hung out over the steps.

"Don't do it, Wake."

"There's still time, honey," he crooned, desperation creeping into his voice. "Hop on, baby. Come on!"

With a blast of the whistle, the train began to roll. Still gripping the blade, Dorie dropped that hand behind her leg as the car with the conductor neared them.

The white-haired conductor called again, in their direction. He gave them the eye as he rolled by. Dorie waved at Wake.

"So long! Come again, Uncle Barney!"

They stood on the platform as the train pulled out with Barnaby Wake first in the doorway, then at the window. Thalia didn't wave. Finally, the last car was gone and the hoot of the whistle faded into the night. The cold made a shudder go through the girl.

Dorie found a cabdriver willing to take them to Kansas City, promising him a fat fee at the other end. They didn't have a dime between them. Thalia complained briefly about leaving her pocketbook and suitcase on the train, then fell asleep before they hit the countryside.

The road rose and fell along the bluffs of the Missouri. Thalia's sleeping face shone in the streetlights of the small towns along the road. She looked peaceful, the face of an innocent child, without worries or cares. Dorie wondered what sort of a child she had been, singing through the house and dancing around the garden. Would Tillie have liked growing up in a fancy house like that, full of toys and pets and grass to roll in? Oh yes. How she would have loved it, the freedom, the beautiful things, attention from servants, parties and delectable treats.

Dorie laid her head back on the seat. The cabdriver was hunched over the steering wheel. "Armenian," he said with a thick accent, "come over with six sisters and a maiden aunt." What had happened to his parents, she wondered.

Would Dorie have loved growing up in that house? She didn't think so. So stifling, full of off-kilter people and a bone-cold chill. And death.

She hoped for Thalia's sake that it hadn't always felt like death.

Close to daybreak, the taxi pulled to a stop in front of Amos Haddam's apartment. A milkman carried bottles to the doors. The driver was too tired to argue when Dorie told him to make sure Thalia wouldn't go anywhere; she was still asleep against the seat.

Amos came to the door in an undershirt, zipping up his trousers.

"What've you got yourself into this time?" He squinted at the curb, where the taxi idled.

"Have you got thirty bucks on you? I'll explain."

"Is that—"

"It's her. Snatched back from the devil's clutches."

He left her on the stoop, returning with his wallet. He found a twenty and two fives. "Where'd you find her?" he called as she ran back to the cab.

Thalia was slow to wake up, blinking and stretching. "Come on, get out, Thalia. Let the man go home."

Dorie draped the girl's arm around her neck and maneuvered her up the walk to Haddam's apartment. Amos held the door as they teetered into the warm living room. She deposited Thalia on the sofa, where she toppled against the arm, head on her hand, eyes closing again.

"Is she ill?" Gwendolyn had joined the two of them as they peered at the heiress. She scuttled off to make tea when no one replied.

"She was on the train to Chicago with Barnaby Wake. I had to disentangle her," Dorie said, not without some pride.

"She doesn't look bruised," Amos said, walking closer to Thalia.

"Took some arm-twisting. Wake didn't want to lose his lunch ticket."

"Where's he, then?"

"Left him on the train at St. Joe. Can't say if he stayed."

Amos nodded. "Let's hope. All the way home to Yorkville." He looked at Dorie appraisingly, eyes stopping briefly on the bulge in her trouser pocket, a sight he was all too familiar with. Their eyes met, hers defiant, his forgiving.

"Thought we'd never see the little brat again," he said, clapping her on the back. "Well done."

At 8:45 A.M., Gwendolyn steered the black Buick up the curved driveway to the Hines mansion and parked in a spot of sunshine.

The air in the car had been strained. Even Thalia had the grace to stay silent as they all contemplated the picture of Eveline Hines on her deathbed.

How bad would it be? She'd looked so far gone these last weeks, it shouldn't be too difficult. But this was different; they all knew that.

A muscular young man in high boots, riding pants, and rolled white sleeves held a garden hose up to Thalia's blue sports car. The day was warming, the sun bright in the cobalt sky, and he'd found a sunny spot to wash the car, rubbing it lovingly with a rag. The new chauffeur. May he live carefully, thought Dorie. He watched them, especially Thalia, as they walked to the door. A sense of roundabout fate—ironic déjà vu—made Dorie's feet lift off the ground for a second.

Mildred opened the door. The stale, cold smell of the foyer enveloped them and the sunshine was gone.

"Thalia dear," Mildred said. "Thank God. We were all so worried."

The girl headed for the stairs. "Is Beulah upstairs? I need a bath."

Mildred's mouth dropped. Gwendolyn and Dorie looked at Amos.

"Young lady. Miss Hines," he said awkwardly. It was as if he'd never met her. "Thalia."

She turned on the first stair. "What is it now?"

"Your mother, dear. We need to see her first."

"Can't I take a bath? I've worn this same suit for days! My hair is a mess," she pleaded, looking at them for confirmation. But a lack of sympathy greeted her. "Oh, all right. I don't see the rush, but—"

Amos took her elbow, guiding her down the hall to the sick-room. Thalia babbled, saying her mother always liked her to look the lady, how she wouldn't want Thalia to run around filthy and unpressed, how she had left her pocketbook and her case on the train and she would probably never get them back. On and on she went, a million miles an hour, irritating everyone who didn't feel gratitude that their own dark thoughts were blotted for a moment.

Mildred pushed open the door. Thalia fell silent, blocking the doorway. Mother Ruth sat bedside, knitting something pink. On the bed, the tiny figure of the Commander floated, lost in a sea of white linens. The old nurse rose, took Thalia's hand, and walked her to the chair. Thalia sat down by the bed. The others hung back near the door.

"Close the door, would you, Mildred?" Ruth said. "The drafts are wicked down that hall."

The door shut behind Dorie. Because they'd called earlier that morning, she knew that there had been no change in Mrs. Hines's condition. She was being given morphine in high doses to keep her comfortable. She hadn't awakened since Saturday night.

Gwendolyn squeezed Dorie's hand tightly. Her first impulse was to pull away, but she let the Englishwoman hold her hand. It was comforting.

Mrs. Hines looked the same now as she had the afternoon of her confession to Dorie: sleeping peacefully in a sea of white. But that day, Eveline had felt she couldn't sleep the big sleep without telling someone about Thalia's parentage. What spurred that confession, she would never know. Dorie felt the secret heavy on her heart as she looked at Thalia.

The girl stared at her hands in her lap. How hard it was to face death, at any age. It shouldn't be required at twenty-one. How often it was.

"Let's leave them alone," Dorie whispered to the others.

Mildred opened the door. She looked older than ever, sadness in her eyes. Amos held Gwen's hand as she trailed behind him. Dorie shuffled behind them, so she didn't hear the footsteps in the corridor until Julian Hines was pushing them aside.

"Where is she?" he shouted. "Thalia? Where have you been?"

His voice blew up the sickroom quiet like a torpedo. He looked wild, his face red, his clothes haphazard—a shirt half-buttoned, cuffs flapping, trousers with no belt, socks without shoes. His thin dark hair stood up as if he'd just rolled out of bed. He flailed his arms madly, as if they were trying to hold him back.

"Get away, let me see her! Thalia! Thalia! Get away!"

Then Amos did have his arm. "Calm down, man. She's visiting now. Let's go outside."

"Visiting? She lives here, you moron." Julian pulled away from Amos and ran to the end of the bed, his knuckles white as he grasped the footboard. "Thalia!"

The girl looked up, her face placid and cold. Mother Ruth stepped next to Julian. "Try to keep calm, Julian, sir. Your mother's sleeping."

Julian gave a mad bark. "My mother's been sleeping for thirty years, you old bat." He shoved her aside roughly and moved next to his sister. "Thalia, I thought you were gone. You came back. You came back!"

Gwendolyn's lip was curled in disgust. Amos frowned, moving behind the mad stepbrother. Dorie had never seen Julian in this kind of state. She had seen few people this dramatic and over-wrought. The room seemed to fill up with his desperation, like a breath straining to be released.

Thalia turned her face toward her mother's, reaching up to take the old woman's small hand. But Julian wouldn't go away.

"I've missed you so much. Where did you go? Talk to me." He lurched forward and threw his face into her lap. His shoulders shook with sobs. He looked up at her pathetically. "I thought I'd never see you again."

Thalia pushed him away, her fingers wide, as if trying not to catch germs from him. He fell back.

"Julian," Amos said, putting his hands on the man's shoulders. "Come away now, son. Let Thalia be with her mother."

With a grace he probably showed only on the golf course, Julian rose, spun, and swung in one fluid motion. He landed a fist on Amos's cheekbone, sending the older man reeling. Amos sat hard on the floor at Gwendolyn's feet. She cried out and stooped next to him.

Dorie stepped forward, fists balled at her sides. "Look, mister. That was uncalled for. I don't know what is going on here, but—"

Thalia rose to her feet. "Get away from me, Julian."

Julian glowed at her attention. "Thalia!" He tried to take her hands, but she stepped back in disgust. "Darling!"

"Don't 'darling' me. If you touch me, I'll kill you, do you hear?" Her voice was very low, and full of menace. "I've told you that often enough, and you never listen. I've had enough of you. Do you understand? I will kill you."

"Thalia darling, how can you say that? I love you."

The room compressed, then decompressed. The air shifted. Mildred let out a squeak, then fainted, hitting the floor with a sickening thump. Thalia's face reddened as her eyes blazed with—what, anger, hatred, embarrassment?

Dorie reached out for Julian's arm. "I'm sure you love her. She is your sister. Now come with me. We'll talk outside."

But Thalia was wound up now. "Sister?" she spat. "Don't be stupid. As much as she—" She scowled at the figure of her mother. "As much as she wanted a daughter. Which wasn't a heckuva lot, was it? No, none of you—"

Thalia bit her lip and stopped. She turned her back to them.

Julian's voice was broken and teary. "Darling, I always cared for you. Even when she didn't. She hurt you, but I was there, I held you when you cried. I love you!"

"Stop it!" Thalia spun back and glared at him. "Don't ever say that again. I hate you. Will you never understand? I hate what you did to me. I never loved you. Don't you know that, you stupid, stupid sot? Never."

Julian fell to his knees. "Darling. Please. Don't say that."

"I told you a hundred times. But you are so dull—so . . . so infected with your own needs, your own desires, you never thought about me, what I felt, what I wanted."

"How can you say that? I always think about you. I think about you every minute of every day. I—"

"Oh, I'm sure you do. You think about me in a most unbrotherly way." Thalia seemed strangely calm. She looked back at her mother for a moment. "And she never stopped you. Never lifted a finger. Never noticed. At least never cared."

His voice was hoarse. "Please forgive me, darling. I love you. I'll take care of you always."

Thalia stepped closer to him, just out of reach of his outstretched arms. "Over my dead body."

She spit on his face. "That's the last piece of me you'll ever have."

Thalia stepped around the wretched figure and out the door. Amos jumped up and followed her, Gwendolyn at his heels. Mother Ruth sat stunned on the floor, Mildred's head in her lap.

Dorie shook herself. She looked over at Mrs. Hines. Could she hear? She looked just the same, her thin chest rising and falling, her face a waxy mask. The Commander, who had told detectives very clearly how much her daughter meant to her but could never make Thalia feel it.

Julian was bent over, kneeling on the rug. His face was crushed in pain; tears streamed down his cheeks. Ruined by Thalia's words, and his own misdeeds. Dorie hated to see men cry. She felt sorry for him, despite herself. He was weak, and crazy. Disgusting, too. He had used and abused his sister.

Dorie looked back at the Commander. Her revulsion of Julian was blunted by the secret Eveline Hines had told her. The one that made their deed a little less hideous.

On the stand by the bed, a flash of gold: the locket, its chain curled in a heap, the hinged door shut, as if the secret was safe. Was it safe now?

She slipped it into her pocket. Someday, Thalia should know. For her own peace of mind, to forgive herself. Even, perhaps, to forgive a mother and know a father.

TWENTY

THE NUMBNESS THAT CARRIED DORIE out of the Hines mansion and across the driveway lay like a wet blanket in the Buick.

Thalia and Amos sat in the backseat, dull eyes staring out opposite windows. Gwendolyn fiddled with the steering wheel, rubbing her finger back and forth over the bumps. Dorie slid in beside her and looked at the copy of the morning paper on the seat. The headline was about London, another attack by the Luftwaffe, women and children buried in rubble. A photograph of a small child standing alone in a pile of bricks, clutching a teddy bear, weeping.

She looked over her shoulder at Thalia. The girl looked drained. The bottled-up hatred for her brother—and everyone else in the family—had been released. She looked hollow and fragile, a feather lying in wait of a strong wind to blow it far from the nest. Would the wind be her own strong will? Or would it be Barnaby Wake's?

Dorie felt a sigh rise in her chest. Perhaps Thalia's will would set her on a new course. Perhaps not. She didn't really care who took Thalia away. She just hoped it was for the best. A bit of luck for the road, then. May it rise up and greet you, honey. God help her, she would need some luck.

Gwendolyn rolled down her window. The cool morning air hung with mist. The sunshine was gone behind a bank of low clouds, turning the day a soft gray. Dorie shivered in the damp breeze, but Gwen stuck her face outside and took a breath. Thinking of England probably. Dorie caught Amos's eye, a solemn glance that gave little away. She frowned at him, trying to decipher his sphinxlike stare, but turned away without getting an answer. She slumped in the seat and stared out the windshield at the dark stain of water on the concrete.

A minute later, little groans and grunts broke the silence. Thalia's face twisted with panic; she pawed madly at her suit jacket and skirt. Amos put out a hand, but she shrank from it.

"It's all right now, dearie," he said softly. "We'll take care of everything."

Thalia wiped her palms down her chest, eyes wide. "A bath— have to take a bath."

"You can do that at my house," Amos said. "You don't want to go back inside. Not just yet. Gwen dear, start the car."

Suddenly, Thalia was out the car door, running with her head down toward the house. Amos and Dorie both jumped out. Amos was quicker, giving his partner a wave to stay. She paused halfway to the house. Perhaps it was better to let him handle it alone. Her distaste for the Hines mansion had never been stronger.

In the front yard, yellowing grass was raked clean of fallen leaves, the shrubs pruned to within an inch of their lives. The chauffeur and the sports car had disappeared. On the outside, things were so orderly. The outside of people, too: often neat, orderly, clean. But the insides, where the turmoil and knots and pain ate you up—the insides were often a wreck.

She put her hands in her trouser pockets. The switchblade was still there, warm and at the ready. Gwendolyn sat behind the wheel, her fingers playing a tune again.

A minute passed, maybe three. The mist fell lower, until the tops of the trees disappeared into the gray.

Then the shot rang out from the house with a force that turned Dorie's stomach.

The door was still ajar. She pushed it open. Whoever had the gun might not be finished. Her breath stopped. Was Amos carrying his gun?

The foyer was empty. She looked up the staircase. Empty. The door to the parlor was open, and a shaft of lamplight yellowed the stone floor. She sidled along the wall to the opening and peered around the door.

Standing behind the sofa was Amos Haddam, still alive. Dorie let her breath out. In his arms was Thalia Hines, sobbing. Amos saw Dorie and glanced to the corner, by the marble fireplace.

Next to the window, slumped by the hearth, was the body of Julian Hines. His hand still held a pistol, used on his temple with unfortunate accuracy. And blood. Lots of blood.

"Pack her a case, would you, ducks?"

Amos might have said it several times, but finally the words penetrated the ocean wave crashing inside Dorie's skull. She pulled her eyes away from the maimed corpse and backed away. Gwendolyn stood frozen on the stoop.

"Go back to the car, Gwen. He's all right. Don't worry. I'll be out in a minute."

When Dorie saw Gwen leaving, she turned to the staircase. In the back hallway stood Mildred Miller, very pale but upright. She had one hand on the wall, as if her legs wouldn't support her. Her other hand covered her mouth. She looked toward the parlor. Dorie put both her hands on the secretary's shoulders.

"Mildred, look at me."

The secretary turned reluctantly, as if in a trance.

"Go back to your office. Call the operator. Do you hear me?" Mildred nodded. "Good. Call the operator. Right now. Tell them to send the police. Tell them there has been a shooting. Can you do that?"

Mildred lowered the hand from her mouth and swallowed. "A shooting. Police."

"That's right. And stay in your office until the police come. That's an order."

The secretary turned and walked toward her office, rounding the corner without a backward glance. Dorie went upstairs and began opening doors. She found the maid she'd seen frolicking in the garden, sitting now on a bed. The cupcake hat bounced on her head, face in her hands. Horrible noises came from her. What was her name?

"Beulah! Get up. There you go. Stop crying. Here, use this. Does Thalia have another suitcase? We need it, now. Yes, now. Start with her dresses. Put in three. Any three. . . . Yes, green is fine. Doesn't matter."

Two hours later, they sat in the car again, waiting. All but the girl. Thalia Hines huddled in the backseat of a patrol car parked around the side of the house. She was wrapped in a blanket. The cops had made sure the patrol cars were hidden behind the hedge.

The numbness was wearing off now. And in its place was the persistent image of the end of Julian Hines. Dorie tried to think of prettier sights. She had already talked to the cops. Amos had been told to stick around. The chief of police, the old G-man Reed, had showed up to throw his weight around. Reporters had started coming, but the cops turned them away.

What was happening with Mrs. Hines during all the turmoil? As she thought this, the doctor showed up. He was a rotund man, bald, scurrying on short legs into the mansion with his kit.

The help now filed out the front door, lining up on the driveway in the chilly breeze. Beulah had lost her cap. She looked pale, shell-shocked. Mildred Miller was ramrod-stiff. The cook was carrying a wooden spoon, as if he'd pulled away from the soup pot. Another maid, another cook, the new chauffeur, some eight servants.

Amos rubbed his ear. In the parlor, he'd been standing close to Julian Hines, trying to convince him to put down the gun, when he'd done it. Amos had spots of blood on his shirt, lapels, and the backs of his hands. His eardrums ached. Gwendolyn sat beside him in the back, white as a sheet.

Up the walk came Dorie's uncle, Captain Warren. She stepped out of the Buick, hoping to catch his eye, but he had his head down, talking to a uniformed cop. They disappeared into the house.

She walked toward the door. Miss Miller looked her way, a stricken look in her eyes.

"Is Mrs. Hines all right?"

The secretary shrugged. "Lined up like criminals. What do they think we had to do with it?"

Captain Warren stepped out of the arched doorway and stood blinking in the light.

Dorie called his name. The old bull looked dazed, and a little shaken. He brightened. "Dorie girl." He squeezed her arm. "Best not to go in there."

"Eveline—is she being taken care of?"

"The doctor and her nurse are there. They say she's not been conscious for several days."

"The noise, didn't—"

He shook his head. "For the best." He peered at his niece. "What's this I hear about you going to court again?"

Her stomach knotted. "I wanted to talk to you about that, Herb. I was set up by these two detectives. Richards and—"

"Richards?"

"What? Is he dirty?"

"And well connected. What are you saying?"

They walked toward the Buick. "He and his partner, Stewart, came to see me at my office. Asked a bunch of questions about the shooting on the bridge, even though I'd already answered all the same questions. Then I got a call from somebody who claimed to be Amos, saying that you and he wanted to see me at the station."

"It wasn't Amos?"

"No. I drive over, and they've got a search warrant. The cops got some anonymous tip that I had a gun in my car."

"And did you?"

"Not one I'd ever seen. But, yes, they found one." She looked up at him, hoping he believed her. "You know I don't use a gun."

"All too well." Herb squinted at her. "Stewart. Beefy, straw-colored hair?"

"That's right. I think they're working for—"

An ambulance pulled into the drive, making its way around the Buick. Three attendants jumped out of the back.

"No hurry, boys," Herb told them. "Sit a spell." And he was gone, striding back into the house.

She stood there a moment, until she began to shiver in the cool dampness. She got back in the Buick. Amos was stroking Gwendolyn's hair as she laid her head on his shoulder. Dorie looked at her wristwatch. It was nearly noon. She slumped down in her seat and closed her eyes.

A few minutes later, a tap woke her. She peered up at Harvey Talbot through the window. He opened the car door and slid in next to her.

"What's going on?" he said cheerfully, looking around the car. "I brought your car back. Couldn't find you at the office."

Haddam frowned at him, glancing at the trembling Gwen. Dorie tapped his elbow. "Come on, let's go for a walk."

The ambulance had been moved while she napped. They passed a uniformed cop in the driveway. "I'll be back in a jiffy," she told him. The cop nodded, glancing at the Buick.

"You'd think there was a Nazi invasion, all these uniforms," Harvey said.

They reached the sidewalk and turned down the hill. The clouds held—if anything, lower than before—but that didn't affect Talbot's mood. His feet bounced along the pavement.

"I have to tell you what happened in Chicago." His face was animated. "It'll be in tomorrow's paper."

She glanced at the Hines mansion, feeling drugged with the morning's events. "Thanks for bringing the Packard," she said. "I could have gotten it."

"Say, your handbag was under the seat. Did you miss it? You gotta hear this. Come on, sit down." He perched on the curb, his feet in the dead leaves in the gutter. She sat wearily beside him, trying to feed off his energy. She felt as dry as the leaves.

"Roscoe Sensa was tied into this Chicago tribe, all into sports betting. So I go up there and talk to this fella I know. He knows the players there. He says Sensa and his friends had been fixing the Monarchs games for years, or trying to. It wasn't working out that well, and people were upset. Sensa wasn't controlling the situation. They couldn't get the players to go along."

"Like Gibson Saunders?"

"Gibson told the other players to keep their minds on their game, not their wallets. They were hassling the team, the owner, all that, to get the Monarchs to forfeit. Or at least hoping some of them would get scared enough to quit."

"Who was doing this?"

"Sensa's boys. Some from here, some from Chicago. You ever hear of Maynard Reilly?"

"No."

"Chicago bookie. He got fed up with Sensa's blunders, and losing money, so they tried to blow him up in his car and take over his action here."

"But got Joe instead."

"They finally got it right, but they still can't put the muscle on the Monarchs. So they decide to teach the other players a lesson and whack Saunders."

"That's disgusting."

Talbot bit his lip, trying to dampen his enthusiasm. He'd finished grieving for Saunders, it appeared, and now was hell-bent on justice. Dorie squinted at him, then laughed at his halfhearted attempt at seriousness.

"Go get 'em, Harve." He grinned. She reached into her pocket for the switchblade. Taking his hand, she slipped the knife back to him, glancing at the cops up the street. "Thanks for the gift. Luckily, I didn't need it."

"But you got her back?"

"She listened to reason."

Talbot's turn to squint. He stared at her, then shook his head. "You wouldn't tell me what happened for a million years, would you?"

Dorie leaned back on the grass, feeling the cool dew through her jacket. The sound of the gun blast was fading from her mind. This was just another pretty day. Playing hooky from school. At any moment, the truant officer would yank you back to addition and subtraction, to structure, to the teacher's paddle. But for just a minute, you had freedom, laughter.

Then she thought about Julian, and the mess inside, the tragedy, the family. She closed her eyes and tried to clear her mind. She looked up at Harvey. There was a distraction.

"Oh, sure, in a million years I'll tell you everything, Talbot."

The sky was white, like heaven. Deep in the clouds, a crow was cawing, telling her to get up off the ground and get warm. But Talbot had leaned down on one elbow and was staring into her eyes.

"What happened to the fascist philanderer?"

"Off to Chicago and points east, I hope."

"You didn't stick him with the blade?"

"Mmm. I wanted to." She grinned. "Would I tell you if I had?"

"No." He laughed.

"You smell like cinnamon, Talbot." She grabbed his brown tie, the one dangling in her face. "What did you spill on here, a candy tray?"

Before he could answer, she yanked him lower for a kiss, just a quick one; then, on her feet again, she brushed off her trousers. He deserved a kiss for that switchblade, but school was back in session. Talbot fell back in the grass, moaning.

"Get up, you masher. There's serious business here." She pulled him to his feet.

"What *are* all these cops doing here?" Talbot straightened, focusing at last. "And there's that bastard Russell. What's he doing here?"

She took his arm and led him back up the sidewalk to the Hines mansion. Nothing good was going to happen there, unless you were a newshound sniffing out a juicy story.

Dorie shook her head in mock sadness. No, it was real sadness she felt, but for Talbot, she kept it mocking. It was shocking how easy it was to be cynical around Talbot.

"Bad news, Harvey. Terrible stuff."

TWENTY-ONE

THE HEIRESS OF THE HINES fortune buried her mother on a Monday, the day before Election Day. The old Commander had clung to life with the same tenacity she'd always had, stringing her remaining family member along for weeks. Thalia had disappeared for days at a time. The detectives from Sugar Moon Agency had learned not to worry. Sooner or later, a report of Thalia singing a naughty number or dancing on tables would reach them and they would scrape her off the floor, or pry her out of some joe's arms. The folks at her regular haunts had taken care of her until they couldn't; then they'd called Haddam.

The rest of the time, Thalia had sat up with her mother or wandered the quiet house. She'd taken long baths and kept to herself. She'd rarely sung at home anymore, Mildred had reported, and they all could see that she was a shadow of her vibrant youth. But on any given night, out on the town, the old self had returned, with such a short, fierce blaze that with time the coals would be stoked again.

Now, at the graveside, Thalia Hines stood straight and solemn, a blond statue of grief as the priest read from the Book of Common Prayer and blessed the ground. A black veil covered Thalia's face. No word from Barnaby Wake, although Dorie had half-suspected him to turn up at the funeral to press his case.

As they began lowering the casket, Harvey Talbot threw a handful of fragrant red petals onto it. Dorie looked at him, wondering where the hell he'd come up with rose petals, and bumped him on the elbow.

There had been a truce in their war since that night at the station. Besides the gift of the switchblade that had brought Thalia home, his sensitive story about the demise of Julian Hines had given her the feeling that he was different from other men. Maybe she'd known this, but her heart was a willful beast. The story was really unique in the rag trade, a suicide story that never mentioned that fact. With some reading between the lines, one knew exactly what had happened. No one offended, children and the religious spared, truth told, more or less.

His other story, the one that connected the murders of Gibson Saunders and Roscoe Sensa to the Chicago bookies, had caused a ruckus among the various jurisdictions, all stumbling over themselves to be the ones to solve the cases and bust up the racket. So far, two lieutenants of Maynard Reilly, the Chicago boss, had been arrested, with more promised.

Across the open grave, Amos Haddam stood alone in his overcoat. The cold wind fluttered the brim on his hat, making him look as fragile as a butterfly wing. He looked like one of the family, so glum was his expression. Gwendolyn Harris had taken the train to Los Angeles two days after the shooting. Nothing Amos or Dorie could say would stop her. It was hoped her aunt lived a sheltered life out there in the golden state.

Haddam said he was resigned to it. But he had changed. No longer strictly accepting of his solitary ways, he looked, and acted lonely now. Dorie had invited him over for dinner at the boardinghouse one night. Carol had burst into tears when one of the bachelors called her a floozy, and Mrs. F. had given young Tony a smack for laughing. That had gotten the rest of them going about hitting children, and dinner had ended in disgust and thrown napkins.

"Entertaining," Amos had called it, "but hard on digestion."

A woman was singing now, her high, quavering voice rising and falling on the wind. Several relatives had surfaced in the last two weeks; this one, Florence, was a second cousin by marriage. The news of Julian Hines's suicide and Eveline's poor health had brought them out of the woodwork. Florence had come from Wichita, and there was no sign of her leaving.

Earlier, as they'd filed into the cemetery, Dorie had seen the urn inside the crypt. The Hines family had a large, moldy crypt, but Thalia had insisted on her mother being outside in the sunshine, and no one had had the nerve to argue with her. But inside the barred door of the crypt, the shiny new cobalt blue urn sat in a carved niche in the wall. There had been no service, no singing for Julian. Another of Thalia's orders. He was gone, vanished from their lives. Dorie couldn't fault the girl's decision. But still, she hoped someone would sing a song over *her* grave.

Once again, the Arlette question nagged at her. She'd spent a considerable amount of time the last weeks looking for her, driving through the colored neighborhoods, asking at stores and restaurants. There had been nothing in the *Star* about a death or the shooting of a Negro woman. Dorie had moments where she thought she'd dreamed it, but the dark stain on the upholstery of the Packard's front seat told her it was real.

One night, she'd actually sighted Dr. Friedkin. He'd skulked out the door of the apartment building and walked to a bar on the corner. But when she'd tried to talk to him there, he'd cursed her, threw a beer on her, and disappeared out the back. She'd never found him again.

Cousin Florence didn't have a bad voice. It must run in the family, thought Dorie. She sang a stiff old hymn—one Dorie didn't recognize—about living forever and heaven and being godly. Relief was Dorie's main feeling, as the Commander was released from her pain. Would Thalia sing a song, too? Dorie couldn't tell what the girl was feeling, her veil did its job so well. The song continued as the men released the straps on either side of the grave.

The sight of the coffin disappearing into the earth caused a sharp, piercing pain in Dorie. Her mother's coffin, in the Atchison public cemetery, only three or four people there, and not one of them willing to sing. Why hadn't she sung? She could have done something, said something, sung something. What song could she have sung? What would you have liked, Verna? *Lavender blue, dilly dilly. Tillie Tillie.*

Harvey squeezed her shoulders. The tears came unwillingly. She lowered her head and tried—but failed—to stop them. Around them, raindrops began to fall in loud splats, hitting the flowers on the coffin, the men's hats, the ladies' feathers, the dry dirt and brown grass.

The preacher hurried to the end of the service and the crowd scattered.

Amos watched the mourners move away in the cold rain. He stood for a moment alone as the grave diggers began to shovel dirt on her coffin.

He'd tried to prepare himself, these last weeks, as she lay unconscious. But the hollowness he felt now told him he hadn't tried hard enough. Eveline was gone, and with her a bright part of his own life. He took a deep breath of the sweet moisture and tried to relax the tightness between his shoulders. A cough made the grave diggers look up.

He walked slowly back to his old Buick. He had to drive himself now. Lennox was back with the newsman and Gwendolyn was gone. He'd gotten a postcard from her. The Santa Monica pier, and a funny note about sunburn and the beach. Good old Gwen. He wished her well.

In front of his apartment house, he watched the windshield wipers go back and forth, then shut off the engine. He was out of the car, feeling the rain on his face, before he saw the bicycle and yellow slicker of the Western Union boy.

Threes. He stood waiting for fate on the sidewalk. The boy pedalled toward him. *Things come in threes.* Eveline and Julian were two. Here, in this telegram, would be the third.

He tipped the boy and went into the apartment. His overcoat dripped on the rug as he stripped it off. His hands were shaking as he dried them in the kitchen and tore open the telegram. Glancing quickly to the end, he saw it was from his mother.

She was alive.

NED FOUND ME STOP NO WORRIES DEARIE STOP NEWS
FROM BERYL STOP IN PORTUGAL WAITING FOR BOAT STOP
CHIN UP STOP MUM

She was alive.

Amos let out his breath, holding himself up against the
counter. His eyes blurred and he wiped away the tears. They were
all alive. There where death rained down from the skies, where
countries disappeared overnight, they all lived.

He slumped into a chair and reread the telegram. He looked
at his watch. He had a meeting in less than an hour.

He was changing his suit when it came to him. The third death.
Wendy Hines, who'd simply fallen off the face of the earth. Lennox had proven that the Silver Shirts were the last to see her. But
he'd never been certain what had happened. Until now.

She was number three.

Dorie leaned forward in her chair to concentrate. She still wore
the blue suit she'd worn to the funeral that morning. Her shoes
and stockings were splattered with mud. The funeral had left her
edgy and distracted, but this meeting had been set up for over a
week. No delaying it.

The assistant county attorney and Wilma Vunnell were talking
in a low tone. She watched the eyes of her lawyer, once again her
friendly victim: Louie Weston, a man she seemed incapable of
avoiding. She no longer found him handsome, his eyes cold, his
hair greasy, his skin dissipated. But he did have a way of charming the officials, her parole officer, the county attorney, the cops.
The only one who didn't seem beguiled by Louie was the fed,
Howie Duncan.

Fortunately, Duncan was eager for the deal anyway. Amos, on
his right, was mumbling to him. Haddam said it wasn't strictly
Duncan's department, this Silver Shirt business, but he wanted to
handle it anyway. Dorie didn't argue. In fact, she'd kept her
mouth shut this whole meeting. Anything to keep the boys happy.

"What's going on?" she whispered to her uncle. Herb Warren flicked his eyes her way and patted her knee.

She sighed, tensing her fists and releasing them. The bag with Tommy Briggs's shirt sat in the middle of the table. No one had touched it.

The prosecutor cleared his throat. "What is your recommendation, Mr. Duncan?"

Duncan folded his arms. "The way I see it, she's offering you a lot more than you got on her. The Federal Bureau of Investigation is ready, as always, to cooperate with the locals on common ground. We'll make this evidence available." He gestured to the shirt. "Of course, we would take possession of it today. And Miss Lennox would have to be available for further questioning and for trial."

"That's not a problem," Louie Weston said.

Assistant Chief Michaels piped up. "There is still the problem of her parole violation, and the weapons charge. I don't see how we can just—"

"I thought you heard," said Herb Warren. "Richards lost his report. Even if he were to refile it, he's retiring next month."

Michaels glared at him, then said, "There's Stewart. He will—"

The county attorney, a thin man with glasses, stood up, buttoning his jacket. Michaels sputtered to a halt.

The county attorney cleared his throat. "Miss Lennox served the majority of her parole in exemplary style. I think we can cut it short now, with the proviso that she not be charged with any further criminal conduct for the next year. And she cooperates fully with both the federal and local authorities in the investigation of the death of Tommy Briggs."

Dorie looked at her lawyer. Did that mean what she thought it did? Louie was smiling, so it must. He nodded around to Mrs. Vunnell, to the cops, to Howie Duncan and Amos Haddam.

"If Mr. Weston feels justice has been carried out, that is," the attorney added.

"Absolutely," Louie said brightly. "All is forgiven."

He turned his grin on Dorie finally. She felt a little sick as she smiled back. Then it was done.

Finito.

Wilma Vunnell caught her in the hallway. "I went to bat for you," the parole officer barked. "Don't make a liar out of me."

"Yes, ma'am," she said, trying to be serious.

"Are you still going to take flying lessons?"

"Does the county have a problem with that?"

Mrs. Vunnell gave an approximation of a smile. "Just flying? None at all. Good luck, dear."

She ran down the steps of the courthouse to her Packard. A great weight had been lifted from her shoulders; then she remembered Eveline Hines. A smidgen of heaviness returned. She should be grieving. She hoped Eveline would understand.

On Charlotte Street, she saw a parking spot near Joe Czmanski's garage. She had a jolt of gin planned in celebration. A big jolt. She'd somehow managed to keep the whole stabbing incident secret from the other boarders at Mrs. Ferazzi's, so there was no one to celebrate with but Amos. He'd gone off with Duncan and Tommy's silver shirt to make sure everything stayed on the up-and-up. Well, a bottle of gin was a good-enough companion.

On the radio, Harry James was playing the "Back Beat Boogie." She drummed her fingers on the steering wheel in time with the music. She would have to buy her uncle a bottle of gin, and Amos, too, for setting up that deal. She felt generous, and wealthy, since they'd all gotten paid off by Mrs. Hines's lawyer. Hell, she'd buy everyone gin.

In the door of the garage, she saw two men talking.

"Just got a call from the hospital about Old Jenny," Joe said after she parked.

"Good news?"

"She's awake. And giving the nurses holy hell."

"Well, get in. Let's go see her."

Joe opened the front door of the Packard. Behind him, the man in the fedora leaned down.

"You, too, Talbot," she said. He climbed in the backseat. She caught his eye in the rearview mirror. "Ready for another tale from Charlotte Street?"

He leaned forward and tugged her hair playfully. "Don't you people ever sleep?"

"Plenty of time for sleep. When you're dead."

TWENTY-TWO

Mᴿ. ʀᴏᴏsᴇᴠᴇʟᴛ ʜᴀᴅ ʙᴇɢᴜɴ ʜɪs third term when Dorie Lennox saw Thalia Hines again.

It was a cold day in late spring, one of those days that reminds one of winter's long icy fingers. A gentle knock on her door from one of the twin librarians who lived next door. A lady and gentleman were calling, waiting in the front hall. Dorie had been asleep, dozing off while reading *Moby-Dick*. Her first evening home in two weeks, as she'd been tailing an accountant suspected by his employers of embezzling funds. Today, they'd fired him.

Dorie leaned over the railing. "Lovely young woman," Nell Crybacker said on her way back to her room.

"Blond?"

"Not originally. Didn't think much of the fella, though."

Thalia Hines wore her powder blue suit again. The sight of it took Dorie by surprise, as if it were last fall again, that day in Eveline's sickroom when she'd last seen mother and daughter together. Before the Hineses' world had imploded.

Thalia looked no different, her cool exterior as placid and unreadable as china. No sign of grief, struggle, or tragedy. The man next to her looked irritated, his good looks dark and a little dangerous. Just Thalia's style.

"Nice to see you again."

"Mildred said I had to come myself," Thalia said bitterly. "She said you were a good friend to my mother, and to Wendy. Wherever the hell she is."

Yes, wherever. Dorie put her hands in her trouser pockets. No one knew where Julian's wife was, but it wasn't among the living. If Wendy had been alive, she wouldn't have missed Eveline's funeral. Not a trace of her had ever been found, and with Barnaby

Wake and his thugs on the run, there was little hope of finding any. Someday, perhaps. Although who would press for answers now?

"What brings you out?"

"We're selling off some things," Thalia said. "Things we don't need. Mildred said you might like this. As a token. It's that Edith woman."

Dorie tore the brown paper off the book. Edith Wharton's memoir, *A Backward Glance.* She opened the cover. Inside it read: "To Eveline, with affection always, Mildred. Christmas 1934."

"Tell Mildred it's very kind of her to think of me."

Thalia sniffed in reply and turned to the man. He set his hat at a rakish angle, holding his arm bent for her.

"Wait."

Dorie felt her heart beating too hard in her chest. She had gone round and round in her mind about this, whether it was right. She'd struggled for months without a clear plan. It was probably wrong to do it now.

Thalia turned back, one eyebrow lifted.

Dorie considered again, but the reasons to stay silent swam into the vortex, leaving her high and dry. This was the only chance. She cleared her throat.

"I have something for you, too. But you have to promise not to ask where it came from."

The girl shrugged. "What's this about?"

She was curious, in her greedy way. From her pocket, Dorie extracted the locket on the chain. Thalia stared at it, frowning.

"That was Mother's. I've seen it. How did you—"

"No questions." Dorie closed her hand and withdrew it. "All right?"

Thalia rolled her eyes. "Oh, good God."

The boardinghouse was quiet. Even Mrs. Ferazzi had turned off her radio set and gone to bed. The man cracked his knuckles impatiently.

"All right. Give it to me."

Dorie handed it over. Thalia opened the locket and stared at the picture. She frowned. "But I thought—I thought it would be Daddy. Or me."

"You recognize him?"

Thalia looked up, her blue eyes troubled. "Who is he?"

"You met him that day with the Willkie people. Teddy Lafferty."

"Oh. Mother's friend." She stared at the tiny photograph. "Much younger."

"About twenty-one years younger. Or maybe twenty-two."

Thalia straightened her back, her neck muscles tensing, nostrils flaring as she let out a hot breath. She blinked, then looked back at the locket. She snapped it shut.

"Teddy Lafferty, you say."

She turned to her boyfriend as she unlatched the chain. He took it from her, moving around behind her to hook it. The locket fell on the swell of her bosom, next to her heart.

At the door, she paused, looking back over her shoulder. Dorie waited, wondering what else could be said. You are not alone, she thought. She couldn't say it.

Thalia reached up and hooked her hair behind her ear. Her eyes were still cloudy with confusion. But in them was also her mother's strength, the ability to hold secrets, to carry on, to make the best of the muddle.

Dorie rubbed the Wharton book with a palm. The boyfriend put his hand behind Thalia's back and pushed her out the door.

To make the best of it. To see yourself out there on life's complicated stage, under the lights, in costume, speaking lines. To imagine the words are your own, that the lies don't matter, that everything fits together. To be a heroine to yourself.

That was all you could do. Then—if you were lucky—all the lies you made up about yourself might come true.